Dream of the Jet ~Black City

Pablo Valcárcel Castro grew up in a bilingual household in the Canary Islands, where he hid from sunny skies in musty libraries and fantasy books. After working as a lawyer and running a small video games studio, he turned his yearning for beautiful and impossible worlds into writing them as well as teaching entrepreneurship to make them happen.

Dream of the Jet ~ Black City

Pablo Valcárcel Castro

ZAFFRE

First published in the UK in 2026 by
ZAFFRE
An imprint of Bonnier Books UK
5th Floor, HYLO, 105 Bunhill Row,
London, EC1Y 8LZ

A CIP catalogue record for this book is
available from the British Library.

Hardback ISBN: 978-1-78512-452-5
Trade paperback ISBN: 978-1-78512-453-2

Also available as an ebook and an audiobook

1 3 5 7 9 10 8 6 4 2

Typeset by IDSUK (Data Connection) Ltd
Printed and bound in Great Britain by CPI (UK) Ltd, Croydon CR0 4YY

The authorised representative in the EEA is
Bonnier Books UK (Ireland) Limited.
Registered office address: Block B, The Crescent Building
Northwood, Santry, Dublin 9
D09 C6X8, Ireland
compliance@bonnierbooks.ie
www.bonnierbooks.co.uk

To Linden, for dreaming with me a world worth living in

The Lands of Niria
Walled Sea
Eriune
Corana
Lorn
Onyxian Domain
Solemn Isle
Venia
Crunia
Gallecia
Tevia
Amalgan League
Amalga

Skala
Highland Marches
Wolven Sea
Faengria
Invernia
Maw Strait
Engrian Peninsula
Lundeyn
The Sunken Library
Damlan
Gentlet
The Valelands
Trevens
Griffinmark
Helysia
Principality of Losianne
The Riven Marches
Duchy of Ilea
Ilea

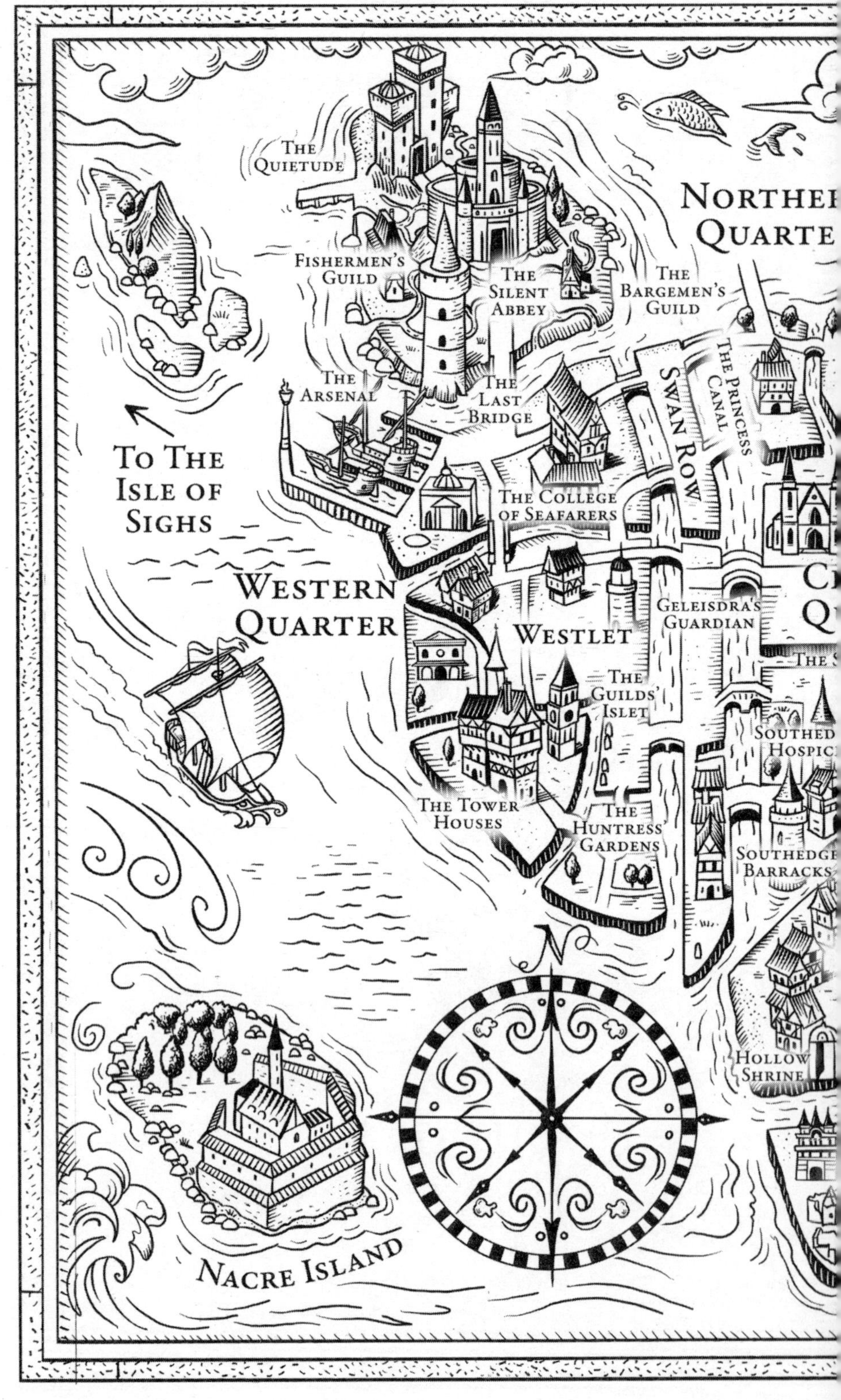
The Quietude
Fishermen's Guild
The Silent Abbey
The Bargemen's Guild
The Arsenal
The Last Bridge
The Princess Canal
Swan Row
To The Isle of Sighs
The College of Seafarers
Western Quarter
Geleisdra's Guardian
Westlet
The Guilds' Islet
The Tower Houses
The Huntress Gardens
Barracks
Hollow Shrine
N
Nacre Island

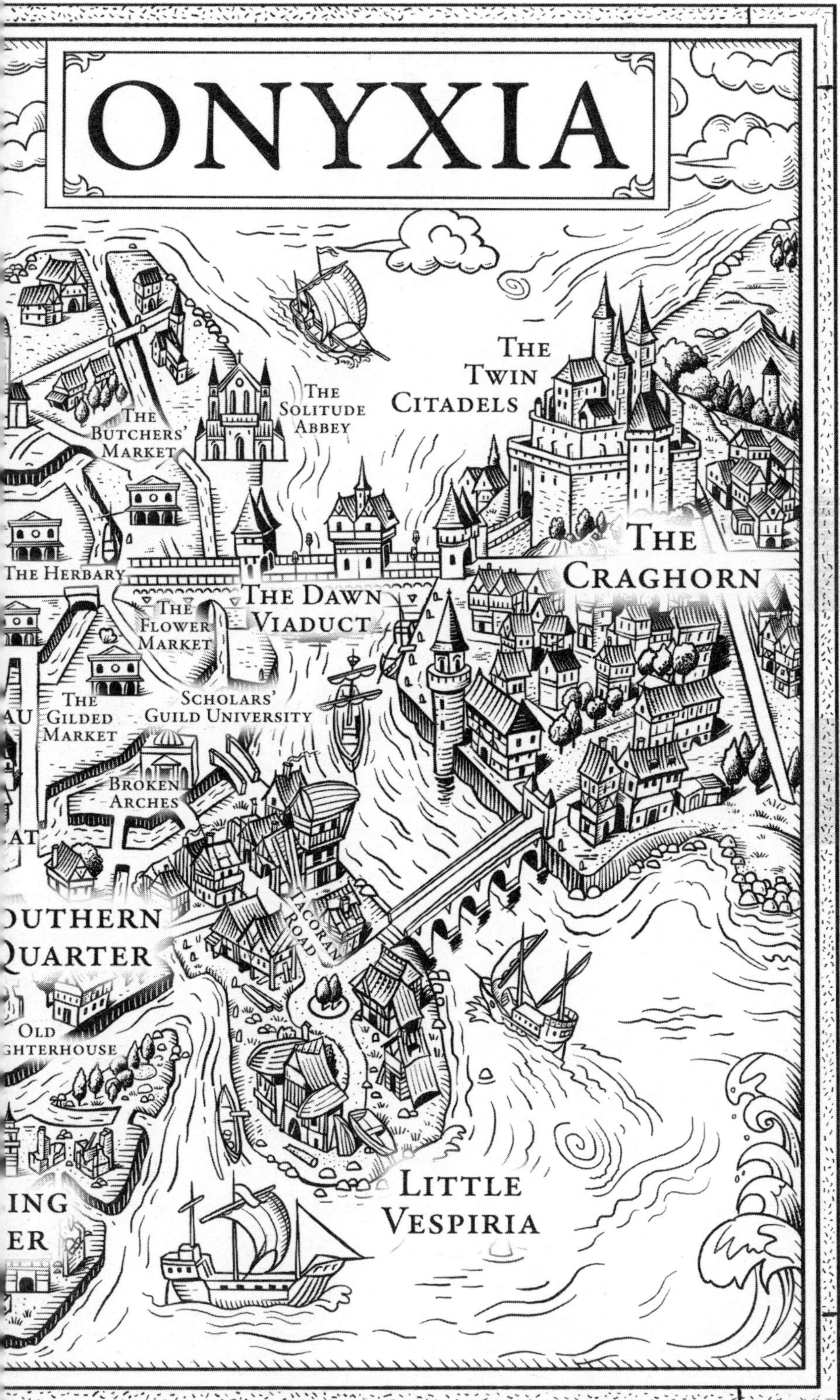
ONYXIA
THE TWIN CITADELS
THE SOLITUDE ABBEY
THE BUTCHERS' MARKET
THE HERBARY
THE DAWN VIADUCT
THE CRAGHORN
THE FLOWER MARKET
THE GILDED MARKET
SCHOLARS' GUILD UNIVERSITY
BROKEN ARCHES
IACORAN ROAD
LITTLE VESPIRIA

Prologue

THE SUNKEN LIBRARY HAD ONCE been home to a hundred thousand books, but in the crooked spires, Ash only sees a drowning mausoleum. Inside, unread and silent, stories are fading into oblivion or, according to his father, turning into living Nightmares.

Which is why they have to rescue them.

This place is cursed, damned. The Philosopher Empress's vision of a home to all the knowledge in the world, dead for centuries now. Stone husks protrude from the water, the ruins of the citadel where copyists, Illuminators and miniaturists once dwelled. Only the colossal library tower has endured, with four darkened towers serving as its flying buttresses. And yet, despite their efforts, the whole structure sags perilously, like a sick oak threatening to drag its offshoot with it.

The boy has known his share of horror already. Before his father traded the sword and siege engines for the types and printing press, the boy followed him through lengthy army campaigns. He's seen gryphons pick knights apart inside their armour, white feathers soaked red. Stryxes guzzling the blood of the battle fallen. Entire cities put to the sword and claw. And yet, his fears are different today.

All such Nightmares were born out of Dreamers' minds – angry, cruel, terrible Dreamers, yes, but still men and women. Here, in the library, the Nightmares have sparked from dying stories, from the anguished echoes of poets and scribes carved into the crevasses of codices.

Even Larens and Rorsen, Father's army friends, feel it. Tough as nails, yet as soon as their boat slides under the spire's half-sunken archways, fear strangles them to silence.

'There!' his father yells, leaping out of the boat, and Ash follows. They splash onto the submerged steps climbing to the library's central vault.

They wade ahead through the cold, fighting the water's pull and the slip of the slimy steps.

The hungry darkness waits. Seeing farther than a handful of yards is near impossible. When the boy casts his lantern's greasy light around, he finds red marble stairways zigzagging upwards, coiled around the colossal columns like snakes. Muck and mud cover the steps like scales, and rotting wood and debris flourish.

'Hurry!' his father says. 'It's less than an hour before the next patrol! Remember to tread lightly and think quietly. The sentinels might have left monstrosities guarding some of the most prized collections, and even if they haven't, the library's listening to your fears.'

'How do we know what to take, Eoinas?' Larens asks, her greying braids glinting silver in the lantern's light.

'Just follow the map I made you and search the sixth floor's vaults for the ancient comedies and tragedies. Then we'll meet at the copyists' hall. That might be the real motherlode.'

'Whole load of trouble for some old books,' Rorsen grunts through his bushy beard.

'You're not just rescuing works lost to history, my good man,' Eoinas replies, then conjures a mischievous smile. 'Once I copy and print them, you'll be turning our fortunes.'

'Now, that's a cause we can all rally behind.' Larens pats both men on their backs.

They part ways, his father's friends on the prowl for plays, while the boy follows his father up the stairs into a musty stone vault. On its lintel, the carving shows a rose wrapped around a lyre, the symbol of poetry. The drizzle outside is the only sound, and footprints on the dusty floors the only trace of life. Most must be from the Nightmare-Hunters that patrol these ruins periodically. The others, colossal, blackened smudges ... he isn't sure.

They work quickly, setting their lanterns nearby and deftly rummaging through piles of scrolls. They need to be handled carefully, lest their ancient skins crumble in their hands. Some still have their pendant seals intact, others he needs to identify by the first lines or, when his grasp of the Ancient Iskian tongue fails him, by unrolling them to find the ending where the author's name is safely sheltered inside.

'*An Ode to the Muse of Melancholy* by Edylas the poetess! Your mother always loved her work, and this is a lost piece!' his father announces with delight when the boy brings him a rare find. 'Find me more from where you got this one.'

A trove of lost names and voices are revealed to them, each assessed by his father. Little does it matter whether these books talk about fiery yearnings, timeless sorrows or furious revenge. If they won't make money, they'll remain in the stillness and silence of dust.

With a good haul, they both hurry down towards the main vault, cavernous and silent, where their boat awaits them.

'We should leave,' the boy says. 'This is worth our trip already.'

'Not yet. We won't get another chance like this. I'll go back to the others; they'll need help carrying all that wisdom,' his father replies, a smile forming under his dark curls. This time, his father stops him when he tries to follow. 'You stay here and make sure the boat's ready.'

Then he wanders into the dark, climbing back up the stairs, leaving Ash to curse and wait about in the shadows with the lapping lagoon as his only company.

There is nothing for a long time, until the darkness groans, rattling his bones like thunder.

The boy is afraid enough, even before hearing the screaming and hacking sounds that come with a fight, even before the desperate running that follows.

'Father?' he calls, dread welling deep within him.

His father takes the steps on the way down in threes and fours. Above, Ash can see something trickling slowly down after him. It oozes and roils like a wave, except then it unwinds into black, liquid shapes, like half-formed ink, that pour down the stairwell.

As his father reaches the landing, Ash notices his sword is unsheathed, the blade cracked in half.

He hurries to untie the mooring line. 'Where are the others?'

'Just cut it!' his father shouts, hauling a sack of books and tools inside the boat. The boy works his knife. Sharp steel gnaws away, tearing each strand of rope from the other. He prays, too: prays to the Motherstorm, to the Solemn Princess, to the divine Philosopher Empress even. Let them be spared, let them escape once more.

As soon as the last strands snap, his father helps him board, working to shove the boat into the water. They just have to make it through the arches and they'll be outside.

'Where are the others?' Ash tries again. Again, without any reply.

He risks a look at the landing and the stairs, lit by the lantern they've left behind. There's nothing.

It's only the black ink and them.

'Get the oars!' his father yells, wading deeper, heaving while pushing the boat.

Something in the water stirs, a shape blacker than night unfurling below them.

'Watch out!' Ash yells.

His father's face twists. Even without seeing, the boy knows; his father must feel it, coiled around his legs. He manages to shove the boat one last time. 'Just row!'

Ash reaches for him, but his father has released the boat and is farther and farther away with each heartbeat. And then the water, and whatever's inside, swallows him.

Chapter One

Ash

Much mourning followed Empress Myrtele's murder, yet none matched her daughter's. Princess Geleisdra cried a Wail of Stone, and every shard of her shattered soul became a jet-black tear, an island, a step into eternity. Her wailing parted the waves and brought forth the onyx islands that would forever be home to her grief and her people.

– *The Life of Divine Geleisdra, the Solemn Princess* by Blessed Elpia

THE MOTHERSTORM ROARED OVER ONYXIA'S spires, and Ash couldn't wait for it to get worse. She was already in labour and soon the skies would light up crimson with firstfall-lightning, the reason he was perched on the dangerous, rain-slick rooftops.

For the devout, this was a momentous occasion. All over the city's hundred jet-black isles, the Wailers from the Sisterhood of Sorrow served as midwives, singing canticles from their abbeys' towers to soothe the Motherstorm's throes of childbirth. For the Lightning-Hunters, tonight meant a chance to make a fortune.

Ash had promised his crew that they'd catch some of the firstfall. Much like fishermen, theirs was an unpredictable trade. The guild caught enough lightning to feed Onyxia's foundries, to heat and light its myriad of cold, dark palaces, yet never enough for Ash's small crew to outrun their debts.

After three months of bad hauls, they could barely afford bread or the damp garret they all shared. Worse, they were about to lose their guild licence and, with it, Ash's means to make a living free from servitude to the Dreamer nobility, the Oneirocrats.

Braving the rooftops on a night such as this was plain reckless. Yet Ash was willing to risk a crippling fall or a lightning strike. Anything was better than suffering the Oneirocrats' yoke.

A firstfall-lightning bolt, though, was the rarest of catches. Its raw anger could power the largest siege thunder-cannons, or light the sacred abbeys during the Ascent Festival. It would afford them more than mere survival.

So long as they didn't die in the hunt.

Thunder groaned loudly again, and Ash crouched at the edge of the aerial colonnade where his crew was camped, scanning the skies with a brass spyglass. The Motherstorm's black heart was hard to read through the rain, with only a glimmer of light from the city's centre farther north . . . There! The sign he'd been looking for all along.

The four of them had spent the afternoon tracking crowcats over Onyxia's southern eaves. Now, a large clowder of the flying felines was forming, circling a palace's dome a hundred yards away. It was rare for the normally solitary cats to band together unless there was a predator around – or unless Ash had guessed right.

He pressed the spyglass into his mentor's ancient, weathered hands and gestured to the airborne clowder. 'Do you believe me now, Rudher?'

'Motherstorm's tears!' the old man cursed. 'I still think this is the wrong choice, with all those gargoyles and worse. Though I admit, I've never seen so many of the rascals together before. What are they doing?'

'They can sense the heat rising! We have to hurry!' Ash yelled, grabbing his gear.

They all sprang to action, any hesitation swept away by the thrill of the hunt. Ash deftly fastened a small onyx globe to the bottom of his copper spear, then helped Rudher do the same. They had hunted together hundreds of times, but tonight they couldn't afford errors.

'Ach. My joints are already aching, and we haven't even begun!' Rudher grumbled.

'Less croaking, more wiggling, old crow!' Yaisa, their young apprentice, jested as she pulled down her hood and leapt onto the nearby shingled slope. She'd taken quickly to the role of pathfinder, not just because she was light and nimble; like many Vespirian immigrants, she'd grown up hopping around steep ravines on her home archipelago.

She led the way, Ash and Rudher followed, while the crew's hauler, a giant of a man named Ghalod, came last with their traps.

The downpour received them with a brutal battering. Ash had tightly closed the straps of his father's old leather jerkin, yet somehow the water still found its way in, down his wool breeches, too. Seeing was near impossible. He swept aside the long dark hair that had fallen from the leather thong at the nape of his neck and tightened his grasp on his spear. Without it, everything was pointless. He splashed through the rooftop's rainwater currents, desperate to reach the dome in time.

He'd fiercely argued with Rudher to give up their usual hunting grounds for the Crumbling District. The city's southmost district had started falling apart when Rudher was young and, as the old man liked to say, like him, its bones hadn't got any younger.

Here, a house's collapse could swallow you whole. Worse than that, there were still a few guardian gargoyles perched on the rooftops of many of the dilapidated palaces. They were blindly loyal to their Dreamer masters and their living stone muscles gave them the strength of men twice their size. Yet another reminder of how much Ash hated the Dreamer nobility, who hoarded every scrap of land.

In the years he'd been living in Onyxia, Ash had seen the impoverished uprooted to the Southern Quarter, where it took a living wage just to pay for a damp, overcrowded room, let alone food. Not just those coming from Vespiria or fleeing poverty in the countryside, but anyone who didn't work for the merchant houses or belong to the artisan guilds had simply been squeezed out by the Oneirocrats' wealth. Even though they had no personal use for them, the greedy nobility refused to part with their ruined palaces in the Crumbling District, instead having their monstrosities guard them against interlopers.

He'd based the plan on something he'd read in Bergos's *Bestiary of Nature and Dream*. It'd been one of the first books his father had printed – that *they* had printed. Even broke, Ash couldn't sell it. Now, he only hoped old Bergos had been right about the crowcats' predilection for hunting in clowders at the eye of storms.

A small island stood between them and their destination: an uneven landscape of cracked slate slopes barely held together by jagged flying buttresses. There were two canals they needed to cross, which meant two chances of slipping into the deadly currents below.

Ash followed Yaisa through a covered arched bridge to the islet, and then up the slate slope. Hurrying to the top, he spotted her searching for a way across the last canal.

He stepped down sideways to avoid sliding. Approaching the rooftop's edge, he noticed the naked patches in the tiling around them. If there were holes in the shingles, the rain had no doubt seeped in and rotted the supporting timbers. He whistled a warning, and the others spaced out to better distribute their weight.

'Isn't there another way?' he yelled to Yaisa over the downpour.

'Not without a long detour,' she replied. Another growl of pain from the heavens deafened him for a second.

Ash cast a quick glance upwards. No eye in the clouds yet, but with the sharp, burnt-wire scent in the air, it had to be imminent.

'It'll have to do.'

Yaisa handed him her spear, backed up a few steps and raced for the edge. She leapt, flying over the darkness separating both buildings before landing on the stone tower overlooked by the dome.

Ash waited for her safe signal before throwing her spear over. She grabbed the catch easily, but his own slid from his grasp too soon and spun without control towards her.

Yaisa reached for it, almost overextending. The spear fumbled from her fingers, plummeting into the darkness of the canals below.

Ash swallowed a curse.

Following Yaisa's lead, he backed up a few steps before running towards the ledge. His old boots squelched as he leapt.

Time felt thick and slow as he hurtled through the air. Above him, a young crowcat, circling the winds in anticipation, eyed him with playful curiosity.

He flexed his legs as he landed, sooty water splashing.

'Ash?' Yaisa asked over the rapping of the rain. 'Should we wait? I think Ghalod has an extra spear.'

Ash looked around. They were standing on an old palace's roof; the highest point was the old dome, likely a family oratory for the residing Oneirocrat to pray to their ancestors' death masks. The rain above them was starting to slow. The moment was coming, but Rudher and Ghalod hadn't made it over yet, and the lightning was imminent.

Around them, the wind suddenly died down. Above, the blackest clouds swirled, and Ash's stomach knotted tightly. He'd gambled their luck, and now his clumsiness was about to cost them everything.

'Please, Yaisa, lend me yours.'

Yaisa nodded, handing him her spear.

Ash sprinted for the dome. Its columns and walls were slippery, but its northern side was covered in bloodvines. He slung the spear onto his back, hauling himself up using the thick foliage.

The higher he went, the stronger the smell of something else. Even with the charged air of the storm, the oratory reeked of an acrid rot. Ash hurried to the apex, only to find that the oculus window in its centre had long ago shattered. The stench rose up from the blackness inside. A creeping sense of dread nagged, but it'd have to wait until Ash was done.

He checked the orb on the spear's bottom. On the neighbouring rooftop Rudher and Ghalod had stayed behind, working to set up the spiked rods of their traps. He felt, rather than saw, frantic movement above him.

He looked up just in time to see the crowcats flying away in unison, like a ripple spreading out on the surface of a pool.

With the Motherstorm spiralling over him, Ash thrust his spear into the air. His breath caught in his throat. A blinding blue filled his eyes.

The long spear shook violently in his hands as the firstfall coursed through it. It was furious, desperate to break free, but it couldn't pierce his thick gargoyle-leather gloves. Ignoring the scorching heat, Ash forced his fists to close tightly around the shaft until, heavy with anger, the lightning sank down towards the bottom, into the onyx orb, a piece of the sacred city itself and the only thing that could contain it.

Ash's insides trembled with the deafening crack of thunder that followed. Still, as quickly as it had begun, it passed.

The orb now shimmered with a bright navy blue, the colour of lightning reflected on the dark sea.

Ash wanted to cry out in triumph, but the celebrations could wait. The newborn storm was unfurling above them, and there was much to do. Before he could secure the orb, a sharp warning whistle cut through the noise.

Lightning broke the heavens above as he spotted Rudher frantically pointing at the oratory's base.

Below, Yaisa was backing away from a hulking figure, daggers gleaming in her hands. They hadn't stumbled into a guardian gargoyle; no, this was way worse. This was a Nightmare, the Oneirocrats' very cruelty given flesh and intelligence to torment or hunt whoever their Dreamer masters asked them to.

Ash yelled at Yaisa to leap away, but she lacked the space to gather momentum. The Nightmare cornered her with two of its long limbs and clawed at her with the third. She narrowly ducked beneath its swipe. Her daggers flashed as she sliced at the arm, but her attack barely chipped the beast's rugose skin. It released a low, hungry gurgle. Ash could make out the shape of the Nightmare's head now, horned like a monstrous goat's, maw filled with rows of sharp teeth like a shark's.

Ghalod joined Rudher at the nearby rooftop's edge. Their spears were too long to be used as javelins but too short to reach the monstrosity from there. Especially without risking hitting Yaisa.

Fighting the Nightmare was suicide, but Ash was the only one who could help her. Yaisa was their apprentice, their responsibility. He'd been the one who'd risked their lives bringing them here.

Ash reached for the orb of firstfall-lightning. Unscrewing it, he dropped the spear at his side.

This was their livelihood, the best haul they'd seen in years, and yet . . . what did it matter if they didn't all make it out alive?

Steadying his feet at the dome's edge, Ash hurled the orb at the monstrosity. It spun until it smashed against the Nightmare with the bellowing of thunder.

The explosion blinded him. Head spinning, he lost his footing and fell. Too dizzy to stand, he remained seated, rubbing at his eyes as his sight cleared.

When he could see again, the Nightmare was gone. To his relief, Yaisa was still there, leaning on the balustrade, gasping for air but alive. He waved at her, and she looked back at him, her face taut with fear.

'Ash, run!'

A claw landed at his feet. The monstrous head followed. Part of its skull had shattered and the remaining horn was ablaze. Such a brutal explosion should have blown its brains out, yet Nightmares spat on nature's laws. It seemed this one needed no brains, only hatred.

Its gleaming ruby eyes fixed on Ash. A gurgle came out of its serrated maw.

Ash rolled to the side as the beast lurched at him, its mouth landing where he'd been an instant before, tearing into the stone and mortar as if it were a crust of bread. Frantically, Ash crawled to the dome's apex, fruitlessly searching for Yaisa's spear, but the rain must have swept it away.

He risked a glance behind him. The Nightmare was climbing after him, steadily gaining ground with its spindly limbs. He couldn't possibly take on a monstrosity made for murder twice his size. He'd have to lose it.

Holding on to the cracked skylight's metallic borders, Ash let his body drop inside the oratory's darkness. The cloying stench of carrion surged from below, making him gag, and he hesitated to let go, not knowing what lay below.

As he hung there, one of the Nightmare's claws slashed through his father's jerkin and a searing pain ran up his arm. Terrified, he released his grip and plummeted into the unknown.

His ankle jolted with sharp pain as he landed, and he collapsed to the ground. He'd fallen into what seemed like a bed of muck and bird carcasses.

Lying on his back, Ash saw the Nightmare peering through the broken oculus above. The firstfall-lightning's blaze was finally dying out, leaving patches of its flesh charred and half melted.

It shoved one of its long arms through the hole, clawed hand reaching for him. Ash writhed away, growling through the pain. The Nightmare's arm wasn't long enough. Unable to reach its prize, the creature withdrew and, as swiftly as it had appeared, vanished.

Ash shoved himself up, his breathing coming in great gasps. Still dizzy, he tried to stand, but the pain in his ankle brought him to his knees.

Thunder rumbled. No, that had been the Nightmare landing on the rooftop terrace.

Ash forced himself to crawl. This *couldn't* be the end. Torn to pieces by some long-dead Oneirocrat's guardian Nightmare.

Lightning struck close by, its radiance filling the dome, bringing a wall fresco to life for a moment.

It depicted a classic allegorical motif: Divine Geleisdra, the Solemn Princess, facing death in company of her majestic winged lion.

The Nightmare trudged closer, but that wasn't enough to drag the picture from his mind. Even after the light faded, the lion's fierce eyes stayed with him.

The image called to him, as if it were waiting to be awoken, waiting to be brought to life. Out of despair, Ash reached out his mind to it.

To his shock, his vision changed.

In the shadows of the oratory, he saw himself as if in a dream: his broken body lying on the filthy floor, a large feline standing over him. A panther of shadows, sleek and deadly, with claws and teeth capable of rending flesh.

The monstrosity hesitated at the archway, sensing a threat.

Ash realised not even a panther would cut through the Nightmare's petrous skin.

Desperate to give it the means to fight, Ash reached for the strongest weapon he could find: firstfall-lightning. The one he'd captured was gone, but its memory still echoed with fresh brilliance in his mind. Holding it in his thoughts, he slammed it into the panther's beating heart, allowing it to uncoil through its veins. Feeding the flames of its hunger.

Then, he let go.

The Nightmare was already upon him, jabbing a claw at his throat.

The panther was fast, a blur of ink with shimmering cobalt eyes.

It leapt onto the Nightmare, toppling it with its strength. The monster spun, swiping at the feline below, but the panther scurried into the shadows. The horned head swivelled as it searched, the Nightmare bracing its many limbs to stand.

Before it was able to rise, the panther was on its back. With jaws like a steel trap, it bit down on the Nightmare's neck.

The Nightmare screeched, stumbling back, but the panther's eyes flickered blue. With a loud crack, its teeth tore off the charred skull. The Nightmare's three arms spasmed blindly before the whole thing fell, limp and useless.

This was all a delirious dream. It had to be. Ash was no Oneirocrat who could bring his dreams to life, just a dying man. He gave in to the blackness.

Chapter Two

Geil

Hunting Nightmares is an art that takes a lifetime to master. The tragedy is that Nightmares are uncountable, while those possessing the courage to take them on are not.
– *On Nightmares* by Ecademus the Nightmare-Hunter

As Geil's ship sailed into port, she wondered if this harbour, far up north at the entrance to the Highlands, would finally be the place that allowed her to escape herself. At the very least, she would be able to avoid the prying eyes and sharp tongues of the marchioness's asphyxiating court. When she'd arrived in the north a year ago, she'd found some semblance of solace until, inevitably, the whispers had begun. What was she doing so far away from her family and home in the jet-black city? Had she made enemies so powerful among one of the parties that she'd had to exile herself to the northern marches?

Geil had started to feel just as strangled there as she had in Onyxia, so when a small commission in a quiet town arrived, it seemed the perfect distraction.

Ayron wasn't the quaint fishing village she'd pictured. Instead, she found a bustling harbour built to feed the ever-hungry provinces that comprised the Onyxian Domain. Two bulky stone wharves stretched like open arms to receive *The Solemnity* and, even this late in the evening, the jetties were packed with sloops, carracks and massive sea-drake-pulled galleys. Beneath the waves, the emerald sheen of their snake-like coils was barely visible, though their crimson eyes shone vibrantly. The air reeked of brine and the foul odour of discarded crab carcasses from the underwater Drake stables. A dozen different stevedore crews laboured to fill their holds with iron, wool and oats. Everyone shouted to be heard, creating a cacophony of noise that was beaten only by the screeching gulls circling above and the sea-drakes' hissing below.

The pious would have found it unnerving that there was no divine storm in the sky; Geil found it liberating. Beyond the Motherstorm's eternal gaze, nobody knew of her loss or her guilt.

As the ship docked, Geil threw her sack over the gunwale and leapt onto the stone wharf.

Pulling up her hood to avoid unwanted stares, she skirted past the approaching harbourmaster. After stopping to ask directions from two exceedingly muscular dockworkers, possibly Dreamblooded like her, she headed towards the cliffs overlooking the city, with the sway of somebody who'd spent the last two days at sea.

Ayron's well-lit roads stretched through the village to facilitate access to the warehouses, but Geil chose to cut through the narrow alleys brightened only by the dirty lamps of taverns. She slid unseen through the crowds of brackish sailors and sooty miners, just another traveller eager to spend their wages on ale and a warm bed. The local cats, though, eyed her with suspicion. They must've noticed her odd scent.

She'd just spotted the stairs that ascended to the citadel when her luck ran out.

'What's your hurry there? What do you have in that sack?'

A sailor, as red and heavy as a bull-lobster, latched on to her arm.

'Hands off!' she grunted, twisting away, but he grabbed a handful of her cloak, pulling her hood down.

'Well, well! And here I thought you were a lad under all that. You should join me for a drink instead!' When Geil snarled, he chuckled. 'Can't be picky with hair like yours. Did they trim you with the sheep, love?'

Geil shoved him hard enough to knock him onto his arse and redoubled her march towards the stairs. Ahead, a gang of rugged, salt-coated men emerged from a shabby tavern. The man shouted over to them.

'Mates, will you hold that sheepie for me?' the idiot called. 'Need a word with her.'

They drunkenly hobbled towards her, spreading out to block the path.

Geil considered the alley to her right. She might be able to lose them there, or outrun them, but her gear weighed as much as a dead man. It would need to be left behind if she wanted a quick escape.

Or she could just listen to *it* . . .

We'll be gentle, I promise, that voice in her mind whispered, cool and tempting. Even though the Drake's thoughts lacked a literal voice, Geil could feel it purring with delight in her head.

She stopped, dropping the bag. The sailor approached from behind, trapping her between himself and his friends, reaching for something tucked in his belt.

'You could have chosen to be nice, but you want it the hard way, is that it? Don't you worry, I can play rough too . . .'

Fool. The Drake crackled like an angry ember.

Geil pulled her left arm from beneath her cloak, revealing the scales that shimmered blackish-blue in the lamplight. She could have chosen a more pleasant form for the journey, Dreamt herself smooth skin instead of showing the scales on half her body, but she was here to hunt and the Drake was more useful than fitting in.

'Wait! She's a fucking Dream-mutt!' the sailor yelled, face twisting in disgust.

'Haven't heard that one in a while.' Geil smirked. Wherever human-like Dreamlings toiled, the Dreamblooded, children of mixed human and Dream descent, eventually followed. 'Now out of my way before you wet yourselves.' Geil spread her left hand, granting the men a good look at her sharp, dark claws.

'Fucking mouth you have!' the man shouted.

He drew a knife, but Geil was faster. Her claws grazed his forehead, a light cut meant to blind him with his own blood instead of taking out his eyes. The drunkard screamed in pain.

A smarter man would have been scared. He, foolishly, thrust at her with his blade.

Too close to duck, she caught the weapon in the crook of her elbow, the steel cradled harmlessly in her scales.

Then, she let the Drake take control.

Geil punched the drunk hard with her free arm. Once to stun, twice to break his nose. As he bent backwards with the pain, she twisted his arm downwards, then shoved the dagger deep into his thigh.

He fell to his knees shrieking. His so-called friends scrambled away, terrified.

'I thought you wanted it rough,' Geil hissed.

At her feet, the man whimpered.

Pluck his eyes out. I bet they're fat and juicy, the Drake whispered.

She certainly could. Who would stop her?

'Please, Master Dreamer! Please, spare me! I didn't know!' he begged.

'I'm not a Dreamer, just a *mutt*, remember?' she snarled. The man's eyes shifted between confusion and fear. He was the sort that'd grovel at the feet of a mighty Oneirocrat like her father but would spit on a Dreamling like her mother.

A merciful death is more than he deserves, the Drake said. She raised her claw, ready to slice his throat.

The man broke down sobbing and drooling. A shudder ran through her. Was this what she'd left the life of a Herald for? From itinerant protector of the Domain to spilling some drunk's blood in a dark alley? To further feed the Drake's ceaseless hunger?

She closed her fist.

'Put your hands on a "Dream-mutt" again and I'll rip them off.' She spat on his bloodied face, shouldered her bag and headed towards the staircase.

* * *

She reached the governor's residence just after nightfall. The harbour stretched below her, dappled in silver moonlight.

Two sullen guards stopped her at the castle gates, and only once her letters had confirmed her trade was she finally admitted.

Inside the citadel, a Highlander servant led her through the draughty halls to their master's study, where a massive fireplace fought a losing battle against the cold. The governor was an older man with wispy grey hair and intelligent blue eyes. He regarded her with caution before offering her a seat. Once she was settled, he set to examining her credentials.

He squinted at the ornate imprint on the sealing wax. 'You're the Nightmare-Hunter from Invernia then?' he asked.

Probably he couldn't make head nor tail of her. Half of her body was the Drake's. Her left arm, covered in scales. Her left eye, a gleaming red orb. With the muddy attire, the half-shaven head, she probably looked more like a thug than a highborn and the marchioness's handpicked envoy.

Not that she cared for his opinion. In the capital, lineage might be everything, but here she could enjoy the luxury of nobody knowing her family name.

'I've come as a favour to Her Excellency.'

Not quite untrue. Yet after months of the marchioness hosting her, shielding her from scandal and shame, it was time to start repaying her debts.

The governor continued to examine her papers. Geil let out a loud yawn and set her boots on his desk.

'The marchioness speaks most highly of you,' he muttered, eyeing her sideways.

'Her Excellency exaggerates.'

'You served as a Herald?' His eyes suddenly widened.

'That was . . . a while ago.' Geil disguised her discomfort behind a polite smile. 'Now, what can you tell me about the task at hand?'

'A Nightmare has been terrorising Striomkala, one of the villages in my province.'

'Could just be a lost one gone feral.' Geil noticed his furrowed brow. 'Yet you think there's more to it.'

'These aren't times to allow discontent to fester.' He leaned forwards to lower his voice. 'The Domain is fraying at the edges.'

The man wasn't wrong. Onyxia's Domain, the lands and peoples under its taxation and rule, stretched all the way from Crunia in the south to the Highlands in the north. The wealthy Valelands in the east had always been in constant turmoil, but it had got far worse in the past decade or so since the Kingdom of Delectia had started meddling there.

King Melandros, self-styled 'King of Thorns', not only coveted the Valelands' wealth, he also despised Onyxia. Where Onyxian Oneirocrats fuelled their Dreams with sorrows and sombreness, the King of Thorns's court devoted themselves to romance and sensuality. The King used this to disguise his ambitions as a crusade to liberate the Valelanders from Onyxian oppression.

Not even two years ago he'd fostered an uprising in Vanday to then seize the city with his host. Nobody believed that'd be the last of it.

Geil pursed her lips. 'Why not deal with it yourself then?'

'I'm afraid that my Dreamcraft is of a different sort.' He gestured at the ornate stone chimney with a nervous chuckle. It wasn't surprising. Many Oneirocrats managed to build a successful public career without ever learning the Academy's trade. To volunteer for its brutal training required either desperation or reckless idealism, just like she'd had. 'Still, it might not be worth your valuable time,' he said, returning her documents. 'I could likely wait until the Academy sends one of their own.'

Geil snorted. 'Be grateful that I'm the one doing this.'

'Why's that?'

'The Academy's Nightmare-Hunters would happily set their own monsters on the village if they thought that was the easiest way to deal with the problem.'

The Governor shifted in his chair uncomfortably. 'Sometimes a heavy hand is needed.'

'Sometimes,' she conceded. 'Sometimes their brutality is what sows discontent.'

'Nothing of strength is ever grown in gentle weather,' he said, unfazed.

Geil nodded; inside her, the Drake snorted. Tall words for a man who'd never known anything but the mildest of drizzles.

* * *

Geil set out at dawn, following the jagged coastline on foot.

Below, waves crashed and lapped at the cliff's feet. The seafoam took on strange shapes, spiralling into ghostly vortexes that disappeared as quickly as they formed. Fishermen's cottages and shacks dotted the craggy land, but the locals shied out of her path. She hadn't bothered to cover her scales and they glimmered in the morning light. She might have to Dream herself a different appearance before she reached the village so as not to scare those she was hoping to protect.

After a couple of hours, she followed a basalt road, a ruin from the ancient Iskians' time Dreamt to connect every corner of their now-defunct Empire with Ravkiria, the imperial capital on the other side of the continent. Its cracked path led inland from the susurrant sea into the rustling slopes of the Highlands.

By afternoon, the wind had picked up, and a Kinstorm rolled in from the south, its drizzle cold and numbing, nothing compared to the Motherstorm circling her home city. She might have lived in Invernia for almost a year, but the capital of the Highlands province was a crude stopper for the gaping hole in her heart. When she'd first arrived, the Jewel of the North was like an unread book, its pages filled with fresh mysteries, but time was relentless at eroding that feeling of marvel.

Now, her quarters at the marchioness's palace felt as narrow and cold as a cell. The city's sculptures were still magnificent, but Geil's eyes had grown tired of their beauty, and the shadows of Invernia's stairwells and columns no longer hid her from the past.

And its gaze was unforgiving.

It glared at her out of the faces of all those she'd left behind in Onyxia: her father's and the Falconess's disappointment when they'd found out she was leaving; Itraya's bitter anger; but most of all, Lanteus's deathly paleness.

As long as she didn't stay still, she could evade her memories. As long as she never returned to the jet-black city.

She just needed to keep moving, outrunning the storm and the shadows it cast. Just a while longer.

And with that, she redoubled her march across the windswept heath.

Chapter Three

Ash

In deep slumber, an imaginative child may Dream a particularly vivid terror or blissful fantasy into existence, but such creations, whether Nightmares, Dreamlings or Dreamchantments, will rarely last until morning. To turn such evanescent imaginings into immanent creations takes will. Refusal to let go of what one has envisioned is the mark of true Dreamers.

– *Dialogues: On Imagination* by Aristan of Ravkiria

As ash rolled sleepily over in his cot, a sharp pain in his ankle jolted him awake. Daylight filtered through the narrow window hole, illuminating the bedroom, which was empty – except for the panther by his bed.

The panther, ears perked, turned, opening its huge maw, and Ash reeled back, slamming his head against the slanted ceiling. The dull pain confirmed he was most certainly awake.

The creature finished a big yawn, then sat on its hindquarters to watch Ash with curiosity.

His racing pulse brought the memories back. He'd Dreamt this creature. Hadn't he? But how? He was no Dreamer. Entombed hells, he despised the Dreamers' arrogance and cruelty with a passion. And he'd never shown the gifts as a child! There had to be another explanation …

Ash squirmed upright, and the feline's eyes widened. Would it attack him? Dreamers knew how to make their creations loyal, but Ash had had no idea what he'd been doing the night before. Some children Dreamt their night terrors into existence, but they'd wither and crumble with morning's light. Permanence required a Dreamer's mastery. So did loyalty.

The feline suddenly looked towards the door. Ghalod entered a second later, holding a clay mug in one hand and a crude walking stick beneath his opposite arm.

'Morning!' The towering man cautiously approached Ash's cot. The panther craned up to sniff the steaming mug. 'Here,' he said, handing Ash some freshly brewed leaf infusion. The stick, Ghalod deposited on the bed. 'One is to help with the limping of the body, the other with that of the spirit,' he said warmly. 'Have you given your new friend a name yet?'

'No . . . I wasn't sure he was even real.'

'Well, you should. I have a feeling that he might be staying with us for a while. Hopefully, he's a good omen of things to come.'

'Omen . . . That's a fitting name.' The shadow-panther's ears perked up, and he looked at Ash as if he understood they were talking about him.

Ash tentatively offered a hand, and the panther sniffed it. He flashed one of his fangs and, for a moment, Ash feared he was about to lose his hand. Instead, Omen just rubbed his maw against his fingers.

'I'd say he likes you,' Ghalod said.

Ash's frown finally turned into a smile.

'Ghalod, have you ever Dreamt something before?'

'No. Nothing this magnificent, at least! Once, as a child, I Dreamt a horrible frog-like thing during a nightmare. The awful little terror gave my parents a good scare. Good thing my dad had his hammer at hand. Come morning, the nasty thing was already rotting away, as it should. Can't stand the sight of frogs since. Luckily, your friend here is handsomer.'

Ash nodded, only then realising how quiet their garret was. 'Where are the others?'

'At the guild, trying to persuade Master Esmus not to rescind our licence.'

'We should hurry then.'

'In your state, you should stay here.'

His right arm, freshly bandaged, throbbed with warm pain. It didn't smell good and hurt worse. Probably why he was running a fever too, he noticed.

'No, it's better if we're all there, even if it's just to inspire pity,' Ash protested. 'Besides, it's not as if we'll be able to stay much longer if we lose our little trade.'

He limped to the basin, washing himself with cold rainwater and tying back his hair, then changed into a spare woollen shirt. His father's jerkin had a fresh tear in the arm, but it would do for now.

He considered leaving Omen behind, but feared their shabby wooden door wouldn't keep him in if he really wanted to get out.

Besides, as soon as he started moving, Omen followed, flicking the tip of his tail.

It was early afternoon when the three of them set out into the bustling streets of the Little Vespiria district. The Motherstorm was deep in slumber, a thick fog seeping through the crowded thoroughfares.

Living space had always been scarce in Onyxia, but these days, even their island in the Southern Quarter, sandy and prone to flooding, was teeming with residents. People kept coming, either driven by the turmoil in the Valelands or in the hopes that the jet-black city would provide them with some meagre livelihood. Yet, somehow, the Oneirocrats' palaces and the merchants' manors in the Central Quarter's gilded islets stood impervious against these waves of newcomers, leaving the rest to be swept like dust into the crowded nooks of the Craghorn isthmus or the squalid crannies of its Southern Quarter.

Still, today Ash cherished every second of their crawl through the zigzagging alleys and around the hunched wooden buildings. Perhaps it was his recent brush with death, or simply that everyone, from the fishers to the woodworkers and child-carers, was quick to open a path for them at the sight of the fearsome-looking panther. Ash was torn between shame at frightening them and pride at his creation.

They crossed over a marble bridge and into the Central Quarter. At least there it was easier to blend into the crowds of merchants and their Dreamling-pulled carts. Soon, the landscape around them shifted, wood replaced with black marble, stone and onyx. The gleaming, dark wealth of the city's central cluster of islets spread all around as they climbed a wrought-iron stairway that coiled upwards to the city's heights.

Only here, high above the covered plazas in the endless expanse of slate rooftops they called the Sea of Shingles, did he feel free. The rooftops were the guild's hunting grounds, and here the Lightning-Hunters' tower lorded over even the Oneirocrats' domed palaces like an angry porcupine, its rocky facade unkempt and overgrown with a mesh of spikes, rods and other lightning-traps.

Ash and Ghalod entered through the forge's cargo bay. There, the guild's glassblowers were busy working onyx harvested from the lagoon's depths into holding orbs.

A narrow staircase took them up to the observation decks. Rudher's familiar voice boomed down the steps. 'Five Octaves? Come on, Esmus! Two full orbs are worth at least two full Onars! How are we supposed to make you any coin if we can't even pay rent?'

Esmus, the guildmaster overseeing them, sounded frustrated. 'Times are tough for us all, and the guild already has enough ill-mannered orphans to feed. Leave the mouthiness to them, Rudher. Five Octaves is more than enough – the other ten are going against the three Onars and three Octaves you owe the guild, so take my offer and let's be done with it. I'll give you a week to pay the rest.'

As Ash and Ghalod stepped onto the open deck, Yaisa hurried to greet them. 'Right on time! This isn't going well,' she whispered.

Master Esmus stood surrounded by Dreamchanted weather-vanes, long-sight scopes and glass containers filled with different types of the Motherstorm's rain to help predict Her moods. He wore a thick woollen tunic under his blue guildmaster smock, but the clothes were too large on him, and his unkempt appearance gave the impression of a scarecrow. Ash didn't really like the man, but Esmus had taken them on as apprentices when no other master would. With good reason: the guild had their pick of the lot from the chimney-sweeper children. Why bother training older apprentices? Particularly when some, like Ash and Rudher, had spent time in the Grand Palace's prisons. Even though Rudher said that Esmus had chosen them out of greediness, he'd betted on them, and for that, Ash was thankful.

'The book-boy is here, Esmus,' Rudher said with a smile, 'and he brings his new friend!'

Master Esmus's sharp face turned towards Ash, his eyes widening at the sight of Omen.

'Do you believe me now, Esmus?' Rudher boasted triumphantly. 'If the lad turns out to be a Dreamer, your investment will be repaid tenfold.'

Ash squirmed at the suggestion.

Entranced, Esmus crouched an arm's length from Omen. 'You'd have me believe you *Dreamt* this?'

'You can believe your own eyes, Master,' Ash replied. He dared to reach to stroke the panther, who perked up at the attention.

'Very well. How much do you want for the beast?' Esmus asked.

'How much can you afford to pay?' replied Rudher.

The master scratched his scraggly beard while musing over the question. 'This might cover all your pending debts with the guild.'

'And the fifteen Octaves from our haul?' Rudher demanded.

'. . . To be paid in addition to that,' Esmus allowed.

Rudher let out a triumphant chortle, but Yaisa cut him short. 'That is if Ash agrees.'

All eyes fell on him. This was the stroke of luck they'd been hoping for. He had the power to free them from debt, to secure their guild status. At a time when so many were drowning, this was a log to cling to, but he felt his throat close at the thought.

'Apologies, Master, but what use would you have for him?' Ash asked. Perhaps if he knew Omen would be taken care of, he'd be able to stomach selling him.

'Me? None!' Esmus rose and brushed dust from his knees. 'Dreamling beasts give me the creeps, but I know of many Oneirocrats who'd enjoy having such a creature in their hunts.'

'As a hound or as prey?' Ash asked.

'That's for them to decide. I'll fetch your payment.'

That was enough money to get them back on their feet. Still, Ash hesitated, and it wasn't just that he was pricing the panther like a cow when he was worth a lot more. The thought of some cruel Oneirocrat pitting Omen against their Nightmares made Ash queasy. Omen had saved Ash's life.

'I'm sorry. He's not for sale.'

Esmus's eyes bugged from his skull. 'What are you playing at, Ash? Do you really fancy yourself a Hordemaster now?'

'I need the panther,' Ash said, 'to keep us safe.'

'Really, Aescyon?' Esmus only addressed him with his full name when chiding him. 'Don't let a foolish fantasy squander this opportunity.' Esmus narrowed his eyes, his face sinking back into its usual dishevelment. 'I'll give you a week to settle your debts. By then, we'll have learned how far your wick goes as a Dreamer. And as a gesture of good will, I'll pay you for last night's haul.'

Rudher and Esmus shook on it, then the master took them to the bookkeepers himself to authorise their payment.

After collecting their dues, the four returned to the Sea of Shingles under a cold drizzle. Omen shifted uncomfortably under the rain, and Ash wondered how he would even take care of the creature with his meagre earnings. Above, skyships floated effortlessly, and Ash watched them longingly, reminded of how far he still was from ever stepping, let alone sailing, on one.

'I'm sorry,' Ash said.

'Like the lass said,' the old man replied gruffly, 'it wasn't my call to make. As for Master Esmus ... Fuck 'em, I say!' The others chuckled with relief. 'If you truly are a Dreamer, lad, soon you'll be swimming in riches.'

'Well said,' Ghalod added.

Ash turned to Yaisa.

'Don't look at me, Ash. You and your furry friend here saved me last night. Old Rhudey here said it best.' She winked at Rudher. 'Fuck 'em.'

Ash felt an immense weight lift from his shoulders.

'This calls for a celebration!' Rudher said. 'What say you that we spend some of this hard-won money at The Biting Ale? Zercas might be there, and I'd very much love to rub this small victory in his face.'

'Perhaps tomorrow.' Ash rubbed the back of his neck sheepishly. 'I'm meeting someone this eve.'

'You're still seeing the Wailer?' Yaisa asked.

Ash's smile was his only answer.

Rudher sighed. 'Lad, for all you've read, you're dumb as a rock sometimes. You know what they say. "Heartbreak and heartache feel all the same to the Sisterhood of Suffering."'

* * *

He was to meet Daerna at The Hanging Lady, a public house in the Western Quarter, home to the city's artisan guilds and many docks. A long walk for him, especially on a bad ankle and weak from the fever, yet a price he was happy to pay. Here, they were afforded a measure of privacy from Daerna's superiors in the Sisterhood.

He found them a secluded table on a balcony overlooking the pub's covered courtyard. It was a cool evening, with the soft wind bringing in the fragrance of the bloodvine-overgrown walls. Nursing a cup of cider, he settled to wait, soothed by the Motherstorm's pattering on the roof.

They'd met only a few months ago. She'd been sitting on a lone bench near the Barley Market, feeding scraps to the crow-cats and reading Saalins's *Songs of the Morrow*. After he'd remarked on her excellent taste in poetry, she'd invited him to sit with her. They'd talked books for hours, and then met again the following day, when a few daring kisses had followed in the rain-scented arcades.

Theirs was a doomed affair. She was a Sister devoted to lofty spiritual pursuits, and he a lowly Lightning-Hunter with only debts to his name. He kept reminding himself to keep his heart guarded.

At least until she walked into the courtyard. She searched for him, black cascades of hair swirling, hazel eyes burning with determination in her pale, sharp face. Those same eyes lit warm hope within his heart, which was why he knew any attempt at guarding against her was hopeless.

He waved at Daerna, and she crossed the courtyard towards him. The patrons turned their heads – at least until they noticed the embroidered black dress buttoned up to the neck. She might not be wearing her veil, but they could recognise a Wailer's habit.

They greeted with a kiss, one that broke suddenly when she noticed Omen.

'There's a panther . . .' she said, eyes wide.

'Dae, meet Omen, my new friend.' He gestured for her to approach the cat, and Daerna did so with her usual poise. Omen watched her with lively, cerulean-blue eyes.

Ash recounted the events of the previous night, and she listened intently, only growing distracted when she grew bold enough to pet Omen.

The panther took a liking to her immediately and was soon spread flat under her caresses like a housecat by a fireplace.

'Blessed Motherstorm's tears! I'm so glad that you're safe! Are you sure you don't need to see a physician?' she asked.

'I've had worse. Besides, I need to save all I can for the guild.'

'Ash, if you can Dream, you won't have to worry about money ever again.'

Ash shook his head. 'I'm not even sure how this happened to begin with.' He avoided Daerna's inquisitive gaze by looking into his empty cup. 'Omen was a miracle – a one-time miracle. I'm no Oneirocrat!' He forced out a chuckle.

'Ash, you know it's not just the highborn who Dream. Maybe you just need to rest before you try again.'

He smiled ruefully. 'I don't think so.'

'If it's not exhaustion, it might just be that your inspiration has waned. Or maybe it's just technique? The Academy's masters could teach you . . .'

'I'd rather die,' he blurted.

Daerna gawked in shock.

'I'm sorry,' Ash said. Whatever scars he carried, she didn't deserve his snapping. 'It's just . . .' Some conversations between them he'd always found difficult. When speaking of love, Ash always feared being laughed at. This was different. Not because of her, rather because the past refused to be dragged from whatever miserable hole it was burrowed inside without screaming and kicking.

'Do you want to tell me about it?'

'I've told you my father died, years ago. Yet not how it happened.' Ash heaved a sigh. 'We were in the Sunken Library, searching for lost books we could copy and print.'

'You mean the ruins of Damnia's Great Library?'

He nodded, avoiding her shocked gaze, then swallowed hard before continuing. 'Some Nightmare grabbed him, and the Academy's sentries just left him to die. They caught me, of course, put me in chains and sent me to the Grand Palace's

Deep Wells. I . . .' He took a deep breath. It had all happened almost seven years ago, but still, even thinking about those days made his chest tighten. It wasn't just his father's look of horror but also how, despite Ash's desperate pleas for aid, they'd beaten him to within an inch of his life. It wasn't just the grief but the weeks spent in the Grand Palace's dungeons, filthy water to his ankles, leeches sticking to his skin whenever he fell asleep: the 'lenient' treatment he'd gotten on account of his young age.

She paused. 'I'm so sorry, Ash, I didn't know.'

'I'll never become one of *them*.'

'Them?'

'The Oneirocrats, the Academy, anyone helping keep the rest of us in chains.'

Daerna reached for his shoulder with a sad smile. 'Ash, I know you enough to tell that you couldn't, even if you wanted.'

'What do you mean?'

'We've spoken about how the world's wrong. Precisely because of that I know you'd never squander such a gift. I know if I were a Dreamer . . .' She didn't finish the sentence, drifting as she focused over his shoulder.

'Aescyon Lightning-Hunter?'

Three people stood behind him, each of them clad in ornate cuirasses engraved with bones, rain-soaked woollen capes and gorgets carved with a crest he knew well. The lone tower, cutting through swirling shadows: the Academy's coat of arms.

'Who's asking?' replied Ash, disguising his fear with hostility.

'Sergeant Dain, from the Academy. You're to accompany us at once.' The man regarding him with cold scorn had a livid scar on his shaven head. His two companions, a slender, golden-skinned woman with a whip and a hulking hooded fellow, only added to the grim picture. He'd been a fool to take Omen out into the streets, to flaunt him. Still, how in the entombed hells were they on to him so fast?

'You've got the wrong person.'

The sergeant scoffed at him. 'Does it sound as if I'm asking? You're coming with us, one way or another.' He grabbed Ash's arm, while his hooded companion produced a pair of manacles.

The sergeant shoved him towards the other two, despite Daerna's angry protestations, but before they could cuff him, a blur leapt from behind a table.

Omen landed on the hooded fellow, who collapsed beneath the panther's bulk. With a snarl, he turned his gaze on the other two.

The woman was ready, though. She flung her hands at Omen and, out of thin air, a web of silver chains took form, trapping the panther before he could leap again.

Omen landed on one side with a heavy thud and a low growl. Twisting and wriggling, the panther fought to be free, but struggled even to lift his head. The metal net was impossibly heavy.

'Impressive,' the woman remarked, helping her fallen companion stand.

'Stupid beast!' The sergeant delivered a harsh kick to Omen's ribs.

'Stop!' Ash yelled, punching him in the back.

The sergeant glared at him, reaching for the sword on his belt. Taking on three people at once was a stupid idea. Taking on three Dreamers at once, unarmed, was suicide.

Still, to hell with them all if they thought they could hurt Omen. Ash might be unarmed, but maybe he could find a weapon elsewhere.

He unfocused his sight and allowed anger to burn through him, filling in the gaps of his vision. It was a leap, a desperate attempt, but anything was better than standing idle.

To his surprise, a grey patina suddenly shrouded the world.

As if on instinct, he drew from his memory the shape of lightning, and he imagined it falling into the middle of the three of them.

Before he'd fully given it shape, the scarred man lunged. Ash saw him move strangely, like a smudge on the watery painting of the scene, hand reaching for Ash's chest. He tried ducking out of his way, but inside the trance his body reacted very slowly.

Horrified, he raised his arms to defend himself, but even that was too much effort. The man stabbed him with the spiked tips of his steel glove. As the metal pricked Ash's jerkin, a red oval on the gauntlet lit up.

A sharp jolt ran through Ash's body, tensing every muscle in a knot of pain and dragging him out of the grey.

He collapsed to the ground, and the lightning in his mind vanished along with his consciousness.

Chapter Four

Daerna

No tear is cried in vain,
If elevated to heaven's rain,
And hearts ground to dust,
And spirits by despair crushed,
Shall be made whole again,
When death lies undone

– *The Song of Sorrows, Canticle I, Neume II,* by Princess Geleisdra

IT WAS SAID THAT WAILING Sisters delighted in misery – that wasn't true for Daerna.

Divine Geleisdra's *Song of Sorrows* spoke of embracing sorrow to preserve it, but many of her fellow Sisters took it to mean that hardships were to be collected like precious jewels. In the case of the Wailers, it was true that a grieving heart might be better able to reach the Hallowed Motherstorm, but Daerna had always rejected the notion that one had to passively endure happenstance.

Tipping up her chin, she blocked the sergeant from leaving. 'He's a member of one of the city's guilds, *not* a child! You have *no* rights over him!' It wasn't just righteous determination that bade her hold her ground. Before leaving the life of a scion of a merchant lineage, Daerna had taken studies at Arvira University. She hadn't just learned about the classics, mathematics and rhetoric, but also a good deal of law. Enough to know there were exceptions to the Academy's right of conscription, and this was one of them.

The man scoffed humourlessly. 'Guildmember or not, if he's an untrained Dreamer, I have every right,' he replied.

She widened her stance. 'You're not taking him until we call for the Lightning-Hunters' Guild and clear up this matter.'

He drew a heavy iron mace from his belt and cradled it lovingly in his arms. 'Don't make me do this, Sister. Better men have tried to stop us, and not once have they succeeded. The Academy always claims its due. Now, you can stand aside, or I can make you.'

He had to be bluffing. Violence against an ordained Sister was enough to earn commoners a hanging. Even Oneirocrats could be punished with exile for such a crime. Then again, the cold delight in the man's eyes suggested that inflicting pain was a rewarding prospect to him. Perhaps that's what it took to rise to such a position in the Academy.

Her stomach tightened. 'Strike me down if you dare!' she yelled. 'Strike down an unarmed Sister and display your cowardice for all to see!'

Some of the patrons of the tavern rose from their seats, drinks forgotten and fists clenched.

'Stay back, you fools! You don't know what you're doing!' the sergeant yelled, but nobody obeyed him. In fact, the innkeeper, a strong, tattooed woman, pulled out a heavy cudgel from behind the bar.

The sergeant muttered a curse, and his eyes went glassy.

Before Daerna could utter a word, a hulking figure took shape right beside her, a crudely carved gargoyle, its stony fangs misshapen but long.

It swung a fist at her, and Daerna barely had time to shield herself with her arms. To her surprise, the blow landed on the table she'd been occupying, splintering the wood.

'Your black habit might protect *you*, Sister, but it won't protect this place, and it won't protect *them*.' The sergeant gestured around the room with his mace.

All around her, the locals' faces twisted taut with fear. Even the innkeeper eyed her with a silent plea. It was one thing to risk her life, another thing all these people's.

'We're not done,' she replied, stepping aside.

After that, she followed them as they made their way to the docks and loaded Ash and his panther onto a large barge with dark sails. The recruiting sergeant shot her a scornful smirk, while the others dragged their captives below deck.

Daerna stood frozen, watching them sail away.

What could she do against the might of the Academy?

Maybe it was the practical blood of her merchant family, but it took a lot more than one defeat to make her back off from a fight.

* * *

When the garret's door cracked open, a skinny, tanned woman peered out at her. 'Ash isn't here.'

Daerna recalled her from a brief meeting in the past. 'Yaisa, right?' she asked, breathing heavily from her run. 'That's why I've come. The Academy has taken him!'

Her distressed face was enough for Yaisa to let her in. Their garret was draughty and damp, tattered pieces of canvas serving as walls. A gangly, grey-bearded man dressed only in a long camisole emerged from behind one.

'What are you talking about?'

'They took him in chains,' Daerna repeated.

'Who took him?' A second man, so tall he had to hunch in the low-ceilinged room, emerged from behind another canvas wall.

Yaisa made the introductions. 'Daerna, meet Rudher and Ghalod. Now, please, will you tell us what happened?'

Daerna recounted it all. When she'd finished, Rudher mouthed a curse and punched the tilted ceiling.

Ghalod slouched in a corner. Yaisa kept shaking her head. 'Ash is no Dreamer. Whatever he did must have been a one-time miracle. What use is *that* to them?'

'Even a lowly Lightning-Hunter is worth something to the Academy if he's got the gift,' Rudher replied.

'And if he doesn't?' Daerna asked.

'Then he'll end up in some Nightmare's belly,' Rudher said bitterly. Then, he clapped a hand to the top of his head. 'I'm a fool! I should have guessed they'd come! Should have kept my mouth shut instead of sweet-talking Master Esmus!'

'Must have been one of the glassblowers. They saw us arrive with Omen,' Ghalod surmised.

'When I find who ratted him out, I'll chop off their tongue myself!'

Growing impatient, Daerna cleared her throat. 'Whatever the reasons, you must get him out of there.'

The Lightning-Hunters exchanged hesitant glances before Yaisa broke the uncomfortable silence. 'It's always about money, isn't it? There must be something we can work out, the right palms to grease.'

'We don't have that kind of money. We'd need to buy a senator or some high-placed official, and it'd take more than a few hundred Octaves.' Rudher massaged his temples.

'Surely you don't think to abandon him now?' Daerna asked, flustered.

'Might be too late . . .' Rudher huffed. 'He could already be on his way to the Academy. And once you cross the Mantle, you're never the same.'

That did send a chill down her spine. The Mantle, the perpetual shroud of darkness that shielded the Academy from the rest of the world, was said to drive a fear so powerful into those who crossed it that it forever scarred their minds. They *had* to save Ash before he left the city.

'They took him on a barge,' Daerna replied. 'They couldn't possibly be taking him to the Academy in that.' She refused to accept that all was lost.

'They've probably taken him to the Isle of Sighs,' Rudher said. At Daerna's confused look, he explained, 'The Academy's citadel on the lagoon's west edge. They hold their recruits there until their ship arrives.'

'Couldn't we try breaking him out?' Yaisa continued.

Rudher barked a laugh. 'We'd need a boat and a captain reckless enough to approach it. Even if we find one, the place is teeming with Nightmares.'

Ghalod shook his great head. 'If Ash was here, he'd figure something out.'

A heavy silence fell on them.

'Does Ash have any patrons that can step in for him?' Daerna asked.

Rudher grimaced. 'The lad's got us, but not much else.'

'How about the guild? Unless I'm mistaken, if he's a Dreamer, your guild has the right to claim him,' Daerna said.

Rudher scratched his balding head. 'Ach. You might be right. Even if somebody at the guild ratted him out, doesn't mean the masters will appreciate somebody stomping all over our rights. It's worth a shot.'

'Let's go to Master Esmus,' Yaisa resolved. 'Will you come with us, Daerna? I'm sure he'll feel more compelled to act with a Sister watching.'

She swallowed hard, considering the invitation. She'd miss her Keening watch tonight and show up exhausted for her chorus practice. No doubt be reprimanded and disciplined. That was if the prioress didn't find out about Ash.

Unlike other Orders of the Sisterhood of Suffering, hers didn't demand celibacy. As long as they touched the Motherstorm with their canticles, they were allowed some peccadillos. Still, many Sisters taught that 'Love's bloom sapped the well of sorrows', that romance was an impure pursuit that deterred from their devotion and ability to perform their Keening art.

'I . . .' She hesitated. This was a terrible idea. Hadn't she already sacrificed enough? Only hard, dedicated work had allowed her to become a rising star among the Keening Choir, and now she was about to risk all of that. For what, exactly? Some young man with melancholic grey eyes and long dark hair? '. . . I'll accompany you, but I can't get involved,' she finished.

'I understand.' Yaisa's disappointment was palpable. 'Give us a moment to get ready, please.'

Following Yaisa's indications, Daerna sat on Ash's empty cot at the back of the minuscule dwelling. It smelled of sweat, of rain and wet cat fur. Around her, books piled up, mostly incomplete, unbound misprints. A rare luxury nonetheless, given they'd be worth what an artisan made in a year. Surely somebody else would have sold them to afford some comforts. Yet he hadn't.

She noticed a worn-out copy of *Songs of the Morrow* by the bed. The book that had connected them. She picked it up and thumbed through it. In the margins, he'd jotted down his own verses inspired by Saalins's poetry.

Her heart ached deeper than she thought possible. Probably because she'd been reminded that, as drawn to his lips as she might have been, it was the heart inside him she longed for. A heart that, like hers, burned with dreams of a different world.

Perhaps she could get involved after all. Perhaps she already had.

Love's bloom might sap the well of sorrows, but heartache and heartbreak certainly replenished it, and nothing made it brim like having love stolen away.

Chapter Five

Geil

Nightmares' shapes are nigh infinite, and they shift with every generation's fears. The Nightmare-Hunter's tools are far fewer. Fortunately, certain stratagems are of universal application on every hunt, and they might spell the difference between triumph or death . . .

– *Mastering the Hunt* by Master Vartus of the Academy

TWO DAYS LATER, GEIL FOUND what she'd been looking for engraved on a milestone. She didn't speak the Highlands tongue well, but recognised the village name: Stiomkrala. She finally left the basalt road for a dirt path that meandered towards a rocky gully. There, on its slopes, rested the sleepy village, its dry-stone houses cobbled together to shelter its inhabitants from the pummelling winds.

Slowing her approach, she Dreamt away the visible scales, leaving rosy skin in their wake. Her arm and face felt naked and alien without them, yet it was best not to frighten the villagers. Wandering the vacant streets, she knocked on the barred doors, four times on each house. A knock for each of Divine Geleisdra's blessed followers and their Orders. Despite the difference in language and customs, religion was the thread binding Onyxia together.

With no response, she headed for the circular clearing that served as the village's market square. There, she sat to wait by the old board plastered with tattered edicts written in both Onyxian and Highlander. She stuck her sheathed sword in the muddy ground and tied her Academy medallion around the cross-guard.

After a while, the villagers trickled in, a sombre crowd wrapped in thick woollen tunics. The tight-lipped men clutched staffs or axes, while the bleary-eyed women held scythes or the hands of their children. Of the hundred or so inhabitants, only two dozen showed up; it was enough.

As they gathered, their whispers grew into a loud murmur. They might not know her, but some recognised the Academy's crest on the medallion. Finally, a grey-haired woman approached her, escorted by a large man.

'I am Calaig, matriarch of this village. Are you here for our children? Or to help us?' Her tone was defiant, and her Onyxian excellent.

'What's this about children?'

'They've been coming every season, three with the sign of the shadowed tower. Like you. Asked about our children. To take them with them.'

While the Academy sought the gift among all commoners, coming so often into the Highlands' depths was new. The masters must've been desperate for conscripts.

'No, I'm here on behalf of the governor to kill the Nightmare.'

'So they sent three for our children but a single woman to hunt a monster? To do the work of a dozen men?' the broad-chested fellow scoffed.

The Drake's blood boiled at his words, but Geil tamped the rage down. She had no interest in beating this man's prejudices out of his head. Besides, he might be a fool, but the people behind him looked scared.

'You can try your luck yourself then.'

Geil stood up as if readying to leave, but the matriarch chided the man in the Highland tongue before turning back to her. 'Please, stay. We'll tell you everything we know.'

It was a familiar tale.

A monster had started preying on their herds. It always came in the thick of night, and was clever enough to, for the most part, avoid their guards and hounds. Some thought it was a sort of winged bear, some that it was a wolf walking on two feet.

'We've found some of our sheep's carcasses in the woods beyond the gap. It must have its lair deep inside them, but that's all its domain now,' Calaig explained.

'Who knows these woods well?' Geil asked.

'The foresters,' she replied. 'Their cottage is on the other side of the gully.'

'And they haven't moved?'

'No.' Calaig's expression soured. Hushed murmurs ran through the crowd.

She didn't ask what upset them; whispered rumours were of no use. Instead, she sheathed the sword.

'I'll need dried meat and a pint of blood,' Geil said.

Matriarch Calaig frowned, asking no questions. Soon, with a satchel full of salted lamb, a blood-filled skin, some rope, tinder and her traps, Geil set out into the woods, then descended down a gully. The Drake suddenly grew restless. It'd caught the same scent Geil had: a faint, feathery whiff, a large bird of prey.

Hefting up the satchel and longsword, she crossed the stream at the bottom, finding several rock pens on the opposite slope. The villagers had taken their herds closer to the village; Geil failed to see what difference the stream would make to a Nightmare that could fly.

Checking near the pens, there weren't any fresh tracks, although she did spot some claw marks on the rocky walls themselves, made by talons as large as a stryx's, if not larger.

The twisted half-owl, half-women Nightmares were known for their unnatural viciousness, which made them a favourite at the Academy. *Nothing nourishes me like tearing a stryx apart*, the Drake murmured, licking its lips, and Geil felt her bile rising. Instinctively, the Drake came to the surface, her skin shifting into sharp blue scales. This was, after all, how and why the Drake had been born.

* * *

It had happened during their first field exam in the Gravelands, one of the Academy's brutal training grounds.

She must've been freshly turned fifteen when her Talon had been dropped into the island's southern reaches. So close to the coast, they should have been able to see the surf, yet only a wall of swirling darkness rose on the horizon. The Mantle, cutting from the sea's rocks to the heavens above, severing them from the rest of the world.

She was on edge, not just because the Gravelands were an ideal hunting ground for Nightmares. The blasted bog was shrouded in a thick mist, tinged grey by the Mantle's dark tendrils and broken by mounds covered in bushes and craggy trees with iron foliage.

But moreover, this close to the Mantle, the land was Vigil-blighted. Nightmares took shape of their own accord, formed by the land or fears you didn't know you had. Sometimes, they thrashed so hard, reality creaked under their efforts.

As soon as the masters had left them, their party had started squabbling. They weren't a proper Talon, not yet, after all. An older boy, Bryon, wanted them to reach their destination by plotting the straightest path possible.

She, Mavis and Lanteus had strongly objected.

'What about ambushes or traps?' Mavis blurted nervously.

'Besides, when have the masters ever given us clear assignments?' Lanteus asked.

Geil had already begun falling for him then. Lanteus was different; he wasn't cocky like some of the older boys, he was brave, and not just for himself. When scrawny little Mavis, the youngest, had been bullied by the others, Lanteus hadn't hesitated to step in the way of the blows.

'Stay with your little lickspittles then,' Bryon had dismissively replied. 'Maybe you three belong together: the fool, the songbird and the coward.'

As the group started moving, Lanteus reached for her and Mavis's shoulders. 'Even an idiot like Bryon can be right sometimes. We'll work well together. Just help me keep an eye out for the rest of the group, will you? We need eyes and smarts, not a hammer.'

'I could watch out for us from above,' Geil said, spreading her grey falcon wings. She was soft and tender back then.

'Excellent! Just watch out for yourself too. It's impossible to know what's hiding in this mist,' Lanteus said.

Geil Dreamt her wings longer and her frame lighter. Beating her wings, she followed their party from above.

They'd waded through the dark crimson waters of the bog, making good progress despite the uneven terrain. Then Geil had spotted a muddy figure hunched over a deer carcass.

'Ahead!' she'd called down.

'It's just some stupid mudghast! Let's take it on!' Bryon yelled.

Something wasn't right about the silhouette, though.

It swayed like a mudghast, but Master Thalder had taught them that mudghasts weren't carrion-eaters.

Geil circled closer. The Nightmare twitched and tilted its head towards her. Its proportions were all wrong; its limbs were human-like, but way too long, with bloodied spurs at its joints. She realised the thing wasn't made of mud, just covered in it. The final confirmation came when she noticed its protracted maw was full of serrated teeth.

'Gouge-hound!' she'd screamed.

Gouge-hounds hunted in packs. Too late, they realised it was an ambush. Others rose from the bogs where they'd been hiding and converged on the unsuspecting cadets.

Before she could land to help, something swooped at her from above. She ducked and heard the frustrated, screeching howl of a stryx. A twisted cross between a woman and an owl, it faced her, cutting a terrifying silhouette of black, feathered wings, large fangs and even larger talons.

And it was coming for her. Stryxes weren't just vicious; they were also fiendishly clever. It might have set up this ambush just for a mere taste of human blood.

She dived like a terrified sparrow towards a copse of trees ahead, hoping it'd offer some shelter. As she came upon it, the stryx struck from above and knocked her directly into the tallest trunk.

She spun through the air, iron branches lashing and cutting at her in her downward fall.

Everything went dark.

When she came to, she was grounded with shattered wings. Breathing hurt, and she had so much blood over her that she couldn't tell where she'd been cut.

Dizzy, she tapped the Dreamchanted gorgon bracer on her left arm, summoning the masters to their aid.

Except the gorgon's mouth moved and bit her fingers, tearing some skin. She let out a shriek. Bleeding all over her forearm, she released the straps and flung the bracer away. The cursed Mantle had twisted it into a threat.

Her vision was blurry. Still, she could make out the shadow circling her above.

The stryx was closing in for the kill.

Too stunned to think how to fight back, she crawled away. As if some bushes would stop what was coming. She called for Lanteus and Mavis, for anyone really, but they were lost to the mist and their own battle.

A searing pain ravaged her back when the stryx's talons dug into her. She heard herself scream, then whimper when the bright-eyed, owlish face sank its teeth into her neck.

The world drained of colour except for the crimson of her own pain.

She was going to die because of Bryon's stupidity. Because of her own stupidity.

Perhaps her masters had been right all along: she was too weak, too frail, a good-for-nothing Dream-mutt.

No. This wasn't because of her weakness; this was because of their cruelty. This was the masters' savagery made flesh and fang.

Curse them all.

She released an angry howl and poured it all into her bloodstream. It filled her heart and pumped into every vein.

This current ran red, not with blood but with burning hatred. It blazed so brightly, so deeply, that she didn't just Dream herself a new skin or new wings; she carved into her very soul.

Here, where reality was porous and fragile, she let go of herself. Her old skin crackled like a chrysalis, releasing iron-like scales. Beneath them, her muscles bulged with renewed strength. Claws burst from her fingertips like knives.

It hurt, except this was her pain. Better to set yourself on fire than be torn apart.

The stryx jerked its head back, drooling with Geil's blood. It was smart enough to realise this was no longer prey, no longer Geil.

She twisted under the stryx's talons, parried the flurry of claws as it fought back.

And then, with relish, the Drake that now inhabited her tore the stryx's chest open, bathing her in pasty grey entrails and black bile.

Later, Lanteus said he and Mavis had found her buried in the carcass, her growls almost a purr. Master Thalder had to knock her out just to ferry her back to safety.

It'd been a miracle she'd made it, the Remakers said. She didn't remember much of it.

What she remembered was Master Davorles, proudly smiling. His words as he admired the Drake's scales. 'Well done, dear. We shall make something terrible out of you yet.'

* * *

Uphill, the slope opened into a grassy dale blanketed by a light mist. Beyond, the mountains spilled into a thick copse of gnarled trees. Not far from the end of the dale, a lone cottage stood, surrounded by a dry-stone wall.

Geil approached with soft steps.

The only sound was a girl's chattering coming from the orchard. There, a young, red-haired lass played with a set of hay-stuffed dolls. She seemed to be talking to them, or perhaps to herself.

To avoid spooking her, Geil walked towards the stone cottage's entrance with much louder steps. The girl's head snapped up, eyes widening as she spotted Geil. With one doll clutched to her chest, she cautiously approached the entrance.

'What are you doing here?' she asked in the Highlander tongue, following with many other questions Geil didn't understand.

'My Highlander isn't good,' Geil apologised.

'Why are you at my house?' the girl asked, cautiously switching to Onyxian.

'Where are your parents?' Geil asked.

'Nearby,' she replied, gesturing at the cottage.

No smoke rose from the chimney, and the silence went past peaceful and into worrying. Still, Geil could hardly fault the girl for lying to a stranger.

'Who are you?' the girl asked.

'A huntress.'

'Why do you look like that?'

'Haven't you ever seen a huntress?'

The girl nodded enthusiastically. 'Grey Glenia in the village. She wears breeches too! But it isn't that.' She leaned over to admire Geil's left arm. 'This!' she said, pointing to the scales. 'And your eye, and your hair! Half of you is different.'

'We can be more than one thing, little one. I'm a huntress now, but I'll be something else before the day is over.'

'Isn't that confusing?'

'Confusing to whom?'

'I don't know ...' She shrugged. 'The people? Matriarch Calaig says we all have paths, and that it's wrong and dangerous to leave them.'

'Paths!' Geil scoffed. 'The world cares little for such things. Your matriarch only says so to tell you who's a good sheep, a strong dog or a bad wolf. You can be many other things than what fits in her head.'

'I don't mind being a wolf,' the girl replied with a bright smile.

Geil chuckled. 'Clever lass. What's your name?'

'Ragdra. Yours?'

'Geil. Now listen, Ragdra, do you know of the monster that has been preying on the herds?'

'The owlet? I've seen it.'

'You saw it?'

Ragdra nodded enthusiastically. 'A big owl! With red eyes and bright feathers. And large talons!'

From her description, it could be a stryx. Although the girl didn't seem worried ...

'Did it attack your home?'

Ragdra frowned. 'No, no! She only eats sheep.'

'And your parents aren't concerned about your playing alone here?'

Ragdra dismissed Geil's worries with a wave. 'I told you! She's an owlet, harmless to us. The village doesn't understand it. That's why Father is selling the wood elsewhere, and Mother forages down at the heath.'

Something was getting lost in translation, Geil feared. Perhaps the girl's family had been cast out, and that was why the villagers spoke of them in hushed tones.

'Don't worry. Soon everything will return to normal.'

With that, she bade the child farewell and headed for the woods.

Ragdra called after her: 'Be careful! If you corner her, she'll lash out!'

Isn't that true of us all? the Drake remarked.

Chapter Six

Ash

To handle Dreamlings, Nightmares and other beasts born from imagination, one needs to learn their nature. Understanding in what regard they transcend the natural is paramount to tend, tame or hunt them.

– *Bestiary of Nature and Dream* by Bergos

ASH WOKE IN A NARROW stone chamber that reeked of urine. It felt like he was underground, but the room had no windows. The only light was the reddish gleam that filtered from beneath a sturdy metal door.

His heart raced with panic. He'd vowed never to return to the Deep Wells of the Grand Palace, and while this might not be it, it was a very similar kind of hell.

What of Daerna and Omen? Shaking, he sat up, swaying weakly. Everything hurt. Not just the swelling of his ankle and forearm but also the burning feeling that the recruiter's glove had left on his chest.

Where was he? The Academy was halfway to the northern provinces, lost in the immensity of the ever-misty Shrouded Sea, days away from Onyxia. And to enter it, one had to cross the fabled Mantle, far too harrowing an experience for him to have slept through.

Frantically, he looked for ways to escape. He could try Dreaming a key or some tool to crack the lock, but it seemed such an obvious stratagem he was sure it would be accounted for.

There must be another way, something less evident. He ran his hands over the cell's walls. Prisoners shared a secret language that he knew well enough. As he thought, there were crude etchings fashioned with hairpins and belt buckles; others were names and dates, both from decades and mere months ago. *Tell my father I thought of him*, one pleaded. *The Charnel Mother will release me*, claimed another, asking for swift death, the only blessing the unholy and cruel deity could offer. Commending oneself to Her wasn't just blasphemy, it was desperate even for those who'd lost all hope.

Some were exquisite pieces of sculpture that must have been Dreamt onto the wall itself: a weeping woman with the inscription 'Mother' below, and a bucolic bas-relief depicting a Highlands farm.

When Ash placed his hand on the latter, the scent of pine trees and acorns wafted over him, and he could feel a soft breeze running over a grassy field.

Ash heard approaching footsteps. After the heavy thunking of someone unlocking and unlatching the door, a man with a lantern stood at the gate, its feeble light enough to hurt Ash's eyes.

'Morning, roof-rat,' said the sergeant who had led the recruitment gang. 'Sleep well? Or did you spend the night bawling like a babe?'

Ash clenched his fists.

The man offered a scornful grin. 'Keep that for later. Now, step out. The commander wants to see you.'

Ash limped into a corridor only a bit wider than his cell. There were doors lining each side, though most of the cells seemed empty.

They headed up a set of worn-out stairs and emerged into a narrow courtyard, the surrounding mossy stone wall tall enough to block his view of anything else. A dozen gargoyles perched atop the battlements guarded the walls. Some of the horned beasts turned their lifeless stone eyes on him.

At least the air smelled better here, and there was wind brushing against his cheek. One of the Motherstorm's tendrils stretched above them, its tears a gentle drizzle. But the clouds were thinner here than in the city's heart. They had to be on one of the islands that dotted the Onyxian lagoon.

'Don't stop!' the sergeant barked.

'Where are my companions?' Ash asked.

'They're both fine. Now shut up.'

'And why would I believe you?'

'We don't beat Sisters, no matter how foul-mouthed they are. As for your feral beast, it's in its cage.'

They entered a turret and climbed a spiral staircase until they reached a roofed arch bridge. From here, Ash saw that the prison stood on a handful of fortified, jagged islets broken into walled plazas connected by arched bridges.

Only when they reached the central islet with its large, star-shaped courtyard did he finally see other people. Most were stern-faced servants, dressed in grey and going about their chores. Here, a woman scrubbing bloodstained linen in a bucket. There, a man carrying a heavy sack of grain. He spotted another of the recruiters too, the slender woman entering what looked like large stables, carrying a bucket full of gutted fish.

He stopped. The stables were dark, but he made out a few massive steel cages along the walls. No trace of Omen, though.

'I told you to keep moving!'

This time, the sergeant shoved him to the ground. Ash's ankle screamed with pain, and his swollen forearm throbbed. Still, he muffled a whimper, refusing to give this bastard the satisfaction.

After limping the rest of the way to a large stone keep attached to the walls, he was led to an office on the second floor where two people waited behind a desk. They both wore the bone-engraved cuirasses, but the woman had a gorget with the Academy's crest on top. The commander, presumably.

Cold green eyes sized Ash up through her lenses. Tall and pale, her presence was imposing despite her intellectual air.

The hunched, bearded man at her side made him uncomfortable too, for different reasons. His robes were dirty, even blackened in places, and his bloodshot eyes were fixated on the dark crusts he attempted to scratch from beneath his fingernails.

'I'm Commander Kardra, and this is Master Galedras,' she said by way of explanation. She picked up a quill and pointedly gestured at the chair across from her. Ash sat down. 'Name?'

'Aescyon of the Lightning-Hunters.'

She scribbled in the tome in front of her. 'Family?'

'None,' he lied. Ash's stepmother still lived. Yet, estranged as they were, he had no desire to see her or have his crew used as ways to torment or pressure him.

She let out a weary sigh without lifting her eyes from the book. 'You do yourself a disservice if you hide anything from us. What if something were to happen to you during your instruction?'

Ash clenched his teeth. Now they feigned concern for his well-being?

'What about your Dreamling?'

'What about it?'

'Who shall we return it to if you die? Or am I to understand that you leave it to the Academy?'

Ash rubbed his wrists. There was no good way out of that one.

Against his better judgement, he played along. 'I'd want Omen returned to the Lightning-Hunters' Guild,' he said. Hopefully Ghalod and Yaisa would keep him out of Esmus's greedy hands. 'I never knew my mother and my father's dead.'

That wasn't quite true. Ash had a few precious memories of his mother from his early childhood. She'd come in, always at night, always with some gift: poems she'd scribbled for him during her journeys, drawings of things she'd seen on the continent. All until one day, she had not returned. His father had taken this to mean she'd abandoned them and barred any conversation about her.

Only at the end had the tide of his bitterness finally begun to recede, and he'd started to blame the whole thing not on lack of affection but on an affliction. 'Kissed by the Muse of Melancholy,' as she'd apparently liked to say.

'Studies? Do you know how to read?'

'I can spell my name with typing letters. Does that help?' he snapped back, his pride injured.

'Watch your tone,' she replied, raising her eyes from the ledger.

'Eoinas Allandra. My father was a printer,' he offered as an apology.

'How did he die?'

The memory pooled in his throat as cold as swamp spit.

'Your father, Eoinas Allandra, the printer,' she repeated, enunciating slowly as if he were hard of hearing. 'How did he die?'

Ash picked his words with care. 'His lungs failed him.'

The commander squinted at him, but the man by her side nodded. 'Ach, blackened lungs are a mark of the printer's trade,' he said, scratching his beard.

Her gaze softened, and she finally let her quill rest.

'I want you to know that we're not insensitive to your predicament. We ask these questions because we care. Training at the Academy is an honour and bestows considerable privileges. But to earn those privileges, one must be found deserving.'

Ash bit his tongue. He had a strong suspicion that being 'deserving' probably had a lot to do with being born in the right family.

'Master Galedras, your turn,' Commander Kardra said.

'Do you have any conditions of which we need to be aware?' he asked. 'Lovesong's disease, frail bones, clogged lungs, that sort of thing.'

Ash shook his head.

'That limping, is it some sort of paralysis?'

'I fell from a rooftop,' Ash retorted.

'Any sudden stiffness of the muscles accompanied by disorientation?'

He realised what he was hinting at. 'You want to know if I'm afflicted with the Wilting?'

He'd seen enough of the Wilting to feel uneasy at the notion, though. It kept eating through Onyxia's poorer quarters like a slow rot. Not two weeks ago, a young woman had died because of it in the building where his crew lived in Little Vespiria. It sucked the strength from whoever contracted it, leaving them confined to a bed and delirious until the palsy killed them.

'Aye,' chimed the bearded man.

'I'm not.'

The commander furiously scribbled a final note. 'I have no further questions. Master Galedras will see to your bone-setting needs. I shall leave you to it.' Rising from her seat, she invited them with an ink-stained hand to enter the adjoining room.

The bearded man led him inside and closed the panel doors after him. The cold room reeked of vinegar, as if it had been scrubbed clean that very same morning. A wooden board hovered, held by chains, above a draining grate on the stony floor. Dark crimson stains had dried on its surface.

'Remove your clothes. When you're done, sit there,' the man ordered, pointing at the table.

'Why?'

'Got to look the horse in the mouth before we decide it's a gift.' The man chuckled.

Ash complied, knowing he had little choice. The cold prickled his skin, and he removed his clothes slowly, all while scanning the room for anything that could help him escape.

Anatomical charts lined the walls, masterful pieces copied from illuminated medicine treatises. Human skulls and jars with balms and leaves filed several shelves. There were some books too: old medical treatises, judging from their spines and binding. None of that would help.

He saw a set of freshly rinsed knives set to dry on a table, but he couldn't see a way to get to them. He ended up settling for something familiar, a small lightning orb set to rest on a spare table.

Pretending to look away, he dropped his pile of clothes on top of it and promptly walked over to the table.

The man examined him from head to heel, huffing and talking to himself. 'Winter complexion. Wiry, long limbs. Plenty of old cuts and some heavy bruising.' He prodded at the ugly, suppurating scab on Ash's forearm, and Ash jerked uncomfortably. 'What's this?'

'A Nightmare got me during a hunt a few nights back. I was lucky. It only grazed me,' Ash said bitterly.

'Lucky? Yes, but not for the reason you think.' Galedras found a jar and slathered a pasty ointment on Ash's wound. Ash clenched his teeth. After a few moments, he felt the injury cool down. 'A claw's rot is deadlier than a sword's cut. Now, what boon do you require?' the man asked.

'Boon?'

'I can Remake your bones, your sinews, your very blood. For beginners, I can stitch that cut up or look at your limping. Only your skull's insides are beyond my reach.'

'I don't need anything.'

The man loomed closer.

'Is it the pain? There's no shame in saying so. I can give you some vespershade to chew. It'll help you bear it while I work.'

His offer was tempting. Few Dreamers could overcome a body's natural resistance to foreign dreams, and even fewer knew how to mend with it. Remakers were, at best, deft surgeons. He might heal Ash, but he'd do so by embedding his bloodstained Dreams into Ash's flesh. Who was to say he wouldn't place something else there as well?

Ash reeled at the thought of it. 'No, thank you.'

The man scoffed. 'Stronger men and women than you have taken me up on my offer. But suit yourself, lad. You're either very brave or a complete imbecile.'

Cold sweat ran down Ash's spine. He dressed quickly, but he was even quicker to pocket the orb in his breeches.

The Remaker ushered Ash back into the now-deserted commander's office and shouted down the hallway, 'Dain! Where in the entombed hells are you?' Seeing no trace of the sergeant, he sighed. 'I should Remake that one's ears someday. Wait here,' he commanded, chuckling at his own joke.

Ash sat down, but as soon as he heard the Remaker in the courtyard, he reached for the commander's ledger.

His entry was easy to find, being the most recent. Sadly, she wrote in a combination of notations and cryptic abbreviations he couldn't figure out. There was no mention of Omen, nor any trace in the previous entries either. By then, he could hear Dain making his way back with the Remaker from the courtyard. Leaving the book, he noticed the bookcase with inventory ledgers by the window. He rushed over and found the most recent one.

Downstairs, the door opened. Ash forced his shaking hands to flip through the pages, his eyes scanning.

Finally, he found the previous day's entries. And there: *Alb/02. Recpt. O. 1. Nightmare. Mottled black fur, feline, 22 stns. Came w. Rec. Aescyon Lightning-H (See log for Alb/02). Night predator? Stored at main hold pending exam by Homt. Thella. *1*

He breathed out in relief and was about to return the book when he noticed the footnote: **1 Alb/03. Homt. Thella reprt disease symptms. Refuses to eat. Sacrifice?*

What was that about? They were considering sacrificing Omen because he was sick? Ash read the line over and over. There was no way around it. He had to do something to help Omen, and he had to do it now.

'Hands off that, maggot!' Dain snarled from behind. 'Thieving piece of shit!' he yelled, shoving Ash out of the office.

Ash fell down the steps and had to roll sideways to shield the stolen orb.

Dain dragged him to his feet, only to shove him towards the dungeons. Ash complied sluggishly.

A needle-like tower stood at one of the star-shaped courtyard's tips. A handful of faces watched him from the barred windows along its height. At first, he thought they were gargoyles, then, noticing they all had childish features and that a boy's skin was shifting from scales to flesh, he realised they weren't beasts but Dreamblooded recruits.

A stark reminder that the Academy's love for Dreamblooded cadets depended on their inherited Dreaming gifts, especially their capacity to mould their shapes.

Ash turned to face Dain. 'I'll do everything you want if you just tell me where you have my panther caged.'

'It's *your* skin you should be worried about,' he said, raising a fist.

'Please, I know he's sick. I can help him!'

Dain's eyes wandered to the stables. 'Hordemaster Thella will decide whether it's to be saved or fed to the gargoyles.'

With the confirmation he needed, Ash reached into his breeches for the orb, but the sergeant's eyes shot to him.

'I knew it. All roof-rats are filthy thieves,' he said as his eyes became vitreous. He reached up and plucked a war hammer out of thin air. It was an ugly thing, heavy and spiked, made to crack open both armour and skulls. 'Hand it over, or I'll teach you your first and last Academy lesson right here.'

Dain spat on the ground and swung the hammer at him. This time, Ash was ready. He reeled backwards, hurling the orb towards the weapon. Dain's eyes widened in confusion, but Ash quickly closed his.

The onyx shattered loudly, releasing the lightning with a thunderous roar. This son of the Motherstorm was old and tired, but the explosion was still brutal enough to knock Ash off his feet.

His forearm hurt, and the thunder deafened him. Only when the blinding light faded did Ash open his eyes and stand. Dain was on the ground, unconscious.

Ash bolted towards the stables, the dull stab of his ankle sending him wobbling, but he soldiered on. From the battlements, the gargoyles shrieked a rocky cry of alarm, and two leapt down to pursue him. Big as bulls, their bat-like wings barely slowed their fall. The cobblestones cracked with their landing.

Despite the pain and the fear, or precisely because of them, Ash ran faster than he thought possible. A claw raked at him, and he narrowly ducked ahead. Almost feeling the gargoyles' breath behind, he slid through the open stable doors.

He spun and closed them behind him. One of the gargoyles slammed against them, and Ash put all of his body weight into holding them closed, yet they shook under the gargoyle's mass. There was no lock, only an empty drawbar rail with no bar in sight.

Heart racing, he forced his mind into the Dreaming, desperate to find a way to secure the doors. To reach for this power made his stomach queasy. He hadn't mastered the Dreaming gift any more than he could master a fire's blaze.

He brought forth the memory of the dark grates in the Grand Palace's prison. A harrowing inspiration, yet fruitful to fashion the heavy bar he dropped into the doors' latches.

Then he poured in the weight of his rage at the Academy, at this prison, and at what they'd done to him in it. The bar coalesced into something as heavy as the behemoths outside.

Drawing a deep breath, he stepped out of the Dreaming and dizzily watched the doors tremble beneath the gargoyles' charge. The drawbar held.

At least for now.

He hurried deeper into the stables, limping. It was dark, and most of the stalls and cages on both sides of the hallway were empty, except for a handful of mules and sheep.

As his eyes adjusted, Ash realised the corridor curved into a descending ramp. He followed it below.

A crypt awaited him, a veritable maze of candle-lit corridors, Dream-carved into the island's rocky bottom. He called Omen's name, and a faint growl answered from the end of one of the passages.

He hurried towards it.

In the penumbra, he passed a caged pair of large Highland hounds, except they had blazing flames instead of eyes, tracking him with curiosity. He came across a large tank filled with green water where a scaly merlass swam in desperate circles, her hair trailing her like reeds. This had to be the pens and holding cells for the Dreamlings.

Finally, he found Omen locked in a steel cage barely big enough for him. The panther weakly rubbed against his hand.

'Don't worry. I'll get you out of here, I promise!'

There was clearly something wrong. Omen's coat, which usually had a sheen of night blue, was sickly grey. Even the panther's previously shimmering blue eyes had darkened.

There was meat and water inside the cage, both untouched.

A loud metallic squeal reached him from upstairs. The drawbar had finally given in.

Omen shifted onto his paws and growled. Footsteps echoed down the corridor.

It was the slender woman with the golden skin from the recruiters' gang, holding the same whip as the last time he'd seen her. This must be the Hordemaster Thella that Dain had mentioned.

Ash leaned closer to Omen, but Thella seemed calm. 'I'd have come for it too. What a beauty. You should be proud of yourself.'

Ash clenched his fists. 'What have you done?'

She shook her head. 'Nothing. It's fading, but it's none of *my* doing. I've tried feeding it, but it refuses everything I offer.'

Ash looked again at Omen, then it struck him. A creature born of lightning wouldn't survive on meat and water.

He opened his hands, raising surrendering arms. The gargoyles' stomping sounds and groans came from the corridor's entrance.

'Please, I'll go willingly! Won't give you any more trouble, I promise. But let me try to help him first.'

She arched an eyebrow, and then lifted her palm to stop the gargoyles in their tracks.

Ash entered the Dreaming again.

He reached into the haze for a memory he knew well, one of pure lightning, the fierce blue of rage, a shriek capable of ripping through darkness itself. But he didn't let it coalesce immediately.

He held on to its raw form and twisted it, coiled it into an oval, heavy and thick with electricity. He swirled it around and poured it into a bowl conjured from a childhood memory. He Dreamt it all inside Omen's cage: a heavy silver bowl filled with lightning cream. Mother's milk for a hungry kitten born from the storm.

He dived out of the Dreaming in time to see Omen lap at the shimmering blue liquid with gusto.

Ash breathed with relief.

Thella approached him from behind. She placed her gloved hand on his shoulder. 'Well done. Fear not, I'll make sure it's well fed, that I can promise.' She looked at him pityingly. 'What I can't promise, though, is that we'll be gentle with *you*.'

The gem on her glove lit up, and Ash felt his every nerve burn.

Chapter Seven

Daerna

No hunting or trading of lightning, nor its thunder or its radiance, shall be exercised in Onyxia, except that conducted by those admitted into this honourable guild.
– *The Onyxian Lightning-Hunter's Charter*, Article I

DAERNA HAD SEEN THE LIGHTNING-HUNTERS' tower many times before, although never from within. To her surprise, its innards were as baroque as its facade. Wrought-iron grates and railings stretched throughout like black veins. The rising fumes of the guild's forges permeated the air, yet were still unable to warm the draughty halls, though it wasn't the cold that made her hands shake.

With every minute that passed, a new concern took root in her mind.

What if the guild was afraid of losing their business with the Academy? Afraid of the Academy retaliating? What if the Academy and the guild were allies on the city's complex political gameboard?

When the crew finally emerged from the master's office, Daerna was unable to read their faces. She followed them into a cramped studio, where Master Esmus, a hirsute and uncouth man, asked her to recount Ash's arrest.

The guildmaster's grimace increased as she related the recruiters' abuses.

'Surely the guild has to do something about this, Master?' she asked.

'I thought the Sisters only concerned themselves with *spiritual* matters. I fail to see why the Solemn Princess, blessed be her slumber, would have any interest in how our guild governs itself,' Esmus replied, politely dismissive.

'Come on, Esmus. You have to help us! You owe us that much!' Rudher pleaded.

'*Owe* you?' the master snapped. 'When was the last time you paid your guild fees, Rudher? You're naught but a pack of filthy, ungrateful crows! You should be grateful I haven't had you expelled already!'

The crew's faces sank with his words. Even Rudher seemed taken aback by the barrage of insults. Esmus slumped into his chair, fuming.

'Master, I'm only here as a friend to the guild.' Daerna tried a softer hand. 'It troubles me to see the Academy stomp all over your charter of rights. Or did the Academy seek the guild's permission before arresting Ash?' Daerna pressed.

Esmus narrowed his eyes. 'You're well-versed in the law, Sister.' He let out a weary sigh before turning to Rudher. 'Tell my assistant we'll need transport. Obviously, the Academy needs reminding that one doesn't pick on a filthy crow, at least not when he's one of our murder.'

* * *

They set off for the Isle of Sighs that same afternoon.

Daerna had hoped they'd take the skyship the guild used for hunting inside the Motherstorm, but their most prized vessel was only to be engaged in their trade. At least Esmus bothered to commandeer a sea-drake-pulled barge instead of an oar-boat.

A fierce wind blew into their faces, but the sea-drakes slithered through the rough waters smoothly. Although her billowing dress kept pulling at her, Daerna refused to go below deck. Instead, she held fast to the gunwale and endured the battering of the wind. Hardship showed the purity of one's sorrow.

When the infamous Isle of Sighs appeared, Daerna found it even bleaker than expected. A handful of islets, meshed into a single island by impenetrable walls and fortified ramparts, as much a jail as fortress.

The battlement's gargoyles howled their arrival alarm. A lone servant rushed from the main gate to help them with the mooring. Their skipper had to coax the sea-drakes to coil around the quays' pillars to prevent the ship from smashing against the nearby rocks.

Daerna disembarked first, Master Esmus and the crew cautiously following. By then, a woman had reached the pier, sauntering towards them with self-assurance, her cloak flapping with the wind, revealing the ornate, bony cuirass beneath.

'I'm Commander Kardra,' was her only greeting. 'Why are you on my island?'

'I'm Master Esmus Alisdra of the Lightning-Hunters' Guild. I'm here to demand the freedom of a journeyman of ours, Aescyon Allandra.' To his credit, Esmus spoke firmly, leaning on his spear for effect, but Commander Kardra just stood there, impervious.

'Demand?' she finally replied. 'With whose authority?'

Master Esmus cockily tapped the ground with his spear. 'The Lightning-Hunter's Charter, of course! Aescyon is under our jurisdiction, and we have a right to claim him if he's a Dreamer. You must free him immediately.'

The commander arched a slender eyebrow. 'I see. I wish I could honour such a request, but he's an untrained Dreamer, and thus a grave danger to everyone. I can't, in good conscience, release him.'

'Request? This is no request. It's the *law*!' Esmus snorted. 'You think we're not aware of how, during the last year, you've been abusing your right of conscription by poaching guild apprentices?'

The crew glared silently from behind Rudher, Yaisa even clenching her fists. Ghalod patted her reassuringly on the shoulder.

'And I say that the Academy's authority to recruit untrained Dreamers supersedes any right of your guild's.' Commander Kardra sniffed. 'He'll stay here until he's sent to the Academy. This is my final word.'

'Final word?' Esmus repeated, his tone growing more aggravated. 'You are making a mistake, Commander. You might be able to pull this off among the simple folk of the provinces, but you're overstepping your reach in the city. We'll take this to the magistrates, to the High Justice, or even better, the High Sage your Grandmaster reports to. We might be commoners, but all guilds have patrons in the Senate, ours being Lady Saorla herself. We'll see what the Captain Regent values most: the friendship of the guilds that help fill her party's chests or a lone and quarrelsome Academy commander.'

The whipping of the wind was the only sound in the heavy silence that followed.

The commander's eyes narrowed. 'I'll let him go if that's what a magistrate orders. Until then, he's a danger, and he's to remain here.' Without allowing Esmus a response, she turned to head back inside.

Daerna couldn't believe that victory would slip from their grasp when it seemed so close. 'Commander Kardra turns her back on the Motherstorm!' she yelled, but Kardra didn't stop. 'She steals from the Sorrowful! From those under the Sisterhood's protection, even!'

Now, Kardra stopped. The commander turned back towards her, face livid.

'*What* did you just say?'

Daerna remained silent. One had to tread carefully between seeming weak and injuring somebody's pride.

'What's your name, Sister?' Commander Kardra asked harshly.

'I am Sister Daerna Eimar from the Wailing Sisters.' A Sister might lack legal authority here, but their accusations on morality always carried a heavy weight. Especially if she was willing to bend the truth. 'And please know that our Order, that Her Sorrowfulness, Abbess Superior Forlaitra, won't abandon the guild in this instance. Do you wish to displease her?'

The commander clenched her jaw and gave Daerna an icy glare that made her skin prickle.

'The *abbess superior* of the Wailers has taken an interest in some lowly Lightning-Hunter?'

Had the commander seen through Daerna's lie? Either way, to turn back on her half-truths was to drown, so she marched ahead.

'No servant of the Divine Motherstorm is too lowly for our aid. But you are right that there's more to this matter. A certain personal friendship between this guild and Her Sorrowfulness. They both live and die by the will of the Motherstorm. I beg you, Commander, is this man worth risking her anger?'

The commander's eyes flared, and her lips curled. 'Of course not . . .' She hesitated, thinking. 'I'll have him brought here. He has a week to get a dispensation from the High Sage's office. I will hold you,' she said, looking at Esmus with disdain, 'responsible for anything he might do until then.'

She was about to leave when Daerna added, 'He's to be returned with *all* his belongings, Commander.'

The commander didn't bother turning this time. Instead, she barked an order at someone on the battlements. Only then did Daerna notice that the hooded recruiter from the previous night had been there all along.

'Tell Thella to bring the Dreamling beast as well.'

They both disappeared, the gates closing behind them.

Not one bell later, a group emerged through the gate. The hooded man carried a battered body in his arms, and the same woman who had captured Omen pulled him on the end of a heavy chain.

Daerna swallowed a curse.

The crew hurried them to the barge. Once Omen was freed, the creature went to lick Ash's battered body. Ash was unconscious, bruised and bloodied all over, but at least he was alive and free. Anything else could wait.

Daerna turned to Master Esmus, seated at the stern. 'Thank you!' she called to him over the wind.

The man offered her a knowing smile. 'Just remind Aescyon that he now owes me three times as much as he did,' he said, before turning his face to the lagoon.

Chapter Eight

Geil

Unto whoever hurts a single Dreamer's hair, damage shall be inflicted tenfold. A limb chopped off for each Dreamer's finger you harm.

– Empress Damnia's Edict on Punishment of Crimes against Dreamers

BY NIGHTFALL, GEIL'S AMBUSH WAS ready. The mist had dissipated, replaced by tendrils of darkness. Fortunately, her Drake half could see just fine.

Geil watched the bait from deep inside a treetop. She'd placed the meat in the clearing below. It wasn't fresh, but that was why she'd needed the blood. Stryxes preferred to drink from warm, still-beating human hearts, but blood was blood.

She shifted uncomfortably in her cradle of branches. Waiting was always hard. At the Academy, she'd learned to endure being still for hours, partly as training to absolutely control her body but also as part of her Nightmare-Hunter training. Nothing gave you away quicker than movement, not that it made her any more patient.

As the hours dragged on, nightlife filled the woods with its sounds. Small game and rodents chittered, but there was no trace of anything larger. She began to fear that the Nightmare wouldn't come.

At the cusp of midnight, the sound of two large wings was accompanied by an enormous silhouette of a bird of prey circling the treetops. The stryx had come.

The Drake stretched out from the depths of her mind. *Let it come. We'll be the ones sucking the leech dry.*

Her pulse was still racing, so she fed that trepidation to the Drake. In return, adrenaline filled her blood, and with it rose her thirst for carnage. 'Fear is a chisel,' her Academy masters used to say. She'd learned to hate their teachings but, tonight, had to admit she had good use for them.

Above, her prey finally gave in to the temptation and swooped down. Geil steadied herself. As soon as it touched the ground, she'd be able to jump on its back. One blow would suffice if she didn't miss. *Pierce the artery and let us gorge on its blood to our heart's content.*

At last, the Nightmare landed in the clearing and dug into the bait. Its feathery back seemed softer than that of a stryx, which promised an easier kill. Geil flexed her legs, but before she could leap, the Nightmare lifted its head and let out a short screech.

She froze. It screeched a second time. The third time, Geil finally realised it sounded nothing like the piercing howls of a stryx. Its face also wasn't nearly as grotesque. Even for an owl, its hooting was too high-pitched. There was almost a sweetness to it. The girl, Ragdra, had been right all along. This might be a Dreamling, but it was no Nightmare. She found a rare, naive beauty to the creature. Whoever had Dreamt the owlet had made it out of fascination, not viciousness.

The Drake didn't care for her thoughts. *Easy prey. Tender meat and soft bones to crush beneath our claws. Show no mercy.*

Still Geil hesitated. She found little pleasure in hunting an innocent beast. Despite the Drake's protest, she took in a deep breath and waited for her head to clear. The owlet deserved better.

She'd do better then.

She let go of the sword and entered the Dreaming instead.

Colour drained from her vision as she Dreamt her eyes anew. She replaced them with large yellow globes like the Dreamling's and curled both hands into gnarly bird talons.

The owlet had finally spotted her, but Geil wasn't afraid. In fact, she used the opportunity to better mimic its shape and colouring. She grew her own mottled feathers and expanded her ribcage. The branch creaked beneath the strain of her new weight.

It hurt, like stretching a limb until it was dislocated. Her human parts always resisted transformation into unfamiliar shapes, but the Drake wouldn't do for her plan, so she pressed on.

The owlet retreated and spread its wings, trying to scare her off with its formidable size, but Geil reached for the memory of Invernia's colossal statues and used it to grow her own set of majestic wings, ripping through the back of her shirt.

When she slipped out of the Dreaming, the owlet had retreated to the clearing's edge. Geil had clearly intimidated it, but it still held its ground.

She'd have to do more than shift her shape, it seemed.

She leapt forwards, spreading her massive wings to ease her fall, her talons reaching for its chest. She grazed it, enough to make it bleed but not to cause serious injury.

The Dreamling shrieked and lunged with its beak, just missing Geil's collarbone. She beat her wings and flew at it.

It hissed furiously; Geil hissed back even louder. The owlet's screech was powerful, but hers was fiercer, sharpened by the years of torment, given weight by angry grief.

It was too loud, too terrifying, for the owlet to ignore. And the beast cowered, acknowledging her dominance.

It retreated, and she gave chase. The angry affair wouldn't end in blood but banishment. That'd have to be enough for both of them.

* * *

It took Geil most of the night to secure the forest by spreading some of her feathers. By morning she was confident that she'd done all she could to dissuade the Dreamling from returning to these hunting grounds.

With a bit of luck, it'd keep to the mountains, hunting shadowdeer and other game. A hard life. Sometimes that was all one could ask for.

She reverted to her natural shape, parting with the wings and letting her scales dapple her left side, then headed back towards the cottage, eager to thank the young girl for her advice. Her muscles were sore after shifting and the long, sleepless night.

A woman was yelling in the distance, and although the morning fog obscured everything, Geil feared it came from Ragdra's house. She dropped her bag and sword and raced towards the sound.

There were a dozen armed men surrounding the cottage, Matriarch Calaig at their head. Their eyes widened when they recognised her.

'You're alive!' Calaig said.

Geil couldn't help but think she sounded disappointed.

'You didn't return at night, and we feared the worst. I decided it was best to follow my suspicions.'

'Suspicions? I've dealt with the beast already.'

Some repeated her news in their tongue, sounding surprised or relieved, but all went quiet when Calaig raised a small doll made of hay and mottled feathers. It looked just like the owlet.

Ragdra and a dishevelled woman, probably the girl's mother, emerged from the cottage. The woman grabbed for the doll and tried to wrestle it from Calaig's hands, but the sturdy matriarch shoved her back.

'Behold! Here's proof! I told you that they were the ones responsible!' the matriarch proclaimed.

Two men reached for the girl. Ragdra's mother shoved one to the ground, but the other clubbed her on the head. She fell, her hair bloodied.

That was enough for Geil.

She called for the Drake, curling her fingers into long claws, then jumped into the middle of the fray.

A man swung his club at her and she punched the weapon out of his hand. He fell to the ground, screaming and sobbing, as she kicked him in the kneecap.

A young shepherd came at her from behind, spear ready, but she dodged the blow, clawing at the weapon's pole, ripping it into sheds with her talons.

'Stop! Stop!' Calaig screeched.

The rest of the men had already backed away, terrified of Geil.

Pity. She was enjoying the fight.

'Leave the girl be,' Geil growled.

'But she's making the Nightmares!' Calaig protested.

'To do so, she'd need to be a Dreamer. Is that what you're saying?' Geil sneered at her with a mouth full of sharp Drake teeth. '"A limb chopped off for each Dreamer's finger you harm."' She quoted the famous edict about the consequences of hurting a child with the Dreaming gift. 'I'd consider my words carefully if I were you, unless you want to be hanged for assaulting an officer of the Domain or watch the Academy raze your village to the ground.'

The reality of what they were doing sank in. If Ragdra was a Dreamer, she wasn't some village freak they could parade about and abuse; she was their better. To harm her, to deprive Onyxia of one with the gift, was tantamount to treason.

'We can't just let her be!' Calaig said shakily.

'That's *exactly* what you'll do,' Geil replied. 'I'll report her to the governor. He'll be the one to pass on word.' This time, she employed a different tone, the trained iciness of someone who'd been taught her place in the hierarchy and knew how to use it. 'Now go back to your homes.'

They collected their wounded. Some kissed the grass at her feet, begging for her forgiveness.

After they left, Geil found Ragdra tending to her mother. The woman had been lucky; the blow had only left a swollen cut, and she was conscious.

'Thank you! Thank you!' she said between tears. 'How can we repay you?'

'Thank me? You don't understand. The villagers aren't what you should be worried about at all.'

'What do you mean?'

'Listen, I won't report any of this to the governor. But if your girl truly is a Dreamer, next time the Academy's recruiters come, they'll take her with them.'

'But isn't that good? She'll serve the Motherstorm's will, and once Ragdra's a powerful Dreamer, my little girl will be able to provide for her family.'

Geil cast a glance at Ragdra. 'You don't *understand.*' She dropped her voice so the girl couldn't hear. 'That place will break her. She won't ever be the same . . .'

Geil held the woman's gaze. She needed her to understand this; even if the training didn't kill Ragdra, it would leave her forever scarred and haunted.

The woman's face slowly drained of blood.

'What are we to do then?'

'Keep it a secret.'

'How? We tried, but . . . everybody knows now.' The woman reached for Geil's hand. 'Help us!'

Geil opened her mouth to explain that there was nothing she could do, but then she felt Ragdra grab her other hand and the words wouldn't come out.

'What's wrong?' Ragdra asked.

Geil and her mother exchanged a glance. 'Nothing,' she told Ragdra. 'I need to get my things, but there's something I want to show you.'

She retrieved her satchel and sword, rummaging through her bag until she found a silver bracelet. She handed it to Ragdra, who held it up and admired the pattern of birds in flight on it.

'They're firebirds,' Geil said.

'They're made of fire?' Ragdra asked.

'They can summon fire, some say because they eat embers, others because they can Dream,' Geil explained. 'The bracelet is Dreamchanted, so if you press your ear to the firebirds, you can hear them sing. See?' She demonstrated, and Ragdra tried it. Her eyes widened.

'It's beautiful!'

'I'm glad you like it. It was a gift from my mother, and now it's for you. They can be friends with your owlets and sing them songs.'

Ragdra's mouth made a tiny circle of shock. 'Thank you,' she said.

'You're welcome. Don't let anybody but your mother take it.'

She pressed the bracelet to her chest. 'I won't,' she said, solemn.

Geil left Ragdra listening to the bracelet.

'I can't promise you anything,' Geil told the girl's mother in a low voice, 'but I'll try to help you. For the time being, hide with other relatives if you can. The bracelet's worth some money, if it comes to it.'

'Thank you,' the woman replied.

She thought of what other advice or comfort she could offer, but there was none. She felt Ragdra tugging at her arm.

'Are you staying with us, Geil?'

'I must return to Ayron to report that the owlet is gone, but perhaps we'll see each other again soon.'

The girl returned her smile, but for her own good, Geil truly hoped this was the last they would see of each other.

Chapter Nine
Ash

Dreaming is different from perceiving. By virtue of imagination, an image arises, yet it is intelligence and science that give it shape. And even then, without will and discipline, mere imaginings they will remain.

Dialogues: On Imagination by Aristan of Ravkiria

ASH HAD NO INTENTION OF leaving his bed. An archipelago of swollen bruises covered his body, each island a different agony. Still, he counted himself lucky Sergeant Dain's beating hadn't broken any of his bones. But there was more than pain keeping him in bed.

Being imprisoned again had awoken old fears in him. His time in the Grand Palace's dungeons had crippled his spirit once, and now he found himself unable to move, drowning under thunderous waves of dread.

Rudher made him some broth, and Ash asked for some of their precious lightning for Omen, since he lacked the energy to Dream more.

'Last of our catch,' Rudher said, handing him a dim orb.

With great relief, Ash discovered that turning it into liquid was easier than conjuring it out of thin air. Omen licked his bowl clean and began laboriously grooming himself. His darker spots shone with intense cobalt tones again.

'Ugh. You don't look so great,' Yaisa said, bringing him some bread.

'Thank you for not leaving me there.'

'Me? Thank Dae! Merciful Motherstorm, she's as stubborn as a Vespirian goat!'

'Where is she now?'

'Back at the abbey, but she stayed all night by your side.' Yaisa winked. 'You really don't want to lose that one, Ash.'

He nodded weakly.

'Don't worry about the dispensation!' Yaisa offered a reassuring smile. 'The guild will help you.'

'From what I've heard, it's only put us into more debt.'

He'd hoped catching the firstfall-lightning would offer them a break, but his fortune was rotten as ever, and his friends were still overworked and drowning in debt. Worst of all, this time Master Esmus would claim Omen, and Ash couldn't stomach losing him again.

* * *

Only angry despair dragged Ash out of bed the next morning. He'd get those damned papers that'd allow him to remain free even if it was the last thing he did. He washed up with rainwater scented with thyme, eager to scrub off any trace of the cage he'd been kept in. The bruises shone purple on his pale skin, so he left his long hair loose, hoping for most of them to remain hidden under it, and buttoned up his jerkin.

Omen seemed happy to accompany him, despite the leash Ash had improvised from a climbing rope. Not that it'd stop the panther, but Ash hoped it'd serve to reassure everyone around them.

It was a long walk that crossed over two dozen bridges, from the humble wooden planks in Little Vespiria to the ornate covered stone passes of the Central Quarter bustling with artisans, servants and the golden-hued sedan chairs of the wealthy.

Until, at long last, the marble archways that crossed the Crown Canal came into view. Gondolas and barges danced endlessly through its connected waterways, carrying supplies into the ever-hungry bowels of the Grand Palace's island. Grand Palace*s* would have fit better as a name, since beyond rose a jumble of onyx domes and towering spires, held by flying buttresses with impossibly pointed arches crowned with the effigies of the Blessed Founders of the Orders and long-dead Oneirocrats.

Here, Onyxia practised its second religion: power. Inside a colossal round basilica, the Senate of Oneirocrats and some gargantuanly wealthy merchants appointed the High Council who managed the Domain, including the joint-Regents who ruled over the army and navy respectively until the foretold day of the Solemn Princess's miraculous return from her hallowed crypt.

But to reach such mighty powers, one had to cut through the black marble morass of the Chancellery halls and archives. A veritable army of bureaucrats worked inside, cleaving the world only with ink, paper and arcane processes.

Ash entered the Petitioners' Pavilion's endless chambers, avoiding the guards' eyes. Hanging lamps shone like stars from the distant vaults. Navigating the twisting corridors proved as challenging as when he'd come here to claim the legal title to his father's meagre inheritance. He had to ask for directions a dozen times, and it took the entire morning to reach the right office.

The stern-looking clerk, after examining Omen as evidence of Ash's talents, sent him on yet another journey. 'Academy dispensations are granted by the High Sage's office. I'll draft you a pass to access the Sages' palace, but you'll have to leave your Dreamling at the stables.'

He ended up wasting another hour ensuring Omen's place. Only when the day was fading was he allowed into the gardens around the island's heart, where at long last he found a basilica surrounded by emerald greenery.

He sat to patiently wait one last time on one of the chamber's embroidered benches, but at least this room had bookshelf-laden walls. Sadly, most of the volumes turned out to be either dull surveys or legal compilations. He was about to settle for a daunting legal compendium when he found an odd gem gathering dust.

The Untrodden Roads by Olati the Bald, an Ilean author. He remembered being fascinated by it as a child. The work presented itself as a travelogue of the remote Cenobian Empire, except it was a work of pure fantasy.

It didn't surprise him that somebody had misplaced it with the cartographic surveys. Such a book required certain imaginative curiosity to be appreciated, something lacking among those concerned only with lining their pockets. He sank into it, only realising an hour had passed when another man was escorted into the room and helped into a seat.

He was handsome and dressed in fine silken robes, the streaks of grey in his long dark hair and beard giving away that he was older than he appeared. His father's age, had he still been alive.

His eyes were silver like two full moons, and Ash wondered whether he was blind. As the servant left, the stranger looked from the book in Ash's hands to his face. 'A strange book, that one. But it does offer some rather unique vistas.'

'You've read it too?' Ash replied, sitting up straighter with interest. 'My father said it was a miracle that it'd been printed at all, but that it was also a map like no other.'

The man cocked his head. 'How so?'

'Take for instance the chapter about the Questing Road that stretches without end towards an unyielding horizon. What is it but a map of unquenchable human desire? Everything Olati describes exists, just in people's minds.'

'A wise man, your father. It can be a literal map too, or a plan, if you will. The roads and cities Olati describes could be built or Dreamt. We can glimpse them in our minds already; only time and will separate us from them.' There was a faint curve to his lips, threatening a smile. 'We might only be able to visit them in the mind, but that doesn't make them any less real. Wouldn't you agree?'

'Who'd want to build them, though? The Domain doesn't care for such things.' For a moment, Ash paused, wondering if this man was a Dreamer. But even if he was, he didn't protest Ash's words. Besides, there was a tiny electric thrill of saying this to someone who might be one of them. 'Dreamers only act out of greed or arrogance,' he finished.

'There can be arrogance in Dreaming ... But isn't it hubris to rebel against what one sees as wrong with the world?' the stranger asked.

'To subvert nature, to replace it with something more palatable to us, that certainly is hubris.'

'But what about subverting the human world? What about Dreaming to illuminate the mind? Or to combat disease and death?'

Ash pursed his lips, considering how to reply.

'I suppose you're right. Dreaming isn't inherently selfish, but few seem interested in Dreaming anything like *that*. The gift might be limitless, but what's the point if everyone's imagination is enslaved to a single purpose?'

'Agreed!' Barely above a whisper, the stranger added, '"Ask not, why do we dream?"'

'"But rather, what light does this dream cast into our shadows?"' Ash finished the quote that he'd recognised by Calodren, the playwright.

'You are indeed well read!' The man smiled, taking years off his face with the expression. 'Now, since we share dear friends, I feel I should know your name.'

'Aescyon Allandra, but please, my friends call me Ash.'

'And I am Nial. Nial Morvander.'

That family name sounded familiar, but before Ash could place why, the doors opened.

A brown-haired woman wearing a magnificent golden dress entered, escorted by two palace guards. The ruby-feathered neck ruff that was draped over her elegant shoulders suggested immense wealth, and the way her blue eyes sized up the room spoke of authority. As soon as she spotted Nial, she hurried towards him.

'Lord Morvander.' She greeted him with an obsequious bow. This man was a *lord*? Strange that he'd been so unassuming when speaking with Ash. Either he'd mistaken him for another Oneirocrat or he was the lone wildflower growing amid the brambles. 'When they told me that you were waiting here, I couldn't believe it! Please accept my apologies for such unfitting treatment.'

'Fear not, the company was good,' he replied, offering Ash a warm look.

The woman turned with a smile for him, which died before reaching her eyes. From his clothes or the way he carried himself, she could tell he was no Oneirocrat worth her notice.

'Her Grace, Lady Saorla awaits you,' the woman said. 'Please, follow me.'

Ash trained his gaze on the book to disguise his awe. Lady Saorla was the captain general of the army and co-Regent, one of the most powerful people in the entire Domain. This man wasn't just any Oneirocrat, but one of notice.

The woman helped him stand and walked with him out of the room. The guards followed and closed the doors behind them.

Shortly after, a servant came for him. 'The High Sage's chief secretary shall see you now,' he said. He led Ash through an office filled with scriveners hard at work copying letters and updating ledgers. A large desk presided over the room, and behind hid the secretary, a thin man of summery complexion and intelligent eyes. He invited him to sit. A scribe brought him a leather folder of records, and the secretary began reading them. 'Aescyon Allandra is your name, correct?' he asked, and Ash nodded weakly. 'Imprisoned for larceny and trespassing on the Domain's property seven years ago . . .'

Ash's face burned with shame. There it was again. The stench he could never wash away. His stomach buckled at the thought of how close he stood to the Deep Wells, the prisons carved into the island's bedrock. He'd spent months there before being let out. Certainly, he could be sent back to them with the stroke of a pen.

'I was exonerated on both charges, sir,' he replied, clearing his throat. And that had only been because they couldn't prove he'd actually been into the library and not just left adrift on the flooded plains around it.

'I see.' The man read on, his expression darkening. 'You're here seeking a dispensation?' he finally asked.

'That is correct, sir.'

The secretary scoffed. 'Why? If you really are a Dreamer, what better chance to clear your family's name than service at the Academy?'

Despite all the years his father had dedicated to the army, they still thought of him as nothing but a criminal.

Ash bit his tongue. 'Please, sir, I'm sure there are other ways to serve Onyxia.'

'To prove you're not a danger, you must pass a mastery examination from the Sages' tribunal. I believe there'll be openings after the Ascent Festivities.'

'Ascent Festivities? Sir, that is in two months! I only have a week to report to the Academy!'

The secretary suppressed a yawn. 'I imagine you'll have to undertake training until then. That or appeal to your Oneirocrat patron. They might offer you tutelage.'

'Tutelage?'

'If an Oneirocrat claims responsibility for you, you can defer Academy conscription. You'll need it in writing, though.'

So that's how the highborn avoided the Academy! Their own families vouched for them until they passed this exam and obtained a dispensation.

Ash left the Sages' palace with a heavy heart. He should have known better than to hope there'd be a way for him to escape the yoke they'd prepared for him.

At least Omen was happy to see Ash when he returned.

And the Wailing Sisters' abbey was close by, so he could thank Daerna for everything she'd done.

At the abbey's gates, one of the servants let out a gasp at seeing Omen.

'He's harmless!' Ash said, pulling Omen's leash to reassure her. 'Will you please let Sister Daerna Eimar know that Aescyon is here to see her?'

Ash lay down on a stone bench in the gardens under the cypresses and hawthorns to watch the grey skies while he listened to the beauty of the Sisters' canticles.

As the sky began to shift into deeper darkness, he felt Omen stir at his side. Daerna was standing close by with a sad smile.

'I'm happy to see you,' he said. He wanted to embrace her, but this wasn't the place.

'I'm happy to see you too,' she said.

They sat together and discreetly clasped hands. Omen was seeking her attention too. Daerna indulged the panther by scratching him behind the ears.

'I can't stay long,' she whispered. 'How are you feeling?'

'Alive. That's good enough right now.'

'Let me see.' She turned to study his face and placed a furtive kiss on his lips. He felt his lungs fully fill again for the first time since he'd left the Academy's dungeons. 'The cut on your lip is healing nicely.' He cupped her cheek, and she placed her hand over his. 'Have you figured out how to get a dispensation yet?'

'I have – what, five days to come up with one? But at the palace they said I'd need two months to get it. And of course, the only way to avoid conscription is by having an Oneirocrat patron vouch for me.' He sighed. 'They're not going to let go of me.'

'Can't Master Esmus get it for you?'

'Perhaps. Even so, that'll only indebt me further to him.'

Daerna fiddled with the tear-shaped charms on her prayer bracelet, something she did when lost in thought. 'I could talk to my family . . .' Her voice faltered. 'They have an Oneirocrat patron, a senator.'

It was tempting to let her rescue him again, but he understood the price she'd be paying. Daerna begging aid from her estranged family would poison their relationship forever.

'No,' he said, and felt lighter when she smiled with relief.

'What then?'

'I could leave. Exile myself. I've heard there are freefolk communities hidden deep in the mountains and the Evenfall Forest.' Sometimes, Ash wondered if this wasn't where his own mother had fled.

'You mean Exarchians?' Daerna surmised.

'Yes, those who live free of rule. And I imagine they must have agents in the city. Perhaps they'd take me in.'

'I thought Exarchians wanted all Dreamers dead.' She looked at Omen.

'They wouldn't have to know.'

'Even if that were true, would you really leave everything behind?'

'Not everything . . .' He looked her in the eyes.

She offered a pained smile. 'We'd never be able to return, and after all I've done to become a Sister, I can't just leave.'

'You're right, I shouldn't be asking this of you.'

'Ash, I know you hate this idea, but why not try finding a patron?'

'And sell myself into servitude?'

'It doesn't have to be servitude! As a Dreamer yourself, you'd get better terms. Besides, they'll want to groom you as a potential supporter. They won't be nearly as brutal as the Academy's masters.'

The thought of binding himself to one of the city's Oneirocrats revolted him.

Still, Daerna's logic was hard to deny: this prospect, no matter how nauseating, was better than the Academy. Assuming he could find a patron in time.

He hadn't been born in a family with such connections, and all his life he'd avoided dealing with the Oneirocrats. As for calling on their palaces uninvited, it seemed as promising as mudlarking for a pittance on Little Vespiria's sandbanks.

Then it dawned on him.

That man at the palace ... Nial Morvander.

'Daerna, have you ever heard the name Morvander?'

Daerna raised an eyebrow. 'Like Morvander's Quietude?'

That was it! Ash remembered now. Early on in his Lightning-Hunter career, Rudher had taught him the dangers of hunting in the Susurrus, a district in Onyxia's Northern Quarter. There, the shadows, ghosts of dead Nightmares according to street legend, whispered into your ear, a distraction better avoided when hunting for lightning. If one had to hunt there, there was a place of solace, a palace known as Morvander's Quietude. The Quietude had been standing for more than half a century. Maybe the man he'd met today, who hadn't looked past his forties, was from that family.

Though it could be the original Morvander. Longevity among Dreamers wasn't uncommon. If you could Dream the world anew, you could Dream your flesh anew. It was a hard and delicate process, and even if you could allay the symptoms of ageing, few Dreamers understood enough to address the underlying roots of senectitude and its ailments, which would explain why the man needed assistance.

He might know one Oneirocrat after all.

'Dae, you might be right. There might be a way.'

* * *

The lamplighters were hard at work by the time he and Omen reached the Northern Quarter. The Susurrus's bridges and narrow passageways were convoluted even by Onyxian standards, but he knew how to navigate the spiral web of canals that coiled around the Whispering Sisters' abbey.

He'd come prepared for the whispers, but they still caught him off guard. Tonight, with the shadows as thick as ink, it was no soft murmur he heard, but a hissing chatter that filled the deserted streets.

Ash was racing by the time he reached the Quietude, Omen jogging beside him, ears pricked. Reaching the periphery of the palace, he felt relief. The colossal fortress was seemingly Dreamt of the same block of jet-black stone as the Onyxian archipelago, but unlike the rocky outcrops where the city stood, Morvander's Quietude was made of one smooth block. To Ash's surprise, its stone gates were closed but unguarded.

Heedless of the drizzle that had started to fall, Ash stood in front of the gates and knocked repeatedly until they opened of their own accord. The door warden greeted him. Wearing a silvery breastplate over a fitted gambeson and with a sword at her side, she seemed more duellist than servant. Her silver eyes and skin of an impossible ceramic paleness revealed her as a Dreamling.

'What's your business at Lord Morvander's house?' she enquired, her eyes shifting between him and Omen.

'Please, could you tell Lord Morvander that Aescyon Allandra is here to see him?'

She stood frozen, as if listening to the whistling breeze. Suddenly snapping into motion, she led Ash into a large entrance hall, then deeper into the palace, through a corridor covered with bas-reliefs of allegorical figures. At the end of the hallway, she ushered him into a chamber with a dark pool at its centre. Morvander waited by it, seated on a wooden stump and dressed in a simple black silk tunic.

'I didn't hope to meet you again so soon, Ash.' He seemed cordial, although his silver eyes looked unfocused.

'I didn't intend to abuse your cordiality, my lord.'

'Just Nial, Ash. How do you expect me to help you face the Chancellery?'

'But how . . .'

'If you had had something to request from me this morning, you'd have used the chance. And I could tell that you didn't know who I was. Now, you hesitate, you scramble about, looking for the right words.'

For a man that seemed constantly unfocused, his perception was painfully acute. 'I have something to request of you, Your Lordship.'

'Patronage?'

The word cut him like a lash. 'Of a sort, yes.'

'I'm afraid I no longer have the time for such things, Ash. I have my own work to tend to.'

Ash sighed. 'Sir, I'll be frank with you. The Academy has given me a week to find an Oneirocrat to offer me tutelage, or I'll be press-ganged into service.'

'And you'd rather sign your service over to a strange patron than try their instruction?'

'You said it yourself, sir. Why do we Dream? I might be able to survive the training, but I fear they'll have little use for my sort of mind. If I were to serve you, on the other hand . . .'

Morvander stood up. 'My work demands everything from me.'

Ash jumped at the chance. 'And if I could assist you with it?'

Lord Morvander's eyes wandered to Omen, then narrowed for a moment.

'Your creation, I take it?'

Ash nodded, and Nial approached the panther, unafraid.

'Interesting . . . very interesting indeed . . . He's most unusual. His make-up combines two seemingly irreconcilable ideas, yet they appear to marry well together. The fine lines of a fierce hunter, the swiftness of lightning – he can blend into the dark or cut through it . . . Perhaps you could bring a fresh perspective after all.'

'How can I prove my value to you?' Ash pressed.

Lord Morvander rubbed his chin. 'Fine. Answer me this: how do you make a person see something they don't want to see?'

Ash struggled to find something to say, but Morvander cut him off.

'Do not make a fool of yourself, Ash. Any idea that you can conjure on the spot won't be something I haven't fathomed before. Give it time, and when you're ready, come to me and deliver your answer.'

Chapter Ten

Daerna

To best serve Divine Geleisdra's will, our followers shall adhere to four strict paths:

I. The Wailers: noble and faithful, to tutor the masses and Keen, to elevate souls to the Motherstorm.
II. The Whisperers: studious and learned scribes, to faithfully preserve every story and life lost in their everlasting archives.
III. The Widows: who know grief and pity, to deliver the Motherstorm's mercy and help others endure loss.
IV. And last, the Wardens: worthy and devoted, to study the Silver Book's portents and ward the Solemn Princess in her Hallowed Crypt until the day of her joyous return.

– *The Rule of the Sisterhoods* by Blessed Merele

At dawn, Daerna dragged herself to the top of Muirtra's spire. Every step made her regret leaving her blanket's warmth, as she moved into the Motherstorm's howling embrace.

Prioress Balachdra had doubled not just her watches but her other duties of reading and helping the Cellarer Sister with some cleaning and provisioning tasks for a month. It was a harsh punishment for missing a day of her watches, although a small price to pay for freeing Ash.

Securing her cloak, she waited for the bells to announce the passing of the hour. As the heavy tolling began, she unbolted the door and entered the cage that faced westwards.

As usual, the view was daunting but magnificent. It was a matter of pride for her Order that Muirtra's spires rose taller than any other in Onyxia, taller than the Grand Palace's and even the Lightning-Hunters' Guild's. Being physically close to the Motherstorm's bosom helped the Wailing Sisters reach Her hallowed heart.

Daerna locked herself inside the singing cage and leaned forwards, taking in the city. A fierce gust hit, shaking the entire cage and knocking her to the soaked planks, her forehead striking the grating.

The Motherstorm was truly wrathful this morning. Was She furious at Daerna too?

Fighting the icy waves of rain pelting her, she forced herself to her feet and closed her fists around the bars. She had endured worse, far worse. She'd endure this too.

Firmly footed, she launched into the Keening.

The prioress had assigned her the 'Salutation to the Glorious Living Lightning', one of the simplest canticles in the *Song of Sorrows*. Picking something with no depth or complexity, something a novice could have sung, was probably part of the punishment.

Still, Daerna gave herself to the holy canticle's harmonies, wrapping her emotions around the rising and falling of her voice, her soul reaching towards the Motherstorm's heart.

By the time she'd completed the first neumes, her fear had melted away. How could she be afraid when her voice was the wind blowing through the Shingle Sea and over the broken waters of the lagoon?

Below, Lightning-Hunters moved apace with her rhythm. Above, crowcat clowders soared with her breathing and skyship sailors saluted her with reverence. The rain had begun seeping through her thick cloak into her very bones, but she felt miles away. She was every gust of wind, every drop of rain. She was the storm's secret harmony.

At that moment, her connection was sublime. In that moment, she *was* the Motherstorm.

Among all Sisters, only the Wailers Keened. Only they sang the canticles daily. This sacrament was an immense honour. Through it, Wailers elevated the souls of the deceased to the heavens for the Hallowed Motherstorm, to rapturously hold them in Her bosom.

But the Motherstorm's colossal power meant that, if left unattended, Her sorrow would turn to brutal anger. Some of it was a gift to harness in the form of living lightning, yet too much would tear Onyxia apart. Thus, the Wailers soothed Her with gentle canticles to keep a perfect balance.

Even on days like today, when they were Keening their care for Her, Daerna experienced the rapturous joy of communing with divine perfection through song.

* * *

For a long hour, Daerna Keened. With effort and art, she worked to tilt the Motherstorm's brawling rage into weeping melancholy.

When the bell rang, signalling an end to her watch, she let her voice lower into a softer chant and then lapse into silence. Not a heartbeat later, another Sister began singing from the spire's eastern cage, allowing Daerna to retreat inside.

Daerna descended the tower in silence. Her throat and her muscles were all sore, but the worst was the ache in her heart.

The feeling of severance after touching the Motherstorm was always hard to bear. Part of it was the sudden return to the body's physical frailty. When Keening, she was raw, pure emotion, her whole being a well-tuned string vibrating with perfect purpose. Now, she felt like nothing but a tired, sniffling lump of flesh stumbling through a dull, disharmonious world.

The descent was long, and she was relieved to find someone waiting for her at the bottom of the stairs with a steaming infusion. And no lay Sister – Daerna immediately recognised the long auburn hair of Sister Dirdra, the abbey's Cantor and Daerna's tutor.

'Here, this'll soothe your throat. Let me take your cloak,' Dirdra said.

Daerna gladly accepted the mug and sat down by a brazier to warm herself. The infusion had both the bitterness of bloodvine and the sweetness of honey. She relished its soothing touch on her throat and the warmth on her hands.

'Thank you, Dirdra,' she whispered.

'I'm afraid I bring more than a throat remedy.' Dirdra frowned. 'The abbess has summoned you.'

'Her Sorrowfulness wants to see me? Why?'

'I was hoping you'd tell me. Either way, we'll find out soon enough. Finish the drink first. You're going to need your voice.'

Daerna drank the rest slowly while she pondered what this could mean. Hadn't Prioress Balachdra already disciplined her? For Blessed Merele's steward, the Superior of their Order and abbess of the most important abbey in Onyxia, to take an interest in her didn't bode well.

Finishing, she followed Dirdra through the stone corridors. As usual, Muirtra teemed with Sisters, busy with their chores, and cats, idle in their slumber. Daerna loved this place, its magnificence, its solace. Normally, she'd treasure a chance to visit the Superior's Hall under the dome's beauty, the silver shine of engraved stanzas shimmering in the candlelight, but not today.

They found Abbess Superior Forlaitra deep in conversation with Prioress Balachdra. A political vulture always hungry for carrion, the prioress was no doubt behind this summons.

Daerna and Dirdra waited in silence while the abbess and prioress finished conferring. Daerna straightened her damp habit. Had she known she was going to meet Her Sorrowfulness, she'd have chosen something other than the humble tunic and belt she now wore. Blessed Merele's rule required Sisters to signal their consecration by wearing habits in the Motherstorm's colours. Amidst the Wailers, many still wore silk scapulars, and even Daerna had fine stark black kirtles and brocaded veils. Hopefully, she'd come across as humble and not dishevelled.

At last, the abbess motioned for them to approach. She might be old and minute, but her bearing commanded respect, and both Daerna and Dirdra hurried to kiss her bracelet of tears. It was marvellously ornate compared to Daerna's: a silver tear for each year of service in the Order and a bejewelled pendant for each canticle she'd composed for the abbey's *Book of Canticles*. There was a lifetime of devotion dangling from it.

'Daerna Eimar, my sister,' the Superior said in her craggy voice, 'you've been called into our presence so you may have the opportunity to explain yourself.'

'Your Sorrowfulness?'

The long-faced prioress was the one to reply. 'I knew you had neglected your duties, but only today did I learn the *true* extent of your misconduct.' Balachdra's greying brows furrowed, shaping her face into stone. 'See for yourself, Sister Cantor, what your protégée has been up to.'

She handed a letter to Dirdra, who grimaced the more she read. Daerna felt a cold sting of fear. Dirdra, being the leader of Muirtra's chorus, could protect her from almost anything. That is, if she chose to.

Daerna craned her neck, trying to catch a better view of the letter. The calligraphy was too tight to read, but she recognised the emblem on the wax seal: the Academy's.

This had to be about Ash, about what she'd done to free him at the Isle of Sighs. She should have known how spiteful they'd be and used a false name.

'Our young Sister here is *so* status-hungry,' the prioress went on viciously, 'that she's willing to impersonate the Order's authorities!' She chuckled scornfully. 'I shall not have our sacred name soiled by some *upstart*!'

Daerna's cheeks burned. The Sisterhood took in women of all statuses, but Muirtra was slightly different in one regard: being the seat of the Wailing Sisters, it exercised an enormous influence on Onyxian politics, and many wealthy families sent their younger daughters to the Wailers both for prestige and to gain power.

But her? She'd had to battle her mother to take the veil. And hearing the prioress speak of the quality of her lineage didn't help her mood. She clenched her teeth, steeling herself while the prioress continued her chiding.

'I've had to apologise and bow to the Academy commander! *Me!* As if I were some lowly fishmonger!' The prioress shook her head. 'This is the only time! Do you hear me? I'll see you *expelled* before this happens again!'

Daerna pleaded with her gaze for Dirdra to intervene. She wasn't allowed to speak in front of the abbess without permission.

'Your Sorrowfulness,' Dirdra began, 'even if our Sister has committed a transgression, we shouldn't hasten into judgement.'

'Her misdemeanour reflects not just on her but on all of us. She's betrayed her oaths to the Motherstorm and the Song. How else would you have us deal with it?' the prioress replied.

The silence grew heavy and thick in the room.

'Your Sorrowfulness, Sister Daerna's Keening abilities are exceptional. To cast her out would be a loss for the Order. Besides, I'm certain that her actions were born out of folly, not of betrayal to our oaths.'

The Abbess Superior gave Daerna a long hard look.

'Is that so?' she asked.

Daerna's heart raced. Defying the prioress was terrifying enough, but if she was going to be expelled from the Order, it shouldn't be for the wrong reasons.

'I didn't betray the Song,' Daerna said quietly.

'Excuse me?' the prioress replied, but the abbess raised her hand.

'Your Sorrowfulness, doesn't the *Song of Sorrows* say that we're to carry the burdens of the world within ourselves? To bear others' sorrows as if they were our own?'

'You dare quote the Sacred Canticles to us?' The abbess's voice sounded stern, but she raised a curious eyebrow. 'How does that justify any of your actions?'

'Your Sorrowfulness, please, consider: isn't it our duty to tend to the suffering masses? Aren't we to speak up when those in power misuse their station to abuse those who have no voice?'

The prioress chuckled with well-practiced scorn. 'Would you have us do the Academy's job instead?' she asked. 'Or is it that you prefer to have wild Nightmares escaped from untrained Dreamers' minds running rampant in the streets?'

'No, of course not.' Daerna chose her words carefully. 'But since we Keen for the grieving masses, shouldn't we stand up for them? Besides, the Academy was transgressing the law by sweeping a Lightning-Hunter off the streets without his guild's permission.'

The prioress laughed. 'Please, we're not interested in your legal opinions! And don't take us for fools! I know that you did it for that lover of yours. I should cast you out and see whether that boy takes you in!'

Daerna felt the tide of battle shifting away from her. With a faltering voice, she appealed to the abbess one last time. 'Please, Your Sorrowfulness, I'm not wrong. The Academy really is violating the laws of the Domain. What will be next, that they drag one of us away if they suspect a Sister of being a Dreamer too?'

The abbess reclined and narrowed her eyes at Daerna.

'Even if we were to believe you, child, you should have come to the prioress first, or at least Sister Cantor Dirdra. Instead, you recklessly fouled the air between us and the Academy. And with the prospect of war with the King of Delectia closer than ever, and the Domain sure to call on the Academy's strength, that was a very foolish thing to do. Balance between the Sisterhoods, the guilds and the Academy has always been delicate. Your childish rashness, taking sides in a dispute that doesn't concern us, threatens our position.'

'I beg you, Your Sorrowfulness,' Dirdra joined in, 'Sister Daerna's recklessness is only misguided devotion. She's too young to understand the delicate hand that is needed to steer the Order these days. With the proper guidance, though . . .'

'There's much you need to atone for if you're to return to our good graces, Daerna,' the abbess finally said. 'But we shall trust in Sister Dirdra's judgement. For your sake, may she be right.'

Daerna breathed in with sudden relief. 'Thank you for your kind judgement, Your Sorrowfulness.'

'Wait.' The abbess lifted a gnarled hand. 'There's something else. We shall ensure you learn a lesson from all of this. You shall join Sister Naida's Penance Procession for the remainder of the week. We hope that seeing the evils they reckon with shall sate your appetite for aiding the impoverished, and hopefully, you'll learn why it's wise to trust the guiding vision of your superiors.'

Did Dirdra grow stiff at the mention of Sister Naida's name? 'Your generosity is an example to us all, Your Sorrowfulness,' she said, bowing low.

Daerna quickly did the same. Whatever concerns she had, they'd have to wait.

* * *

Daerna was to remain in her cell until the procession. The impromptu trial had left her partly shaken, partly ashamed, but mostly angry: at herself, for being caught, but even more so at the Order.

While studying music as part of her curriculum, she'd found that she craved to do more than shift money around. Inspired by the help they offered the city, she'd left her studies and joined the Order, renouncing her future as the helm of the Eimar family.

As an ordained Sister, she'd dreamt of saving souls, achieving transcendent communion with the Motherstorm and being able to use her position to shape a better world.

Transcendent communion had been found. Under Dirdra's tutelage, she'd quickly risen inside the abbey's chorus. But she had yet to find any sign of being able to shape a better world. If anything, it seemed that her new family was becoming as power- and wealth-hungry as her own mother had been.

In the three years since she'd joined the Order, she'd seen a sickening obsession within the Sisterhood grow, one of nepotism and political machinations promoting only the 'right names' into the abbeys. Where once their ranks had been seen as a counterbalance to the excessive greed and cruelty of the Oneirocrats, it seemed that under Abbess Superior Forlaitra, they were willing to become their silent enablers.

Worse, when for once Daerna had the chance to use her position to fight injustice, she'd ended up facing her very own Sisters.

Dirdra came to visit her shortly after dusk, carrying a basket. Inside was a hunk of bread, some cheese and a single egg, a sparse dinner that Daerna wolfed down quickly.

'Did you know of Sister Naida? I suppose she's a discipliner.'

'Yes, that and a zealot. We actually studied together,' Dirdra replied with a frown. 'She's very devout, but as inflexible as a rock. During our second year as novices, our chorus Keened at some Oneirocrat's wedding. Their manor's sculptures had been crowned with bright flower garlands, and Naida thought that it was an affront to the Motherstorm's sorrow.' Dirdra sighed. 'They caught her red-handed, defacing the sculptures with hammer in hand . . .'

Daerna's eyes widened. 'Why wasn't she expelled?'

'Because she's a Marsael.' Daerna knew the name, one of Onyxia's founding lineages. 'She was exiled to minor abbeys in the provinces. There she made a name as a very effective discipliner, which is why she's now in charge of the Penance Procession,' Dirdra continued. 'This is their way of keeping her from stirring up trouble in the wrong places. Everyone knows she poses a danger.'

Daerna swallowed hard.

'Don't worry, Daerna. She's dangerous, but so am I.' Dirdra let out a burst of deep laughter and ran her long nails through her hair. 'I'll let her know that you're my apprentice.'

'Thank you, Sister Dirdra. How can I repay you for all of this?'

'By staying safe out there. And that means not letting Naida Marsael get under your skin.'

* * *

At first glance, the fabled Naida Marsael wasn't particularly imposing. She had a stern frown and grey rivulets in her brown hair despite not being much older than Dirdra. Then Daerna noticed the whip and mace that hung from her belt, alongside the manic gleam in her eyes.

There were a dozen women in total, the majority Wailing Sisters from smaller abbeys, one of them reeking of wine, but two belonged to the other Orders.

A tall young woman, pale as snow, wore the mist-white habit of the Whispering Sisters, a rare sight given how small their Order was. Her long fingers were ink-stained and her lips painted white, reminders of her Order's consecration to chronicling and silence.

There was a Widowed Sister too. About Daerna's age, the young woman wore a simple grey habit of breeches and a leather jerkin. With her dark hair cropped short and her hands on the pommels of twin quillon daggers, she seemed more like a street mugger than a Sister.

Unlike the aristocratic Wailers or the scholarly Whisperers, the Widows, the largest of the four Orders, also drew their members from the common folk, including former soldiers that now served in a militia to protect their hospices.

The biggest surprise was discovering a familiar face from Muirtra. A wiry young woman with golden-brown skin, whose habit was a bit too big on her and whose large doe eyes were expressive enough to speak for her. Daerna stepped to the petite woman's side. 'I believe we studied Keening together two years ago. Roshia, was it?'

'Yes!' The girl's fawn face lit up with relief at finding someone familiar, a sentiment Daerna shared. 'You're Daerna, right?'

Before they could catch up, the Widowed Sister interrupted them: 'Daerna? You're the one that went to the Isle of Sighs to get her lover out?'

'Pierla, leave her be!' Roshia said.

'I'm just getting to know her.' The Widow smirked at Daerna. 'Tell me, lovey-dove, was it worth it? What's so special about him? Pretty eyes or a pretty cock?'

'My reasons are none of your damn business,' Daerna snarled back.

'The little dove has a sharp beak!' Pierla chuckled, stepping into Daerna's space.

'Dove, you say?' Daerna replied, placing her hand on the anlace dagger she carried. The habit might protect her these days, but before being a Sister, she'd belonged to a family of means, and that had afforded her a fencing tutor growing up. Violence wasn't the Sisters' way, but damn it if she was going to let some brat bully her.

A loud crack quietened them.

They turned to see Sister Naida glaring, whip in hand.

'Silence, foolish girls! Had you put as much energy into your duties, you wouldn't be here! Now move!'

With another crack of her whip, the procession was set in motion. They poured out of Muirtra into the plateau's drizzle-misted streets.

From there, they marched east.

Sister Naida led them into the Craghorn peninsula. Unlike other charity rounds Daerna had experienced, Sister Naida seemed to have little interest in ministering the Motherstorm's mercy to the suffering masses. Her interest was instead on Her hallowed wrath.

Sister Naida was quick to chide and admonish those consorting in the narrow alleyways of the neighbourhood, haranguing the locals on their many moral failings. Their procession she herded with an equally stern fist. She didn't shy from using the whip either, as an older, inebriated Wailer found out when she stopped for a moment, receiving a lashing to the back of her hand.

* * *

The following nights didn't prove any easier. Sing too loud and be lashed for the sin of self-enamoured vanity, remain quiet and be punished for remiss obeisance.

Roshia and Daerna learned to watch out for each other. Skittish as she was, Daerna's friend had an uncanny skill for reading Sister Naida's moods, thus allowing them to mostly stay out of her path. For her part, Dae ensured that if one of them did catch her eye, she received the blame.

The Widow did the same for the impoverished folk they crossed paths with in the streets. Whenever a sickly or old resident was about to receive some ministration of Sister Naida's whip, Sister Pierla was quick to make some crass joke that would draw punishment to her instead.

Seeing the purple markings and scars on both her forearms, Daerna developed a begrudging respect for the Widow. And judging how Pierla stopped teasing her, she suspected it went both ways.

* * *

For Daerna's final night of penance, Sister Naida decided to head into the Scab, the most dangerous of the southern districts.

It hadn't always been like that. Once, the Southern Quarter had boasted the most luxurious palaces in the entire city. Then, the southmost islets began sinking back into the lagoon. Even then, the High Council had tried to save the district by Dreaming huge steel chains to tether the islets above the waters.

The effort proved fruitless. The Crumbling District barely held on, and the Oneirocrats moved farther north into the plateau, while their servants and the guilds followed. Only the poorest and most stubborn who had no place else to go held on to the dying bits of the district, now covered in a web of rusting chains. Soon that same rust began spreading everywhere, tinging the entire district red, earning it the nickname 'the Scab'.

Nowadays, the Scab was a crowded maze of humble dwellings carved into the carcasses of other buildings, sewn together with rusting metal and rickety bridges. The grimy and shadowy alleys served cutpurses and cutthroats equally.

Graffiti in many tongues covered the walls. Sister Naida stopped occasionally to read them, sermonising on the sins contained within and allowing their procession brief respite, before leading them deeper into the Scab's entrails.

At their passing, shutters were drawn closed, while even shady individuals loitering under the arches fled from them.

Soon, lost in the depths of the winding lanes, the only light was the Whisperer's orb-lamp. The wooden houses hunched over their procession, their flaking facades dark and silent. The group's lamentations became mournful echoes, and even the rain sounded muffled on the muddy streets.

Sister Naida's attention was on a trail of scribblings on the walls. They all followed her down a narrow close and into a cobbled plaza surrounded by a thick ring of stone buildings, perhaps once some palace's inner courtyard. The ground-floor rooms were entirely bricked up, while the covered upper balconies were but rotten husks. A large well stood at the centre, closed by a mossy grate that did nothing to stop the reek of stale refuse.

Naida ordered a halt to their march, and the Whisperer placed her orb-lamp on the well's edge. While most Sisters sat to rest their sore legs, Daerna's attention was caught by a flicker of light. In the corner, she found a statue niche had been turned into a shrine of sorts.

A wooden effigy of a skeletal figure stood over melted candlewax. The figurine was lying on her back with her legs spread open wide. The bones were varnished black with ashes, while the skull was smeared with a dark red liquid. At her feet, someone had placed rows of small skulls from various birds and rodents. Cold fear rushed over her.

Naida approached, pausing to kick over a bucket placed at the shrine's feet. A dozen rotting pigeon corpses spilled out.

'What under the Storm?' Roshia whispered. Some of the other Sisters gasped in shock. Like Daerna, they must have recognised the effigy of the Charnel Mother.

This wasn't just some foreign religious figure; this was a proscribed cult. After Empress Myrtele's murder, the Divine Empire was partitioned, and different forms of worship became the norm. Then the simmering rivalries of the Divine scions boiled into open war during the Sibling Strife, which tore apart the heavens and the seas. Yet nothing was as fearsome and brutal as the emergence of the Charnel Mother and Her host.

Etedros, the Pale Prince, had Dreamt Her to unbirth every living being and suck blood, sap and air from existence. The Charnel Mother's host of jubilant dead had swept the continent and reduced every city in their path to cinders.

It'd been Princess Geleisdra who'd stopped them, stood against her brother and defeated the Pale Prince's host in battle near Ludeyn and banished the Charnel Mother from the world.

Yet somehow, the Charnelite Cult still thrived among the desperate and the broken.

Tales spread of heretics collecting bones for their hidden ossuaries, where they prayed for the Charnel Mother's grim deliverance from the world's many cruelties. Daerna had hoped they were mere rumours.

'Behold, Sisters!' Sister Naida addressed them. 'Rotten idolatry has taken root in our very home! Fear not! We shall rain righteous anger and thunder upon it, to wash away the filth from our jet-black city!'

As she spoke, Daerna noticed Pierla reaching for her daggers.

'What are you doing?' Daerna whispered. Pierla gestured up with her chin, and Daerna saw them: a group of ragged figures skulking in the shadows of the balconies above.

Naida noticed them as well and climbed atop the grated well to use it as a pulpit. 'Are you the heretics responsible for this filth?' she called into the darkness.

A wrinkled man, his head shaven and painted red, leaned over a balcony. He carried himself with authority despite his ratty clothes. 'You're not welcome here, daughter of Geleisdra! Stay away from our shrine, and we'll let you part in peace.'

A handful of others crept forwards, carrying clubs and daggers. A woman painted black with ashes began descending a stairway. Some Sisters backed towards the plaza's entrance, until Roshia's cry cut their retreat short.

'Watch out!'

Glancing over her shoulder, Daerna saw two other men with their faces smeared in ashes blocking the way out. One carried a spiked club, the other held a cleaver.

Daerna's stomach knotted. This could easily turn bloody.

She slowly drew her stiletto, ensuring that the gleam of her blade was hidden in her own shadow.

Heedless, Naida kept berating the priest. 'To think I'll allow this rot to fester! The arrogance! Come down here so I may chop off your viperous tongue myself!'

'You don't belong here!' the old man spat at her. 'Step away from the Mother or pay her tribute with your flesh.'

Though Naida's face was pearled with glimmering sweat, her eyes were lit with twin fires and her lips were twisted with delight.

'She's going to get us all killed,' Pierla muttered.

Daerna nodded and tapped Roshia on the shoulder. 'We can't just stay here. Follow me.' Quietly, the three crept towards the exit.

The woman who'd descended tried sneaking closer to the shrine, but Naida took out her iron mace and raised it threateningly.

Daerna pressed on towards the exit, her dagger carefully hidden behind her. The man with the club stepped into her path.

Naida was yelling from behind. 'You think we're afraid of rats like you? I'll teach you what happens to those who defy the Motherstorm!'

Daerna kept her eyes on the men blocking the passageway, but the cracking sound and the crowd's roar said it all. His eyes and mouth widened in sudden, furious horror. This was her chance.

She swung hard, punching him in the face with her dagger's guard. The blow connected against his temple, and he fell like a sack of rocks.

'This way!' she yelled, pressing ahead.

Too late, she realised that the man's companion was on her. She raised her blade to block his cleaver's swing, but she moved far too slow.

The dirty blade neared her face, then bounced away. Pierla parried the blow with one of her daggers. With the second, she stabbed the man's side. He shrieked in pain and retreated into a corner.

The mob rushed downstairs for them. Roshia bolted for the exit, calling for her Sisters to follow, and bumped into a third man, twice her size, who grabbed her in a bear hug.

Roshia kicked at him frantically, while Daerna searched for an opening, but he held Roshia like a shield.

Someone flung a cobble over Daerna's shoulder. It was a magnificent shot and struck the man in his face. He leaned over, forehead bleeding, and Roshia kicked him in the groin. He released her, gurgling, and fell down. Pierla kicked him in the face, knocking him out.

Daerna turned and saw the pale Whisperer with another cobble in her hand.

She turned to Roshia, who was still gasping from her ordeal. 'Get the Sisters out of here!' she cried.

'Follow me!' Roshia yelled, her voice wavering with fear but still strong enough to carry. She started towards the exit, and the Sisters followed, doing their best to avoid the men on the ground.

Daerna looked around. Were they all safe? No.

Sister Naida was still in the square, fending off those who'd come down to defend the shrine.

To her credit, Naida skilfully swung both her mace and whip. A young man had fallen under her blows already, and she'd managed to keep most of the mob bottled on the stairway.

But it was only a matter of time before she was surrounded.

'We have to leave!' Daerna yelled.

Without acknowledging her, Sister Naida leapt towards the exit. A handful of men followed her, armed with axes and short, rusty swords.

'Next time I'll feed you to the lagoon crabs myself!' Naida yelled before smashing the orb-lamp with her mace. Thunder and lightning exploded in the square.

Daerna staggered blindly into the exit passageway, only to trip on a loose cobble.

'We have to run!' Pierla shouted.

Blinking to shake the flash off, Daerna ran after Pierla, who in turn was chasing after Naida through the alleys and wynds.

The furious mob followed close behind. Any wrong turn and they'd come face to face with them.

'Motherstorm's dark bosom! Who's leading us?' Naida growled. It was a question Daerna shared.

As they caught up with the rest of their group, they found Roshia at its head. She seemed to know the way out, which was lucky because Daerna couldn't remember for her life which curving lanes led where.

When they came in sight of the chained bridge that had brought them to the Scab, the mob lagged behind. The Sisters crossed over its rocky curve, and Daerna turned to find all the pursuers had disappeared back into the night. The women stopped at once, completely out of breath. One of the older Sisters collapsed with exhaustion, and another vomited into the canal.

'You have much to be proud of, girls!' Naida announced, ecstatic. 'May this be a lesson: those who show unwavering resolve and devotion to the Motherstorm are protected no matter what.'

Daerna and Pierla shared a grimace. If they hadn't reacted quickly and fought their way out, they would have all ended up brutally beaten, or worse.

Eventually, Sister Naida lined up the company and sent them marching in procession back towards the abbey.

During the march, Pierla stepped to her side.

'Perhaps you aren't a silly dove after all,' she muttered.

'Perhaps you're not the browbeater I took you for,' Daerna replied.

'I hope tonight has helped you realise how different things look from the gutter. Talking about one's discontent is easy; caring about people, even those who hate you, is something else.'

'You've seen what I'm capable of.'

'Good. Some talk high and mighty, then run scared at the first whiff of trouble.' Pierla eyed her. 'But *some* aren't afraid to speak the truth, even if it angers the abbesses.'

'Some? Who?'

'Sisters, like us, but ones who deal only with trusted friends. I could introduce you to them . . . if you're interested.'

Daerna nodded without hesitation. 'Introduce me.'

Chapter Eleven

Geil

Blood runs thicker than Dream.

– Old Nirian proverb

GEIL FINISHED HER ALE AND, even though it tasted like barley watered down with piss and brine, ordered another.

The tavern whirled around her, flooding her senses with smoke and drunk chatter. She wanted inebriation to wrap around her like a blanket, to smother the nagging ideas pecking at the back of her mind. The drink alone wasn't doing it.

The governor had toasted her when she'd shown up to collect payment for dealing with the owl Dreamling. 'Vanquisher of Nightmares!' he'd called her. If only it was true of her own nightmares.

She'd lied to him, omitting Ragdra's role in the owlet's creation. How long until a trader or a villager carried the news to someone else? Sooner or later, the Academy would come to snatch the girl away.

Maybe if Geil hadn't given up on the promises she and Lanteus had made to each other when they'd left the Academy, none of this would be happening. If they'd changed things like they'd planned, Ragdra wouldn't have to face being viciously chiselled by the masters' hands.

For the past year, Geil had found respite, losing herself in the Highlands' melancholic moors, living only for the marchioness's next ball, the next drunken stupor, the next forgettable affair. Now this incident had woken Lanteus's spectre, and not all the ale in the world, nor all of the lovers, would quiet him down.

Winning your own battles is hard enough, muttered the Drake, impervious as ever. It was tempting to embrace its philosophy. Let Ragdra and her family find their own way. Didn't Geil have enough to deal with already?

The hearth was dying, reduced to a few silent embers that produced more smoke than warmth. Just as her hopes were fated to.

But she also knew that letting this dream die was to let Lanteus finally disappear from her world.

They'd sworn they'd put an end to the Academy's cruelties. That a day would come when they'd return and become better masters. That if they ever had children, they'd spare them the suffering, prove they could teach without scarring young Dreamers.

The Academy had stood for centuries, preceding even Onyxia. Its rebellion had helped shatter the ancient Iskian Empire into warring nations, which had taken the extraordinary might of Damnia, the Philosopher Empress and grandmother to Divine Geleisdra, to bring to heel. And even she hadn't been able to change its brutal nature. How could Geil expect to do any different?

Maybe the two of them together would have achieved something. Yet such dreams had crumbled to dust the moment Lanteus was killed. What was worse, even if Geil hadn't been the one wielding the blade, she might as well have, given her betrayal.

A rush of self-hatred ran down her spine, and she shattered the ale jug with her claws, the noise so loud that everyone fell silent and turned, a glint of fear, mistrust and hatred in their eyes.

She dropped a handful of Octaves on the table and left.

Dragging her feet through the harbour, she searched for the Skycouriers' post. It was a half-formed idea, reaching out to Marchioness Nisdre. She had the power and influence to find a suitable patron for Ragdra. Of course, Geil would have to pay for it, probably accepting patronage from the marchioness herself. The idea of another year of service at Nisdre's pleasure weighed on her, but her father's name carried enough weight to negotiate favourable terms.

A chained Drake only flies so far. The little girl's weakness is a heavy load for us, her other half protested. Geil ignored it.

The Skycouriers' post was a sturdy guardhouse with its own turret. That such a small harbour possessed such an imposing post was testament to the Chancellery's bureaucratic apparatus's efforts at controlling information and money in every corner of the Domain.

Swinging the door open, she walked into a room tinged blue by hanging orb-lamps. Even at this late hour, the place was busy, captains and traders sending reports or collecting bundles of letters. When her turn to approach the counter came, she spotted a woman wearing the Academy's bone cuirass at the other end of the room.

The long-faced clerk cleared her throat impatiently. 'Are you here to collect or send a letter?'

Geil hesitated. Was the Academy agent a recruiter? Would she overhear Geil's request and deduce that she was trying to hide a Dreamer? She glanced over her shoulder. The stranger seemed absorbed in the documents she held, but Geil still felt off balance, cold bile swirling in the pit of her stomach.

'I'm here to collect any letters addressed to me,' she said, trying to stall until the Academy agent left.

Geil offered the clerk her travel papers, and the clerk's eyes widened. 'There's a letter waiting for you. Let me fetch it.'

That was unexpected. When the clerk handed it over, Geil saw that it'd been forwarded by the marchioness. Then she noticed her father's seal on the back.

When her mother had died, he'd lost himself in his work, and he'd never fully returned. She'd seen little of him in the past few years, and only received rare letters from him since she'd left for the Highlands. They hardly ever bore good news.

She cracked open the seal and devoured the words inside. With relief, she saw that nothing terrible had happened. He was still in good health. In fact, he'd written to tell her that he was about to turn another corner in his work. *Come home*, the letter ended.

'Does Your Ladyship have a reply?' asked the clerk.

Geil waved dismissively, then an idea came to her.

Perhaps there was a way around Ragdra's situation that wouldn't be so costly. Perhaps her father was right, and it was time to come home.

She and Onyxia had parted ways miserably. It wasn't just that Lanteus was dead. Even without saying it, many blamed her for his death. Entombed hells, she blamed herself for it too. Which was why she'd sworn never to return.

Yet his ghost was calling her. Asking her to aid Ragdra.

'On second thought, yes,' she said.

Chapter Twelve

Ash

Even without the gift, all beings who sleep possess a measure of imagination. It's this imagination that shields them from another's Dreaming, especially when it flares in deep slumber. Even the Undreaming are naturally resilient to Dreamers' attempts to influence, harm or heal them. And yet, even humankind must bow to cats on this. Stubbornness and slumbering prowess make them immune to any attempts to change them.
– *Dialogues: On Imagination* by Aristan of Ravkiria

ASH SOON REALISED THAT LORD Morvander's challenge was a daunting riddle, if not impossible. How was he to make people see what they didn't want to see?

It wasn't as if he could pry open other people's minds and observe their thoughts. And even if he could, how would he carve them? It'd be like trying to sculpt smoke with a paintbrush.

The next morning, he requested his crew's assistance, and Ghalod was the first to volunteer. For years now, his revulsion of frogs, the same creatures that had led him to suffer many nightmares as a child, had troubled him.

Since Ash couldn't simply erase Ghalod's fear, he tried focusing on his friend's eyes. Ash attempted to Dreamchant them, to embed into them the notion of frogs as beautiful creatures. However, altering Ghalod's eyes proved impossible; Ash could imagine all the changes he wanted inside the Dreaming trance, but none of them took root in their world.

Ash had read about this in Aristan of Ravkiria's writings. Every living being with dreams had a natural resistance to a Dreamer's influence, especially when they slept. Ghalod wasn't a Dreamer, but his mind had a solid idea of who he was, and changing it was nigh impossible.

By the end of the day, Ash had only managed to give both him and Ghalod immense migraines. And if anything, Ghalod blamed frogs for it.

The next day, Ash tried a different approach. Books, music, wine and plenty of other creations influenced the mind. Why not use them as a lever? He just had to Dreamchant them.

Rudher agreed to lend him his flute to experiment with. Inert matter was easier to tamper with even when Ash's lack of musical education made it exceedingly difficult to envision changes that weren't cosmetic. Only after several failed attempts did he manage to crudely Dreamchant the flute.

This time, when Rudher played for them, the tune pulled Ash and Ghalod into a dance, but their movements were blundering and forced. It was like their limbs were being moved by an unskilled puppeteer, and it hurt. Their bodies tried to fight the enchantment too, and soon Ash's bruised legs cramped up.

In the end, only Rudher's mood was lifted, and only because he'd got a good laugh at them.

Ash was exhausted, but felt Dreamchanting had to be the way; he just needed to figure out the right angle.

Finally, he asked Yaisa for her wooden pendants, then set to Dreamchanting them with an impossible gift: the wearers would be able to hear each other's thoughts. This would open the door for one mind to persuade the other.

It took him hours of trial and error, until eventually he managed to move from vague impressions to clear emotions.

Still, even then, the result was muddled. He'd hoped he would be able to hear Yaisa's voice in his head and vice versa; instead, her emotions bled into him directly.

It was an unsettling experience. Yaisa's emotions felt untrue and alien in his head, and his in hers. Plus, the enchantment turned out to be ephemeral. By evening, the only trace that he'd ever altered the pendants was the gleaming blue light that ran through them like veins.

Yaisa tried to cheer him up. 'I bet they'll fetch a good price now!' But Ash's mood had irremediably darkened. He was out of ideas, and time trickled like sand through his fingers.

* * *

With only two days left, spending one at the Grand Palace's library felt like a risky gamble, but he needed to enlist the aid of greater minds than his.

A librarian, the best pathfinder in the maze of imaginings and voices, helped him navigate the black-and-gold halls. Ash thanked her for her efforts.

The tomes she recommended became hard enough to reconcile, though. Aristan of Grotto, the ancient Iskian philosopher, wrote in *Study of Rhetoric and Sophistry* that humans were rational beings. To him, 'Reason was the sole and supreme arbiter . . . and persuasion merely the discourse needed to bring us to it.' While sophistry was concerned with the appearance of reason and truth, persuasion employed logic.

Centuries later, Damnia, the Philosopher Empress and the founder of the Divine Empire, had acknowledged that the human mind was imperfect and unable to grasp objective truth. The truth of a queen wasn't the truth of a shepherdess, and it was an empress's duty to present loftier ideas in humbler trappings to make them palatable. There was something to her notions, even if they seemed dated and idealistic.

Malchiavos's pamphlet *The Oneirarch* was thought-provoking. The infamous adviser to the King of Delectia, he advocated plainly for ruthlessness in governance. In a rather frontal assault to the old tenets, he posited there weren't objective truths to begin with. Rather, truth was what the collective accepted in opposition to the individual, which was held as a lie. Thus, rulers could employ propaganda leaflets and rumourmongering to reshape their own lies into the collective truth.

While Malchiavos's tone was callous and provocative, Ash couldn't say he was entirely wrong. He'd seen it first-hand working the printing press. Many came to them to print pamphlets to incite fear or hatred to achieve some political gain.

His father rejected them, mostly because he thought they lacked any meaningful substance. Books were almost a religion to him. He'd believed that they spoke to the mind directly, sometimes even allowing the mind to speak for itself, and that, in such conversations, a discerning eye could sift through the grains to find if not truth at least lucidity.

Ash felt on the verge of some epiphany, though something was still missing for it all to crystallise in his mind.

He reached home late in the afternoon, and he was so eager to begin his experiments on new Dreams that he almost missed the fact that his door was slightly ajar. What he didn't miss was Omen's growling.

He entered the apartment warily. Yaisa was nervously petting Omen, who growled at a large, burly man clad in a leather vest and thick gauntlets sitting on a stool behind the door. The other intruder, slouching on a chair by their brazier, was a familiar, scraggy figure.

'He's here!' Yaisa announced with relief.

'Master Esmus? What are you doing here?' Ash asked.

The master rose from the chair, no smile on his face.

'Business, Aescyon. What else? It's time for us to settle our pending debts.' He motioned at the man. 'Get your chains.'

The hulking man reached into a sack and produced a heavy set of steel chains and a muzzle. The chains were speckled with white spirals and spikes: Dreamchanted.

'Wait!' Ash replied desperately. 'Let me settle my business with the Academy, then I'll repay you in full!'

'I can't wait that long, sadly,' Esmus said. 'What if they spirit you both away? I can't take that risk.'

'I said no!' Ash stood between them and Omen. 'I won't let you!'

'Are you going back on your word, Aescyon?' Esmus asked coldly. 'Fine. Shall I expel your crew from the guild then? I can bar them for life, if that's what you want. You might have a life after the Academy as a Dreamer, but you'd do well to think on what will happen to those you leave behind.'

Ash's stomach sank at the reality of the situation. Omen looked at him, awaiting his orders.

He took a step back, and Esmus's man approached Omen with caution. The shadowcat was tense and growled, but Ash shook his head, and Omen allowed the man to set the heavy collar around his neck.

When he looked at Ash, Omen's gaze wasn't one of anger, just confusion and sadness. Ash tried to stomach it, to ignore the stabbing pain in his heart.

The man began securing a horrible muzzle around Omen's maw, and the panther growled, uncomfortable and afraid. Ash had to find a way out of this.

He looked around the room in desperation. Was there anything worth more that he could offer? He could try Dreaming something, but nothing ephemeral would be worth as much.

Moreover, Master Esmus was too money-minded; a simple trinket wouldn't do.

And then it struck him.

'Wait, Master! I do have something for you!'

'One of your misprinted books? I have little patience for those who try to cheat me . . .'

'No, no, it's not that. This is different. You'll see.'

He went into the communal quarters and fetched the sooty mirror kept there.

'A mirror?'

'Just give me a moment.'

He saw himself darkened through the Dreaming once more.

Esmus shifted in front of the mirror, while his man reached for a dagger. Omen readied himself, gleaming lightning pulsating through his veins.

Ash focused on the mirror's surface, its mercurial thickness thawing at his touch. He blew into it, and ripples broke over its surface. Then he narrowed his mind's eye to study the ripples and the many reflections that echoed within them.

From inside the mirror, the ripples were coloured, each one with its own hue, tinged with their own shade of truth. He reached for one with the right shade of gold, a single truth out of the many possible ones, and stretched it with his hands over one half of the mirror.

It coalesced like a thin caramel coating until the mirror had two faces, two truths in its bones.

Ash took a breath, letting the Dreaming go. The light flooded back, and his temples prickled with buzzing pain.

'What have you done to it?' Esmus asked while he studied the mirror. Ash saw that it carried his Dreaming Imprint now, the blue, marble-like veins.

'Look for yourself.'

The master's furrowed brows softened, and he glanced at the mirror warily.

Master Esmus stood, admiring himself in the mirror's surface for a long while. His eyes narrowed. He chewed on his lip. He looked at Omen, as if weighing his options. Finally, his bushy beard cracked with a yellow smile.

* * *

When Ash returned to Morvander's Quietude, the door warden in armour greeted him at the gates. This time she didn't ask anything, just led him through the silent corridors to the same reception hall as the last time. Ash waited by the dark pool, Omen by his feet.

Morvander appeared shortly after, guided by a thin chamberlain.

'Aescyon! I didn't expect you so soon,' Morvander said.

'I didn't have much time, my lord ... I have something to show you.'

'I'm listening,' he said.

'The thing is, in addition to natural human stubbornness, truth is complex, partly because minds are shaped differently, which means they'll be receptive to different truths.'

Ash had hoped that beginning with some of Empress Damnia's sayings would buy him some credibility, but Morvander winced and cut him short. 'I know. That's precisely why it constitutes a challenge.'

Ash swallowed hard. 'Indeed. What I meant is that you can try fooling them, but truly changing their minds in a lasting way ... that takes a lot more. That's something they can only do by themselves.'

Morvander's silver eyes widened with interest. 'Go on.'

'At best, you can present them some fragments of truth and hope that they'll have the will to try and assemble them. There are more prosaic details, but allow me to illustrate my point.'

He unveiled the mirror.

'My guildmaster showed up to collect Omen, my Dreamling, as payment for certain debts. How could I persuade a greedy man to refuse a prize worth a lot of Onars? I couldn't ... But he could convince himself. I just needed a way for him to speak with his own greediness or – in this case – a mirror that'd show him what he believed his future could be if he collected on the debt later down the line.' Ash went on to recount the entire episode, and as he answered Morvander's questions, the Oneirocrat's face lit up.

'Fine work, fine work indeed! I wasn't wrong about you . . .'

He clapped, and Ash held his breath. Did this mean that he'd passed the test?

'Come tomorrow. There are some friends I'd like you to meet. Then we can talk about your apprenticeship.'

Chapter Thirteen

Geil

EIDOLON: Time and death are the two gates barred to all Dreamers. Dreaming a corpse alive will only offer a wretched parody of the deceased.

Eidolii (singular, Eidolon) stand as a rare exception. When a loved one is on their deathbed, powerful Dreamers can sometimes Dream accurate replicas of them, meant to live as a twin sibling to their original.

– *Bestiary of Nature and Dream* by Bergos

THE SKYSHIP SHOOK UNDER THE Motherstorm's breathing. It was a fast skysloop of long wing-sails meant to travel quickly between Invernia and the capital, but its speed meant it shook like a sparrow's heart in a strange hand. Though that wasn't what was making Geil's insides boil.

With dawn seeping through the Hallowed Motherstorm's dark curls, tinging the black spires and the domes of the city below a blue hue, she realised the city hadn't changed, hadn't forgotten. And that terrified her.

She hoped to secure Ragdra's dispensation and leave before the day was over. Her father didn't even need to know of her arrival. There might be a time to return home – she could admit that to herself, now – but this wasn't it.

Thankfully, the Motherstorm was blissful that morning. On the skysloop's deck, she stretched to fight off the cool air's bite, and then, with a jump, perched herself on the worn, rain-mottled railing.

A gust of wind shook her, and she crouched to keep her balance. Dreamblooded or not, a fall could break her neck and kill her in an instant. But the Drake wasn't afraid. On the contrary, the height thrilled it.

'Mistress, get down!' a hirsute sailor cried.

'Stay away, I'm about to shift,' she grumbled. His eyes widened in fearful understanding.

Eyes closed, she plunged into the Dreaming and called to the Drake. Her skin rippled like mercury as the scales grew thick. She flexed her talon-tipped fingers and lengthened her back to make room for two large, scaly wings.

Two blood-red eyes opened to take in the city.

Feeling a high wind rising from the canals, she dived into the sky and soared over the city.

Below, the Central Quarter gleamed with the morning dew, while Lightning-Hunter, thatcher and chimney-sweeper crews worked over its slate surface. The open-air market plazas bustled with hawkers and merchants and the beggars that hovered nearby.

Veering away towards Muirtra's elegant spires, she caught the beautiful singing of a Wailing Sister and her canticles. As always, a reminder of those grieved, like Lanteus.

This once, tormenting herself could wait. She'd come to fight for his dreams – their dreams – even if he was no longer here to see them through. To save one girl, even when so many others still suffered.

She propelled herself against the currents towards the Grand Palace's magnificent domes. The familiar balustrades and expanse of balconies in the Skycouriers' pavilion tugged violently at her heart.

This was home. The place where she'd built herself, found a family, a purpose. Where she'd been deeply, unapologetically and relentlessly happy. Until she'd burned it all down.

She dived away, towards one of the grand entrances that faced south. Shifting back into a presentable shape, she marched through the crowds of supplicants until she found the right clerk. Geil's family name proved to be a powerful key that opened many doors, and, in a pleasant surprise, she was swiftly ushered to the Sages' palace and then to the High Sage's personal chambers.

Lady Malvedra was old blood, with kind, smiling wrinkles around her eyes. Her dress was a sumptuous crimson velvet, with a neckline edged in gold with inlays of precious stones, yet they were nothing compared to the round headpiece garlanded with yellow topaz. All exceedingly ornate, in contrast to her silver bracelet of office.

'Lady Morvander, what a *pleasure* to finally meet you! I'm told you're interested in obtaining a dispensation, is that so? Who might this be for?'

'Ragdra of Stiormkala in the Highlands March.'

Lady Malvedra gestured for her assistant to write the name down along with other identifying details. 'You're most charitable, my dear Geil – may I call you Geil?' The High Sage chuckled with melodious indifference. 'This fortunate young woman will be residing with you here in the city?'

'I have yet to sort out the details. Isn't my vouching for her instruction enough of a guarantee?' Geil asked. She stood, eager to leave, but her relief was short-lived.

'My dear Geil, of course it is. For me, at least! Alas, my hands are tied! The Sages' tribunal calendar is full until after Ascent. Her dispensation will have to wait.' The High Sage leaned onto her arm, as if she were an old friend imparting a confidence. 'You must know I'll do everything in my power to expedite the process. I only pray I have enough time, *especially* with the upcoming expiration of the High Council's term. I fear if the Senate were to appoint a new High Sage, they would have a far harsher view on dispensations than myself.'

And there it was. Lady Malvedra wanted to exact a political toll in exchange for her favour. Geil regretted having come here at all.

The High Council positions were a legacy from Princess Geleisdra's court. Blessed Elpia, founder of the Whispering Sisters and former imperial scribe, was said to have been the first High Sage. If so, those who followed in her footsteps did so with far less nobility of spirit. The High Sage not only controlled the archives and university curriculums but appointed and recalled lecturers and Academy masters. Enough control over Dreamcraft matters to, even with a two-year mandate, afford a measure of power. Which was why Lady Malvedra sought support from senators like Geil's father for her re-election.

'I see . . . My father might be of help with that.' Geil gritted her teeth. 'In the meantime, I'd ask you to keep this between us.'

'Of course, Lady Morvander, you can trust me,' Malvedra replied.

Geil strode angrily out of the office, doing her best not to curse. She'd stumbled into this trap all by herself.

Without her thinking, her feet carried her up from the gardens to the stairs to the Skycouriers' headquarters.

Geil emerged on the terrace, immediately drawing the guardian gargoyles' gazes. Their leader, a hulking creature known as Moss-Eyes because of the green of its ancient eyes, soon stood in her way.

'What brings you here, Lady Morvander?' it asked, its voice like the grinding of old stones.

'Moss-Eyes, would you please announce to the Falconess that I'm here requesting an audience?'

The old gargoyle offered a stiff nod, before marching inside the barracks.

Geil entered the arcades and peered through one of the windows into the dining hall. The place hadn't changed one bit. Ornate silver lamps burned brightly, and young Skycouriers, dressed in cerulean doublets and light plate armour, sat on benches, toasted loudly, practised with their swords or talked about their recent travels.

Strange to think that hardly a year ago, she herself had been one of these wains. Not that she was much older than them, but they all seemed so joyful that she felt decades older.

She could hardly blame them. She, Lanteus and Mavis – their closest friend at the Academy – had truly been enamoured with the Skycourier ideals.

Skycouriers were more than messengers; they brought justice and law to every province. Heralds like Geil had even assisted local magistrates in their investigations, or passed sentences where there were no magistrates.

'To be a Courier is to rise above the ground's miseries and dishonour,' she'd been told. In the end, she'd been the one who'd fallen into the muck, and got Lanteus killed.

Here, he still felt alive. They'd often sat together in this very portico to watch dawn break over the city. Any minute now, she'd hear his booming laughter and see him walking towards her with his confident stride.

She missed him.

She missed leaning against his broad shoulders, his stable frame, a breakwater against the tides of uncertainty. She missed his lips, planting the softest kisses despite his scraggly beard.

She missed the certainty of being the two of them against everything else.

Thinking of him was torment. So was her fear of forgetting him.

'Geil Morvander treads among us again?'

Geil turned to greet the familiar figure of the Falconess. Her long silver braid hinted at her age, but her wiry physique was as formidable as ever.

When Geil had resigned her position as Herald, the hardest part had been disappointing this woman. 'Couriermaster Mathana.' Geil bowed. 'How are things up in the blue beyond?'

'Always chasing the horizon, Drakelet.' The old woman's worn lips curled into a smile. 'These days, the High Council's got my hatchlings flitting about in a frenzy.'

'Because of all this talk of war?' Geil ventured.

'It's not just talk, I fear. The King of Delectia craves another jewelled flower to adorn his crown, and his minister Malchiavos sows lies and unrest everywhere in the Valelands.'

'I'd have hoped he'd choked on Vanday,' Geil said.

That was one of her last services for the Falconess. She'd brought plenty of alarming dispatches from the Valelands. When the wealthy burghers of Vanday on the frontier with Delectia had risen in arms, they'd quickly placed themselves under the King's 'protection'. A series of brutal skirmishes on the frontier had followed, yet war had never fully erupted.

'What have *you* heard?' A grey eyebrow curled like a weed.

'Me? Not much since the front quieted down.'

'Isn't Lord Orles Brakte of Harlyn a frequent guest of your father's these days?'

'I haven't really spoken to my father this past year,' Geil admitted.

With every single report of importance passing through the hands of her couriers on their way to the High Council's table, the Falconess was one of the best-informed people in the Domain. That didn't excuse the shame Geil felt from vanishing from her father's life, nor how she'd ignored her father and his efforts to reach her.

'Fret not, Drakelet. I meant nothing by it,' the Falconess said, placing a calloused hand on Geil's shoulder. 'Your father does well in forging alliances. Ill winds are brewing here too, with the Traditionalists demanding a stronger hand with the Valelands and open war with the King of Thorns.'

'It's always been like that, Falconess,' Geil said without much conviction.

'It has . . . And yet, I fear it's worse than ever. The two factions have set their roving bands of agitators to the streets. They won't be happy until there's blood on the cobblestones. Politics are dangerous right now.'

'They always were.'

The Falconess nodded. 'Then, allow me to ask, if not for your father, why are you here?'

'A personal matter. I'm seeking an Academy dispensation for a young friend.'

The Falconess's grey eyes widened. 'A friend that's got you running their errands?'

'It's for a very young girl from the Highlands. Her family can't afford to lose her.' Geil sighed, thinking of Ragdra and her mother. 'I thought my family name could be used for good. The High Sage was quick to remind me that in these times, everything comes at a price.'

The Falconess snorted. 'Of course she did. Somebody needs to fund Lady Malvedra's fondness for rare vintages, Dreamchanted silks and her equally delectable companions! Let me guess: she wanted you to promise your father's vote to her in exchange for your dispensation.'

When Geil nodded, the Falconess clicked her tongue against her teeth. 'I am to meet with the High Justice now, but I'd be happy to offer some advice if you're still around later. Besides, there's something else I'd like to discuss with you . . .'

'Of course, Falconess.'

The Falconess tapped Geil's shoulder. 'I might try re-enlisting you, though. Don't hold it against me. You always had a good head on those shoulders, and that's a rare enough gift these days for me to not let you go without a fight.' She let out a croaky laugh before heading for the stairs that led down into the Grand Palace.

A warm wave of relief washed over Geil. She'd half expected bitterness and scorn from her former mentor and had found none.

She stood at the Skycouriers' mess entrance, hesitant. The room still held the same varnished-wood smell, still served the same watery ale. And as if her memories had come to life, she spotted a familiar armoured figure.

It was Mavis, but he seemed worse for wear than the last time she'd seen him. His usually clean-shaven face was now covered in a russet beard, and deep shadows sat under his eyes. The past year must have not been gentle to him, either. A year ago, Mavis had been like her little brother, but there was barely anything left of that now. Lanteus's murder had shattered that bond forever. When he'd found out, Mavis had lashed out against her, spitting bile and recriminations both in public and in private.

Geil had cut all contact with him to avoid the very specific kind of hatred he held for her.

Let him come to us, teach him that we can bite back, the Drake teased her. She opted for just turning around. She might lose it, and they might come to blows. Besides, Mavis couldn't teach her to hate herself any more than she already did.

Striding away from the mess, she stumbled into a large figure.

'Geil?'

It was Itraya.

The Skycourier looked almost happy to see Geil. *Almost.* When Geil straightened, Itraya kept her arms crossed.

'It's good to see you,' Geil offered, conciliatory. Itraya's handsome face, her powerful frame beneath the cuirass, were exactly the same. Something had hardened in her eyes, though. 'You haven't changed a bit.'

'Not quite,' Itraya said, pointing at her blue armband. 'I'm aide to the Couriermaster now. Are you back to report for duty?'

'Not quite. I'm just passing through.'

'Passing through,' Itraya repeated scornfully. 'I should've guessed. You shouldn't wait here then.' Looking down her nose, Itraya murmured, 'You should be somewhere you belong.'

Geil knew she shouldn't reply, but her heart was too raw for the Drake not to jump at the chance of a fight. 'Somewhere I *belong*?' Geil snarled.

'With your father or with whoever's willing to put up with your whims.'

The Drake wanted to slap her, but Geil bottled the impulse. 'Look, Itraya, we all have regrets. Let's leave it at that.'

Regrets Geil had in abundance. She'd run away from Itraya without even a goodbye. 'Give my excuses to the Falconess,' she said as she turned away.

'Yes, Geil, run like you always do, damned coward,' Itraya muttered at her retreating back.

Geil quickened her pace. She'd been a fool to think she could ever set foot here again. Forming wings, she pulled herself into the sky, turning her back on the Grand Palace's silhouette.

She headed west for the docks. She wanted to leave at once. Fly away, ride the Motherstorm's gales as far as she could. Or let Her lightning set her ablaze. Anything but this, anywhere but here. She beat her wings furiously, struggling to keep high because of the rainfall that battered her like guilt.

The Drake doesn't bend; the Drake doesn't yield, not even to the storm, the creature roared in her head.

Below, the city was full of memories, ready to tear her apart. Even in the rain she could make out the greenery of the Huntress's Gardens, where she and Lanteus had lived together, burned together in a shared bed and fallen asleep under the rapping of the rain in their own garden.

That was also where she'd betrayed him with Itraya after too much wine. Where Lanteus's mother had screamed at her and tried to claw Geil's eyes out after hearing her son had been found dead.

Where she'd watched Lanteus's funerary procession perched from a rooftop. She'd felt her body tear itself apart when the honour escort of Skycouriers slowly descended from the heavens carrying his shroud. She should have been one of them, yet she couldn't bear the shame, Mavis's bereaved anger, Lanteus's parents' disgust. Her own loathing at herself.

Grief and guilt hadn't been outrun. All this time, they'd been patiently waiting for her return.

She heaved, running out of breath.

Let them come, we can take them all, the Drake's gentle growling promised.

The Drake was wrong. She was drowning, she couldn't fly or breathe or live.

When her father's palace appeared in view, she beat her wings desperately to gain altitude before gliding towards its sky dock, only to find the stone gates firmly shut.

She tried prying them open, yet they wouldn't budge. She called and yelled to no avail.

Without the Dreamchanted bracelet marking her as a member of the household, the Quietude, her own childhood home, wouldn't recognise her. She was unwanted even here.

An angry howl ripped from her throat. She punched the doors – once, twice, three times, a dozen. Her fists burned and bled. They hurt, yet not nearly as much as they could, as they should.

Geil's legs began to tremble. Her chest felt too tight. This was the moment to fall apart, but the tears wouldn't come.

She jerked away and hid her face in her hands. Perhaps if she clawed the skin from her face, she'd lose in blood what she wasn't able to cry in tears.

'Geil?' her father asked. He was standing at the threshold. The gates had silently opened.

He looked the same, wiry despite his thinness. His eyes, two silver moons, focused on her. His beard cracked with silver streaks and his mouth twisted in concern.

She stood there, heaving, unable to answer. Unable to find the words.

'I'm sorry,' she finally muttered.

Leaning on the railing, he walked to her side and crouched to touch her.

'What is wrong?' he asked.

'I shouldn't have come back.' Her breathing was still ragged.

'What are you speaking of? You're my daughter. This is your home.'

'This isn't my home! This city can't ever be my home again! It's got only spite, and, and—' She struggled for air.

He remained still, watching her with concern.

'I'm sorry, dear. Our home, this city, they're full of shadows for me too. We must walk alongside them. One must comprehend loss in order to co-exist with it.'

'Oh, spare me your pity! You never got over Mother's death. Why should I be any different?' she snarled. 'This is why I didn't reply to your letters! You're like Grandmother, entombing yourself alive!'

Her father staggered at her words, and Geil realised she'd been too harsh.

She pressed her hands to her head as if she could stop the rage, the hatred, the grief from seething inside by sheer force.

She felt her father's hand on her shoulder.

'You're very strong, Geil. Stronger than me. As strong as your mother.'

'I wish she was here to teach me her strength,' Geil whispered.

'She is, Geil,' her father replied, gently tapping her temple. 'Here, in the islands and canals of your mind.'

'That's not enough.' Both her mother and Lanteus were gone. Forever. And the pain of their losses was the only thing she had left of them.

'It is not,' he conceded with a sad smile. 'They can never come back to us, but they left a lot of themselves in our minds, entire archipelagos.'

'You're saying the pain keeps us from forgetting them? But how are we to endure this?'

He stroked his chin and looked up as if he were reading the answer in the skies. 'I'm saying that even if you forget them, they'll still live on through you. They've already shaped your mind. Their memories might be islands frozen in time, but the waterways they carved, they're entirely alive. Every day you think, talk or behave in a way shaped by your mother, she breathes through you. Their ways of seeing the world, of feeling it, of understanding it – this is what we must nurture. That is how you keep them alive.'

'But isn't that just a reminder of what they never achieved? Of what they'll never see done?'

'Yes,' he said sadly. 'But the actions they inspire are a way for them to reach from old memories to the new.'

There was something soothing in thinking that death and grief couldn't conquer everything, that Lanteus couldn't be fully erased from the world while she lived. That his dreams, *their* dreams, weren't dead, not while she could still do something about them. It wasn't enough to fix the pain, but it helped to think the agony could be turned into purpose, given a measure of meaning.

'Dear, I won't even ask you why you came back. But maybe you can spend the night?' her father asked. 'It might do us both some good.'

Something about the softness of his request shattered Geil. No one could understand her loss like her father. And if she stayed, she might still be able to help Ragdra. 'Maybe I could stay . . . for a few days?' she asked tentatively. 'I don't have my bracelet anymore.'

'Yes, you do,' he replied. As he reached into his loose sleeve, Geil saw that alongside his own house bracelet of darkglass and steel, there was a second one. One that Geil instantly recognised because of the adornments she'd added to it, including the emerald Lanteus had given her.

She'd thought it lost, but her father had kept it.

As he unclasped it to place it gently around her wrist, Geil felt it pull her down, down into the ocean of grief she'd barely kept her head above for so long. It swallowed her like an ocean.

The Drake doesn't bend, the Drake doesn't yield, not even to the storm, the creature thrummed inside her, but for once Geil thought there was no need to silence her inner turmoil. No need to fight it.

She could just cross it, weather it, embrace it.

As a reply, she embraced her father, her whole body shaking.

In silence, her father embraced her back.

Tears came, burning like streams of molten lead down her cheeks. She didn't mind the pain. In fact, she felt lighter because of it.

Chapter Fourteen

Ash

For the Undreaming, there's no higher purpose than serving the Oneirocrats. By their exertions, whether mercantile, agricultural, artisanal or any other, they spare their betters unpleasant burdens, honour them and add greatness to their city or state.

– *The Oneirarch* by Malchiavos

THE FOLLOWING MORNING, ON ASH's last day of freedom, he returned bright and early to the Quietude. His new patron had agreed to offer tutelage and had asked for one night to draft a contract of patronage.

As always, Lord Morvander's palace offered a welcome respite from the Susurrus's whispers, but today Ash also felt that it rose like an ominous wave of black amidst the neighbouring sea of turret-houses. The future – his future – approached too fast, threating to sweep away his plans and principles.

The palace's gates began opening, and Ash hurried, thinking the door warden had spotted him milling about on the bridge, but another woman emerged, dressed in breeches and a simple shirt. A jet bracelet with the crest of house Morvander and an emerald gem marked her as someone of importance.

She'd been escorting another stranger, an older man with streaks of ashen steel in his braided black hair and fierce scars on his umber-brown face.

'You must be Aescyon. Early bird, aren't we?' she said, offering a strong hand. 'I'm Geil Morvander.'

'A pleasure, Lady Geil.' Ash shook it, hoping she wouldn't notice his sweaty palm.

'Here, allow me to introduce Master Thalder, a—'

'An old dog that carries around trouble like fleas,' the man interrupted to say, and Geil laughed. Thalder shook Ash's hand firmly, his brassy eyes gleaming vitreous for a moment. Another Oneirocrat? He seemed more of a huntsman, given his mud-splattered cape and leather jerkin. 'Silence is the armour of the slighted,' Thalder said, flashing a white grin before striding away.

Ash watched him go before Geil whisked him inside and the gates closed.

'What did he mean by that?' he asked.

'Master Thalder? Nothing. He's got a sharp wit,' she said as they climbed the steep steps to the palace's heights. 'You're alone? I was looking forward to meeting your renowned panther. Father says it's a magnificent creature.'

'Sorry, I left him somewhere safe.'

'I respect a man that takes care of his friends.'

It was reassuring to hear her give words to Ash's fears. 'Those who live surrounded by prodigies soon grow oblivious to their value,' had been one of his father's many criticisms of Oneirocrats, but maybe that wasn't true of Geil and her father.

Despite Lord Morvander being an Archdreamer, an Oneirocrat who'd raised his own islet in the lagoon and thus earned a prestigious seat in the Senate, so far, he'd defied Ash's expectations. Instead of luxuries and countless servants, his palace's sombre corridors were hollowed out and deserted.

'My apologies,' Geil said, stopping to read the carvings on a lintel. 'Sometimes even I get turned around. The palace has changed a lot since the last time I was here.'

'I thought it'd been here for decades.'

'It's unchanged on the outside, perhaps – but my father Dreamt this place with a malleable nature. The palace reacts to his mind, as well as his moods.'

After finding the right door, she renewed their brisk pace. Down a spiral staircase, they came to a chamber with a red door, guarded by twin sets of armour.

'Here we are. This is Father's workshop. If you don't know where to find him, this is always a good guess.'

She knocked. Shortly after, Balchod, the scrawny chamberlain, appeared. Unfamiliar voices echoed from inside.

'Aescyon Allandra, you're expected. Please do come in,' the chamberlain said.

'Silence is the shield of the slighted,' Geil whispered, repeating Thalder's strange warning, before the chamberlain ushered him inside.

The workshop was large, holding as many forges as the Lightning-Hunters' tower, but also sculpting blocks and water collectors. Chemistry benches and botanical shelves lined the walls, while a drawing table overflowed with sketches and plans.

Ash followed Balchod with utmost care, wary of where he stepped. As they passed by the designs, Ash realised that they all shared the same strokes and lines – probably Lord Morvander's. It seemed the man had mastered both art and science, but then again, if he was as old as the legends said, he'd have had the time.

Lord Morvander waited on the hall's other side, surrounded by a company of richly attired Oneirocrats Ash did not recognise.

Ash's mirror was on display nearby, reflecting the red morning sun. From what he'd seen, most of the palace lacked windows, but the walls, made of something resembling smoky quartz, adjusted their opacity to let in light.

Morvander bade him approach. 'Aescyon, please meet Lord Orles Brakte, senator for Damlan in the Valelands and head of the Harlyn merchant household.'

Ash thought he heard sarcasm in Morvander's deference, but Lord Brakte seemed not to notice. It wasn't surprising for Lord Morvander to count senators among his friends, but one hailing from the ever-rebellious Valelands was unusual.

Ash's time in the region, following his father in military camps, had taught him that the Valelanders' desire for independence ran far and deep.

The Valelands might nominally be one of the Domain's provinces, but every few years their restless merchants and artisans would revolt against their Onyxian governors, always with the support of the King of Thorns.

Lord Brakte, for his part, seemed no docile sheep. He was a towering man who looked more a grizzled corsair from the Sea of Wolves than a merchant prince. Perhaps he was both.

Ash offered a slight bow as Brakte looked him over coldly. 'Who's this, Nial?' he asked.

'My soon-to-be apprentice.'

Brakte arched one of his golden eyebrows. 'Apprentice? What are you playing at, Morvander?'

'If I am to finish my work in time to aid your people, I'll need assistance.'

Brakte's glare was icy. 'Tell me, Aescyon, what's your household known for?'

Another Oneirocrat who believed that only those of a certain lineage were worthy of Dreaming. That all Undreaming were beneath notice and deserving of miserable treatment.

Sadly, he had nothing to offer. He lacked noble blood, and as far as guild reputation went, the Lightning-Hunters were seen as little more than 'roof-rats' by many. In other circumstances, he could have spoken of his father's army service. Officers were respectable, if poor, but he remembered the hostility with which most Valelanders regarded the Onyxian army.

'My father was a printer,' he finally offered, ignoring Brakte's smirk.

'A printer's son?' he scoffed, turning to Morvander. 'Is this a joke, Nial?'

Ash had expected as much, yet the words still felt like a punch to his gut. Little did it matter that Ash had grown up surrounded by an endless stream of wildly different books at his father's printing shop, or that his father's previous service as an army officer had allowed Ash schooling by the residing Wailing Sisters at the Twin Forts. To them, he was a servant at best, a roof-rat at worst.

'Have you been trained as a Dreamer?'

'I have not, my lord,' Ash replied.

Brakte sighed and leaned towards Morvander. 'Nial, I know I've insisted that for us to make progress fast, you should enlist aid, but there're plenty of trustworthy Dreamers in my household. Take Josod and Lucre,' he said, gesturing at the pair seated by his side. The woman had a dignified clay complexion, while the smug man caressed his blond curls. 'I handpicked them from a hundred candidates! Now, with Josod's mind and Lucre's eyes, I can see everything. Tell me what you seek, and I can find the best.'

'I appreciate the offering, but I'd rather take a mind that's unblemished,' Morvander replied.

'So, you plan on, what? Training him yourself?'

'If that's what it takes,' he said indifferently, pouring himself a glass of wine.

'If you yearn to pass on your knowledge, I can find you a better student. To train a poor mind impoverishes one's own,' Brakte protested.

A shiver climbed Ash's spine. If this man convinced Lord Morvander to rescind his offer of patronage . . .

'I feared you'd say something like that,' Morvander said with a sigh. 'Especially since I've had to offer him tutelage to snatch him from the Academy's claws.'

'Why would you do such a thing? Lady Saorla's coalition is fragile enough! Why undermine it further by poking at the

Academy?' Brakte raised his voice, and his eyes flared. 'This isn't the time, with High Council about to be renewed, to start a quarrel with her other allies!'

Lord Morvander winced at that. Ash had never much cared for politics beyond his guild's. Since the Senate was only open to the Dreamer nobility and the wealthiest of merchants, the commoners' only involvement was to publicly demonstrate their support for their patrons and their patrons' causes. Ash lacked the former and had no love for the latter.

Still, the city and the Domain existed in a tenuous balance between the two parties, and nobody could afford to antagonise one faction without having the backing of the other.

Traditionalists, the 'Blues', led by Lord Stalcar of Lorn, were made up of the oldest Oneirocrat families and the powerful merchants who backed them, both interested only in upholding their privileges. As the member of a guild, that had left him only one real alternative.

The Reformers, known for their white caps and emblems, at least pretended to care what the guilds thought. Their current leader was Lady Ines Saorla, the Starspun Maiden, named so by the glimmering golden stars embedded in all she Dreamt. Not that their Oneirocrat senators did enough for the plight of the common folk. More than anything, they were a way to keep the Traditionalists from further crushing those below them.

Ash cleared his throat. 'One of my creations is here, Lord Brakte. Perhaps Your Lordship can see for himself what I have to offer.' He pointed at the mirror.

'Is it now?' Brakte twisted his lips into a smile, then gestured to his companions. 'Josod, Lucre, tell me what you make of it.'

The two Dreamers went to examine the mirror. First, Josod tapped his fingers over its surface. Ash feared it would crack, but it merely rippled like water.

Josod snorted. 'It is but a crude copy of the Gentlet mirror-cabinets that were all the rage two years ago.'

Of course there were bound to be similar designs to his. Especially in the Valelands, renowned for their Dream artisans and fine craftsmanship, but to suggest he'd just created a cheap copy was insulting.

'Sir, I assure you that it's my own design!' Ash protested.

'If you say so. I suppose that explains why it's such a poor piece of work. This is a child's trinket, nothing more,' Josod said, shooting Ash a scornful smirk.

Ash wanted to lash back, then remembered the warning: 'Silence is the shield of the slighted.' This was a test, had to be. Breathing in, he swallowed his anger.

'In Harlyn, Dreamers sell mirror-cabinets that allow you to pick the most splendorous version of yourself. A thousand Onars a piece!' Brakte commented boastfully, but Morvander's moon eyes remained on the woman. There was a hint of a smile on the corner of his lips, as if he anticipated her answer.

She reached into her purse for an eye-mask made of interlaced veins of dark metal and embroidered with eye-shaped rubies. She donned the mask ceremoniously, as if preparing for a formal dance. When she gazed into the mirror, the rubies lit up like embers.

'The Dreamcraft is flawed, there's no question of that,' she said, curling her lip.

'See? A waste of time,' Brakte said.

'With your permission, Lord Brakte,' the woman continued, 'there's more. It's not quite like a mirror-cabinet. Its design is flawed, yes, but also far more ambitious. It's not just a vanity piece, it intends to elicit reflection.' She looked at Ash with curiosity.

Brakte grumbled, reaching for Morvander's arm. 'People will hear that you've taken on an apprentice, Nial. They'll ask what you're working on. Drawing attention to our endeavour will only invite meddling. Have you formalised the patronage contract?'

'No,' Balchod said.

'Then there's no harm done. You're risking it all for, what, compassion? Give him a bundle of Onars and send him on his way!'

Ash felt sick. His only chance of escaping conscription was close to going up in smoke.

Morvander placed his chin on his interlaced hands. 'Or you could ensure that this is worth our time: help me train him.'

Brakte's face reddened with sudden outrage. 'Are you trying to play me?' He rose from his seat, holding his cup in a fist. He seemed about to smash it.

Ash clenched his own fists, ready to step in to protect Lord Morvander. Yet before he could react, Lord Brakte broke into thundering laughter, and Morvander joined him.

'You old fox!' Brakte placed the cup on the table. 'Have it your way then. If your mind is set on this, we'll make sure he won't waste your time. Lucre, Josod, you are both to help train the young Dreamer. Make sure he becomes useful!'

They nodded, Lucre politely and Josod with a barely concealed scowl. After that, Lord Brakte and his entourage bade their farewells and Balchod saw them out.

Ash's heart was still racing, but his dread turned back to anger. They thought of him as less than nothing. He clenched his fists, mad at his own helplessness, at the fact he couldn't even talk back to them.

'Sit, Ash,' Morvander ordered.

'I'm good standing,' he replied bitterly.

Morvander sighed. 'I apologise for Lord Brakte's manners, and I appreciate your showing restraint. I assure you this was necessary.'

'What, exactly, was necessary?' Ash blurted out despite himself.

'It was necessary to make them feel invested in your education.'

'Why?'

'Orles Brakte's tongue is like a scorpion's sting, but the man's got a sharp mind. Part of his brilliance is knowing how to surround himself with people smarter than him. What better tutors could you have than his handpicked apprentices? I intend to help you, but, as you've heard, my work is demanding enough, and I'd do a poor job of tutoring you. So, this is the way we shall do it. Now, let's sign the deal.'

On cue, Balchod entered and handed him a contract. The document was long – five pages, tightly scribbled, and compiling a minutiae of considerations.

Ash dived into it. The language seemed deliberately obscure and vague: . . . *The Apprentice shall provide all services required from a Dreamer to his Patron. In doing so, the Apprentice will exercise extreme diligence and shall maintain in utmost secret the affairs of the Morvander household* . . . The penalties for breaching the contract sounded ominous too, but Ash refused to let himself be intimidated. What he needed to know was the length of his service. Such apprenticeships often lasted ten to twenty years, which seemed like a lifetime to him. However, this contract stated he was to conduct his service until he'd passed his dispensation examinations.

'I don't understand, Lord Morvander. When will my service finish?'

'You'll be in my service only during your training. You said your exam is in two months? I'd say that's a fitting estimate.'

It felt too good to be true. There had to be a catch he wasn't seeing.

'And if I fail?'

'You won't. That's why we've just recruited such accomplished tutors. Besides, that's the time I've given myself to achieve results. Time is of the essence for Lord Brakte and his people, too.'

Ash stared without blinking. What secret endeavour merited such penalties and had such a pressing time limit?

'Do we have an agreement, Aescyon?'

Ash gave a weak nod.

Morvander took a quill offered by Balchod and proceeded to sign on all the pages, including a letter of tutelage that Ash snatched right away. In the meantime, Balchod opened his purse and began counting out a hefty sum of Onar notes. Once he was done, he placed them on the table in front of Ash.

'What's this?'

'Half of your stipend to be paid in advance, as per clause seven of the patronage contract,' Balchod replied.

'But this is . . .' Ash counted it twice. It couldn't be. 'Fifty Onars?'

'Isn't it enough?' Morvander arched an eyebrow.

'No, it's *very* generous! It'll cover what I owe the guild and more!'

'Of course, we must think of your guild. Balchod, amend the contract. Let's make it eighty Onars. I trust that'll be enough to cover all of your outstanding debts and allow you to buy new clothes? We can't have you looking all tattered,' he said.

That remark stung, but only because he'd worn his father's recently patched jerkin today. Though it was true that for too long he'd neglected such matters. Still, the amount seemed obscene.

'Lord Morvander, this is too much. I can't accept it.'

Morvander's countenance turned stern. 'Too much? I'll ask a lot of you, Ash, so don't be quick to dismiss it. Now, please sign.'

The quill shook in Ash's trembling fingers.

He swallowed his growing unease and signed. His father would have hated him if he'd seen him. Good thing he was dead and Ash could no longer disappoint him.

* * *

Ash left the Quietude feeling lightheaded. This early in the afternoon, it wasn't the Susurrus's whispers that bothered him; it was everything else.

The letter, the contract and the money, tucked away inside his belt, felt like a load of bricks. Eighty Onars amounted to six hundred and forty Octaves. This was more money than he'd ever seen in his life.

The prospect of settling their guild's debts and giving his crew a break by sharing some of the spoils would alleviate some of his shame. First, though, he needed to present the letter at the Grand Palace, then he'd be taking the money to his crew.

Crossing the skeletal marble bridge leading back to the Central Quarter, he noticed that somebody seemed to be following him. Their face was hidden under a wide-brimmed hat. Maybe Ash was imagining things . . . or maybe the Academy had set somebody on his trail now that his time was about to expire.

Turning back, he ran into four watchmen, and one man he recognised wearing an Academy cuirass.

'Aescyon shit-eater,' Sergeant Dain said with a smirk, emerging from the shadows. 'Put him in chains!'

'Wait, I have a patron!' Ash fumbled at his belt to produce the letter of tutelage; Dain snatched the papers away. He skimmed them before crumpling them and dropping them to the floor.

'Fucking fool. Lord Nial Morvander, really? Why not Lady Saorla, the Starspun Maiden? Even she would have been more believable. But Morvander? The man must be a mummy by now, if not dead. Too bad you got greedy, roof-rat.'

A guard reached for him, but Ash shoved him away, and the man fell into a puddle. Contract or no contract, he'd be through the Mantle by the time Lord Morvander heard what had happened. Ash had no choice but to try to escape and sort this mess out later.

Dain pulled a many-tailed whip out of his belt. 'Seize him! Break his legs if you have to!'

Ash feinted one way, then pivoted at the last minute, scooping up the papers and squeezing through two of the guards. He ran.

There was only one way to get out of their reach: the Sea of Shingles.

He headed towards the building to his left, a two-storey house with wrought-iron balconies. Clenching his teeth, he swallowed the pain before jumping.

He grabbed on to the railing and was pulling himself up when a guard latched on to his leg. Ash dangled perilously in the air. Another pull like that and he'd fall.

Lungs burning, he clung to the railing and furiously kicked his free boot into his assailant's face. His heel connected, knocking the guard loose, and Ash pulled himself up.

The railing was slippery, but with determination, Ash reached the top of the balcony, and from the corner of his eye saw another guard draw a crossbow. He froze. Dreamer or not, a bolt would kill him. To his surprise, Dain shoved the crossbow away.

'He's of no use to us dead, fool!'

Ash didn't wait for them resolve their differences. Reaching for the roof's edge, he began climbing, stopping short at what perched above.

A large gargoyle of coalesced ash. The Nightmare, with its long talons and sharp bone horns, swiped at him.

Ash reeled backwards. A talon brushed his forehead, piercing his skin. Warm blood ran into his eyes.

He slipped, pinwheeling his arms to no avail. The roof was gone from beneath him.

He fell.

His ribs slammed into the balcony's railing, knocking the wind out of him. Worse, he felt something crack.

Coughing, he tried to stand, but the gargoyle landed on the railing, grabbing his arm.

Dain taunted from below. 'Pity you didn't bring your kitten. I'd have *loved* to tear it apart.'

Ash was trapped. This time, when they flung an iron net at him from below, all he could do was weakly shield himself.

The net hit the gargoyle, and it toppled over the railing, releasing Ash's arm.

Shocked, Ash looked down. The guards were just as confused as he was. There was someone else in the alley: the wide-brimmed hat that had been trailing him out of the Susurrus.

'Geleisdra's blood! What do you think you're doing?' Dain yelled at the newcomer.

'Don't you recognise me, Dain? After all the fun we had together at the Academy, I'd expect you to remember your favourite master. Is this what Grandmaster Ranndra has you doing now you've run out of cradles to rob?'

Ash's rescuer took off the hat, and he recognised the man from the Quietude.

'Thalder? What in the rotting hells are you doing here? Shouldn't you be drinking yourself to death in some pigpen with your carrot-fondling friends?' Dain tossed his shaved head backwards with laughter.

Thalder put himself between the bailiffs and Ash. 'Carrot-fondler, is it? You want some of my stick then? Remind me again . . . How did you get that scar? Was it me, or was it all those feisty crabs you liked to tumble with?'

One of the guards chortled, and Dain slammed his elbow into the man's chest. He fell to his knees, wheezing.

'You don't scare anyone, Thalder,' Dain sneered. 'Yours was a dying breed at the Academy even before the High Sage removed you all. Me, though? I'm now part of Grandmaster Ranndra's new order of things. I'm happy to teach you how we deal with weaklings such as yourself.' He pointed his whip at the man.

'Will you? Or will you shit your pants like you used to?'

Dain seemed about to jump him, but Thalder produced a black sigil-bracelet on his left arm. It was pure onyx, with a black swan as a crest.

The guards recognised it and backed away. 'Apologies, sir. We were told that Lord Morvander's signature had been forged.' The sergeant of the guard bowed his head at Thalder.

'You're going to regret this, Thalder. The time for the likes of you is coming!'

'Give the Grandmaster my regards and tell her to stick herself with the biggest carrot she can find while you're at it.'

Dain shot one last glare at Ash before turning on his heel, his gargoyle limping behind him.

Ash dropped down, landing in the mud and splattering his clothes.

'Thanks,' he said, offering a hand to Thalder.

The man shook it vigorously. 'You carry your trouble like fleas, don't you? We dogs are going to get on well, then!'

Chapter Fifteen

Daerna

The Wandering Sisters eschew all of our rule. Refusing responsibilities, they spend their lives as vagrants, wandering from community to community. Their lack of obedience incites unrest and rebellion among the lowest echelons of society. As for their unlearned preachings, it is better to be silent than to speak.

– *A Condemnation of the Wanderers* by Aleena Forlaitra,
Abbess Superior of the Wailing Sisters

DAERNA PICKED OUT HER OLDEST woollen cloak, worn enough to offer a good disguise in the seedier parts of the city.

By the time she reached the Barley Market, the grain merchants were beginning to pack up their wares and pull their carts away. The only stragglers were porter women haggling for evening deals and beggars camping early for the night.

She feared the Sisters might have left without her, then spotted Roshia on one of the market's benches and joined her.

'I'm sorry it took me so long.'

'To be honest, I was kind of relieved nobody came.' Roshia let out a nervous chuckle. 'It made it easier to forget the whole thing.'

'Come on, are you going to get cold feet now?'

'Now that you're here? No. But it was nice daydreaming about not getting in trouble so soon again.' Roshia let out a weary sigh.

It struck Daerna how little she knew about Roshia. They were roughly the same age, but their careers inside the Order had taken them in different directions. Although they'd shared some of their instruction and the chores of the novices, Roshia had then followed on the scholarly path, becoming an apprentice to those who taught at the university.

'Roshia, may I ask how you ended up at the Penance Procession?'

'A fairly ordinary transgression, I'm afraid . . . I missed some of my classes.'

'Did you know that nothing says more about an individual than the reasons why they miss their chores?' Daerna teased.

Roshia grinned shyly. 'Fair enough. I've been helping my parents with their work. They're physicians in the Craghorn. It doesn't pay a lot, but it's necessary work. And lately they've needed all the help they can get.'

'I'm sorry to hear that,' Daerna said.

'Are you finished chatting, ladies?' Pierla called from behind them.

The young Widowed Sister was leaning against one of the columns with her usual smirk.

Without a gesture for them to follow, she exited the market through the nearest alley. Roshia and Daerna had to run to catch up with her. Pierla set a quick pace, heading southwest, veering away from the giant chains anchoring the southern islets to the plateau.

'This isn't the way to the Scab,' Daerna said.

'Are we going to Little Vespiria, then?' Roshia guessed.

'Not that far.'

'University Square?' Daerna tried, then she thought of a better option. 'We're going down to Broken Arches!'

'Clever lass! Let me guess, you attended university?'

'For about two years, but I knew the Arches from before, when they were called the White Arches Market.'

She'd seen it as a child, when her parents had still owned a warehouse there. Back then, it'd been the main merchant hub in the city: a maze built above and inside a particularly rocky island. A faint recollection came to her, of playing up and down the stairs, chasing after her sister, Phania. Happier times before they'd drifted apart because of their mother.

However, as soon as the High Council funded the construction of the huge tower-houses of the Western Quarter, her mother, along with most merchant households, moved their warehouses there and settled on Swan Row. The canal connecting the western islands with the plateau soon became the largest trading hub in the city.

After that, the High Sage arranged the purchase of the old market buildings for the creation of a university to rival Arvira's, and many of the vice-peddlers that had operated in the Southern Quarter swooped in, eager to take the abandoned and 'broken' warehouses by the canal and the silos below; thus, the 'Broken Arches' was born.

'I should have smelled the money on you,' Pierla said with a grin.

'That was a lifetime ago,' she replied dryly.

And she meant it. It'd only been a few years ago that she'd quit her studies, but as they entered University Square, she didn't recognise herself in the students loitering around the arcades, drinking and engaging in loud debates.

The back alleys beyond University Square reeked of stagnant water and refuse. That much hadn't changed. This was still the frontier between acceptable society and the downtrodden of the Scab and Little Vespiria, the perfect place for slumming.

They followed Pierla into the decaying hive of meshed brick buildings that was the Broken Arches. The place had changed, and for the worse. Between the old warehouses, families dressed in rags huddled inside wooden hovels.

A formerly open square had been quartered. Wooden planks and canvas walls now sectioned off taverns, gambling dens and brothels. Smoke clung to the eyes and the nose, painting the figures around them in a sinister light.

Here, a man retched against a lone column, his vomit thick and reddish, hopefully just from wine. There, a group of young teens lurked together, watching them with sunken, sullen eyes. And everywhere, pale rats scurried about, collecting their rent from the scraps among the refuse.

A young lad approached them when they stepped inside, his honey eyes shining with curiosity. He wore a muddy rag as a cap.

'Need a sparkler, misses? Half a quarter Octave for a tallow candle! A quarter Octave for two and this!' He proudly displayed a blackened candle-holder in front of them.

'Sure, lad! Here, give me one. The ladies are paying,' Pierla said.

Daerna grunted, reaching for her girdle-purse. She offered the young boy half a full Octave. 'Keep the change.'

The boy gawked at her. 'Th-thank you, miss! You need a guide too? Charcoal knows all the good dens, the ones where they won't rip you off!'

Pierla chuckled. 'Sure, lad, why don't you take us to the healing house?'

'Right on it, miss!' Charcoal reached for the sack on his shoulder and withdrew a fresh tallow candle that he lit with a flint. Then he deftly led them deeper inside the maze, and finally to a jagged ramp that descended into the rocky underground.

They descended quietly into a series of darkened underground vaults.

The air was musty, and it all seemed strangely deserted given the overcrowding above.

'Who would hide here?' Roshia grimaced with discomfort at the paint peeling off the walls and the mould that seemed to grow all around them.

'Those who have no other options,' Pierla said bitterly.

The sparkler led them onwards. When they turned a corner, they spotted their destination at the end of a corridor where a large woman guarded a double wooden door. Her hard face, her scars and the sword in her lap spoke of one accustomed to the Arches' sharper ends.

'Here! Charcoal will wait for you upstairs, near the entrance, miss!' The boy handed them the candle. Daerna thanked him, and the lad was quick to disappear the way they'd come.

The guard stood as they approached her, sword at the ready. 'Sister Agonea doesn't like visitors,' was her ashen greeting to Pierla.

'I vouch for these two,' Pierla replied.

The guard shrugged and knocked on the door behind them five times. Soon after, someone unbarred it from within.

Pierla led them into what looked like an old warehouse repurposed as an infirmary. Cots littered the floor, and half a dozen women in ratty grey uniforms that resembled those of the Widowed Sisters laboured, preparing herbal infusions and applying lard ointments to the sick who filled the room.

Daerna's rudimentary medical knowledge came from her natural philosophy classes and her conversations with medical students at university. Still, it was enough for her to tell the patients shared the same symptoms: they were haggardly thin and writhed in agony in their cots. More importantly, they were feverish, drifting between silent stupor, violent convulsions and bouts of delirium.

'They all have the Wilting,' Roshia muttered, confirming what Daerna thought. 'My parents have started seeing many new cases at the Craghorn.'

Pierla waved at the sick. 'The Wilting's sapping their life to the point at which they can barely move. And once the palsy sets in, it's often a matter of days, if not hours, until they're gone.' She led them to the other side of the room, where a grey-haired woman wearing a worn Widowed Sister's uniform awaited them. 'Agonea, I've brought some friends.'

The woman sized them up with hard brown eyes. Tapping the gem in the centre of her necklace, she spoke. 'New faces often invite prying eyes.' Her voice sounded metallic, and even though she was moving her lips, the sound came from the vibrations of her Dreamchanted collar.

'These two new faces have capable working hands,' Pierla replied.

Agonea stiffened, eyes now on Daerna. 'Is that so? Why are you here?'

Daerna paused. 'Pierla says that you know what's happening at the Scab.' Nothing changed in Agonea's face. 'We were attacked by Charnelites there a few nights ago.'

'You want to know why the people are desperate enough to embrace the Charnel Mother's heresies? Look around you.' Agonea waved at the ward behind her. 'For all the talk of charity, the abbesses are quick to abandon those who're deemed beyond saving.'

'That can't be,' Roshia protested. 'The Widowed Sisters have a hospice across the Chain Bridge. I'm sure they tend to those who face disease in the Scab, don't they, Pierla?'

Pierla snorted. 'Why do you think I'm here? I used to work the almoner processions in the Scab myself. At first, the disease was a trickle, but it soon became a flood. Then, half a year ago, Abbess Mortre, our own Superior, made us stop. We were to *deny* our aid to those with the Wilting. Now, our hospices will take anyone but them, and they're left to die in their burrows.'

Roshia groaned loudly.

'What sense does that make?' Daerna replied.

'They're deemed "morally corrupt", and thus "undeserving of the Motherstorm's mercy",' Pierla quoted bitterly.

'There you have it,' Agonea said. 'The simple and ugly truth: the Charnel Mother reaps what we sow. Their priests do not shun those afflicted by the Wilting; they even see it as a blessing. A special kind of death to liberate us from our mortal coils into their macabre mother's embrace.'

Daerna was reeling. How could the abbesses let this be? '"Whoever suffers deserves consolation."' She angrily quoted the *Song of Sorrows*. 'We have to help them!'

'Talk is cheap,' Agonea said.

'We're willing to do whatever you need us to,' Daerna said.

Agonea arched an eyebrow. 'I shall be the judge of that. Come with me.'

She led them to an adjoining chamber, one that hadn't been cleaned in ages judging from the mouldy walls, the rat droppings and the rotting pieces of wood littering the floor. 'There are some buckets and rags in the adjoining cellar. Show me how much you're willing to *help*.'

Daerna didn't let the challenge intimidate her and immediately set to work with Roshia's help. This was novice's work, but it wasn't beneath her. If she had one thing to thank her mother for, it was that, despite her obsession with wealth and appearances, she'd raised her daughters to fend for themselves no matter the circumstances, and that included a healthy dose of household chores when they were growing up.

They laboured in a silence broken only by the coughs, moans and whimpers coming from the infirmary. Luckily, some other stairs in the back climbed upwards to a nearby quay, and they took turns fetching water from the canal. They scrubbed and rinsed the floors with vinegar until their knees ached.

By the time they were done, Daerna's back burned with the strain of being hunched for so long, and she stank of sweat and sour water.

They were both trying to wash the smell away when Pierla came to fetch them. 'Who knew that you two would make such good housewives,' she said, grinning, and waved for them to follow her. 'Come on, we're about to have supper.'

They followed her up and then outside to a quay, where Agonea, the guard and some other Sisters had gathered to break bread.

'Come sit with me,' Agonea ordered.

They settled by her side, and she offered them some hard bread and a bowl of watery fish stew. Daerna was so hungry that, despite the strong smell, she swallowed a few mouthfuls before giving up on it for being too salty.

'I can see you have questions,' Agonea said. 'Ask.'

'You're helping those with the Wilting, but you're not working with the Widows. Why?'

'They already have me! Who else could they want?' Pierla joked, and the other women laughed.

'A lot of us used to belong to the Widowed Sisters, actually. Take myself and Mirna, for example,' Agonea said, gesturing at the burly guard. 'And to their credit, many of our brethren still aid us on occasion. What little vespershade we can get for the soothing infusions comes from their gardens.'

'So, the abbesses are content to just let these people die?' Daerna asked.

'The city watch is to deal with them.'

'What? That makes no sense! What do the guards even know about healing or hospices?' Roshia asked.

'Nothing.' Pierla frowned. 'When someone is too ill, the guards drag them out of their house and send them to the Quarantine Islet, south of the lagoon, where they fade away out of sight.'

'You have dozens of people here! Do they plan on banishing them all?' Daerna asked.

'Oh, believe me,' Agonea said sullenly, 'they've already shipped these numbers and more! They still refuse to call it a plague, despite the way it keeps growing. Since it's ravaging the

Southern Quarter, nobody protests too much. The poor haven't got many friends in the Senate normally, and it's even worse since the upcoming election has them bickering like crowcats over cheese.'

'What's the whole point of the Orders if we're to stand idle?' Daerna huffed.

'I feel there are others in the Wailers who would want to help,' Roshia added.

'Not a word to—' Agonea broke into a fit of coughing.

Mirna, the guard, chimed in while she recovered. 'Agonea is right. If the Superiors find that some Wandering Sisters have set up a hospice behind their backs, it won't be them coming for us but their jackals . . .'

'So, you're Wanderers, then?' Dae had heard of them before, and even then, her superiors in the Order were always suspicious of the errant holy women.

'That we are,' Mirna replied. 'Wandering Sisters, or "the vagrants", depending on who you ask,' she said, feigning a bow with her muscular arm. The rest laughed at her gesture.

'Truth is that our ranks are filled with all kinds of Sisters who grew tired of their Orders' rigidness,' Agonea continued. 'Our only rule is that of the charity we offer and receive. We live as humbly as Divine Geleisdra did when she exiled herself from Ravkiria's imperial court. It's an unrooted life, but one with a lot of freedom. Freedom to bring justice to this world, no matter the cost.'

'But that is . . .' Roshia didn't dare finish.

'Reckless? Heretical?' Agonea's suggestion cut them all short. 'Say it, little sister. I care not. The abbesses' rules only serve to keep us under their heels and, in turn, for the Orders to keep the masses under the boots of the powerful. This is why they despise us, and why we ask you to keep our presence here a secret. If they find out about what we're doing, we'll all feel the lash. Knowing this, can we count on you?'

The request in Agonea's words felt heavy. The sensible thing to do would be to step away from this door, not open it, and certainly not to cross it.

And yet. Daerna couldn't deny what she'd seen in the Scab. What she'd seen here. This was why she'd joined the Order in the first place – for a chance to help.

Daerna looked at Roshia, then replied with a subtle nod.

'You can,' she said.

Chapter Sixteen

Ash

In the end, the same Dreamer Guilds that had helped ancient Iskia rise above all other kingdoms were its downfall.

Nightmare-Hunters, Wind-Riders, Light-Artisans and Delight-Forgers eventually commanded more power, land and riches than the Ravkirian monarchs.

Their rule might be long over, but their rival philosophies have shaped the modern world. Delectia's obsession with beauty, as well as the Valelands' excellence in trade, are the inheritance bequeathed by the Delight-Forgers, as much as Onyxia's mastery of the most terrifying Nightmares is a legacy of the Nightmare-Hunters.

– *The Rise and Fall of the Dreamer Guilds* by Henriod Esturos

'A LITTLE BIT OF FEAR KEEPS the mind clear,' the old saying went. If there was any truth to it, Ash had come well prepared to his first lesson.

He worried his new tutors would humiliate him and feared disappointing Lord Morvander even more. Only the idea of failing the exam and being sent to the Academy was more terrifying. Omen could feel his anxiety, and paced around Ash, ready to lash out at any threat.

Josod and Lucre awaited him in the Quietude's hall of mirrors. The gallery encircled one of the palace's highest floors, letting in light through the translucent walls and reflecting it into its hidden recesses.

Just seeing the Valelanders' lavish satin and velvet fashions made him uncomfortable. Josod, in a ruffled golden doublet, wrote back and forth with someone through a Dreamchanted messaging journal. Lucre wore an orange-and-gold dress with elegant quilted sleeves. Ash's patchy, moth-ridden attire made him feel even more beneath them. Though he now had the funds to buy new clothing, in the past few days, he'd only found time to help his crew sort things with the guild. Debts needed to be paid, and his upcoming absence needed to be planned for. The tailors could wait.

Lucre watched him as he approached. He hated Josod's arrogance, but if anyone could reveal him for the fraud he was, it was her.

'Tell us, Aescyon, what do you know of the dispensation exam?' she asked.

'I've heard it's like the guilds' journeyman exams,' he said nervously. 'You're taken to a tribunal of masters to answer their questions and demonstrate your understanding of the theoretical principles. You also demonstrate your Dreamcraft by presenting them with one of your creations.'

'Essentially correct,' she offered with a poised nod. 'A tribunal of five. Two university lecturers knowledgeable in natural philosophy, two Academy masters and the High Sage presiding.'

'Why does the Academy have any say in this?'

'That is an excellent question! The boy's not so dumb after all.' Josod chuckled. 'The Academy's a relic of a bygone era. The Senate think their Hordemasters are the key to keeping us Valelanders in line, but a nation of brutalised sheep rarely produces anything of value.'

Ash shared Josod's dislike for the Academy but, clearly, they were coming from different places. In the same way Onyxia had inherited the old Nightmare-Hunters' Guild, the Valeland cities had absorbed much of what was left of the Delight-Forger schools. The rival philosophies had led to warring societies. Not that either cared for people like him.

'Enough!' Lucre commanded. 'What matters here isn't whether the exam is fair but how to beat it. Since there's three of us, we'll split the work. I shall school you in Inception: strengthening your imagination's eyes by teaching you the theoretical foundations of the gift. Josod, for his part, will tutor you in Conception.'

'That is, precisely, technical Dreamcraft,' Josod explained as if Ash were slow. 'Any child can have a vivacious imagination, but finesse is what sets a Dreamer apart.'

'And Master Thalder?' Ash asked.

'Hopefully not Volition,' Josod said with a smirk.

Lucre glared at him. 'He'll train you in the principles of Nightmare-Hunting, a traditional subject at the Academy.'

'Should we wait for him, then?' Ash asked.

Lucre dropped her eyes. 'He must be busy elsewhere.'

'Busy floundering at the bottom of an ale jug!' chimed in Josod. He slammed his ledger closed, walked over to the table and poured himself a cup of a warm charcoal infusion from an ornate silver teapot.

Ash followed his example and poured two cups, one that he offered to Lucre and another that he kept for himself despite Omen's interest in it.

'The truth is that Nightmare-Hunting is a waste of time! Unless you plan to make a living as a rat-catcher, that is.' Josod dropped back into his chair and slouched. 'Anyone with a brain can find more fruitful pursuits to invest their time in. A proper Oneirocrat has other means of defence, if that's what worries you.'

Lucre shrugged. 'As I said, the tribunal will have masters from the Academy. Thalder was one of them, so he knows what you can expect.'

'Let me make one thing clear.' Josod leaned forwards. 'I'm not here to wean you. Either you learn to swim or you drown. Do you understand?'

'Yes.' If this man thought he'd be daunted by the prospect of harsh schooling, it was because he knew nothing about Ash's childhood, the Lightning-Hunter training or life on the Sea of Shingles.

'Good. Let us begin then. I assume that you've mastered the basics by now. Can you enter the Dreaming trance at will?' Josod asked.

'Yes, and I've Dreamchanted a few things already.'

'Let's test you. You have seen a tree in your life, I assume?'

Ash nodded coldly. Gardens might be a luxury in the barren, salt-coated jet-black city's islets, but there were some open to all. Again, Josod conflated poverty with stupidity.

'Dream us a tree, then!'

They both stared at him expectantly. Ash gestured for Omen to get out of the way, and the panther found a spot against the warm, translucent wall to lie down. Ash unfocused his eyes, letting his vision blur and his imagination spill out of his mind.

He pictured a sombre willow growing at the centre of the gallery. It was modelled after one he'd seen in an engraving in a Highlands travelogue. He got the rough shape right but realised that it was hard to picture the leaves' contour or the bark's folds. The details scurried like fine sand through his mind's grasp, possibly because his memory wasn't very fresh.

Still, he forced himself to give it a solid trunk, with layers and rings, and a rough texture, like the logs he'd fed to the hearth at his stepmother's house. He Dreamt the branches like a woman's lush hair, thick with dark leaves tinted blue.

When he'd finished, he stepped closer to admire his work. Cobalt-blue veins traversed both leaves and wood. Ash's Imprint, his innate signature. Omen approached with tense caution.

'What's wrong, boy?' Ash asked.

Omen bared his long fangs. He'd caught the scent of some threat.

Ash checked the tree more thoroughly and found a golden ivy had sprung up. In a matter of moments, the tree began wilting, the veins losing their colour. The more it withered, the more the ivy seemed to grow.

Ash scrutinised the tree until he found the cause. The ivy had grown thorns to claw through the bark and sap the tree's life.

'A brave yet foolish attempt.' Josod's disapproving voice came from behind. He approached the dying composition. 'There's so much wrong with it, I can hardly decide where to begin. Look at these roots! They aren't porous enough to find any nourishment, and where's the soil? Without foundations, there's no room for growth, only decay. And what's the point in giving it these leaves? You've squandered your efforts on the wrong thing.'

'The wrong thing? Every tree needs leaves to breathe.'

'These ones are insufficient to that end, so why bother with a worthless cosmetic trait?' Josod pulled a leaf from the tree and one from his ivy. 'Yours smells of soil and grass, they're dull in colour and probably inedible. But mine?' He displayed the golden leaf proudly on his palm. 'This! This I could sell for ornaments to garment merchants! All your talents must be put in service of perfection and unity of purpose. If they don't serve your vision, it means they're worthless.'

'I thought there was a certain beauty in making it natural,' Ash replied.

'Beauty is in the buyer's purse! And rarely in what's common. Replicating nature squanders your gift. Imagine how much more valuable your pet would have been with fangs of steel and an armoured coat!'

'Some of those things might have made his life a torment. Besides, Omen's already a formidable hunter!' He could take Josod's criticism, but he wasn't going to let him insult Omen.

Josod scoffed at him. 'I've trained with actual Hordemasters, and there are a dozen flaws in your creation. Everything you Dream is to *serve* you! If you're going to invest your will and inspiration in a long-lasting toy, you should at least make it fulfil its purpose. Otherwise, it's a waste!'

'Omen is not a waste!' Ash snarled, clenching his fists, but Josod only seemed emboldened by his reaction.

'Do you think that by talking back you're going to learn anything? Maybe in your miserable guild you were a mighty lion, but here . . . here you're a worthless roof-rat until we say otherwise.'

Ash felt his cheeks burning with anger, wanting to punch Josod in his smug face.

'That's enough,' Lucre interrupted. 'Josod is out of line, but he's also right. Your current technique is crude. If you want to improve, you'd do well in taking our advice. Otherwise, why have us here?'

'I . . . I understand. Thank you . . .' It was hard to say the words. To speak them and mean them. Lucre was right. No matter how much he despised their lack of manners, they were his best chance at passing this exam and earning his freedom again.

'Good lad,' Josod said gleefully.

Ash glared at him but bit his tongue and kept his composure.

Lucre let out a loud sigh. 'Josod, you may leave us. I'll spend the rest of today's session going over the basics of Inception.'

* * *

When Thalder finally showed up that afternoon, Ash's vision had become blurry out of sheer exhaustion.

'Now tell me, what have you learned?' Thalder asked, lolling in the armchair and nursing a bottle of wine in his lap.

At least he promised a change of pace, which Ash welcomed. He wanted a win, some encouragement, the slightest hint of approval.

After Josod left, Lucre had had him enter the Dreaming trance and recount what he experienced there, only for her to point out the lack of detail and nuance in his own perception. After that, she'd questioned him about his knowledge of the Dreaming arts, and then corrected his many omissions and glaring mistakes. As it turned out, books weren't a perfect substitute for actual schooling.

She'd left him with more questions and the promise to deliver some treatises for study. Perhaps Thalder's lesson would be easier.

'I can craft you a Nightmare,' Ash said. How difficult could it be? He'd seen enough of them.

Thalder yawned loudly. 'A bed-wetting babe can Dream a Nightmare. Show me something else. How about you Dream me an apple instead? I'm kind of hungry.'

'An apple? I thought it was dangerous to eat anything made of Dream.'

'It is. Mess it up and you might poison me, so better be careful.'

Ash felt a painful concentration settle on him as he entered the Dreaming trance once more. His head was throbbing with a growing migraine, but he still managed to craft an apple from nothingness. He even made sure to conjure the right texture and flavour in his mind. Short of Dreaming an apple tree, it was the only way he could think of to ensure it was safe.

He handed the apple to Thalder, who wrinkled his nose at it. 'Another one! This one smells rotten!'

Again, Ash entered the Dreaming under the curious gaze of Omen. This time, he refined the same formula he'd employed. He captured the memory of sweet cider and spread it evenly like a mantle on the apple's paper-like skin.

'Here, see what you make of this.'

Thalder didn't deign to even take a whiff of it. Instead, he made it spin in his palm.

'This one's wrong too. Too symmetrical. Real apples aren't symmetrical.'

Ash crafted yet another apple. The new creation was uneven, unbalanced. It wasn't pretty, but the small imperfections in the skin made it somehow more tangible, more real.

'This one's too ripe! I want it juicy, not bitter and dry. Another one!'

He tried again.

And then again.

And then once more. Omen had flopped on one side to sleep by then.

Every time, he found it harder to Dream. Harder to focus and draw on recollections or even his own imagination. It was as if his mind were becoming sore from too much use.

Every time, Thalder rebuffed his attempts. 'Too green! Too small! Too knobbly!'

Ash's migraine worsened, and his eyes grew bleary and itchy, but he refused to give up. He had to succeed at something.

He tried once more, producing a perfect apple. The right size and scent. The right feel of the skin and the perfect shape.

For once, Thalder picked it up with what seemed like genuine curiosity. After he couldn't find anything to comment on, he took a knife and cut a slice off. He held the sliver into the light of the lamps.

It looked disgusting. The surface was natural and healthy, but the inside was a grey paste, closer to sooty tallow than to an actual apple.

Ash felt the cold sweat running down his back.

'Are you trying to poison me? Another one!'

Ash tried to reply, but although he heard the words, suddenly he didn't understand them. The room turned around him.

'Come on, lad, I don't have all day . . .' Thalder's voice was a hollow droning, and when Ash tried entering the Dreaming trance, everything went black.

He floated in the wet obscurity for a while, feeling light, untethered, free from the migraine and the throbbing in his temples. Then he felt a sharp pain on his cheek and heard a crack of thunder.

Ash opened his eyes to see Thalder leaning over him. Omen was by his side, watching with concern.

'Ash! Ash!'

Thalder slapped him again, and Omen snarled at the man.

Ash forced himself awake to prevent a disaster. 'It's fine, boy,' he grunted. Omen licked his face, and Ash scratched the panther behind the ears.

'Your friend is very loyal. Good thing you gave him some patience too,' Thalder said, offering a nod of respect to Omen. 'Now, how are you feeling?'

'I'm fine, I think. What happened?'

'That was my fault,' Thalder said, running a hand through his braids. 'I pushed you too hard. If it's any consolation, you lasted longer than many of my former students.'

Thalder offered him a hand. Ash took it, and Thalder pulled him up and helped him to a chair. Omen followed, concerned. When Thalder offered him a glass of cool water, it practically evaporated in his mouth.

'I don't understand. It's like I've lost it all of a sudden.'

'Don't be foolish!' Thalder gave a belly laugh. 'Once a Dreamer, always a Dreamer. You could spend a hundred years without creating anything, and the fire would still be within you, embers burning silently at the bottom of your soul. No matter how much they try to crush your spirit, they'll never put out that fire.'

Ash felt Thalder was talking to himself as much as to him. In a suddenly sullen mood, Thalder poured himself another cup of wine.

'Then what's wrong with me?' Ash asked.

'You've just run out of fuel. The mind is a forge. Keep it burning long enough and the flames will die out. At least until you rekindle them with more inspiration.'

'But the apple …'

'Lad, what do you know about apples? Clearly not enough. First lesson: pick your battlefields. A Dreamer might be able to Dream anything, but to excel at it, you must know the subject matter. While we're at it, the second lesson: the Dreaming is infinite, but your inspiration isn't. Thus, nurture it. Now, this is your task for the rest of the day: replenish your strength. And I'm not just talking about a hearty stew, although that won't hurt. Go see a play in the Craghorn, pick up a lute or chase some pretty lips.'

Ash stood up and woozily headed for the exit.

In the streets, the Susurrus's taunts bit into him. *Worthless … scum … hollow mind, unable to conceive anything worthwhile … You deserve nothing but to spend the rest of your days in silent dungeons … an empty sack of bones, incapable of doing what needs to be done …*

By the time he reached Muirtra's gates, he was exhausted. He sent Daerna a message through one of the abbey's servants, and then went to the gardens to wait. Under an oak, he sank onto a stone bench with Omen at his feet.

He dropped his head into his hands. The migraine was receding, but now the emptiness and gnawing fear nestled in his brain. Before he could sink farther into despair, he felt Omen press against his legs, warming him.

Ash stroked his head and drank in the garden's sweet petrichor. Everything stood still and quiet.

And dark.

He shook his head to keep himself awake.

'Ash?'

Daerna approached, wearing a brocaded black shawl. His heart lit up at the sight of her, like a trap catching lightning, and she greeted him with a kiss.

Omen also rose to greet her, rubbing his large head against her legs. It was always delightful to see him behave like a big house cat when Daerna was around.

'I don't have much time, I'm afraid,' she said.

'Don't worry, neither do I.'

They sat together, ensconced under the canopied arch.

For days, he'd been anticipating the moment of sharing everything that had happened, but now, it felt like a waste to use the little time they had to discuss Lord Brakte's humiliating remarks, his last encounter with Dain or Josod's arrogance.

'You don't sound that well,' she said, giving him an assessing look.

'I'm sorry, I'm so tired,' Ash said. 'Lord Morvander has picked some tutors to help prepare me, and they're . . . difficult. What about you?'

'I too am having difficult days.' She rubbed her temples.

'The prioress is still bent on flogging you?'

'Among other things.'

'Dae, if there's anything I can do to help, I'm here for you.'

She squeezed his hand. 'Right now, we must each focus on our own battles. You should be preparing for the exam. My trouble can wait.'

Ash breathed with relief. 'To the entombed hells with the exam! I care about you a lot more than about any of this.'

'I know.' She smiled and leaned against him, resting on his shoulder. He kissed the top of her head. Her hair smelled of lavender and rain – her scent had become hope to him.

Here, with her and Omen, he longed for nothing, except for time to stand still in the perfect solace of this shared moment.

Chapter Seventeen

Geil

. . . For the Domain can provision both a mighty army and a deft navy, but both will fail without a captain general and admiral worthy of their command. I mean not just in the force of their Dreamcraft, but also in their knowledge of military matters, their authority and their magnanimity. Rare it is to find a person in which these four talents co-exist; rarer even to find two individuals. That is why they are to share the Regency, since it is upon their conduct that all wars depend, and it is the mastery of war that conjures peace.

– *A treatise on Onyxian Honour* by R. Erringsod

NACRE ISLAND'S LIGHTS GREW CLOSER on the dark horizon. Soon they'd arrive at Lady Saorla's palace, and Geil would have to brave the tempestuous waters of Onyxian high society.

If Ragdra were to get her dispensation, Geil needed influential allies. And this time of the year, that meant attending one of the Ascent Festival's fatuous masquerades.

The festival itself celebrated the founding of Onyxia with a city-wide canal parade, but the previous week offered Onyxians a rare opportunity to engage in debauchery where the streets became a stage for performers and festive revellers, where palaces filled with masked balls, music, wine and other usually frowned-upon delights.

And not one was more prominent than Lady Ines Saorla's. She wasn't just the Captain Regent, one of the two most powerful people in the Domain and leader of the Reformer Party, she had a well-earned reputation for hosting uniquely scintillating celebrations.

Ahead, the lantern-laden barges of merchants and Oneirocrats queued like a swarm of fat fireflies, but Geil's darkglass gondola darted past them like a wasp. Her knuckles went white with tension as they prepped for landing.

'You know that you don't have to do this. We can turn back, and you can have a tutelage letter signed and shipped to Ayron's governor before the night is over,' her father said.

When Geil had finally explained the reason for her return, her father had offered immediately to take Ragdra on as an apprentice. Yet she'd refused it.

Sure, Ragdra would have a comfortable life in their household, but at the cost of leaving her family and life behind, reshaping herself to fit into the jet-black city.

No, Geil wanted to do better than that.

'Don't worry, Father. I've fought wyverns. I can handle some senators.'

'Ines Saorla is a lot more than a simple senator,' he said.

'Which is why she's the person who can help me.' Instead of that scheming worm, the High Sage.

'If you feel overwhelmed . . .' Her father trailed off as their young pilot skilfully approached the white-stone quay and the servants helped secure their boat.

'I'll handle it,' she replied, adjusting her brocaded eye-mask.

Balchod opened the cabin doors, and they emerged to loud complaints from the boats behind them, quickly followed by surprised gasps from those who recognised them. So much for Geil's hopes of mingling unnoticed. Against the other guests' pale embroidery and bejewelled masks, her dark crimson doublet stood out like a fresh cut on a smooth face.

As much as she reassured her father, the prospect of facing hordes of courtiers made her stomach queasy. They'd come for her seeking blood and scandal.

Let them try, the Drake snarled. *Words can't cut like we do.*

A servant, finely attired in a pearl-white silk tabard, escorted them uphill, lighting their path with a nautilus lamp.

All of Nacre Island was a masterpiece of Dreamcraft. Onyxia might not lack in Dreamers, yet only a few could call themselves Archdreamers. Such a title was only awarded to those who'd Dreamt their own island in the lagoon's waters, either because they'd flocked to Divine Geleisdra's service in the early days or because they'd raised their own in the centuries since. Even then, those who did usually chose to lift the lagoon's onyx bedrock, like her father. Not Lady Saorla, though. She'd Dreamt her whole domain on pale limestone and white marble. A political declaration that the future of the Domain could be built on different foundations than its past.

Geil and her father walked into a ballroom as radiant as the morning sun. A formidable assembly of human and Dreamblooded performers had taken over every corner, playing music, reciting poetry and performing theatrical pieces. Lady Saorla's servants moved throughout, filling cups with fragrant spiced wines.

She kept a step behind him, hiding in the anonymity afforded her by the mask. It didn't last long.

Some nearby guests chattered about her, many barely pretending to whisper. A few were innocent enough, but others came like a shiver of sharks chasing the scent of blood.

Yet not nearly as terrible as the pack of courtiers with lapis lazuli–painted lips that spouted the worst speculation of all: 'I heard she had her lover murdered . . .'

Geil closed her fists. *We could choke them, show how blue their countenances can get*, the Drake urged. Before Geil could indulge it, the crowd parted, but it was only to make room for their magnificent host.

Her pearl-white hair was cropped short, and the golden silk of her fitted vest and breeches was covered in pearls connected by silver thread in patterns that evoked constellations, a reminder of her moniker, the Starspun Maiden. A cloak of coalesced mist sparkling with diamonds trailed her. Even her consort, a handsome, broad-shouldered captain with the warmest brown eyes Geil had ever seen, felt like an ornate piece of jewellery. The Drake wasn't easy to impress, but in Lady Saorla's presence, even it stayed quiet.

'Lord Morvander! And here I feared we'd miss your company another year!' She grabbed his arm, though even in her welcoming manner, Geil noticed her dominating presence.

'I must admit, I've missed your magnificent parties, Lady Saorla. I'm most grateful that my daughter persuaded me it was time to experience them once more.'

Lady Saorla turned to her. 'Then allow me to thank you, Lady Morvander, for your generous contribution to our shared delight.'

'Thank you, Your Ladyship. And please, just Geil.'

'Will you be staying with us for a time, Geil?' Lady Saorla asked.

'Hopefully,' her father replied.

Geil offered a worn-out smile. The Drake was squirming under her skin, itching for a way out, and they'd only just arrived. No, she'd come here for this. This was her chance to make her case.

'Lady Saorla, if I may, there's something I wanted to ask your advice on.'

Her eyes gleamed with delight. 'Of course, dear. Walk with me.'

Geil followed as she strode elegantly out a door that overlooked the palace grounds. There were attendees who would kill for this audience.

As they settled into a gentle walk outside, Geil said, 'I approached the High Sage's office for help with a personal matter, but Lady Malvedra seemed eager to . . . charge heftily for her aid.'

'Hardly surprising,' Lady Saorla lamented, leading her down a path of white-marble statues representing allegorical constellations that glowed with encrusted amber pieces like captured stars. 'When the Senate goes back into session after the Ascent Festival, their first order of business will be to renew the High Council. Since the High Sage oversees the Academy, their election will be very contentious. A year ago, Lady Malvedra's tepidness made her a perfectly palatable compromise candidate. Now, the Blues are clamouring for open war against the King of Thorns, threatening to drown out all voices and other concerns.'

'Who do the Blues want to replace her with?' Geil asked.

'Prioress Balachdra of Muirtra Abbey.'

'A Wailing Sister to serve as High Sage?'

'You'd be surprised. She studied at Arvira, and has strong opinions on how to reform the Domain's universities to only allow entrance to those deemed morally acceptable by the abbesses.'

Geil frowned. It seemed that those who opposed change had grown, if anything, emboldened in the past year. 'So that's their grand vision? Keeping the masses from immoral texts and sinful ideas?'

'Spoken like the prioress herself.' Lady Saorla's smile was warm. 'It's not only that, though. The abbesses' voices can sway many in the Senate. With this gift, Lord Stalcar ensures their support to his other appointments and policies.'

'We should be fostering literacy and easing access to universities and schools, not stifling it!'

The lady arched an eyebrow, now curious. 'You have your father's ambition; I like that! Tell me, Geil, have you ever considered elevating yourself to the Senate? You could take on your father's empty seat, or even your grandmother's. We need bold minds like yours.'

Geil was briefly tempted. *We'd quickly wither in that cage*, the Drake groaned. Often, those who meant to climb over the walls of politics ended up being just bricks in those same walls.

She cleared her throat. 'I lack the right temperament for politics. If I had to hear the Traditionalists denounce the dangers of literacy, I'd end up breaking somebody's jaw.'

Lady Saorla laughed, melodious and confident. 'I can't fault you for that. Then let us speak of other ways in which we can aid each other. Your father's voice carries enormous weight among the Susurrus's Oneirocrats, and some of the Valelander senators, wouldn't you agree?'

'I suppose, yes. And he has a long-standing friendship with Lord Brakte,' Geil acknowledged. Unlike others, she'd never enjoyed flaunting her family's influence, but this wasn't for her benefit. 'And my parents' efforts to aid the Fishermen's and Bargers' guilds, as well as aiding in the hospices, mean we carry some support with the commoners, too.'

'Allow me to extend a friendly hand, then. Such support could greatly help Puglius Zerandra, my candidate for High Sage. Of course, such confidence would be handsomely repaid by involving you in the drafting of ambitious policies to enlighten the Domain.'

'I could see that working to everyone's advantage,' Geil admitted. This was far more tempting than taking her own seat. 'But I'd need to meet Zerandra before agreeing.'

'Where did you think I was taking you all along, dear?'

Lady Saorla had guided them to an open-air terrace overlooking the hidden face of the island. Beyond, marble steps flowed like a stream into a mist-wrapped copse of pale trees, some bearing golden fruits that echoed the starry light above.

She led Geil to a middle-aged man with a red beard who was regaling an enraptured audience with ingenious tales.

'Master Lecturer Puglius,' Lady Saorla said. 'Please meet Lady Morvander, the sort of person whose support and counsel could lead you to great heights.'

Puglius flashed her a seedy smile. 'A pleasure to make your acquaintance, Your Ladyship.'

'Master Lecturer? At which university?'

'Onyxia's very own! Although there are few I haven't known myself either as master or student. I studied medicine in Ilea and the Iskian Classics in Amalga, then taught both subjects in Helysia while I took philosophy studies. Not to mention rhetoric with the harshest masters of the continent: my two grandmothers!' he added to general merriment of those present.

'Impressive,' Geil admitted. 'And as for your views of the position of the High Sage?'

'We must pursue progress, yet always with prudence, lest its own growth unroot its foundations,' he replied, deftly dancing away from anything controversial. She wouldn't let him get away that easily.

'What about the Academy? For the Domain to pursue progress, our Dreamers must be allowed to become more than hoarders of monstrosities or the swords that put them down. Moreover, I have on good authority that the Academy are overreaching their remit – taking younger children, breaking guild laws – surely you agree their conscription powers need to be curtailed?' Geil tried.

'Certainly.' Lecturer Zerandra cleared his throat. 'The Valelander burghs should have a say in how their Dreamers are trained. Academy conscription should be put to an end there. Instead, Damlan University could train those with the gift according to the Delight-Forger Dreamcraft traditions.'

Polite clapping and nodding followed.

'Why not stop conscription *altogether*?' Geil asked. She could practically hear the shocked gasps in the concurrence's minds. 'Why not let those with gifts choose what stirs their ambition?'

'Lady Geil seems intent on outdoing the Philosopher Empress herself!' Puglius jested.

'Isn't limiting their education a way of limiting our future too?'

She expected Puglius to offer some witty retort, but colour suddenly drained from his face as if a cool wind had blown in. Even the music died.

'Ambition is always to be praised,' a man said behind her. His voice was hard like stone. Geil turned to the older man. Even with the green coral kraken mask covering his chiselled face, it was easy to recognise him.

Lord Stalcar of Lorn, Regent Admiral of Onyxia and leader of the Traditionalists. And perhaps, more importantly, the Leviathan-Maker, one of the most powerful Dreamers alive. He was taller than she remembered, but the air was as heavy in his presence as it always had been, an echo of an ocean's deep, cold darkness.

Even the Drake quivered, as if sensing a much larger predator. She had to force the words out.

'So, you agree then, Regent Admiral?' Geil asked. Nearby, Lady Saorla's eyes flicked past her conversational partner to her political rival; it wasn't far-fetched to imagine he'd come to speak with her. Or *at* her, as the case may be.

'Changes are needed. And they will be made. But changes to strengthen the Domain. Schooling won't protect our ships when the King of Thorns razes every single town and city in the Valelands. Our fleet will, but lasting peace can only be conquered by inspiring unsurmountable dread in our enemies' hearts.'

Lecturer Zerandra was about to retort when the shrill braying of some colossal sea-drake came from the lagoon's waters.

'Apologies,' Lord Stalcar said with obvious delight. 'My loyal mounts grow restless without me. You were saying?'

Whatever Lecturer Zerandra had been about to say had slipped away. Geil's Drake too was restless, yet she refused to be intimidated. 'Your Lordship, training every Dreamer for cruelty, like the Academy does, will ultimately starve us. Unless you expect monsters to build cities, raise bridges and tend to trade and harvest, of course.'

Lord Stalcar's stare sent a shiver down her spine. 'The Academy's mastery of Nightmares is paramount for Onyxia's dominance of the seas – and the trading routes, of course,' he added for the benefit of those around them.

Geil snorted. 'Paramount for the Academy's wealth most of all.'

'In that, we agree. It is long overdue that that ancient institution is disbanded once and for all.' He chuckled with a sort of fatherly approval. 'Its knowledge should be shared between the fleet and the army, to be put to better use.' Lord Stalcar's eyes wandered to Lady Saorla, who had extricated herself from her former conversation and stood as if waiting for him. 'A wonderful conversation, Lady Morvander. We'll have to continue some other time,' he said, excusing himself to speak privately with his co-Regent.

As soon as they'd both wandered off, some of the Whites in the crowd began trading barbs with those who'd arrived with Lord Stalcar. There was a venom that Geil had rarely seen before. Veiled accusations of cowardice and stupidity were followed by veiled threats from one faction to another to not stray into the wrong quarter of the city, 'lest some untimely accident befall them'.

If she'd returned hoping there was change for the better coming, she'd been mistaken. At least she'd got her night's entertainment.

Or so she thought. A familiar guest dressed in lavish ice-blue silks and wearing a snow fox mask, complete with silver jewellery, opaline earrings and a thick white fur cloak, darted towards the woods at the back of the palace, past startled servants.

She recognised the silver bracelet of her office. It was Lady Malvedra, the High Sage.

Geil shadowed her at a distance. Lady Malvedra cast only the briefest of glances behind to make sure she wasn't being followed, then disappeared into the wood's pale shroud.

Carefully, Geil crept after her. Inside the copse, citrus and the smell of lush grass assaulted her senses. In the distance, she spotted the shape of a sequestered spire with a dome-shaped top, lit by gleaming golden lamps.

Although Lady Malvedra had only been a bit ahead, Geil had lost track of her. She had seemingly vanished.

She won't lose us so easily, not here, not to hunters like us, the Drake whispered eagerly.

Geil shifted, letting the Drake's senses take over. Her eyes could now read the warmth where the High Sage had trodden, her nose pick up the clove of her perfume lingering on the air. She followed both deeper into the woods, where the shadows had grown impossibly thick. Suddenly, the darkness rippled around her, and she saw everything as if submerged in a lightless pool. On top of that, something grazed against her mind, like a long fingernail tickling her brain.

It reminded her of what crossing the Mantle to enter the Academy's lands felt like. Perhaps that was why, instead of being scared, it made the Drake's anger flare. She determinedly trudged through the blurry shroud and emerged inside a hidden copse. Sounds of conversation suddenly reached her, as if the darkness carried its own heavy silence. Lady Malvedra was talking to a thin individual clad in a cape of smoke. On his head perched a horned dragon mask.

'—because of the wretched rats!' she cursed. 'If you want me to keep helping you, you'd do well in ensuring my future on the High Council.'

'We have paid you handsomely for the privilege,' the dragon-masked man explained dismissively. She knew his voice only too well from her time in the Academy.

Well done, dear. His proud smile. His fingertips hovering over the Drake's scales. *We shall make something terrible out of you yet.*

His mask was not meant to be a dragon; it was a wyvern, the symbol of the man's family, which he wore only too proudly at the Academy.

'It's not coin that I want anymore! You must have filth on all of them. Use it! Use it to secure my position, if you want me to keep aiding you.'

'Hush!' the man hissed before looking in her direction. 'Who dares?'

Geil stepped into view.

'Apologies, I didn't mean to intrude,' Geil lied.

'What do you want?' Lady Malvedra demanded, voice fraying with outrage.

Geil thought about snapping back. Instead, the Drake delighted in showing her fangs. 'I believe you know what I want, Lady Malvedra.'

'I . . . I'll reward your discretion, Lady Geil,' Malvedra said with badly disguised anger. With a look at the masked man, as if dismissed, she departed. He waved his hand, and the unnatural darkness began dissipating, or rather coalescing into his cloak.

'It is quite the surprise to see you here, Geil,' the man said, his sharp, waxen face broken up by a thin moustache and grey-green eyes.

'Master Davorles,' she mumbled, facing the man. Nicknamed 'the Wisp', he was one of the Academy's most renowned instructors. The master prized himself on knowing his students better than anyone else, only because it meant he could tailor his Nightmares to each one's individual fears.

'Actually, it's Vice-Chancellor Davorles now. I'm head of the Secret Chancellery.'

So that's what Lady Malvedra had meant. The Secret Chancellery was the twisted, ruthless twin of the Skycouriers. They kept spies in every port, and its agents, the Stone-Masks, had the authority to arrest and torture the enemies of the Domain. Their sinister moniker came as much from the gargoyle-leather half-masks they wore as the symbol of their office as from their ability to watch at will through the eyes of the Dreamchanted stone lionheads spread throughout the city.

No wonder Lady Malvedra expected him to have access to a trove of others' secrets.

'It's good to see you again, Geil. I take it you too have had private dealings with the High Sage?'

'I'm no longer a student of yours, and my business with her is my own,' Geil found herself snapping. The last thing she wanted was the ruthless Davorles sniffing around Ragdra.

'You wound me, child. My former students hold a very dear place in my heart.' He cupped her shoulder with his right hand, and her stomach squirmed at his touch. 'You should know, when I heard about Lanteus, I immediately volunteered my aid. How do you think those vermin were put to the sword so quickly? I only wish you could have heard their screams.'

Despite herself, the Drake licked its chops at that. She wished she'd been there to see them being torn apart herself.

'Thank you,' Geil mumbled, caught in the image Davorles painted.

'If only it had been in my power to cleanse the Scab before that . . . Though what Lanteus was doing in such a low-down place, one can only guess . . .' Davorles mused, gaze fixed on Geil.

She said nothing.

'You could help me save others, though.'

'What?' she asked, snapping out of her trance.

Davorles went on: 'The Secret Chancellery could use someone of your skills, Geil. Many of your fellow students from the Academy have already joined me.'

She cleared her throat. 'There are plenty who learned brutality at the Academy better than me. I'd be a disappointment.'

'Please, Geil, who do you take me for? There's so much more to the trade of secrets than working the rack. What I require is agents who can ascertain truth through any means necessary and who are willing to keep the Domain safe in these uncertain times.'

'For someone who's spent a lifetime beyond the Mantle, you seem very invested in this. And here I thought your only love was Nightmares, Master Davorles,' Geil joked.

He scanned her with hard eyes.

'Believe it or not, I was raised in Onyxia. I carry long memories of everything this city gave my family . . .' Here it was, his secret pride: the same reason he wore the mask in a way that only those who knew him would connect to his family's crest of the wyvern rampant. 'Besides, here I can still dedicate myself to my love of Nightmares. Some of the sweetest fears are kept secret. The beauty of a Nightmare is that they can be crafted to listen and watch anywhere.' He flicked his gloved hand.

The smoky tendrils of his cloak rippled, and Geil followed them down her former master's back to the ground and then all around them. That was the wall she'd hit earlier. She'd seen this before.

'It's like the Mantle. Clever.'

'Like the Mantle?' Davorles teased. 'It's a very piece of it.'

Was that even possible? Could he have carved out a sliver of the unending darkness shielding the Academy as a sign of vanity?

'Think of it as a reminder of how the Academy protects one's own. And perhaps of the hardships that made us grow.'

She cleared her throat. 'Some of us grew into something *very* different to what we were.'

'Hardships strip us of our excesses, leaving only our true selves,' he said. 'The Academy forges swords, and you're among the best it's ever produced. What would Lanteus think if he saw you squandering your talents?'

'I don't think you'd know much of what he'd have wanted,' she snapped.

'I think he'd want those he cared about protected, wouldn't he?'

'I wouldn't dare presume anything, Master Davorles.' She kept using his former title to provoke him; if he noticed, he didn't mind. 'Now, you'll have to excuse me.'

She offered a curt bow and walked away.

The shroud of darkness had dissipated. To avoid seeing Davorles again, she pressed on to the tower she'd spotted before in the distance. The sounds of the palace dimmed behind her, replaced by the murmur of a waterfall in the gardens. She only realised what the tower was once inside. The domed roof was made of transparent Dreamchanted glass, and a circular desk at the centre overflowed with astronomical charts, astrolabes and sketching materials. An observatory.

There was a rustle of fabric as a pale young woman entered the room, wearing an exquisite vermilion dress embroidered with pearls and thread as golden as her hair.

'I hear you single-handedly chased off Lord Stalcar,' the woman said with a grin.

Geil swallowed hard. 'I'll have to apologise.'

'Don't! He deserved it!' The woman placed her hands on her shapely hips. 'For too long we've indulged the Traditionalists' short-sightedness. Printing has changed the world. Rivers of ink now flow freely and no dam will hold them back. What sense is there to hide books from the masses? We should be opening schools to teach every single commoner in the Domain!'

'What of the dangers of sowing perilous ideas in unprepared minds?' Geil asked sarcastically.

'Then arm the people with a robust understanding to make sense of what they read.'

'Well said!' Geil replied. Of course, this young woman might just be saying what Geil wanted to hear.

'Have you come to hide here as well?' the woman asked.

'I just like the view.'

'Really? I thought I was the only one who enjoyed looking at the skies. Most Onyxians pay more attention to what they have in front of their faces.'

'Well, you have to watch where you're going, otherwise you're going to have a dip in a canal. You don't want to swim with the lagoon crabs. I speak from experience on this matter.'

The woman threw her head back in laughter. Geil wet her lips at the sight of her slender neck, then forced herself to look away.

'So, what about you?' Geil asked. 'Are you also hiding, or have you come for the view?'

'How about hiding in the view?' Seeing Geil's puzzled face, the woman pointed out a star through the glass dome. 'See that one? It's Lyre. The ancient Iskian sailors who named it thought on a still night you could hear its melody. It'd keep them sane on long voyages. Legends, of course, but it's true that if you pay enough attention, you can see a musical pattern in its light.'

Perhaps it was the effect of her words, but Geil thought she saw something resembling a rhythm in its twinkling. 'It's beautiful. Now I wished I'd had the patience to learn music when my mother tried teaching me to play the lute.'

'There's always time,' her companion said with a smile.

'I lost her, many years ago now. To a blood disease.' Geil cleared her throat.

The lady reached for Geil's hand and held it between hers. Her delicate fingers were warm through the thin brocaded gloves. Her eyes were deep like diamonds, but to Geil's surprise, there wasn't any false pity in them.

'I'm sorry. I can teach you if you'd like.'

And with that, she began singing, her voice like a stream of honey. Geil found she couldn't tear her eyes away, and listened, enraptured. Even the Drake was silent.

A servant cleared his throat, interrupting them. Geil had no idea how long it'd been. 'I beg your pardon, Lady Morvander, but your father has been looking for you. He's ready to leave.'

Geil pulled herself away and looked back at her companion, a question on the tip of her tongue.

'Liadra,' the woman offered. 'And you are Geil Morvander.'

'At your service,' Geil said with an exaggerated bow. 'Thanks for hiding me here, Liadra.'

'Thanks for hiding with me. Might not be the last time if you keep dealing with my sister's court. Next time, I do hope you'll provide the entertainment, though,' Liadra added with a mischievous smile.

'Your sister?' Geil asked.

'Well, Ines Saorla, of course.'

Geil half staggered, half nodded. When she left, she could feel the Drake's growling protestations building inside her head, but that didn't temper her own silly smile.

Chapter Eighteen

Daerna

It is the manner of the custom during the week preceding the Ascent Festival for the citizens to enjoy masked revelries on the canals from evening till midnight. More importantly, the masks allow all classes of society to assemble and abandon themselves to the people they could have been.

– *Portraits of the Onyxians* by Kairik of Fredsen

Daerna paused her scrubbing. Her knees hurt from kneeling at the quay, but it was the rash on the back of her hand that stopped her short.

It was probably nothing. Everyone was certain that you couldn't get the Wilting through contact. This had to be her skin reacting to the vinegar after washing the floors of the Wanderers' hospice day after day.

Sitting down to rest, she admired the passing barges' garlands and religious effigies. Even from here, one could hear the revelry in University Square.

Growing up, Ascent Carnival had been her and her sister's favourite time of the year. The entire city became a wondrous place: flower garlands and flags hung from bridges and arcades, and the streets became a constant masquerade. For a whole week, everyone could play at being someone else behind their masks – the sad at being mirthful, the graceful at being grotesque, the shameful at being liberated.

Even the Sisters partook in the celebrations. Keening watches were shorter, dedicated only to elevate Canticles of Solace and those funerary dirges that couldn't wait. Above, the Hallowed Motherstorm was ushered to peaceful quietude, while below, Onyxians embraced the joys of living.

For a moment, Daerna worried life was slipping through her grasp. She should be attending masked balls with Ash instead of writing him ever shorter letters between her even shorter breaks. She should be focusing on her Keening practices with Dirdra instead of neglecting them.

'Ready?' Pierla asked, standing above her with a basket full of washed sheets.

Daerna joined her. It felt good to stretch after hunkering down for so long. They trudged back inside, carrying their heavy baskets. Inside the chamber they'd cleaned, Roshia had finished clearing one of the clotheslines.

Roshia looked ragged, with deep shadows under her eyes. Just like Daerna, she was fraying at both ends. 'Don't worry, I'll hang yours,' she offered. 'Can you take the clean bandages to Agonea, though?'

'Of course, Your Grace!' Daerna joked, but still picked up the wicker basket and carried it into the main hall.

The infirmary seemed fuller than during her first visit a week ago. Some in the early stages of the disease, before delirium had set in, had improved and returned to their families. Sadly, the majority had still faded away despite the Sisters' attentions.

For all her wisdom, Agonea had no magic cure. Daerna had seen four people die, and each one had been worse than the last. Even then, this was better than letting the watch immure them in their hovels. At least here, Agonea's Wandering Sisters kept them comfortable. Their lard ointments relieved the rashes' pain, and feverfew and vespershade infusions helped with fever and ravings respectively.

Still, it crushed Daerna's heart to watch the sick grow grey and lifeless. It was even worse to see that they kept coming. There was no day when someone didn't turn up at their door begging for a cot.

Other people too had begun showing up at odd hours. Rugged men and women who spoke in hushed voices with Agonea and carried swords under their cloaks.

At first, Daerna had thought them a criminal gang, demanding tribute for operating within the Broken Arches, but then she'd noticed that they'd brought sacks of grain, bundles of feverfew, linen and even wine and vinegar barrels to help their work there.

Roshia, who spent every moment she could helping at the hospice, had told Daerna that one night, the strangers had barged in, bringing two of their number badly injured. Agonea had sent Roshia away immediately, but not before she'd overheard the strangers cursing the Charnelites for some bloody clash at the Scab.

When Daerna saw Agonea bickering at the entrance with a wiry young woman dressed in leather garments, she hurried to the door, tiptoeing around the cots filling the floor. Maybe this was her chance to learn who these people were.

Except the young woman was no mysterious stranger. She was Ash's friend Yaisa.

'I'm begging you!' Yaisa was yelling. 'We'll pay for your services. Here!' She tried pressing a handful of Octaves into Agonea's hands, but the Wanderer refused them.

'Yaisa!' Daerna called.

Yaisa's jaw dropped. 'Daerna, what are you doing here?'

Daerna squeezed past Sister Mirna's towering figure to hug Yaisa. 'I'm helping the Wanderers. Why are you here?'

'It's Little Vespiria! The Wilting's got really bad there. So far, we've managed to keep most of the sick hidden, but soon the watch will find out. If Sister Agonea helped us—'

'Don't you realise that'd endanger us too?' Agonea snapped, throwing up one hand while pressing the other against her metallic collar. 'We can make space for two, three at most.'

'Three? There's more than a *dozen*! The majority can't walk. They're bedridden with fever.'

'That's all we can do, lass. Our cots are full, and we've pushed our luck enough as it is.' Agonea rubbed her sore hands uneasily. This wasn't just her usual cautious self, rather, she seemed on edge.

'If you don't help us, nobody will,' Yaisa begged.

'I can spare some of our ointments and some vespershade wine,' Agonea said.

'I can take it there,' Daerna offered. 'If nothing else, I can assess the gravity of the situation. Besides, what good is putting out one fire if there's another blaze close by?'

Agonea frowned, then sighed. 'Tread carefully, Daerna. There are worse things than the city watch out there these nights. I'll fetch you some supplies.'

* * *

Daerna had never been to Little Vespiria's southern half. There, the poorest among the Vespirian immigrants had pieced together a shanty town from ship wreckage and driftwood. Many avoided the area, considering it a shoddy and dangerous slum, but Daerna just saw hardworking people trying to earn a living however they could.

It'd been more than a decade since the Onyxian fleet had seized Vespiria.

Now, the Domain's westernmost possession served as a lynchpin for a lot of new trade. Daerna knew this well, because her family's fortunes had risen when her mother bought a charter to trade with the golden kingdoms in the south. Then traders had started to sail in number from the west, which was when everyone's fortunes had truly changed.

As for the Vespirians, it didn't seem that their lives had got much better. Their Dreamers might have joined the ranks of the Oneirocrats, but even then, they'd had to renounce their religion, customs and names. As for the Undreaming, poverty and famine had chased them. Waves of immigrants had flowed into the city, crashing into a different sort of poverty on the easternmost isle of the Southern Quarter.

Despite the prejudice they endured, they'd laboured hard to gain a foothold in the city. They'd even reclaimed a sandy bank from the lagoon's waters, turning it into the Southern Quarter's latest addition. As far as Daerna had seen, they just wanted to live in peace and be left alone.

Tattered children watched their approach with curious eyes. Sisters were a rare sight here.

She was grateful that Roshia and Pierla had joined her, especially when a group of men abandoned their knucklebones game to block their path. They held sturdy staffs, fashioned in the Vespirian way for fighting and pole-vaulting, and had knives tucked in their sashes. One of them, tanned and muscular, waved a sharp cleaver sculpted from hardened wood.

'You can't be here,' he said with suspicious eyes.

'They're with me,' Yaisa said, waving at them. A loud argument in Vespirian ensued.

Daerna's rudimentary command of Vespirian was enough to grasp that Yaisa was pleading for the men to let them in and that the man kept saying the word 'secret'.

Perhaps it'd be easier to just stay out of this as Agonea had suggested. Except, wouldn't that prove the Charnel Mother's cult right, that the Sisters weren't interested in the suffering of the truly desperate?

To the entombed hells with all of them. Let them refuse her.

'We'd be honoured if we can enter,' she tried in her crude Vespirian. Hopefully, showing some respect would go a long way.

'More flea-ridden *gihires*, like the Charnel Mother's children,' he said to Daerna stiffly.

Yaisa turned to the man. 'These women are my guests; don't you dare disrespect them.'

The man studied Daerna, then replied in Onyxian: 'They said they knew the disease was spreading, and they could help us with it to appease their vulture spirit of a goddess. They thought we'd be afraid of them or their bone daggers.' He slapped his cleaver. 'We taught them better.'

So, this was why they were being so protective. Agonea was right in her suspicions. Where the Wilting struck, the Charnel Cult seemed to follow.

'We come not to preach but to listen and help. And I assure you, we'll respect the words of your *Harymawadas*.'

The men exchanged surprised glances at her use of the Vespirian term for sacred women. As if on cue, an old woman angrily shook her staff at them, ordering the men to let them through.

'Do as the *Harymawadas* tell you, Sister. And not a word to anyone,' the man said, and Daerna saw the desperation in his eyes.

'We swear it on her divine grace,' she offered solemnly.

The man ordered his gang to make way for them.

Yaisa guided them expertly through the muddy streets.

'I'm sorry,' Yaisa said. 'Everybody's on edge.'

'If things are getting this bad, why not try letting the watch know? Might give them something else to focus on other than your sick.'

'Perhaps. Can't trust them, though. They might use it as an excuse to cleanse the entire district of our people.'

'Miserable asses!' Pierla cursed. 'They prey on you because you don't have strong patrons, don't they?'

'Precisely. Little Vespiria might be as poor as the Scab, but believe me: we're treated even worse than them,' muttered Yaisa.

A stranded carrack's carcass awaited them at the end of the alley. The locals had carved a hospice out of it.

'There are other places, but none as bad as here,' Yaisa said, leading them into the main hold. Every inch of the floor was covered in cots. In some cases, mothers watched over sick children, and in others, sons and daughters watched over elderly relatives.

'So many children,' Roshia gasped.

'So many orphans,' Pierla corrected her.

'She's right,' Yaisa said. 'This hospice harbours those who have nowhere else to go. Some of the children are raised by the elderly and are half adopted by the families here. Better that than the criminal gangs taking them.'

'Why has the disease affected so many here? And so young too?' Daerna asked.

It was painful to see all these emaciated younglings sinking slowly into the Wilting's delirious embrace.

The four of them sprang into action. They had brought rags to make bandages and vinegar and soap to clean, but they lacked food to strengthen the patients. Daerna administered cold compresses and shared out their supplies. Agonea had taught her that keeping the afflicted clean and comfortable made a difference. The fight against the disease might be spiritual, but caring for the body helped the odds.

The elder women's sullen glances gradually softened as they watched the Sisters work. It was obvious they were desperate for anything that might help them fight the disease.

When the Motherstorm outside began raging, the entire structure trembled with the rain's pummelling. Soon icy water trickled into the room. Some burrowed deeper into their damp blankets, while many of the caregivers placed themselves among the convalescing for heat.

Daerna's insides tangled into a knot. She began singing the first neumes of the 'Water of the Spirit' canticle. Soon, Roshia joined in and, to Daerna's surprise, many of the caregivers hummed along.

The canticle spoke of the hallowed tears of heaven, every drop an echo of eternal loss. It spoke too of the kindness of consolation. Melancholy, when reconciled with hope, opened the path to solace, and that was the grandest of rewards. This was what she sought: solace in the act of singing, in creating harmony over the world's miseries.

For a second, despite the disorganised form of their singing and distance to the Hallowed Motherstorm, it seemed that She was listening. The rain slowed to a soft tapping, and even the shivering and squirming of some of the raving children eased.

Eventually, a dissonance crept into their song. The notes felt wrong, tilted off their axis, and Daerna's tenuous connection with the Motherstorm began ebbing away.

It was something about the place, as if the despair hanging in the air had thickened and, in a virulent reaction, was strangling sound itself. It was like swimming beneath the surface of a lagoon, its waters thick and dark, swallowing all light.

She resisted its pull, clinging to the song, reaching with her voice to the storm's tendrils far above. When an icy drop of rain fell on her face, she faltered. The water was cold, but worse than that, it felt greasy, tainted and devoid of the Motherstorm's purity. It was enough to make Daerna lose her concentration.

Once she faltered, the singing soon died out.

Exhausted, but also frustrated with her own inability to help, Daerna stepped outside to breathe and the others followed her. She saw Yaisa perched atop the upper deck and climbed to join her.

Not even there was she able to shake off the slimy heaviness suffocating her. It threatened to bring her down with the entire sagging structure.

Thinking of that, Daerna ran her eyes over the deck and, for the first time, noticed the mouldy cracks in it. They ran deep and dark and stretched down the sides and into the soil, seemingly into the hospice's very foundations.

'These cracks . . . have they always been there?' Daerna asked.

'I'm not sure,' Yaisa answered.

'Can you ask the caretakers?'

Yaisa went back downstairs to do so. While they waited, Roshia came over to examine them.

'What are you going on about?' Pierla asked.

'Don't you think they resemble the cracks in the Broken Arches?' Daerna asked.

'Cracks are squalor's adornments. Perhaps they're not a normal sight in Muirtra's *pristine* walls, but trust me, sooner or later, the Motherstorm's constant rain takes a toll on all buildings. And mould grows whenever there's darkness and water.'

'Pierla's probably right,' Roshia said, rubbing her chin. 'Though, I'd also swear that Agonea's hospice looks worse now than when we first arrived.'

'You're both imagining things,' Pierla snorted.

Yaisa returned shortly. 'We're in luck, one of the women was actually a woodworker. She said that the building has always been unstable and that they're going to have to reinforce the timber soon. Another reason to get these people out of here.'

'See? It's just the rain,' Pierla said.

Yaisa interjected, 'She also said the cracks and the rotting seem to have grown very quickly in the past two weeks. And that it came from below, from the foundations.'

'Even if that was true, what would that prove?' Pierla replied.

'I'm not sure . . .' Daerna struggled to explain herself. She was afraid of sounding like a fool. 'What if there was something external to the disease? What if it is breeding in these places?'

'You mean like a foul fume corrupting the air?' Roshia tried. 'It's true that these living conditions invite all sorts of them, but my parents are both trained physicians and they haven't found a clear explanation as to what sparks it. Which should concern us all. Lack of evidence isn't evidence of absence either.'

'Besides, wouldn't someone else have noticed if there was something like that?' Pierla asked.

'That's a good point.' Daerna turned to Roshia. 'Doesn't Muirtra keep records of those lost to the disease? If there's a pattern, there might be something to find.'

Roshia shook her head. 'I'm afraid our archives only compile the religious services where a Keening has been performed. There are the elevation dirges, but those are too poetic and vague to have the sort of specifics you need.'

'The Widowed Sisters might have something,' Pierla said, 'but I doubt it, given their current stance on the disease.'

'What about the Sisters of Silence?' Daerna asked.

Roshia nodded. 'The records of the Whisperers are extremely thorough. Perhaps if we could study their archives, we'd find something?'

'What was the name of the Whisperer that was with us at the Penance Procession?' Daerna asked.

'Indre, Indre of . . . Skala? I think,' Pierla replied.

'Would she help us?'

'I don't know. Lass has got nerve, that's for sure. You could try, I suppose.' Pierla shrugged.

For Daerna, it wasn't even a question. If they had a chance of fighting this at the root, they had to take it.

They left soon after, heading for the Central Quarter. They parted ways with Pierla near the Flowers Market. There was a post-house there that Daerna's mother used frequently.

In this part of the city, the decorations for the Ascent Carnival were magnificent. Even the ominous Dreamchanted lionheads of the Secret Chancellery had been crowned with garlands of purple and copper.

Luckily, the postmaster still had their table set in one of the square's corners. Daerna asked for pen and paper.

Dear S.Sl. Indre of Skala,

We don't know each other well, but your aid during our time together under Sister Naida's care hasn't gone unnoticed. I feel we share the same inclinations in change.

I wonder if you could aid me in finding something I seek in your abbey's records? There's something that could help a great deal in this city.

Your Sororal Servant,
S.S. Daerna Eimar

'It'll be delivered tomorrow morning,' the postmaster said.

Daerna had done what she could for now. While Roshia headed to her family practice in the Craghorn, she returned to the Muirtra for the evening Keening. She could tell Roshia was burning herself at both ends.

Daerna thought about begging her not to overexert herself. But truthfully: was she the best person to judge Roshia for doing whatever she thought necessary to help others?

Chapter Nineteen

Ash

The school shall train children between the ages of eight and fourteen, Onyxian born, poor and orphaned, for four years in the arts of piloting, seamanship and sea warfare, so the Domain can call on abundant and experienced sea-folk.

– Foundational Charter of the College of Seafarers

'EXPLAIN TO US, AESCYON, THE theories regarding the phenomenon of subtraction,' Lucre said from the front row of the lecture hall.

Blinded by the lantern on the stage, Ash couldn't see the audience but could feel their gazes. He clung to the lectern to disguise the trembling of his hands.

He understood the question, even knew the answer, but his throat went dry at the fear of misattributing their authors. Was Pheidios a Sculptorist? Or was he a Caster?

It wasn't the presence of his tutors that made him nervous. By now, he'd become accustomed to Josod's harsh reprimands and Thalder's snarky retorts. It was everything else. The strangers' gazes. The oppressive opulence of the College of Seafarers. The feeling that he'd stumbled into a trap.

The College of Seafarers was both guild and school. The powerful guild of sea captains, pilots and shipbuilders had its home in an imposing palace built by the city's large shipyards of the Western Quarter. Unlike other guilds, though, they didn't just train their members but had a school for orphans. All of this made them immensely influential and a critical part of the Reformers' power. Their Ascent feasts were renowned, and to be invited to them considered a high honour.

Dressed in a fine blue velvet doublet, fresh from the tailor, Ash had waltzed in as part of Lord Morvander's retinue. The guests, from guild captains to powerful Reformer senators, had welcomed him, and he'd been offered all kinds of delicacies, Valelander cheeses, Vespirian sweet wines and even pine-fruits from beyond the Furious Ocean, the vast expanse beyond the Walled Sea ruled only by the twin furies of the tempests above and the sea dragons below.

His fascination had soon led to unease, though. The lavishness of the meal sat wrong with him. Just yesterday he'd finally been able to visit his old garret, and despite Rudher's and Ghalod's jovial demeanour, they were still risking life and limb for the next lightning haul. Ash's money had allowed them to trade fishbone soup and crusts for fish pies and fresh bread, but extricating themselves from the draughty and damp garret was going to take more than that.

Nonetheless, he hid this discomfort. He'd been given a chance to remain free; the least he could do was to put up with this.

He'd mingled as he was expected to. He'd even shaken hands with some senators from the Reformer Party, who approached him when Lord Orles Brakte praised him publicly on several occasions.

He should have suspected there was a catch.

When one of the guildmasters suggested that Ash demonstrate what he'd learned in the past few weeks, instead of turning the offer down, Lord Brakte had quickly taken on the invitation and proposed they conduct a mock examination in the college's lecture halls.

To Ash's dismay, Lord Morvander and his tutors had been quick to agree. The event had soon drawn dozens of spectators, and Ash realised that if he failed, it'd reflect poorly not just on him but also on Morvander.

Thalder loudly cleared his throat. Ash had to answer with something.

'Well, there are three main theories to explain the phenomenon of subtraction. Pheidios's Sculptorist theory posits that the Dreaming mind carves matter in the same way a chisel removes rock, and that any subtracted matter is returned to its primal imaginary state in the Dreaming. Contrarily, proponents of the Casting school of thought argue that the removed matter is consumed, purged in the act of creation ...'

To his surprise, he remembered more than he'd thought.

He might have lacked the Oneirocrats' tutors growing up, but a lifetime of reading beside his father had compensated for that lack. He'd studied Lucre's suggested readings until his eyesight had blurred. He'd sacrificed seeing Daerna, seeing all his friends, for this.

Once he gained footing with his first answer, the ones that followed weren't as hard and he began speaking with more confidence.

'That's enough,' Lucre said after he'd successfully answered the fifth question. Her tone was hard to read, but Ash thought she sported a smirk of pride.

'Now, will you show us what you're working on, Ash?' Lord Brakte suggested, grinning eagerly.

'I haven't brought—' he began, the words dying in his throat as Balchod approached the stage with a satchel.

Clearly, the whole thing had been a set-up from the beginning.

He was retrieving his creation, a black stone egg, from the satchel when a commotion began at the back of the room. A group of newcomers had settled somewhere in the middle benches. Ash couldn't make them out in the chamber's darkness, but a guild servant ran down the stairs to announce their arrival.

Morvander and Brakte exchanged troubled looks, but Morvander gestured for Ash to begin.

Ash held the egg above the lectern. It was as large as his head, so he hoped everyone would be able to see it. He pulled it to his lips and whispered, 'Open your eyes . . .'

The only reply was a pecking sound from inside. Cobalt-blue cracks spread over the egg's upper half as its inhabitant fought its way out.

Ash held his breath, at least until he saw the falcon's head emerge. It was more beautiful than he'd anticipated, its plumage gleaming aquamarine under the lamplight. It craned its head, curious, then let out a piercing cry as it spread its wings, tearing the rest of the egg apart.

Omen jolted awake from his slumber at Thalder's side. Feline eyes fixated on the gleaming bird, and Ash feared he'd underestimated his friend's predatory instinct, but Thalder grabbed him by the scruff.

'Take flight!' Ash commanded.

Free from the shell, the falcon took to the hall's darkened heights. It circled above the audience's heads a few times before swooping back to the stage to perch atop the lantern hanging at the centre.

'It seems that your bird was born tired!' Josod called, eliciting some chuckles from the audience.

Ash felt a cold sweat run down his spine. 'It's landed there because it can sense the lightning.'

'You mean it's seen the lamp?' Lord Brakte asked, arching a golden eyebrow.

'No – I mean, yes! There's more to it. Its brain senses the movement of the storm and smells the lightning before it happens.'

'To guide Lightning-Hunters?' ventured Lucre.

'Yes, yes, precisely! Part of the problem for the Lightning-Hunters is knowing where the lightning will strike.'

'Doesn't it always strike on rooftops?' Josod objected. 'What difference does it make?'

'The difference between a bountiful hunt or an empty purse,' Ash said, stretching his arm. 'Here!'

The falcon swooped down to land on his arm.

'What's the point of it understanding verbal commands it won't hear in the thick of the storm?' Josod asked, unfazed.

'It understands the Vespirian whistling tongue too.'

'The bird can work as a language tutor if everything else fails,' Josod scoffed.

Ash hadn't expected them to clap, but shouldn't they be at least somewhat impressed? A month ago, he wouldn't have been able to Dream something this delicate and complex.

'How long did it take you to craft this?' Lord Brakte asked.

'A month, I think.'

'A month!' Brakte snorted. 'Imagine . . . a month of your work to sell it to the Lightning-Hunters' Guild for how much? Fifty Onars? One hundred?'

'That's about right.' Ash was briefly encouraged by that. One hundred Onars still sounded like a fortune to him – Brakte's frown clearly said otherwise.

'That might be a lot for a lazy Lightning-Hunter, but it's a waste of a Dreamer's time. If you want to make something beautiful, you might as well Dream something that sells for at least a thousand Onars! For that, it must be something that will serve those with money. Imagine what you could Dream for the Seafarer's College, or the merchant houses.'

As the hall filled with murmurs of assent, Ash's nervousness slowly gave way to simmering disgust. Of course, through the lens of wealth, the fortuneless were invisible.

He looked at Thalder for support, but his tutor was grimacing as if he'd seen a ghost, at the sight of a stranger striding confidently towards Ash. No doubt he was some powerful Oneirocrat, given not just his armed escort but the way shadows trailed him like a cloak.

'Master Davorles, you honour us with your presence!' Lord Morvander said.

Ash squinted, trying to make the man out as he came closer. He wore a sober earth-coloured surcoat. A painstakingly pencilled beard framed a vulpine smirk. Behind him, two guards with grey leather masks followed. Stone-Masks, the Secret Chancellery's enforcers.

'It's Vice-Chancellor of Secrets now, my lord. But it gladdens me to hear that you remember my service at the Academy. I have very fond memories of your daughter . . . Now, with your permission, may I offer the young man some hard-won wisdom?'

Lord Morvander nodded, and Vice-Chancellor Davorles walked onto the stage. He was imposing, not because of his gangly physique but because of the way the air felt murky around him. His grey-green eyes fell on Ash. 'Allow me to see for myself,' he said, and then called the bird to his gloved left arm. After a brief examination, he muttered, 'Beautiful feathers.'

'Thank you, my lord,' Ash replied.

The man waved one of his gloved hands, and suddenly a tendril sprang from his cloak to engulf the falcon. Trapped in what looked like a dark sphere, the falcon fell to the floor with a heavy thunk.

The solid orb sat there, unmoving, and Ash's heart froze with horror. 'What have you done?' he gasped.

'It's not dead.' The man smiled. 'But it will be soon if you don't free it.' Ash could hear the falcon wriggling and pecking violently inside the sphere.

Ash knelt and seized the globe, shaking it, searching for an opening. He punched at it, but it was hard as metal. He'd only managed to hurt his hand.

'Omen!' he called, and this time Thalder let the panther go.

The Stone-Masks reached for their swords, but Lord Davorles cried, 'Let it through!'

Omen approached. Once again, the panther's mind seemed to pick up on Ash's intentions instinctively. He clawed at the sphere, sending it spinning away. At least the panther had cracked it, Ash saw, picking up the orb.

'Again!' he commanded. If Omen missed, he might slice some of his fingers, but to the entombed hells with them if they thought he was going to let the falcon suffocate for their amusement.

Omen stilled, as if calculating. Then, rising on his hindquarters, he delivered a blow that fell like thunder. This time, his claws tore through one side of the sphere, slicing it open. The falcon immediately hopped out and took to the air, battered and terrified but still alive.

Breathing heavily, Ash looked up at Lord Davorles. 'I don't understand . . .'

The man stepped back, addressing the entire room like a lecturer. 'May this serve you as a lesson. You gave it fancy feathers when you *should* have given it sharp claws. Your feeble bird was an ornament, not a predator. Lucky for you, your other creation has proved closer to the truth.'

'The truth?' Ash repeated.

Davorles turned back to face him, and for the first time, his smile reached his grey-green eyes.

'The truth is that Master Thalder should have taught you better. Your other tutors talk a lot about money and aesthetic value, but their Dreams are fragile. The truth is that for everything of beauty, there's a Nightmare growing in its shadow. Strength can yield to beauty or trample it, and yet fear rules them both. Because fear can sway and command, because it can grow even in the absence of what caused it. That is the truth.'

'With all due respect, my lord, shouldn't it be capable of doing more than one thing?' Ash tried to stay composed, his stomach taut with anxiety.

'A blade wielded for too many tasks soon loses its sharpness. Lord Morvander would do better by sending you to the Academy.'

Brakte glared at Davorles but said nothing.

'I'm sure my apprentice will thank you for such fine advice. As for now, it's apparent that he has much left to learn,'

Morvander said. He sounded colder than usual. Probably disappointed by the spectacle Ash had offered, and that hurt him more than any of Josod's remarks.

'Thank you, my lords,' Ash said, hiding his flushed face with a deep bow.

It was all over then. Vice-Chancellor Davorles left, and the audience melted away with relief. Morvander and Lord Brakte soon followed. Ash watched them depart from the floor. Only Lucre bade him farewell with a sympathetic look.

In the now-silent room, he called the falcon to him. The creature flew back to his arm. He'd been a fool to think they'd treat it with anything more than cruelty. Like many in this city, it deserved something better. It deserved to be free.

Not that he could provide any of that with his crude skills and poor imagination. He wasn't even free himself.

Oneirocrats' only interest in nature was how to tear it apart and replace it with a set of sharp, soulless tools. If he was to endure here, he'd have to become another tool for them, a prospect that nauseated him.

He was gathering his things when he realised someone hadn't left the room.

'Where are you going, boy?' Thalder asked gruffly.

'I have plans . . .' He'd barely seen Daerna in weeks and felt the distance between them growing inexorably larger by the day. Same went for his crew.

Thalder scoffed. 'You clearly haven't understood *anything* of what's happened here today. It's not good that Davorles has taken an interest in you.'

'Friend of yours?' Ash asked.

'Not precisely,' replied Thalder with disgust. 'They say the Wisp dances with the Reformers these days; I don't think a scorpion like him changes his poison so easily. What you should be wondering is, if a "friend" of ours has been so harsh with you, what do you think you can expect at your dispensation exam?'

Ash snorted angrily.

Thalder went on: 'You know what we have in abundance in the jet-black city? Bitterness, rain and people full of themselves.' Thalder paused. 'Like you, Ash.'

'What are you saying? I'm *nothing* like them!' Ash glared at him.

'You hearing yourself? Who's "them"? The Oneirocrats? The merchants? The powerful?'

'Aren't they all one and the same?'

'Do you want to pity yourself? Go ahead! Sog yourself in wine while you're at it, just share the bottle.'

'Enlighten me then! What's so wrong with me?'

'Simple, boy. You still treat the world as if you were a scorned lover. You think that you know better than the Valelands' soft lords and ladies because you don't soil your imagination with utilitarian concerns. You think you know better than that sadist Davorles because you realise there's more to the world than cruelty and strength. And you're right. However, that doesn't make them *wrong* either. Onyxia's Domain is maintained by Onars and Nightmares. What you have is as much a curse as it is a blessing.'

'You mean Dreaming?'

'No, *imagination*, and by that I mean a will to think for yourself. The way they see it, wanting to think for yourself is an act of defiance against them. Their natural "order" of things isn't meant to be questioned. Those of us who do, whether by thinking, speaking or just plain existing, better get ready for what's coming.'

'So I should stop questioning things? Go with the current? That's why nothing ever changes!'

'No, I'm saying that if you're going to be a little *arseling*, you'd better start learning to hold your own in a fight. And I don't mean with your fists, although that doesn't hurt. Having powerful friends like Lord Morvander draws powerful enemies, and they never play fair. Do you think what happened today was chance?'

'What, the Academy set up that ambush for me?'

'Not for you, you big-headed ox! They used you to get to Lord Morvander and Lord Brakte!'

'But why?'

'With a new council coming, even allies are flexing their muscles and jockeying for power. They'll use you to get to Lord Morvander. Worse, they'll use others to get to you. At least with the gift, you have a shot at protecting them, at keeping yourself alive. But you need to be ready . . . which will be the point of today's lesson.' As Thalder said this, he undid his sword-belt and handed Ash his weapon.

'Today's lesson?'

'To teach you to defend yourself. Because they're coming. With all their might.'

Chapter Twenty

Geil

The Ascent Day ceremony, on account of its splendour and the vast concourse of people attracted by it, constitutes the chief and most pompous festival to be seen in Onyxia. Beginning at the Guardian's Arch, the waterborne parade celebrates not only the Solemn Princess's raising of the city from the waters but also her great vanquishing of the Pale Prince and the Charnel Mother.

– *Portraits of the Onyxians* by Kairik of Fredsen

ONCE THE *NIGHT SWAN* HAD reached the skies above the Central Quarter's plateau, Geil changed the opacity of the hull with a wave of her bracelet, turning the floor translucent.

Below, the jet-black city shone like a constellation. The Ascent Carnival parade was in full swing. Every barge and gondola was bejewelled with gleaming lamps, and they were all converging on the Princess Canal that cut the city between the Eastern and Western Quarters. From up here, it looked like a drunken fire Drake dancing down the canal's length.

At each bend, the crowd pressed together, cheering the dallying barges. In turn, the paraders gifted them with songs, candied figs, garlands, lead medals of illustrious personages and, on rare occasions, Dreamchanted mirages.

The barges slowed at the Guardian's Arch, allowing the masked revellers to toast the colossal winged lion sculpted into it. Tradition had it that those blessed by the Solemn Princess's Guardian would be safe from harm until the next Ascent Carnival.

Around the *Night Swan*, other skyships loomed in the evening sky, teeming with the wealthiest Oneirocrats' entourages. Geil's was the rare exception, almost empty.

The Drake turned restlessly inside her skin, yearning to flee the cacophony of sound and lights below, itching for the still darkness of the hunt – or perhaps just the freedom from human stupidity and ritual.

That's what the wine was for, to muffle the Drake's complaints while she showed public support of House Morvander for Puglius Zerandra, and implicitly, Lady Saorla's Reformers. She was here for Ragdra.

With that consideration, she filled her cup again.

A bronze skysloop glided into view, flying white banners with an embroidered golden star, Lady Saorla's house emblem.

That was her cue. Geil hurried to the pilot's deck, where the captain kept watch over the wheel.

'Please bring us to the side of Lady Saorla's skyship. Slowly, so everyone can see.'

Geil hastened to the prow to get a better look at the deck. It teemed with guards and servants, wearing elegant nacred uniforms. Dreamlings with amethyst skin moved back and forth from the celebration tent to the lower decks.

Through the open curtains of the tent, Geil made out the guests. Many were Reformer senators she'd met last week on Nacre Island. Puglius Zerandra was there, his red beard visible under the golden horns and golden beak of his mask, laughing with exaggerated movements.

Someone else caught Geil's eye: the harpist in a snowy-silver silk dress playing near the prow.

Her slender neck bore a close-fitted pearl necklace with a central golden star-shaped medallion that matched her heavy earrings, her face hidden beneath a pearled half-mask; despite that, Geil recognised Liadra by the long golden braid trailing over one shoulder.

As Geil's skysloop descended to the same level, she readied herself, smoothing the wave-like wrinkles of her dark blue doublet with sweaty palms.

Instead of waiting for the servants to lay a bridge for her, she jumped on the gunwale and, from there, leapt towards the other ship.

It was a reckless way to make an entrance, but precisely what the Drake wanted.

Geil landed with a cat's grace on the opposite deck, rising with a smile, and found herself surrounded by Saorla's startled squires.

'Stop right there, ruffian!' A towering squire violently seized her shoulder.

'I'm here as Lady Saorla's guest,' she replied coldly.

'I very much doubt it,' the man snarled.

Flaring with anger, the Drake punched him in the face.

The other guards shouted and drew their rapiers, but a woman stepped between them. 'Stop! She's indeed our guest!'

It was Lady Liadra, Ines Saorla's sister. Her face was as radiant as Geil remembered it from the night beneath the stars.

The men backed away, offering ashamed apologies and bows. Geil waved them off while she focused on reining in the furious Drake.

Liadra was clearly mortified by what had happened. 'I'm so very sorry, Lady Geil . . .'

'I shouldn't have startled them,' Geil offered with a conciliatory smile. 'Not that any Exarchian assassin would fall from the heavens, I hope.'

'No, no, it's just that with the renovation of the High Council imminent, tempers are high. Not a week ago, some Blue-capped agitators assaulted one of our senators' palanquins with stones. And just yesterday there was a quarrel at the Crown Bridge between our supporters and theirs. Two men ended up stabbed. This is why my sister keeps me mostly out of sight.'

'That explains why I had such a hard time placing you when we met,' Geil replied.

'Who did you think I was?'

'I don't know what I thought. Some philosopher or poet? It's rare to hear a highborn advocate for the opening of literacy schools for the commoners. Rarer even to hear someone care to arm them with understanding.'

Liadra's laughter was like her voice: ethereal, high-pitched and melodious.

'That was quite the entrance! What a delight it is to see you again, my lady,' Lecturer Puglius Zerandra greeted her. He'd waltzed into their conversation, wearing an open jerkin that left little to the imagination. 'And immediately you begin speaking of arming the commoners,' he said, amused.

'Don't you think it ambitious, Master Zerandra?' Geil asked.

'It is indeed ambitious! But ambition alone rarely stirs the hearts of the senators, Lady Geil.' He twisted his mouth despondently.

'It stirs my heart and those of the Susurrus. I thought you wanted our support.'

He cleared his throat, taken aback by the comment. 'Your Ladyship misjudges me. I believe in the nobility of your purpose, but consider this: there's a reason why the schooling of commoners is left to the guilds and Sisterhoods. Who'd pay for it otherwise?'

'The High Treasurer's coffers seem capable enough of paying for the Academy's voraciousness, not to mention two universities,' Geil retorted.

'Your Ladyship would be surprised how difficult it is for the Treasury to keep meeting its obligations as it is. And it's mostly the merchants who pay for our universities. As for the Academy, you well know that the Senate can afford their excesses in exchange for the protection they offer the Domain.'

Clearly, she'd come ill prepared for this conversation, while Puglius seemed to be enjoying himself. Like a master duellist sparring with a clumsy child. Still, she wasn't going down without a fight, not when a group had gathered to listen to them.

'More educated minds will bring more Dreamers. Don't you think that a good protection of the Domain?' Geil tried.

'You know well that the Traditionalists believe the Dreaming gift runs in the blood. "Just like with currency," they'd argue, "by increasing its number, you devalue its worth."'

Zerandra went on, pontificating about the best way to entice the Senate to reinforce the schooling already offered by the guilds and strengthening the existing universities.

Then, Liadra interrupted, 'What about creating literacy schools and libraries in every city of the Domain? And new universities for Dreamers too?'

'Your Ladyship surely jests! Commoners need trades, not lessons in philosophy. Not to mention the cost would be astronomical. And what would be the point of creating specific universities just for Dreamers? It seems to me that there's enough knowledge at the Academy and in the Valelander guilds.'

'That's precisely the problem!' Liadra exclaimed. 'Dreaming could be far more than Nightmare-Hunting or Delight-Forging, yet we keep following the same old paths set down by the ancient guilds. As for the cost, if we have more Dreamers, they'll create more wealth. Even better, you could save some Onars by reforming the Academy and transforming it into a university!'

Geil let out a delighted chortle at that.

'Even if you—' He tried to cut in, but Liadra pretended not to hear. The group that had gathered around them nodded along with her.

'As for how to stir the enthusiasm of the senators, consider how it'd greatly benefit the Domain to train people in literacy for speedier communications, more qualified scribes, a greater pool of administrative staff to support the Domain's growth.' As she said it, her eyelashes fluttered, and she lowered her gaze, appearing suddenly and deliberately demure. 'Of course, it's a simple idea. I'm sure you can polish it with the varnish of your accrued wisdom, Lord Zerandra.'

Geil was trapped by her eyes, not just the way they shined but what set them aflame. She found herself wanting to gaze deeper into them, to see what else they saw.

A roar rose from the canal below, and the conversation cut short as all the guests craned over the gunwale.

Geil joined them and spotted the reason for the excitement. A chariot rode the canals, pulled by a colossal creature. It slithered through the water like a bloated sea-drake, except many heads emerged when it reared. Unlike a hydra's, all its faces were different: one, that of a snake-like eel with unending rows of sharp fangs; another, a dark stallion with aquamarine eyes that breathed fire; a third one bellowing from its blind, horned maw. Each monstrosity was fearsome and magnificent, but most impressive was that they inhabited the same body. There was no question that this was Lord Stalcar's design. The Regent Admiral was not known as the Leviathan-Maker for nothing.

The man in the chariot wasn't him but his son, Beiros of Lorn. He whipped the beast with a lash of fire, and the Nightmare obediently coiled to a sudden halt, sending a wave ahead as if even the water were afraid of it.

The heads bellowed, roared and neighed, only to then sink into silence. The crowd went still with astonishment, but after a heartbeat, even those who'd got splashed cheered the

Leviathan-Maker's name. This was a show of strength. His reminder that he was Regent Admiral because of his supreme ability to rule over the waves through his own horde of sea-leviathans.

Beiros waved at them with a smile and then looked up and blew a kiss.

Liadra waved back.

'A close friend?' Geil asked.

'In a manner of speaking,' Liadra replied.

'More of a suitor, I take?' Geil asked, feigning mere curiosity.

'Such a match would make *many* happy, I can tell you that,' Liadra whispered, rolling her eyes.

Geil remembered Lord Stalcar and Lady Saorla speaking privately at the party; had this been part of their discussions? 'I suppose it would unite the Domain's two most powerful households,' she said, turning her body so that the two of them could speak privately.

'Don't get me wrong, I want peace. I just think it's naive to believe all this quarrelling will stop because of one marriage. The rift runs far deeper than that. A marriage could seal a peace between our factions, but how is it to be reached? What compromises will be made?'

'And what do *you* want?' Geil asked.

'I might lack the gift, yet I feel there are ways in which I could serve my family other than being married away for some dubious alliance,' Liadra admitted bitterly.

'That's why I joined the Academy as soon as I could, and later became a Herald.' Geil sighed. 'I figured that if I found a purpose early on, I'd spare my grandmother the temptation of marrying me away to some lord or lady interested in climbing the ladder thanks to the Kerentes name.'

'I envy that you were given the freedom to do so,' Liadra said longingly. 'I've begged Ines to allow me to become more involved in politics, but she refuses.'

'She doesn't trust her own sister?'

'It's not like that. She just thinks that a head held too high is a target for arrows.'

'Can't say I disagree with her.'

Liadra's hands curled into fists. 'But there's so much that needs to be done, so much I could help with!'

Geil found herself smiling. Curiosity got the better of her. 'Why does education interest you?' she asked.

'My family isn't without failings, but if Ines has risen the way she has, it's in no small part because we both attended university at Arvira. Lecturer Zerandra knows this even if he won't admit it. To learn a trade is valuable, yet it should be a choice. I do believe the gift is found more frequently among the highborn only because we're afforded the luxury of having time for our minds to roam freely. It's the confluence of true passion and technique that sparks Dreamers.'

Geil nodded, but remained quiet.

'Do you know what I'd like to see?' Liadra said passionately, her eyes glittering once more. 'A thousand schools! We have two universities, three if you count Damlan's, but most people can't afford them. We should be Dreaming schools to elevate the talents of the Undreaming. A thousand schools to reach every corner of the Domain!'

'A thousand schools indeed!' Geil repeated with glee. 'I say that you'd be a better High Sage than many others.'

'You do me great honour, Lady Geil. My sister would never agree, though,' she replied.

'Perhaps, but then again, you seem like a woman who gets what she wants.'

'You don't know the half of it,' Liadra said, shooting Geil a mischievous grin and leaning closer. Her perfume of roses went straight to Geil's head.

Another roaring cheer rose from the canal. Lady Saorla's barges had arrived, and the crowd chanted her moniker. 'Starspun Maiden!'

With a wave of Lady Saorla's arm, birds made of light floated from a dozen coffers, filling the canal like shooting stars. They flew directly into the hands of the crowd, where they sang melodious songs. Some shifted their forms to become gleaming jewels, others turned into ripe fruits. Some even laced their tails around arms, becoming strands of exquisite golden silk. The display of sheer power and Dreamcraft was impressive in and of itself, but more importantly, trinkets or not, all these things were valuable gifts.

The crowd roared in adoration. They might have admired Lord Stalcar's Nightmare, but as they screamed Lady Saorla's name, Geil saw why the Traditionalists hated and feared her so much.

'Isn't it beautiful?' Liadra asked.

'It is . . . but also reckless . . . Nothing beautiful lasts long in this city.'

That had been the way of every prized thing in her life, except perhaps for her father. Or maybe this was melancholy speaking, too deeply rooted in her bones for her to grow anything other than sadness in her heart.

'Perhaps this time,' Liadra whispered, taking Geil's hand, 'it'll be different.'

Maybe it was her touch, heady as wine, but Geil dared hope that, for once, it would be.

* * *

That night, when she walked into her room, Geil's mind was still at the parade. She walked the elated walk of someone steered by their heart and fell into her bed, her insides still as warm as melted wax.

It wasn't just the wine that had gone to her head, but all the bright ideas she and Liadra had discussed.

Moreover, her forearm bore the touch of Liadra's fingertips, like prints in the sand, a vibrant, sparkling sensation.

Then she noticed the letter in her message bowl. It was unsigned on the outside.

She forced herself out of bed and opened it.

I haven't forgotten Lanteus. I hope you haven't either. Sunset. The Last Bridge. Two days from now. Reparations must be made. -M

Mavis, their Talon-mate. She'd avoided him since returning home, but it was clear he was intent on talking to her.

She tossed the letter aside and tried to hide in the memory of Liadra's sweet touch, but even that wasn't enough to shake the ashes that the letter had blown into her heart. In Onyxia, the dead might burn, but the past rarely burned with them.

Chapter Twenty-One

Daerna

Only through faithful dedication to silence will we protect the Sorrowfuls's stories.

Yet this wilful burden knows of exceptions: speak if you must, with few words and with quiet voices; speak too, Sisters, about matters affecting the work. Speak especially when listening to those recounting loss. For one to understand, one must indeed ask questions.

– The Precepts of Blessed Elpia for a Life in Silence

DAERNA COULD HEAR THE CROWDS roar from the Princess Canal. She and Roshia had left before the grand finale, racing through the deserted bridges and canalways.

After the Oneirocrats' parade finished, the Orders' barges would carry gifts and offerings to the lagoon in honour of Divine Geleisdra's raising of the Onyxian bedrock from the depths.

This was the climax of the Ascent Festival's parade and an important occasion for the abbesses. There would be much Keening and speeches at such an important celebration, which gave them at least two hours unseen.

The Silent Abbey's spires rose up from the star-shaped building like a skeletal hand grasping the Susurrus's skies, their lack of Keening cages a testament to the Whispering Sisters' silent work.

The Wailers' Keening touched the Motherstorm Herself while the Widows' charity cared for the people, but only the Sisters of Silence could offer everlasting remembrance. At their locutories, anyone could recount their life with the certainty that they'd be recorded and kept forever. Those archives were precisely what they sought.

Indre had written back that she was willing to hear them. Yet first they needed to get to her.

They hurriedly entered the abbey's nave. Tonight, the row of wooden locutories on the latticed wall facing them stood deserted. They knelt on one of the hassocks, and Daerna rang the calling bell.

A Whisperer opened the locutory window from within, her worn-out tunic almost as grey as her hair. She sized them up warily, pursing her white-painted lips, the symbol of their consecration to Blessed Elpia's precepts for silence. Such were the harsh strictures that merited them their position as scribes of the world's sorrows, something Daerna had always deeply respected.

'Hallowed Ascent, Sister!' Daerna said. 'We bring a life testimony to consign to Sister Indre of Skala.'

Through the grille, the Whisperer searched for a letter in Daerna's hands. Not finding it, she huffed.

'Sister Indre has other duties tonight.'

'Is that so? One of our superiors at Muirtra asked us to request her exquisite calligraphy.'

The old Sister arched a snowy eyebrow then let out a sigh. 'Wait here.'

'Or perhaps you could lead us to her? I've always wanted to admire your marvellous temple from within.' Daerna offered her most reassuring smile. She knew their plan dangled on a thin thread.

'Come, then. Behave with respect.'

The Sister opened the small wooden doors reserved for visitors on the right side of the latticed screen separating the nave from the inner sanctum, then led them inside.

Both the Silent Abbey and Muirtra had been built at the same time with the archipelago's onyx. Except this design was Blessed Elpia's, one of the Solemn Princess's followers who'd Dreamt it as a secure place for her disciples to archive all records of the suffering masses' sorrows.

The ancient abbey's narrow passages spiralled inwards, and they struggled to follow the old Sister. Several layers of books lined every wall, while only a handful of thickly caged orb-lamps lit the dark corridors.

The scribes' hall at the abbey's heart, in contrast, was vast, populated by hundreds of work desks. Tonight, because of the festival, it was empty except for a lone pale figure at her desk: Sister Indre.

She gestured for them to approach and sit with her, then silently watched their guide with narrowed eyes until she left.

'I agreed to help. What is it you need?' Indre muttered through her painted lips.

'We've been working with those afflicted by the Wilting, and we thought we could ask you for help tracing its origins.'

Since Sister Indre didn't reply, Roshia went on. 'The records,' she said, her sunken eyes lighting up. 'Muirtra's archives hold records only of our canticles and the religious rituals we perform: birth and wedding blessings, funerals and memorials. Your Order records everything, especially deaths and testimonies about their circumstances, correct?'

'Blessed Elpia demands thoroughness,' Indre conceded in her raspy voice. 'What do you need my help for?'

'We need someone who knows the archives to find what we seek, someone we can trust,' Daerna said.

Indre rubbed her chalky chin with ink-stained fingers. 'You think you can trust me?'

'Sister Indre, I don't presume to know you, but I can imagine that you were at the Penance Procession for the same reasons we were.'

'And what reason would that be?' She massaged her fingers, which cracked loudly.

'Because you ask your own questions.'

Indre's eyes narrowed with interest, and Daerna pressed on. 'You've seen the Charnel Mother's followers thriving in the Southern Quarter. We believe it's because the Wilting has spread deeper than anyone truly knows. Worse, even though the Widowed Sisters know the gravity of the problem, they've been ordered to ignore it.'

Indre's hands stilled. 'A serious accusation, Sister Daerna.' Her eyes wandered over her chewed nails as she pondered their request. Finally, she took a deep breath. 'What would you need to prove it?'

'Anything regarding the circumstances surrounding those who passed to the Wilting. Where they lived, worked, and how many recorded cases there have been.'

Indre fetched a journal chain-bound to her desk, scribbled something into it, then set to checking the shelves. Within minutes, she placed tome after tome on their table. As it turned out, the Sisters of Silence had a formidable indexation system: their registry books were written with Dreamchanted ink that linked them to compilations and records. The journal Indre used listed the ledgers that the words they sought were contained in.

In less than an hour, they'd pulled and consulted a hundred different records on Wilting-related deaths. The majority were the sparse obituaries recounted by the Widows after funerary rites, but a dozen were true memorial accounts of lives. Sadly, if Daerna had hoped for details on the dwellings of the afflicted to confirm her suspicions, she was soon disappointed.

The accounts described squalid dwellings or impoverished conditions, but nothing else. Luckily, Roshia's keen eyes found something else.

'The accounts, they keep growing in number. Decades ago, cases were but a dozen per year, but they've increased since. Just in the past three months, there have been almost three hundred recorded deaths! And look at how it's spread.'

Daerna glanced at the list that Roshia had noted.

The notations were sparse, but looking at Roshia's compilation of registries, it seemed evident that the disease wasn't just growing rampant but also that it had a clear focal point in the Scab.

'There are deaths reported as far north as the Susurrus, but over two-thirds come from the Scab. One-third alone comes from an area called Hollowshrine,' Roshia explained excitedly. 'And now guess: where did the first victims live?'

'Hollowshrine?' Daerna ventured.

'Exactly!'

'The timing, the concentration of cases . . . They both suggest that some initial spark started in the Southern Quarter. How could this have been missed?' Daerna pondered.

'Perhaps it wasn't,' Indre said, holding one of the index books.

The registry was exhaustive, and Daerna would have got lost if Indre hadn't pointed at a certain line.

There, the index referenced something other than the Whispering Sisters' records: a decree from the Consistory of Sisters Superior, which included a portent from the Warden Sisters.

'Pierla told us that the Superiors had decreed the Widows were to stop administering assistance to those afflicted with the Wilting, but what's this about a portent?' asked Daerna.

'It comes from Divine Damnia's Silver Book. Sometimes they consult it in search of guidance,' Indre explained.

The Silver Book wasn't just a sacred symbol, it held a trove of holy wisdom. Some university scholars even argued that it'd been control of the Silver Book, and not that of the crown, that led to the Sibling Strife.

'I thought it took years to decipher a single one of the book's hallowed mysteries,' Roshia said.

'A select few Wardens train for this, from what I understand. They serve as oracles and decipher the Silver Book's portents,' Indre said. 'Sometimes they even advise the Consistory of Superiors and the High Council on spiritual matters.'

'So someone has noticed after all! Why ask them to consult the Silver Book otherwise?' Daerna surmised. 'Where is this portent?'

'According to this, the original writ is kept in the Warden's Abbey on the Solemn Isle.' Indre chewed on her thin cheeks while she kept searching. 'It looks like our vault also holds a copy . . .'

'Is there any way to consult it?'

Indre stared at Daerna. 'Only Sister Archivists are allowed inside. To enter its guarded halls is nigh impossible. Just the attempt would carry severe punishments.'

Daerna sighed loudly. They were so close. 'What if this portent explains why they've decided to ignore the problem?'

Indre snorted. 'We'd still need the master key, the one hanging from the Sister Provisioner's neck.'

Indre stood and headed to the elevated desk that oversaw the room. On her way, she picked up a chisel. Climbing onto the dais, she put one hand on a chest that sat on the table.

'Fortunately for you, tonight of all nights, the Sister Provisioner is at the festival, and I know where she keeps her keys.' Indre stuck the tip of the chisel into the lock. 'Now you two keep watch while I get it for us.'

* * *

The vault's entrance was at the bottom of a staircase behind the scribes' hall. The gate was solid steel, thick as walls and tall as trees. An ornate bas-relief of a lush garden covered its surface, but there was no apparent lock.

Indre efficiently felt her way around the carvings until she found a cavity inside the furrows of an engraved bush. There was hidden a metal lock that one could only reach by putting their arm inside.

'It looks . . . uninviting,' Roshia said.

'Blessed Elpia Dreamt this gate to be the first guardian of the Order's vault. The key reaches the lock, but *she* must deem you worthy of admittance. It'll recognise me as but a novice. Perhaps you'll have better luck,' Indre replied.

Daerna held out her hand for the key. 'I'll try.'

She took a deep breath and inserted her arm into the passage. The gap was as cold as the lagoon's waters in winter.

As she struggled to turn the key, she heard a sudden rustling of leaves. The bas-relief shifted, as if ruffled by a gust of wind.

'What's happening?' Daerna asked.

'Hold still under the gate's gaze,' was Indre's vague reply.

Daerna felt an icy finger run up her spine until it reached the back of her head. There it sank into her skull and blossomed into a thought.

Daerna's mind's eye opened in a stone chamber, where an ornate chimney's fire had just died, leaving only embers.

She was seated on an old stool of ancient design by a dusty floor harp. A woman stood by her side. Even in the grey penumbra, she shone with her own light. Her long russet fingers reached out, pointing to the harp's metallic strings.

'There are songs written on these strands of silver.'

Something about her was familiar. She wore an ancient tunic of exquisite make: a veritable garden of winding silk brambles and lush pomegranates. The diadem around her black braids was crowned by a topaz that glowed like her eyes.

Just like Blessed Elpia was portrayed in effigies and paintings.

'Now show me,' the woman said in a deep, steely voice. She stood impervious to the rain, to the rustling of shadows, to the growing whispers.

Daerna wasn't skilled at playing the harp, but she'd studied enough music to try. She fought to play the chords. They resisted her, the sharp metal piercing her fingertips. It took blood, but she managed to make them sing.

A loud metallic click followed, and the gate opened wide. Daerna barely had the time to jerk her arm away before the door pulled her with it.

'Are you alright? What happened?' Roshia asked, pointing at two droplets of blood on Daerna's wrist.

A sudden breathlessness hit Daerna. Had this been a vision, a miracle or just delirium? Whatever it was, explanations could wait. 'Later,' she replied.

She traded Indre the key for the orb-lamp. Another set of stairs awaited, sharply descending downwards . . . into the deep core of the Susurrus's rocky bed. There was no way to close the gate behind them.

'At least we won't get trapped inside,' Roshia said.

'Yes, but we must hurry. As soon as somebody sees it like this . . .' Indre trailed off.

They descended as fast as the light allowed them. The place was dark as a crypt, but at least there were clear signs of usage on the baroque engravings.

'Thank you for helping us, Indre,' Daerna said.

'Thank me? Thank providence, Daerna.' Her blue eyes burned fervently. 'You've led us through the gate. I thought I'd never get another chance.'

'You've entered this place before? What for?' Daerna asked.

'What do you know of the books on the Dreaming of the dead?'

'Necromantic tomes? The vault holds copies of them?' she asked, uneasy.

'You'd be surprised what the restricted section of the vault holds.' Indre curled her lips. 'My Order possesses extensive chronicles on the Sibling Strife and the depredations of the Pale Prince's host and his Charnel Mother. We preserve them because they're knowledge of the enemy, and also of what was. Some are written on dead leaves, some etched in flayed skins.

Some are even carved in marble slabs from Ravkiria, the old imperial capital itself, if you believe the tales.'

Just mention of the old city that had become a hellish, entombed prison sent shivers down Daerna's spine.

'Why are you interested in them?'

Indre stared into the distance. 'I was barely a woman when the Faengrians raided Skala. They killed my parents and all my siblings. I joined the Order to preserve their memories, their stories. Last year I found mention of books that said that I could do more than weep for them, more than wait for Divine Geleisdra's return. I wanted to read them, to see for myself what was meant by that.'

Daerna felt Roshia's concerned glance and ignored it. That Necromancy was soul-condemning heresy was clear. Yet if reading heretical texts helped Indre bear her grief, who was she to judge? Daerna too was ignoring her own strictures.

Passing through two massive wrought-iron gates standing ajar, they entered a subterranean basilica, as large as if not larger than the abbey above. It was a gargantuan archive. Colossal columns stood like giants hunched by the immense weight of the vault they held, caught in an almost infinite web of wood and metal. The thousands of shelves probably held millions and millions of records and books.

'The code is old, different from the one in Muirtra,' Roshia said, trying to read the plaques on the shelves. 'How will we find anything in here?'

'Follow me.' Indre navigated the maze by following the plaques' cryptic notations. Finally, she pointed to an ornate wooden shelf, bent like an ancient oak, at the end of an aisle. 'This is the one. Up there.'

Daerna climbed a wooden ladder until she reached the correct height. She focused her eyes on the task at hand, ignoring how far the floor was, skimming over the dozens of scrolls there, all sealed with silver ribbons and arranged by date.

Finding the one she was looking for, she brought it down with her. Indre had seemingly vanished, looking for her own forbidden text. At least she'd left the lamp behind, which Roshia was now holding. They both set to reading the scroll.

They'd expected the decree to contain some arid theological discussion, but to their surprise, it began with the summary of the portent the Warden Sisters had gathered consulting the Silver Book:

As feared, the plague afflicting Hollowshrine and beyond isn't new; it springs from the same fracture that tore apart the Garden District a century ago.

The book revealed to us that this too is one of the oldest, deepest mysteries of the Wail of Stone. All of Divine Geleisdra's sorrows took shapes of hallowed onyx, all alike in holiness. And yet, different woes took different shapes and cast different spiritual resonances.

Hubris and arrogance undermined the abodes of the mighty in the Garden islets. Now other woes come as a punishment to these people living around Hollowshrine and the rest of the Scab's islands.

'What's this Garden District? Isn't that an old name for . . .' Daerna trailed off.

'The Crumbling District!' Roshia exclaimed. 'None of this makes sense. How can a spiritual disease cause the structural collapse of some islets, and then a century later bring a physical malady to the residents?'

She was right. Then again, Daerna had come here because she'd seen the disease heralded by black mould and cracks in the Broken Arches. Now, more and more, the evidence pointed to some common, invisible cause.

Daerna scanned the rest of the document. What followed was the summary of the positions of the Sister Superiors, and as she feared, it'd been their own, Forlaitra, who'd cast the harshest possible interpretation on the portent:

Let us remember, as one of Geleisdra's Hallowed Dreams, Onyxia is meant to shape us. In any affliction it elicits, there's a lesson, an echo of our own failings.

If the Wilting malady ravages the indigents and lowlifes of the Southern Quarter, it is only because of their *failures of morality.*

To protect our holy city, we must remain strong in our convictions. A century ago, this affliction demanded that our predecessors cut off the Garden District, like a gangrenous limb, to preserve the greater good. The same must be done with those afflicted with the moral decay of the Wilting.

Let us agree to begin the toil with processions and penance and deny the Motherstorm's mercy to those unworthy. If those tools prove insufficient, as per Vice-Chancellor Davorles's advice, let us use the sword and the gauntlet, the Nightmare and the storm. Heavy is the toil that shall follow. Let us all bear this punishment with dignity and severity.

Unsurprisingly, the Superior of the Whisperers had followed this counsel, while the Superior of the Wardens had remained quiet. Only the Abbess Superior of the Widows had stood against her: *Let us appeal to the Holy Book's wisdom to find a more merciful solution that might address the underlying fracture of the city's spirit.*

Daerna was astounded by all of this. The idea that the Southern Quarter was prone to spark these crises because of some spiritual lacking was hard to swallow; harder even was how the abbesses' treatment could be so callous. Especially since the Abbess Superior of the Widows believed that the Silver Book could offer solutions to the deeper root causes.

With Vice-Chancellor Davorles's advice, they'd been content to let the afflicted die and the disease worsen because they believed the people of the Southern Quarter as beneath saving? No. This couldn't be.

'There must be more in other documents,' Daerna said.

As she returned the scroll, they heard a loud metallic growl from the entrance, followed by a chorus of chattering whispers from the hidden heights of the vault.

'What was that?' Roshia asked, voice quavering.

Hurried footsteps approached. It was Indre.

'We have to leave!'

The three Sisters rushed towards the exit. Above them, something followed, flickering in the darkness.

'What is that?' Daerna asked, doing her best to swallow her fear.

'I told you, these halls are protected.'

Indre's vagueness about the vault's guardian must have been deliberate to entice them, but it'd been her own eagerness that had blinded Daerna to the danger. Whatever they were, their voices were low growls that sounded like the distorted Susurrus shadows, now echoing all around them.

They ran through the stacks as fast as they could. One wrong turn, and Daerna knew they wouldn't make it out in time. When they finally saw the iron gates in the distance, they were already half closed.

She chanced a glimpse at the corridor behind them, swarming with the guardian Nightmares that were growing ever closer. Darkness coalesced into worm-like shapes, broken only by rows of white teeth and scabrous tendrils. They coiled and uncoiled, weightless, to crawl along the walls and shelves. Some sort of olfactory organ resembling a crimson chrysanthemum pulled them after whoever had roused them from their slumber, and thus were they fixed on Daerna.

She pushed herself onwards, one foot in front of the other, until her lungs felt about to burst. They were close, very close, when Roshia faltered, falling behind.

Indre crossed the dwindling threshold. Daerna grabbed Roshia's arm and dragged her along. Reaching the gates, she shoved Roshia through before her.

Daerna could feel the Nightmares' furious whispering filling her head, threatening to overwhelm and drown her. Just when she feared it'd crush her skull, a sudden silence.

She squeezed through the slender gap at the last moment, the mighty gates snapping closed just behind her.

Breathing heavily, they clambered up the stairs. The relief of escaping the vault was short-lived; above, they heard distant noises, conversations and footsteps. The Whisperers had returned.

'Pull your veil down,' Daerna said. Roshia followed her example.

Bidding farewell to Indre, they hurried towards the exit, skirting past any Whisperers they happened to come across. No one stopped them.

Until they came to the exit gate. The same old Sister who had let them in now called after them. 'You two, why are you running? Stop!'

Daerna pretended not to hear her. She followed Roshia over the threshold and into the night.

* * *

Daerna had slept poorly thanks to the previous night's revelations. She soldiered through the morning Keening, fell asleep during lunch and once again found herself late to chorus practice.

Gathering her skirts, she ran up the staircase that led to the Chorus Hall, but upon reaching the door, she stopped short. Something was wrong. There was no Keening, only the gentle rumbling of the Motherstorm's drizzle.

Opening the door, she found the hall empty except for Dirdra, who stood behind her lectern in deep concentration. The rain formed rivulets on the window behind her.

'Come in, Daerna,' she said without lifting her head from her hymnary.

'Where is everyone?'

'I suspended today's practice.'

'Oh, I didn't hear.'

'Hardly a surprise given your recent absences.' Dirdra sighed.

Dirdra was always a picture of perfect composure, but Daerna picked up on the slight downturn at the edge of her lips. She was angry.

'Sister Naida wrote to tell me about your new friends, the Wandering Sisters. And I suppose you wouldn't know anything about the two members of our Order seen last night fleeing from the restricted areas of the Silent Abbey?'

Daerna froze. They couldn't know it'd been them unless Sister Indre had confessed.

'Who said that I'm involved with the Wanderers?' She held her head high, playing up her outrage and steering the conversation away from last night.

'One of the reasons Naida excels at her position is that she doesn't lack eyes or ears among the devoted. It really matters not who told her. What matters is if it's *true*, Daerna.'

Daerna looked over her shoulder. The door was still closed. They were alone.

'I don't want them to be punished on my account.'

'*Them?* You should be worried about yourself, Daerna!' Dirdra shook her head angrily. 'Don't you worry about Agonea. That old fox has been playing the same game for years. She likes to bark loudly, but as soon as she wakes up the lioness, she scurries back into hiding. Once Abbess Superior Forlaitra takes notice of them, they'll be banished from the city, and that'll be the end of it.' She dropped her voice to a whisper. 'Soon they'll be gone with the wind, leaving others to answer for their transgressions.'

'What will happen to those in their hospices? They've been helping those afflicted by the Wilting!'

'Motherstorm, give me temperance! If you want to destroy everything you've built here, don't do it on a whim!' Dirdra rubbed her forehead with a closed fist. Her anger wasn't loud, but it burned hard. Daerna had plenty of experience disappointing her mother, but it was different betraying the trust of someone she admired. 'There are other ways to help the downtrodden if that's what you want. You could be Keening at one of the Widows' hospices, for example. Please, don't squander your talents this way!'

'I'm sorry. I didn't mean . . .' Daerna was flustered, and a knot had formed in her throat.

'And I'm sorry I didn't warn you about Sister Agonea before.' Dirdra's rage was cooling. She touched Daerna's arm. 'She almost got me cast out too.'

Daerna could barely fathom the story between her mentor and Agonea, but she trusted that Dirdra's pain and concern were genuine.

'Sister Dirdra, may I be frank with you?' Daerna asked.

'Please.'

'When I left the university, I expected that, from within the Sisterhood, I'd be able to better help those who were suffering. And then, when I realised that I could help by Keening, I hoped that it would be enough. But it doesn't feel like that anymore after what I've been seeing on the streets.'

'Are you telling me that you've lost your faith in our art? You, of all people?' Dirdra shook her head. 'Daerna, you have a *gift*. Many can learn the canticles, many can practise the intonations to reach the Motherstorm; however, few truly deliver their hearts into the songs like you do. You must know this! How many times have you told me that you've felt the Hallowed Motherstorm listening to you?'

'I still believe in our art and I'm grateful for everything that you've taught me. It just feels *wrong* to ignore what's happening in the Southern Quarter.'

If being a Wailing Sister meant devoting yourself in heart, mind and soul to this sacred art and ignoring everything outside these walls, then perhaps it wasn't enough for her anymore.

'I could be doing more. *We* could be doing more! I know the Wilting is getting worse, I know that we've given up on those afflicted by it, and I know the Charnelites are sweeping in as we abandon them.'

'You can always bring those concerns to the prioress, Daerna. And I'd happily back you.'

'That won't be enough! Some of the Widows already did that, and instead of helping they doubled down on the decision to abandon them!' Daerna protested.

Dirdra cocked her head, giving Daerna her full attention. 'There's something you're not telling me.'

Could Daerna reveal what they'd found in the Silent Abbey? To explain her concerns was one thing, to confess to breaking into a restricted vault, a very different one.

At the same time, if she couldn't share her worries with Dirdra, who could she tell?

Daerna cleared her throat. 'What if there was something else, something in the city helping the Wilting spread like a plague? I've been in two different hospices, and in both places, I've felt the same dissonance, seen the same darkened cracks. I don't have an explanation, but I'm certain of what I've witnessed.'

'Is that why you and Roshia snuck into the Silent Abbey's vault?'

Daerna saw no point in hiding it any further. 'Yes. We saw their records. The Superiors know how the Wilting's worsening through the Scab and Little Vespiria. Despite acknowledging it, we found a portent writ from the Warden Sisters cautioning the Orders not to do anything, even if the Silver Book indicated "other paths".'

'This is all hard to believe ... Why would the Wilting suddenly be getting worse?' Dirdra asked, sucking her teeth thoughtfully. 'As for the rest ... It could be that the Superiors are considering a political dimension to the issue that we're missing. Still, Sister Naida would never allow the Charnel Cult to profit from this. Perhaps we should discuss it with her.'

Dirdra's grasp of politics made Daerna hesitate. She could be missing a lot. And yet, she couldn't shake either the outrage or the dread at abandoning all these people to their misfortune.

She met Dirdra's eyes. 'You might be right about the politics and the Wanderers. I still fear that unless we do something soon, a lot of people will suffer and many will die, because of both the disease and the Charnelites.'

Dirdra looked upwards, her reddish hair cascading behind her like a mane. 'If that is what you believe, I shall protect you. I'll speak to Sister Naida and vouch for you and Roshia.'

'Thank you, Dirdra.' Daerna breathed out with relief. Immediately, it felt like a weight had been lifted from her shoulders. 'What will happen to you?'

Dirdra shook her head. 'It might spell the fall for both of us, though I suspect Prioress Balachdra doesn't have conclusive evidence to accuse you or she would have already. Besides, she already has a culprit, a young Whisperer who claimed to act alone.'

After everything, Indre hadn't betrayed them. Daerna should seize the opportunity she'd given them.

Except letting Indre take sole blame was the cowardly thing to do. All of this talk about Sister Naida had got her thinking. Maybe there was a way of forcing the Abbess Superior's hand on this after all.

'Can I ask you for one last favour?'

'What?'

'Please tell Sister Naida that I'd like to atone for my transgressions. There might be a way of righting two wrongs here.'

* * *

Once again, they'd joined Sister Naida on her search for heretics, except tonight, they were the hounds.

With Dirdra's aid and a lot of careful spinning, Daerna had managed to weave the right tale for Sister Naida Marsael. She'd presented their incursion into the Silent Abbey as misplaced fervour rather than disobedience, that they'd just wanted to stop the Charnel Mother's heretics.

That was the perfect prize to dangle. What did their little transgressions matter when compared to the spread of this infamous heresy in their own hallowed home?

The plan had worked, if anything too well. Sister Naida would take them, together with some Sisters who'd indulged too much in the previous week's revelry, in the next Penance Procession into the Scab, and they'd lead her to the heretics. Except this time, it would be a hunt.

Sister Naida requested a score of militant Widowed Sisters. Those who, like Pierla, had been recruited from the military. Instituted to fight against the Pale Prince's host of jubilant dead, the Order's precepts didn't allow them to shed blood of the innocent, but seeing their battle maces decorated with passages of the *Song of Sorrows*, Daerna knew they'd break bones liberally.

Sister Naida even went to the Southern Quarter magistrate, who, horrified at the accusations of having allowed heresy to fester, immediately joined their party, bringing along a city watch patrol: a dozen men armed with swords, halberds and crossbows.

And then, at the head of the march, were the familiar faces of her penance friends: Roshia, Pierla and, now, Indre of Skala.

The Scab's maze of coiled alleys stood eerily quiet. Some of it had to be the hangover that followed the Ascent Festivities, some of it she wasn't so sure.

'I should have known better than to get mixed up with you quarrelsome hens,' Pierla grumbled.

'Come on, we're birds of a feather! Tonight, we can put all our troublemaker skills to good use! Also, you didn't have to come,' Daerna replied. Indre's lips drew into a smile at that. Daerna was very relieved that Indre didn't resent her for the trouble they'd caused.

'And let you all wander around like chickens with their heads cut off?' Pierla quirked a brow. 'Fuck that. Those pus-festering pillocks owe us from last time.'

'And how are we going to find them?' Roshia replied in a trembling voice.

'If I'm right, the worse the Wilting, the more physical signs on the landscape. Even if the Charnelites don't know that, they surely follow the stench of death. Where the Wilting is bad, they follow.'

'Agreed, but the Scab is huge,' Indre replied in her raspy voice.

'Which is why I suggest we head for the belly of the beast: Hollowshrine, where it all began. Can you take us there, Pierla?'

'I can if you don't mind the meandering walk.'

Pierla deftly led them through the Scab's nooks and crannies for a long half hour. Disease-struck homes had multiplied since the last time. On every street, it was hard to miss the doors marked white by the watch.

Perhaps that was why, at first sight of them, the locals split like oil in a stream of water. They saw the armed guards alongside the grim-looking Widowed Sisters in chainmail and rushed home before getting swept up by them.

After a dozen sharp turns and many ruinous bridges held together only by rusty chains, Pierla announced: 'There. There begins Hollowshrine.'

Hollowshrine felt older than the neighbouring patches of city. Around them, alleys coiled into a snail-shell-like spiral, and ancient marble walls were half buried by the brick houses built on top of and around them.

At first, it was hard to find anything in the mesh of haphazardly built shacks and crumbling buildings. The whole island was victim to all kinds of maladies, from scabbing to woodrot, yet all explainable as perfectly natural decrepitude.

Then, Daerna felt a familiar heaviness in the air, like acrid smoke sticking to her vision.

'There's something around here,' she said, 'but I might need a moment to find it.'

'I'll take care of our fearless leader,' Pierla said, 'and you ladies do the work!' She went back to the main body of their company.

'Sister Naida! I think I've seen some heretical scribblings in that alley!'

'Show me!' the greying-haired woman demanded.

Pierla led her and her enforcers into a clogged alley, while Daerna and the others slipped away to examine the nearby houses. Only decaying and deserted abodes surrounded them. One had even collapsed in on itself, the upper floors fallen into the ground floor.

'Here!' Indre called from nearby.

They'd found what seemed to be a hidden square. Old carved pillars stood amidst it, like a fractured ribcage.

Daerna crept through the disjointed and cracked archways into what had been the main nave of some sort of monastery. With some hesitation, the others followed.

All the columns and nearby walls were covered by tar-like veins of mould sprouting from near the ground. In some places, it'd met with the Scab's rust, causing veritable wounds on the building's tissue, fractal cracks that bled an oxidised stone.

Underneath their feet, the floor was peeling away, shedding its cobblestones and revealing naked bedrock.

'It feels heavy,' Indre muttered.

At first, Daerna thought she meant the reek of refuse in the dust-laden air, but she soon realised what Indre was alluding to.

The air hung heavy over her head. It was as if a cloud of dread had nestled into the ruins.

'This is what I felt in Little Vespiria's hospice. And I'm certain that the same thing is happening in the Broken Arches too,' Daerna said.

'Blessed Merele's bones!' lamented Roshia. She'd halted in front of a frescoed wall. At first Daerna thought it was the worn-out and faded painting that had decorated the nave's chancel, but this paint was fresher than that.

The fresco depicted a vision of deliverance, but not by Divine Geleisdra. The Charnel Mother, cloaked in crimson red, stood over a field littered with decaying corpses. She trampled them all, from crowned Oneirocrats and Sisters in their habits to warriors clinging to their swords and peasants their tools. Her arms were held upwards, filling the heavens, circling the skies, embracing the naked souls of the fallen. Lepers, the ailing and beggars knelt at Her feet, kissing the naked bone. Their eyes were lit with joy, imploring the grim figure for an end to suffering.

'They've consecrated these ruins to their heresy!' Roshia remarked. 'Did they cause this?'

'I don't know,' Daerna admitted.

They had to cut their conversation short when they heard Pierla call for them. They hurried back, fearing Naida had noticed their absence, but instead they found that the discipliner had stopped some locals for questioning. A man, a woman and two girls, sharing a family resemblance. Likely Faengrians, judging from their clothes.

'What are you hiding in there?' Naida waved her mace around, pointing at their heavy baskets and travel pouches.

'It's all my family has left. We want no trouble!' the man protested. He spoke in accented Onyxian.

'Creeping about at this late hour, laden like thieves?' Naida chuckled sardonically. 'Scoundrels, that's what you are.'

'Priestess, please!' he begged. 'We were just leaving! The Mother of Bones is coming! You should leave too!'

'"Priestess"? Only a heretic would speak thusly! I bet you're smuggling false idols in those trunks!'

A militant Widow with the arms of a stevedore wrangled a basket from the woman and poured out their belongings: some ragged garments, a handful of carpentry tools and a skin of dried bread and salted fish.

Daerna grabbed Naida's arm. 'Sister Naida, please, I don't think they mean ill to anyone.'

'Don't you dare interfere in the Motherstorm's wrath, child!'

'Please, Sister, they're just a scared family!' Pierla said, stepping in between them.

'How dare you?' Naida stared at the two of them, wild-eyed. 'I thought you had learned last time! Heretics lie! Now step aside before—'

To everyone's shock, Pierla drew her daggers. Yet they all soon understood why.

'There!' Indre said, pointing at two armed men crouched atop a nearby rooftop. Their faces were smeared with red. The loud argument must have drawn them.

'Seize them!' Sister Naida commanded, and one of the armed Widows and two watchmen went chasing after them. Roshia discreetly used the distraction to usher the Faengrian family away into the night.

A horn cried out somewhere in the nearby alleys. Distant chanting grew louder as it approached.

'Let's end this! With me!' Naida yelled. 'We'll arrest them all!'

They marched into a larger street, only to stumble upon a waiting mob. The bearded priest they'd faced last time led the group in chanting an ancient Iskian funerary hymn.

Sister Naida addressed them. 'It's time to face the Motherstorm's furious judgement, heretics!'

The militant Widows formed a line with the guards at their sides and the crossbowmen right behind.

Sister Naida began singing the 'Guided by the Mighty Guardian' canticle, and Daerna and the others joined in. Their Keening was poor, but the rain fell harder on the thoroughfare.

'I told you they'd come!' the bearded priest called to the crowd. 'Even now, with the final reckoning soon approaching, they deny the Pale Prince! But this is your opportunity to prove yourselves!'

One of the guards shot his crossbow, missing the priest but piercing the neck of a man behind him. The mob wavered.

'Don't fear them! The Midwife shall protect us!' the priest said, looking above.

Daerna followed his eyes and spotted, atop a nearby balcony, a tall woman dressed in a ragged gown-like garment of sooty and filthy purple silks. It resembled some ancient, moth-eaten houppelande. Even from this far, Daerna could see that her gaunt figure was misshapen: bony spikes protruded through her ghastly skin and hairless head.

'Deliver them to us!' She spoke to the mob as if from a pulpit. 'Deliver their skulls to the Charnel Mother, and She shall absolve you in your time of judgement.'

'Fetch the heretic!' Naida yelled.

The 'Midwife', as the priest had called her, lifted a hand, and something large shambled out from a nearby alley. A Nightmare, tall as an oak, with a body of thick bone and a head made of skulls meshed together that wheezed through their gap-toothed grins. Its heavy frame was like a thornbush of pointed ribs and weighed the monstrosity down so much that it could only move by leaning on its long, clawed arms. They'd come expecting a fight, but not against a Dreamer.

'We need to go, Sister Naida!' Daerna pleaded.

'We defeated them once! We shall do it again by the grace of the Motherstorm!'

'You damnable fool!' Pierla snarled. 'We barely made it out alive last time! And there's an army of them now!'

'Nonsense! As soon as they feel the Motherstorm's righteous fury, they'll scatter like the rats they are!' Naida turned to the Sisters in the procession. 'Raise your voices to the Motherstorm! Ask for Her righteous retribution! Magistrate, put that monster down!'

The Penance Procession closed ranks, while the wizened magistrate mustered enough grit to order his crossbowmen to aim at the Nightmare. They fired a volley of bolts, most of which sank into its torso.

No blood, no screaming; it only wobbled for a moment, the head of its many skulls turning towards the guards. Then, to their horror, it renewed its march, lumbering towards them.

'Hold!' Sister Naida called.

Daerna turned to Roshia and Indre. 'Run back to the main bridge and call for reinforcements!'

'A-are you sure?' Roshia asked.

'Go! Every second counts!'

They both ran towards the bridge. Daerna had to fight the urge to bolt with her friends. This was where she would die. The creeping certainty seeped in. Even then, she wouldn't abandon her Sisters. They too felt it, and their Keening wavered.

Daerna stood behind Pierla, Sister Naida and the line of Widows. The Nightmare picked up speed, coming faster and faster, and behind it, the mob, reassured by the inability of the crossbows to stop it, followed.

She began Keening again, not 'Guided by the Mighty Guardian' but her own formless song, a wordless prayer of desperation. Spurred by anguish, she threw the full weight of her heart into it and ended up dragging the rest of the group with her. This was not calculated harmony; this was their plea for help.

The more she poured into the song, the more she felt the world fade into a blur. Soon, the rainfall became Daerna's melody. She looked up, searching for consolation or perhaps a sign, and thought she saw a clowder of crowcats circling above them. Even higher, an eye seemed to be opening.

Was the Motherstorm listening to their plea? If She was, She'd better aid them soon.

Daerna sang on. She raised her voice in melancholic supplication, asking for courage as well as mercy. She lacked the words and her throat was raw, but to her surprise, she felt the Motherstorm resonating with her.

Lightning landed on a rooftop not far from the Midwife. She screeched an angry howl. 'We shall rip out your throats!'

The Nightmare charged, smashing against their line. Some fell backwards; some flew into the nearby walls.

A crossbow bolt pierced one of the skulls, but the Nightmare trampled the shooter. Pierla and three other Widows swarmed the Nightmare, furiously swinging their maces and chipping away at its legs. It teetered but remained upright.

A claw swiped at them. Pierla ducked to the side, but an older Sister, slower, found her neck torn open. Spurting blood, she fell.

Their line wavered as many screamed in fright, and one of the guards bolted, dropping his halberd. Others buckled, stunned by the clash. Sister Naida leapt forwards, waving her mace and screaming invectives. One of the heretics charged her with a hatchet, and she brought her mace down, crushing his cranium inwards.

The Widows and disorganised guards tried in vain to hold the undaunted heretics at bay while hacking at the monstrous Nightmare. They struck at it to little avail. The sergeant who'd been trying to pierce it from below with a sword was seized by the head and then shoved against an opening in its ribcage. To the group's terror, the pointed bones closed on the man's front half like two rows of teeth.

The world blurred and darkened at the edges of Daerna's vision. Some Sisters ran, but she held her ground, clinging to her song. She conjured her desperate pain and fear into an aria, begging one last time for the Motherstorm to save them all from a pointless and brutal slaughter.

Something above tugged at her. She'd touched something with the raw potency of her frayed heart.

The sky turned black. A breath of electric anger filled the air.

Then, the blinding clarity of lightning followed, lighting up the night and striking hard, striking fiercely.

When she opened her eyes, the Nightmare was on fire, flames and smoke emerging from between its rib-rimmed mouth. It clumsily braced itself, trying to hold itself together, then collapsed against a building, broken like a lifeless statue.

All around, people tried to escape the falling debris of masonry, dust and bone shards. Daerna bolted out of the way into a nearby alley, her feet skidding on the muddy street. She saw a bridge ahead, through the rain, and with it the promise of escape.

A promise cut short when the Midwife, taller than the tallest man she'd ever seen, blocked her way. Her mouth was cracked open in a misshapen smile, twisted by zeal and the bony spikes of her cheekbones and jaw.

'Pierla! She's—' Daerna cut off as the Midwife seized her neck and squeezed, pulling her off her feet. Nails like talons dug into her skin.

Struggling for air, she fumbled for her dagger.

'We are marvelled with you, child,' the Midwife said. Reddened and serrated rows of fangs twisted her face into a mask of cruelty. 'Quiet unbirth, we shall grant you.'

Daerna's numb fingers found and gripped the hilt of her knife. With a shaking hand, she drew it. Her vision blackening, she barely managed to stab forwards. The blade bit into something, the Midwife screeched and Daerna fell to the ground, the wind knocked out of her.

She was in the mud, dazzled but breathing. She pushed herself up and, coughing, staggered and turned to run the way she'd come. She saw someone coming her way with a dagger and hesitated, squinting in the rain.

It was Pierla, covered in mud and blood, battered but breathing. Daerna smiled at her, until she noticed that Pierla was screaming at her. The Midwife had chased after her instead of retreating.

Only when the long claws pierced her side did she realise how close behind she'd been.

Chapter Twenty-Two

Ash

Just as she vanquished the Charnel Mother, one day Divine Geleisdra will release us all from death and undo every loss since the beginning of Onyxia. Until then, we can only weep for those lost to us.

– *The Life of Divine Geleisdra, the Solemn Princess* by Blessed Elpia

ASH DROWSILY HURRIED AFTER BALCHOD. Lord Morvander's chamberlain had roused him after he'd collapsed in sleep over Joshian the Errant's travelogue, *The Forever Currents*, but he wasn't clear on what the hurry was. This late, it was probably one of Thalder's strange exercises.

He followed Balchod into the vestibule, carrying his boots in one hand and suppressing a yawn with the other. When he realised Lady Geil was there with a hooded woman, he hurriedly tucked in his shirt, almost tripping on Omen in the process.

'He's here,' Balchod announced.

Geil looked at him with furrowed brows. 'I'm sorry, Ash.'

'Sorry about what?'

'You're Daerna's lad?' The other woman raised her bloodshot eyes to look at him.

Under the murk, he recognised a Widowed Sister, half of her face caked in mud, bloodied bruises showing through the furrows cut by the rain.

'Who are you?'

'I'm Pierla, a friend of Daerna's. I was with her when . . .' An anguished shudder wracked her.

'What are you talking about?'

'Cursed charnel pigs ambushed us.' Pierla winced. 'There was some Dreamer with them, and she stabbed Dae.'

The young Widow's head sank as she recounted the assault, but Ash's temples started throbbing with dread to the point he could no longer hear her clearly.

No. That was impossible. Daerna was safely asleep at her cell in Muirtra. This was someone else. Someone who'd been stabbed in some dark alley – not Daerna, not her.

'The Widows at Southedge Hospice are doing everything they can. The claws cut deep enough to pierce her lungs, so they fear they won't be able to save her . . .' Pierla's voice faltered again.

Cold fear flooded his veins. His breathing became unsteady, agitated. Omen stared up at him with concern.

'She's still alive?' he finally managed.

Pierla nodded, red eyes glistening.

'I'm a Dreamer. There must be something I can do, right?'

He looked at Geil, but she lowered her gaze. 'We could call for our family's Remaker and physician.'

'Please!' Ash cried.

The chamberlain turned to Geil instead.

'Do it, Balchod! You have my authorisation!' Geil snapped.

'Balchod, wait.'

Morvander stood in the shadows of one of the hall's entrances. He was worn out and sweaty. He'd probably been in his workshop until moments ago.

'This late at night, it'll take hours for the physician to arrive,' Morvander said. 'It'll all be over by then.'

'Please, I beg you! I'll do anything, but please, help her!'

'Anything? Who is she to you?'

Ash took a deep breath, barely able to admit it to himself, let alone anyone else. 'She's hope, peace, love, my lord. She's *everything*.' Ash knelt in front of Morvander. 'Now please, will you call for a Remaker?'

Morvander's brows furrowed deeply. The seconds moved too slowly and yet too quickly.

'No,' he said.

The words landed like a slap. Ash shook his head, dazzled. 'No?'

'Ready the skysloop, Balchod, and have Tarna load my current sculpting block. We leave at once,' Morvander replied. 'I'll need you as my apprentice tonight, Ash. I might be able to save her, but I'll depend on your help. Now get ready.'

* * *

Ash leaned over the *Night Swan*'s prow, stroking Omen's head as they watched the black clouds unfurl below. He'd longed for a chance to sail aboard a skyship; now he just wanted it to be over.

Sister Pierla was praying beneath her breath: 'May the Motherstorm embrace my sorrows in her regard, may She carry them away to burn in the night.'

As if summoned, the Widowed Sisters' hospice emerged into view, a sturdy stone building with a narrow cloister at the plateau's southern tip. Farther south, the Scab was shrouded in eerie silence, broken only by an occasional howling and screeching.

Pierla had told them how, after the assault, the Southern Quarter's magistrate had set guards on all its bridges. The Academy's Hordemasters had been called to unleash fresh Nightmares on the Scab's streets to hunt down the Charnel Mother's followers.

Ash feared the Nightmares wouldn't discriminate between the innocent and the guilty in their purge. Admittedly, such concerns were secondary to him now.

Captain Bentor skilfully lowered the skysloop to the hospice's only spire, where a lonely skywharf protruded. Ash didn't wait for them to be docked, leaping from the gunwale and landing on the stone horn. The ground was more slippery than he'd anticipated, yet dread carried him forwards as if with wings. With Omen close behind, he rushed into the tower and down to the hospice's cloister.

The halls were overflowing with dozens upon dozens of injured from the Scab's attacks and the overworked Sisters tending to them. He searched for Daerna in every bed. Here, a matronly Sister sobbed on a cot, her swollen face as purple as a grape. There, an older Wailer struggled to breathe through dried blood. Farther down the ward, a grey-haired guard whimpered while a young Widow rinsed his many wounds with vinegar.

Where had they taken Daerna?

He spotted a group of Wailing Sisters sobbing around a bed. A young woman lay ashen and still amidst them.

No, please, Motherstorm, no. He felt a hammering in his head as he approached.

It wasn't her.

Someone called to him from an adjoining hallway.

'Aescyon?'

It took him a moment to recognise the woman. Dirdra, Daerna's tutor. He'd met her in passing at Muirtra, but her dignified presence wasn't easy to forget.

'Merciful Motherstorm! Pierla found you!' There were heavy shadows on her face as she stepped into the ward's dim light. All colour and hope seemed to have been sucked from her.

'Where's Daerna?'

'Come. She might not be awake. They've given her Mother's Tears for the pain.'

'Have the physicians seen her already?'

Dirdra lowered her gaze. 'They have. They've done everything they can to give her peace.'

They hurried through a seemingly endless stone corridor. With every step, Ash felt himself sinking deeper and deeper into the reality of this nightmare. When Dirdra stopped, they'd come to a small chamber with two beds. One of them was empty.

Daerna lay on the other with two young Sisters, a Wailer and a Whisperer, watching over her.

Daerna's dark hair stuck to her sweat-covered brow. Air wheezed through her cracked lips as she shuddered in the bloodstained bed.

When Ash took her hand, she turned her head. She was awake after all, and tried to say something but instead burbled blood.

'I'm here, my love. I'm here.'

She was pale and grey, too much like the corpse he'd just seen.

'I'm sorry,' she managed before breaking into a painful cough.

Omen paced, turning his head towards the door. Pierla barged in and hugged the others. Geil shuffled after her, carrying a burly chest in her arms, straining with effort. Morvander followed, stopping at the foot of the bed, his moonlike eyes wandering from face to face.

'I need only three other people in the room. My daughter, my apprentice and the most accomplished Keener. The rest should leave.'

Pierla and the others seemed about to protest, but Dirdra ordered them out in a tone that allowed no retort. 'What now?' she asked.

'I'll try to help her, but you must all understand the risks are high. For all of us. What we're about to do here could get us all executed should it become known. I need your oaths to keep this secret.'

'You want me to swear to something, and I don't know what it is,' Sister Dirdra protested. 'You're not speaking of Necromancy, are you?'

'It's not. Yet I fear it could be seen as such by those who don't understand. Such is the danger. However, I fear this is her only chance. Now, will you swear?' Lord Morvander asked, rubbing his temples.

Daerna wheezed in a breath, blood bubbling on her lips. Sister Dirdra looked at her, hesitating. Ash wanted to scream. If there had ever been a noble purpose to Dreaming, a purpose at all, it was this.

'Please, Sister Dirdra, I beg you. Whatever it takes, I'll carry any blame. Say I forced your hand, say anything, but please let us try!'

Her eyes narrowed. 'Fine,' she said after a moment. 'I swear to keep your secret.'

'Thank you,' Lord Morvander replied. 'Geil, open the chest.'

To Ash, the contents looked like a block of the jet-black stone that was the bedrock of the city.

'Is that . . . ?' Dirdra trailed off.

'Geleisdra's Wail of Stone? Not exactly. This mirrormatter, as I call it, is my own formula, my own refinement of Onyxia's bedrock.' Morvander touched it, and its surface rippled like water.

'Just tell me what to do,' Ash begged.

'You and I will Dream a replica of her body using this sculpting block.'

What was he talking about? 'You mean an Eidolon? You said you'd save *her*!'

Morvander huffed with impatience. 'No, an Eidolon lives in place of the deceased; here we'll ensure the replica dies instead of Daerna. I'll need your help for it to work. Remember the challenge I set for you?'

'The one about changing someone's mind?'

'Precisely. For me to heal her, we need to overcome her natural resistance to my Dreaming. Specifically, we need Daerna to feel, to see herself in the replica. She must believe her pain, her very injuries truthfully reflected on this other body.'

Ash's mind flooded with questions. The idea was outlandish enough, but something in specific troubled him. 'You want her to feel the replica, the injuries in the replica as part of her ... Doesn't that mean she'll feel twice the pain?'

'It's the only way for this to work,' Lord Morvander admitted. Ash's blood froze in his veins.

'I'll sing to her. She might find it soothing. And if we fail ... she'll need me by her side,' Dirdra said, swallowing through the hesitation.

'It'll all be for naught if her body doesn't *believe* the lie. That's why I need *your* help, Ash.'

'You're a far more accomplished Dreamer than I am!'

'You're the one who knows how she thinks. The only one here who can speak the lie with an element of truth to her soul.'

Ash's mouth ran dry. If he failed, they'd be increasing her torment for nothing.

Sister Dirdra had already begun singing a gentle canticle. Her deep voice was soothing and steady like an anchor.

'Now, you two, turn her on her side. The closer I am to the wounds, the easier it'll be for me to replicate and mend them.'

With Geil's assistance, Ash removed the bloodstained sheet and turned Daerna on her side.

She was wrapped in a bandage that was so soaked in blood it'd started pooling at her back, staining her undergarments.

'I must sculpt quickly, so you'll have to keep her still for me. Otherwise, I might miss or rip apart tissue.' Morvander, one hand on the jet block, placed the other on Daerna's back. His pupils suddenly turned red, swirling with blood, and his whole body tensed.

Daerna began heaving, and a violent spasm followed.

Ash and Geil fell on her to keep her still. Omen paced around the bed, concerned. Together, they managed to hold Daerna still, but blood frothed at her lips.

Sweat was running down Lord Morvander's face as the mirrormatter block slithered like clay animated by expert hands. Slowly, it began to take human shape. First bones, then tissue, organs and veins weaved together into an unseen tapestry, tattered by terrible cuts covered in skin.

A perfect replica of Daerna's bust was being chiselled into the dark block with swift, invisible strokes. Right when Lord Morvander seemed finished, he carved stab wounds into it.

Daerna screamed and fought furiously to free herself.

'Keep her still or this will definitely kill her!' Morvander hissed.

Her body, her whole being, fought back against Lord Morvander's Dreaming.

Geil leaned over Daerna's legs, forcing them still, but Ash was losing control of her upper body.

His legs wobbled.

'Ash!' Geil yelled at him.

Blood dribbled from Daerna's lips.

'Forgive me,' Ash mumbled, holding Daerna as strongly as he could with his own body.

Sister Dirdra's soft Keening continued in the background, and Ash steeled himself. Like her, he had to remain focused.

In Daerna's ear, Ash whispered, 'We'll leave this place, you and I. We'll see the golden plains of Amalga, the scarlet eaves of the Evenfall Forests.'

She convulsed with pained, shallow breaths, while burning tears rolled down his cheeks.

'I'm . . . sorry . . .' she managed.

'There's nothing to be sorry for, my love. I'm here with you,' he continued. 'I'll always be here to Dream the skies and sea anew.' Fire rain on him from the heavens, sea-drakes chew his bones to dust, he would never leave her.

She violently coughed blood as her lungs struggled in vain to find air, her head hammering against his clavicle.

He clung to her desperately.

Daerna's wheezing turned into a gagging noise through her blood-soaked lips. She was asphyxiating.

'Now, Ash!' Morvander shouted. 'Dream for her!'

Ash plunged headlong into the Dreaming.

Her light was as dim as a candle about to extinguish. They were out of time, and he didn't have much of a plan.

He had to Dream away the pain, but he couldn't do it by fooling her. He had to build a bridge, not a trap.

He wove a mesh of silver threads from her mind and heart. From the Keening that hung in the air and moved through him, every small tendril a caress.

He built a ghost, a sketch of who she was, between her and the mirrormatter. He added the ethereal smudge of her Keening. The image of her hugging him and caressing Omen's head. The brightness that he felt when he was with her. He drew the bridge in the air, made of nothing.

She had to cross, not him.

'Please, stay with me, Daerna,' he pleaded, hoping she'd hear him.

Inside the grey room, Daerna calmed. The light within her reached from her body to dance along the threads he'd strung, illuminating them one by one.

At once, the replica of Daerna's body animated, mimicking her movements. The threads between the bodies turned blood red.

'Now, sever her away!' Morvander called.

Ash snatched for the threads and ripped them apart, destroying the bridge he had so carefully built.

As Ash came back to his waking senses, Daerna's body collapsed in his arms, still and pale.

Dirdra's song broke.

And Daerna sucked in a deep breath.

'Let her breathe!' Geil said, pulling Ash away.

Daerna coughed, but no longer did a stream of blood run from her lips. She was alive, taking in deep, panting breaths that came easier with each heartbeat. The jet-black replica, on the other hand, had frozen in a contorted effigy of death, a mortuary sculpture of a final moment that hadn't come.

Daerna cleared her throat and leaned over the side of the bed to spit the blood clot into a pissing pot.

'My lord,' Sister Dirdra whispered, 'this is a miracle! How can we ever repay such kindness?'

Morvander collapsed in an empty chair, exhausted. 'Your silence is enough,' he said grimly. 'Even if *you're* now persuaded of my work's virtues, others won't be as generous. They'll accuse me of Necromancy, or worse.'

'They'll think you're trying to violate the natural order,' Geil said, eyes widening. 'That you're desecrating Geleisdra's legacy by using it for your own creations.'

Ash was speechless with elation, but also astonishment. He could barely envision all the implications, yet he was certain this was a miracle. Tonight, they'd cheated death.

'I promised you my silence. No matter the price, you'll have it,' Sister Dirdra finally said.

Morvander slowly caught his breath. 'Thank you. Now please take me to the rest of the injured. Whatever relief I can provide with my Dreaming, I'll offer.'

He leaned on his daughter as they followed Sister Dirdra out of the room. Ash covered the replica with a sheet, then returned to Daerna's bed.

'You came back,' he said, squeezing her hand, kissing it, afraid she might slip from his grasp.

She managed a weak smile. 'I did . . .' Her voice was hoarse. 'It was mostly for Omen.'

She lowered her other hand, and the panther rubbed against it. Ash laughed the tears away at that and kissed her. Blood had never tasted better.

Chapter Twenty-Three
Geil

To rise beyond the blue,
bright as comets,
our road the skies,
until ashes we become,
that's our solemn vow.

– Oath of the Skycourier

THE LAST BRIDGE TAVERN STOOD by its namesake bridge connecting the Western Quarter with the Susurrus. The dimly lit inn reeked of burnt fish, brine and ale-stained wood, but it wasn't the smell that had the Drake uneasy. The problem was Mavis.

Geil felt it was past time to plant her feet on solid ground and take what she had coming. She couldn't keep running from her past, not when she was entertaining thoughts of staying in the city, of rebuilding a life here.

If nothing else, she owed Mavis a drink for old times' sake.

Lanteus had been the one to invite Mavis into their Talon. Back at the Academy, that wasn't a decision made lightly. Your Talon didn't just face the trials alongside you; it was your family. They were the ones to put themselves between you and the masters' Nightmares, to carry you on their backs to the Remakers when you were bleeding to death.

Upon his arrival, Mavis Calanthas had seemed like nothing but gouge-hound food. He was too soft-hearted for Nightmares, too clever to be brave and too unimaginative to sidestep the Academy's dangers. The Calanthases were a well-respected lineage, but theirs was a setting sun that no longer carried much influence.

Despite all of that, Lanteus took him in, probably because he loved lost causes. Ones like her.

By the end of Geil's second drink, Mavis still hadn't shown up. She ordered another one, drowning the Drake's grousing with a deep gulp of black ale.

A tattered sparkler girl approached her table. 'Light, milady?'

Geil found it hard to say no to her sooty face. 'Sure. Give me your best.'

The lass collected the money and handed over a candle wrapped in paper. She lit it and then hurried back into the street.

Geil was only half surprised to see there was writing on the paper. Out of habit, she unfolded it discreetly, pretending not to look at it while she read it from the corner of her eye.

The Fishermen Guild's Oratory. Try not to be followed. -M

What was Mavis playing at?

She nursed her drink for a bit, eyeing the room. It was a slow night in the inn. A couple of old men nagged at the innkeeper and some sullen-looking fishermen rolled bones in the back. Geil took a final swig, burned the handwritten note and slid like a cat into the cool of the night.

The bridge was empty this late, the dark reaching tendrils into the alleys and canyons below. As soon as she entered the Susurrus, the shadows lapped and lashed at her. Had she not known better, she would have sworn Lanteus was calling for her from under the bridge.

Soldiering on, she found the Fishermen's Oratory, a tower with a colonnaded staircase spiralling around it. It was pitch black, but the Drake could make out the open door.

During the day, this was a place of solace and remembrance. At night, it could very well be home to remorseless cutthroats.

She had no sword on her, so instead she strengthened her scales and sharpened her senses. The Drake picked up the musky smell of sweaty clothes and the sound of shallow breathing coming from one of the chambers.

If this is a trap, it's about to spring, the Drake growled. Geil slowed.

Crouching, she skulked up the final few steps and entered the chamber with her fists at the ready. Mavis rose, startled.

'Were you followed?' he asked, watching her with deeply shadowed eyes.

'What's this about, Mavis? I thought the last thing you wanted was to ever see my filthy face again.'

'Hopefully, that's what they'll think,' he replied. 'Now tell me: were you followed?'

'No! What do you want, Mavis?'

'Justice. For Lanteus. As much as he can get, anyway.' He chuckled bitterly. 'It's time to make those who betrayed him *pay*.'

Was that a jab at her? 'What the fuck are you saying?' The Drake bellowed the words through her.

She grabbed him by the throat and slammed him against the entrance.

A small push was all it'd take. The fall would break his bones. That would make him understand.

He's had it coming a long time, the Drake thrummed.

'Please, Geil, please!' he pleaded.

He let out a weak yelp, like an injured pup. Just like he'd been when they'd met. That they'd both been before the Academy had broken them. Except this time Lanteus wouldn't be around to fix either of them.

For once when the grief came, it was an antidote, cold and sobering. Geil pulled Mavis up and helped him back inside.

'I'm not blaming you – it wasn't *your* fault, Geil!'

That's where Mavis was wrong. That was the truth that stung deeper than any arrow. If Mavis had seen Lanteus's broken look when he'd found her in bed with Itraya, he'd know. Perhaps she'd feared this moment because Mavis would forgive her when she knew she couldn't be forgiven.

'I failed him too,' Mavis tried, rubbing his throat. 'Many times! But it wasn't us. *They* killed him!' He gestured towards the darkened skies beyond the lagoon. 'The masters did it!'

'What? Nonsense. It was those Scab criminals. They killed them all. Davorles found them, he told me.'

It'd been rotten luck. Rotten luck and the pain and shame she'd caused him blinding Lanteus to what was coming. Mavis was fooling himself if he believed there was anything else to it.

'How *generous* of Master Davorles.' Mavis chortled sardonically. 'Not only did he *happen* to be in the city, he also *kindly* lent his services to the Southern Quarter magistrate, all to find some convenient scapegoats to slaughter before they could protest.'

'What are you talking about? They found Lanteus's house sigil at their gang hideout in the old slaughterhouse.'

'You think those criminals were stupid enough to take on a Skycourier and then have proof of their deed conveniently lying around? Davorles placed it there! Don't you remember Lanteus's injuries?'

Of course she did. She'd been called to identify the corpse when they'd dragged him from the canals. The purple flesh, the blank stare. She'd reached out to touch the ghastly wounds on his chest, as if she could somehow kiss them closed and restore him to life. Suddenly, she found it hard to breathe. 'What of them?' she blurted out.

'Whoever killed him came at him straight on. You think some cutthroats took out Lanteus while he was on his guard? No. This was a Nightmare or a Dreamer.'

'No. It can't be. Why would Davorles and the masters want him dead?'

'Mother of lightning, Geil! You really don't know, do you? He was an *Exarchian*!'

She froze. Lanteus, an Exarchian? Even if he had been distant those last few months . . . The notion was ridiculous.

'You don't believe me? Fine, you can at least believe *him*.' Mavis produced a folded document from inside his jacket. 'Here. You tell me what this means otherwise.'

She snatched it out of his hand and walked towards the stairs to steal some light from the nearby streets.

The broken seal on the document was from Couriermaster Mathana; she felt a pang at recognising Lanteus's handwriting. Was this what the Falconess had wanted to discuss with her when she'd first returned to the city?

It was a testament, dated the day before he'd left on his final mission, about a week before his death. The writing was succinct, befitting a military will, granted under the Falconess's authority. Why would Lanteus write one unless he feared something might happen to him?

That wasn't even the strangest thing. He'd named Geil executor of a specific legacy: two thousand Onars, to be bequeathed to some orphanage in Logria, not a day's travel east from the capital.

'What's this? And how come I'm only hearing about it now?'

'Lanteus's family. That legacy is a small fortune, so they fought the provision in the testament tooth and nail. The Falconess wouldn't give up on it, though. She suspected, in fact, that it was the whole point to it.'

'What's this place? Oldcourt's Orphanage?'

'One of the many Widowed Sisters' orphanages,' Mavis whispered. 'Or so it'd appear. But I've been keeping eyes on it for some time now. Armed groups come and go in the night, and I've also seen them bringing in loaded carts that depart empty, or worse, carrying children with them. My guess is that they're Exarchians "liberating" them from the Academy's conscription.'

'I don't understand. None of this explains why Davorles would bother covering up Lanteus's murder, least of all kill him.'

'Here's the thing, and the reason why I got involved. The night he was murdered, after . . . whatever happened between you two,' Mavis hurried to explain, 'Lanteus sent me one of his Dreamling ravens asking me to meet him near the Scab's southmost quay. He might have just wanted to drink and talk it out, but he did ask me to make sure that "nothing else stuck to my shadow". I waited for him for hours, only to find out the next morning that he'd been murdered.'

A chill ran down Geil's spine. Davorles's moniker wasn't casual. His Imprint, his Dreamer signature, was the presence of unnatural, living shadows. And their former master always used them to spy on his students.

'Why are you only telling me this now?'

'I've only known about this for a month, since the Falconess sorted the matter with the magistrates. I was planning on taking care of this myself, but when I heard you'd returned, I hoped you'd help.'

She heaved a sigh. 'Why not go to the magistrates? Better yet, the Falconess? She knows of the testament, and Lanteus was under her command. She even has the ear of the High Justice.'

'Don't you think I've considered it? What if I'm wrong, though?' Mavis said angrily. 'Even if some Exarchians are hiding in that orphanage as a front, I don't know why Lanteus left that sum to them. And if I'm right, he intended for *you* to find out by naming you his executor. I need *your* help, Geil!'

'What do you expect me to find that you haven't?'

'*Everything.* I only got so far with the Sisters who run the orphanage, but if you show up as executor to Lanteus's estate? They'll open the doors for you! And if I'm right and Davorles had something to do with his murder, they might know something about why.'

To think that if she hadn't been with Itraya that night, not only would he not have been murdered but also would have told her about whatever this was, asked her to come to the Scab with him, was a bitter draught to swallow.

Despite their acrimonious parting, Geil had always wanted to believe that, with time, Lanteus might've forgiven her. That they both might've found a way back into each other's hearts. Death had robbed them of that chance. Or perhaps not death – the Wisp.

We'll hunt them, and when we find them, they'll pay. In bone and blood, in time and pain, in everything they took from us, the Drake roared.

Chapter Twenty-Four

Ash

The Silver Book contained all of Empress Damnia's wisdom. As Divine Geleisdra's legitimate birth right, she claimed it after the vanquishing of the Pale Prince, as a symbol of her legitimacy but also to guide her people in times of need.

– *The Life of Divine Geleisdra, the Solemn Princess* by Blessed Elpia

AFTER THE ATTACK, ASH DEVOTED his days to helping Lord Morvander with his work. Only in the evenings did he scurry away to visit Daerna at the hospice. Her steady recovery was a relief, proof that manufacturing more mirrormatter was of the utmost importance.

Sparing life-threatening injuries would aid many, yet what Lord Morvander truly sought was a theriac, a universal cure to disease and injury. If he could help Morvander produce mirrormatter and, more importantly, figure out a way to help Remakers use it effectively, they'd be able to help hundreds – no, *thousands* of people.

That was precisely why Lord Brakte had come to Lord Morvander for help to begin with, as, for the past year, sickness had spread in the eastern Valelands as plague-winds and foul humours rolled in from the Evenfall Forest mists.

Sourcing the onyx wasn't the main challenge. Raising the palace itself from the lagoon's bedrock had led Lord Morvander to discover some of its Dreamchanted properties and also to secure an ample supply with which to experiment. Not only was it extraordinarily malleable, but also among its innate properties was its ability to react to the human spirit.

He'd refined his own alloy from it, first for the Quietude, but then based on the same principles for the healing replicas. After the success with Daerna, Morvander felt he was close to perfecting the formula.

No, the challenge lay elsewhere: to aid the injured, they had to accept the replica as part of their own self. One would believe the mind eager to part from its pain, but as Morvander wisely put it: 'Pain shapes us as much as happiness. That's why our souls refuse to let it go, and why I need you to find a way to bridge this gap, just like you did with your mirror.'

'I thought Josod said other mirrors had achieved the same results as mine,' Ash replied.

'The Valelands' mirror-makers cater to the perception of our external self, but yours touched on something deeper: our inherent desire for improvement. Your eyes are still fresh, Ash. Keep them that way and see what you can create.'

Ash spent hour after hour Dreaming mirrors, canvases and books that would allow one's mind to see itself reflected in the mirrormatter. He pricked and cut himself to feel the necessary pain, and even when he succeeded in replicating the injury and feeling the replica's pain alongside his own, it only added to his mind's natural rejection.

These half-focused efforts weren't enough. He'd need months of dedication, years even, to find a solution. Right now, his only success was at failing to prepare for his exam.

Thalder was still training him in the foundations of combat against Dreamer and Nightmares, and while he used his visits to the hospice to catch up on the readings Lucre had assigned him, Ash was nowhere closer to producing the piece of

Dreamcraft mastery required. This lack of progress led Josod to eventually give up on him. Lucre took over his duties, but even with her help, Ash felt he lacked both imagination and inspiration.

If only he had time to sleep, to rest. If only he could postpone the examination a year, or half a month even. Sadly, there was no time. Ascent had come and gone, and the Senate had already begun their endless debates to appoint the new High Council.

When his summons finally came, it was for an extraordinary hearing to be presided over by the salient Lady Malvedra just before the Senate had agreed to vote on the new High Sage.

The political implications were clear even to Ash. She was trying to force Lord Morvander to support her.

Let that woman choke on her own greedy bile. Ash wouldn't be used as leverage, especially to stop whatever reforms Lady Geil was trying to launch. Neither would he let her or Lord Morvander down.

If he had to face a hostile Sages' tribunal, so be it.

He'd have something for them, something with enough cruelty that the Academy masters wouldn't be able to reject it.

Even if that meant stealing his father's designs.

His father might not have been a Dreamer, but he'd known the trade of war and sieges like few others did. During his service in the Valelands, he'd worked with some of the best Nirian engineers of war and devised his own contraptions based on their work, designs Ash would be able to Dreamchant or build upon. So long as he could get hold of them.

* * *

The Craghorn had become his home when he and his father had first settled in the city and started their printing business. Ash had learned to love it then. Weathered wooden houses filled the craggy peninsula's crevasses like a thick mortar, squat buildings climbing onto each other's backs for light and air.

Tonight, it didn't feel like home.

His old neighbourhood felt more silent than ever. He hoped to find the tavern he sought quickly, quickly enough to avoid being seen.

The Jolly Nag was still there. The windows were shuttered and the doors closed, though. The city watch had nailed their curfew notice on the door. After the attack on the Penance Procession, the Secret Chancellery was bringing order to the streets at all costs.

Ash paced about the building, seeking any sort of light inside. Nothing.

He banged on the door loudly.

The long silence was broken at last by muffled cursing, then a bar being removed and finally the door cracking ajar.

'Ash?' It was Isande, the girl he'd played with as a young boy freshly arrived in the city. Her father was a former comrade of his father's, so they'd banded together. The tavern was dark and seemingly empty.

'You've chosen the worst night to drop in for a drink,' she said.

'I'm sorry for the trouble, Isande. Where's your father?'

'In Her dark bosom,' was her reply.

Ash staggered. Just like that, another link with his past, tinged with the memory of his father, had snapped. He'd promised himself he'd make time to visit, to get some stories from old Telmos about the past. But the Lightning-Hunter trade had sucked all the energy out of him. 'I'm so very sorry. I wish I had been here more often. He was a good man.'

'What did you want to see him for? Or is this to do with the breaking of yokes?' she added, lowering her voice.

'Sort of. I've come for my father's things.' Both Ash's and Isande's fathers had had Exarchian sympathies, enough for them to share and discuss political pamphlets. They were the sort of documents Ash had wanted to keep at arm's length after this arrest, like everything connected to the Sunken Library.

Isande sighed. 'I suppose one doesn't choose when to be visited by one's past. Come.'

She led him into the pantry. There, under the light of a candle, she pulled open the trapdoor to the cellar, and he followed her below. It was cool and quiet, filled with hanging herbs, salted fish and meat, jars with grain and barrels of ale.

'In there. Behind the loose piece of slate. I'll leave you to it.' She left a candle and climbed back upstairs. Ash crouched between two barrels to laboriously remove the stone from the wall.

Inside a hole was a pile of letters and old documents, smelling of soil. The years, humidity and dirt had taken their toll, but he could still read them. He sat by the candle to go through them.

There were hundreds of pages, either written or annotated by his father. He hadn't really gone through these after Eoinas had died. It had hurt too much, and he'd always found other, more pressing concerns.

There were drawings of cities and landscapes in the Valelands, but also in Gallecia and of ships and people, too. And so much more than that. Designs for printing presses, sketches for types.

'Envisioning a better world is the duty of everyone with an imagination,' his father had liked to say. That'd been his curse and ambition, the root of his idealism and his bitterness: to fall in love with the dream of a better world, only to have his heart broken by his failure to build it.

Ash flicked through the stack of papers, and to his relief, he found what he sought. His father's old sketches.

The campaigns in the Valelands his father had participated in had been grim affairs involving lengthy sieges and plenty of waiting. There were quite a few sketches of the landscape, canals, rivers and mills . . . and also of the business of war.

That's what he sought: drawings and notes on siegecraft, from tunnelling devices to grappling hooks to modifications for thunder-cannons. They possessed the sort of practical cruelty the Academy-dominated tribunal would value. Ash needed only to Dreamchant them.

There was another sketch journal, one Ash regretted opening as soon as he did. It was filled with other haunting images well known to him. His father's notes on his studies on the Sunken Library. Why had his father been so obsessed with the place? Why was he willing to chase this obsession to the point of risking both his and his son's lives to this foolish endeavour? There were safer ways to make money on old books. He would have angrily demanded answers from his father, had he been alive. But he wasn't, and so these notes had to do.

Against his best judgement, Ash soon found himself lost in them. Reading them was like rubbing an old scar to see if the pain was still there. And it was.

Here were the highlights of a lifetime of obsession: quotes from Illuminators and travelogues, fragmentary sketches of floorplans and incomplete attempts at compiling its gargantuan catalogue.

And yes, he had been interested in the trove of books that had been left behind. But as Ash read, he discovered something else.

His father had scribbled some of his own conjectures regarding Empress Damnia's Silver Book of Wisdom. He'd obtained a crumbling journal allegedly belonging to an Illuminator who'd hastily worked to copy the book during the Great Library's final days. Some of her sketches, focusing on the challenges of engraving Dreamchanted silver, suggested that the attempts had been partially successful.

He'd also noted how the legendary poet and philosopher Joshian the Errant had entered the ruins a century past to find that the books were miraculously intact. Outlandish as it sounded, Ash's father seemed convinced that a partial copy of the Silver Book had been forgotten in the library's forsaken collection.

Even a partial copy of the Philosopher Empress's masterpiece would have made them rich beyond measure, but from

Eoinas's fragmentary notes, it was evident that wasn't why he wanted it.

If the copy were still there, it could be replicated, and Damnia's motherlode of wisdom taken to the masses with the printing press . . . It would arm their minds and allow them to form an army in which they could dream unrestrained . . . It could be the key to bringing justice to the Undreaming, to free those who have nothing and are kept under the Oneirocrats' yoke. Isn't that a dream worth pursuing?

Ash reread the lines over and over again, but he could find no other interpretation. Enlightenment and the ideals that only existed in the perfect prose of books had been the real purpose of their trip, not just some cheap score.

A noble dream or a fool's errand? In the end, Eoinas had failed. And why had he kept this a secret from Ash? To protect him? If so, he'd failed at that too. Ash's heart burned with years of bottled resentment, but there was nobody he could yell at.

'Found what you were looking for?' Isande asked. Ash had been so absorbed by the reading he hadn't heard her return.

'Yes.' He paused. 'And more,' he said, packing the documents inside a large leather pouch. He headed for the stairs, Omen following, but was stopped by Isande. 'I owe you for this.'

'Don't fret. My father would be happy to know that they're finally being put to some use. Sometimes, building on the foundations they left us is all we can do,' she said, gesturing to the inn.

Ash could do nothing but nod and leave, the papers both a relief and a heavy weight.

Chapter Twenty-Five

Daerna

Losing a friend cuts your soul not just with sorrow but also with longing for the conversations that you'll never have.
– *Contemplations on Sorrow* by Empress Myrtele

The sound of music seeped into Daerna's uneasy sleep. She rolled over in her hospice bed, hoping to see Ash, but when she turned, she faced a woman playing a floor harp.

And then she remembered where she'd seen the woman before.

'Blessed Elpia?' she mumbled.

The woman smiled, her lips shimmering silver white.

'You're ready to *see*,' the woman said.

Petals began raining from the darkness above, except when they touched Daerna's skin or her bed, they turned to scraps of paper bearing words smudged with ash.

'I don't understand,' Daerna said.

'Her song is written in sorrow and hope, but they don't feel it. Her song is in the clouds and the rocks, but they refuse to touch it. Her song is written on silver, but one must sing it, not just repeat it,' the woman replied.

Blessed Elpia was holding a heavy tome of silver pages. Daerna reached out from her bed for it, and someone seized her arm.

She turned to see a veiled Wailing Sister by her side. The stranger gripped her forearm, digging her nails in, droplets of blood welling up. Except it wasn't her nails but sharp fingers of bone, trying to tear through Daerna's habit and her skin too. Under the veil, the Midwife's eyes bored into her.

Daerna screamed herself awake, partly because of the nightmare, but also because of the dull pain in her sore ribs.

Omen was nuzzling her.

'What's wrong?' Ash asked, closing the sketchbook on his lap. 'You screamed in your sleep.'

Her muscles still felt as if someone had bludgeoned them, but she could breathe almost normally. Besides, in only a week, hers was a miraculous recovery.

'I just keep having these dreams,' she managed.

'About what happened?'

'About something I saw at the Silent Abbey, but fear not. I'm better.'

'Here, drink.' Ash held a mug to her lips, filled with a medicinal infusion. Daerna forced herself to down at least a draught of the bitter liquid before sitting sideways on the bed, her naked feet caressing the cold floor tiles. Omen rubbed against her leg.

She reached down to stroke his head, only for the room to spin around her.

'What's wrong?' Ash asked, again.

'Just a dizzy spell.'

He frowned.

'I'll be fine. Besides, Omen won't let me go anywhere on my own, not even to the lavatory.' They laughed. 'Please, just continue studying. I'll be back shortly.'

Ash sank into his book again as Daerna slipped from the bed and then the room, Omen marching protectively ahead of her.

She paused to look through the windows open to the inner courtyard where some of the Widows' militia talked and cleaned their maces. A lot of them had been brought in to protect the hospice. The curfew might have brought stillness to the night, but not peace.

She'd heard from Dirdra that while the Charnelites had all been hunted down by now, the Academy's Nightmares still prowled the streets at night, erring on the side of destruction. Bargers came in day in, day out with the injured and dead.

Mother's Tears were given to those who needed them, and the Wailers sang their funerary dirges to elevate the souls of the deceased almost every hour. Above the aerial pyres, black clouds cast a perennial shroud over the hospice.

The whole thing made Daerna's stomach queasy.

Omen grumbled at the sound of footsteps on the stairs. A novice, a young girl with frizzy hair, reached the landing and gasped upon seeing the panther.

'It's fine!' Daerna hurriedly placed her hand on Omen's head.

'You're Sister Daerna Eimar?' she asked, unable to take her eyes off the big cat.

'Yes, why?'

'Sister Dirdra of Muirtra has sent you an urgent message.' The novice placed a letter in her hands, then hurriedly vanished down the stairs.

It was about Roshia. And it was the worst sort of news.

* * *

The hospice's Sisters returned her habit, but even after washing the blood and the mud off, there was still a hole where she'd been stabbed. She was only able to disguise the worst of it thanks to Ash's cloak.

They set out into the cold, overcast streets. Walking, she ran out of breath easily, a reminder that she wasn't fully recovered, but Roshia couldn't wait. Ash kindly offered to pay for a barge to take her to Muirtra, and she gratefully accepted.

Watching the city slide by from the canals felt strange to Daerna.

On the southern side, the streets seemed empty. People darted through alleyways, keeping to the shadows, while others angrily confronted the guards blocking the bridges. In the Central Quarter, life went on with a forced normality, but even there she saw cracks.

Some graffiti denounced 'Lord Stalcar the tyrant' for the brutality of this repression. Others accused Lady Saorla of weakness for 'inviting the heretics and criminals into our home'. Even now that new senators had taken office, everything was a battlefield to elevate councillors of their party's persuasion.

The pigeons and the crowcats perched above the lionheads watched the tensions between Reformers and Traditionalists, but also between those who had bread and those who starved.

The city felt balanced on a knife's edge.

Muirtra's tall spires appearing gave her some relief. Despite everything, this was her home, and the onyx steeples and lush gardens were a welcome sight for her sore eyes.

She found Sister Dirdra in the chorus chamber. She looked even more tired than the last time she'd seen her.

'Daerna? What are you doing here? You should be resting!'

They hugged, forcefully enough for Daerna to feel the flaring burn in her ribs, but also to silence her mentor's concerns.

'Fear not, I'm fine, given the circumstances. Thanks to you and the others. Speaking of which: where's Roshia?'

Daerna caught a glint of fear in Dirdra's eyes. 'In her cell. Sister Herbalist Skiara is tending to her. I didn't mean for you to rush here. I'm hopeful whatever the malady is, Sister Skiara will treat it adequately.'

If she had to guess, Daerna would bet that Roshia had been working twice as hard in the past week to cover for her absence.

They hurried downstairs. Roshia lay in her bed, her eyes lost in contemplation of the grey light that came in through the arched window. The rosy-cheeked Sister Herbalist stood up from the chair by Roshia's bedside.

Daerna hurried to the bed. Something had been worrying her since she got the message. Roshia was conscious, but her gaze was unfocused. 'How are you feeling?'

'I'm sorry, Dae ...' Her voice was a weak croak.

'I'm here!' Daerna clutched Roshia's hand. It was limp and clammy.

'I'm sorry, Dae,' she repeated, her eyes wandering aimlessly over Daerna's face as if not truly seeing her.

'How long has this been happening?' Daerna asked, although she feared she knew the answer.

'The fever only a few days,' the Sister Herbalist replied. 'But she was acting strangely before that ... There were moments in which she seemed a bit dazed.'

Daerna felt Roshia's forehead. The fever was already quite high. She pulled up her tunic's sleeve to examine her arms and found a rash.

No. No. No. This couldn't be.

'Sister Skiara, would you leave us alone with Roshia for a while?'

The Herbalist looked at Dirdra, who nodded. As soon as she'd left them, Daerna stood up and paced the room, searching for the tell-tale stains on the walls and the floor.

The cell, sparsely decorated, was pristine for the most part. Roshia had always been the tidy type. Clothes neatly kept in her chest. Books and letters discreetly arranged against the wall on her worktable. Even her lesson notes seemed organised. Daerna was about to give up when she noticed an odd mark near the back of Roshia's worktable.

'What are you looking for?' Dirdra asked.

Daerna pulled the table from the wall, her ribs aching in protest, and found the same dark mould she'd seen at the hospices. Fear bloomed cold in her heart, sending shivers through her body.

'How long has this been here?' she asked, pointing at the mould.

Dirdra looked at it in confusion.

'I don't know. A few days?' Dirdra answered. 'That's how long she's spent here. What is it?'

'I've seen it appear before in the dwellings of those afflicted with the Wilting.'

'But how could that be?'

'This past month, we've spent a lot of time among the afflicted. We must act now, before it gets worse! Once the palsy sets in, it's too late!'

Dirdra breathed deeply. 'Are you certain? This goes against everything we've been taught about the disease.'

'The symptoms are the same, and the risk is . . .' Daerna couldn't finish, neither the sentence nor the thought. This was Roshia that they were talking about. Young, happy, bright Roshia . . . This couldn't be happening.

It shouldn't be happening.

'There must be something we can do about it,' Dirdra said.

'Yes. We'll help her fight it off. We need to have someone care for her at all hours. And if the tremors begin, they must let me know immediately.'

'I thought if that happened, it'd mean it was too late.'

Daerna felt a knot in her throat.

'It won't be,' she said, ignoring the heavy darkness that loomed in the air. 'I won't let it be.'

Chapter Twenty-Six

Ash

And when the Solemn Princess heard of Empress Myrtele's death at the hands of her power-hungry cousin Prince Arcos, she walked into the black, breaking waves and she cried a Wail of Stone, and every shard of her shattered soul became a jet-black tear, an island, a step into eternity.

– *Life and Miracles of Divine Geleisdra* by Blessed Elpia

THE MORNING BEFORE HIS EXAM, Ash's work ground to a halt when Daerna came to the Quietude. She had deep bags beneath her red eyes.

'We're losing Roshia,' she said, sinking into his arms. 'The paralysis is setting in. Her breathing has become erratic. The others still hope for a miracle, but I fear that she's extinguishing. I don't know what else to do, Ash.'

Her voice cracked.

'I'm so very sorry,' he said, hugging her.

'The Song says we're to be strong, to harness our own sorrow and wear it proudly like a crown. But I can't. This is all my fault!'

'No one can control the Wilting, Dae.'

Daerna's head sank onto his shoulder, and she smothered a whimper.

'Come on, let's try to find that miracle,' Ash said.

He led her upstairs to the workshop where Lord Morvander toiled. Half a dozen masks floated in the air, their opaline eyes allowing him to oversee a dozen different variations of the mirrormatter. The freshly Dreamt replicas were piling up in the workshop, despite Tarna, the door warden's, best efforts to haul them down to the palace's massive cellars.

'Ash? What's this about?' Lord Morvander asked, clearly exhausted from his work.

'My lord, I've mentioned the condition of Daerna's fellow Sister, Roshia. We fear she's getting worse. Stiffness has started to set in.'

'I'm sorry to hear that. The palsies often come with the swelling of the blood vessels in the brain. These ultimately lead to thrombosis and death. There are remedies that can ease her pain, though.'

'I was hoping,' Ash said, 'we could try using the mirrormatter to save her . . .'

Morvander fell back onto his workbench with a sigh. 'I fear that would be reckless. In such a delicate state, the strain of the process might kill her. Not to mention we've never attempted such a thing. We're still struggling to transfer something as tangible as a physical injury. How could we capture something so elusive as the Wilting?'

'We could try treating its physical symptoms,' Ash replied.

'Even if we could overcome the afflicted's natural resistance, I wouldn't be able to help her any more than a skilled Remaker could. And from what I've heard, in the case of the Wilting, the symptoms shortly reappear.'

'Maybe with the mirrormatter it'll be different! Perhaps transferring the symptoms would allow us to isolate the disease!'

'You might transfer some symptoms, but not the root of it. The replica mirrors the body, not the soul. A spiritual ailment is something we can't attack.'

'What if the spiritual disturbance is consequence and *not* cause?' Daerna interjected. 'What if there's an external force causing and propagating the disease?' Ash and Morvander turned to her in surprise. 'Over the past few weeks in the Scab and Little Vespiria, I've found a black mould spreading wherever the disease festers. What if it taints the air around to cause the Wilting?'

Lord Morvander straightened. 'You're suggesting it's a physical cause and that every single physician and Remaker in the city is wrong?'

'Not suggesting, I *know* there's more to it. The oracles of the Warden Sisters know this. I've seen the evidence.' Daerna's voice hardened.

Morvander arched an eyebrow. 'The oracles. You mean those who study the Silver Book for "portents".'

'Indeed. I know for a certainty that they believe the Wilting is connected to the rot I've described.' Lord Morvander's eyebrows arched at that. 'They even believe it to be connected to the Crumbling District's collapse decades ago. They wrote that it's connected to the Wail of Stone's spiritual echoes in the different islets.'

Daerna had told Ash of her incursion into the Silent Abbey before, but only now was he realising the gravity of what she'd discovered.

'Why . . . of course.' Morvander pressed a hand to his forehead. '". . . and every shard of her shattered soul became a jet-black tear, an island, a step into eternity"!' Morvander said, and Daerna nodded emphatically.

'"She cried a Wail of Stone,"' Daerna said, finishing the quotation.

'I don't follow,' Ash said.

'All Dreams have hidden kernels, but Geleisdra's hallowed miracles have even deeper mysteries at their hearts. These, it would appear, have to do with Divine Geleisdra's many different sorrows,' Lord Morvander replied. 'There's a reason why the lagoon's onyx has proved an ideal receptacle for maladies.'

'Then, wouldn't investigating the Wilting offer us an opportunity to improve the mirrormatter's design?' Ash asked eagerly. This had to be the opening he needed to win Lord Morvander's aid.

'Perhaps. Though researching this mould would take time.' Morvander stroked his beard. With a flick of his bracelet, the room's walls grew darker. 'I've made sure that no one can overhear us, so tell me, Daerna, how did you learn of this?'

She hesitated. 'It's fine,' Ash said, placing a reassuring hand on her shoulder.

Daerna took a deep breath. 'The Sisters of Silence's library. Inside their vault, they keep copies of the Warden Sisters' portents. It's all there! They also said that the Silver Book holds more answers.' She shifted from foot to foot. 'Lord Morvander, you're an Archdreamer. Couldn't you go to the source? Ask to consult the Silver Book yourself? I know that other Archdreamers like Lord Stalcar have been granted the honour of visiting the Solemn Abbey in the past.'

'Impossible,' he said sullenly. 'The Wardens are extremely selective of whom they allow to consult the Silver Book. I assure you I'd fail their purity tests. And I won't risk their scrutiny, not when our work is at stake. You know the risks I've already taken.

'Besides, even if you were right, who could we trust with this? Start asking the wrong questions, or worse, throwing accusations without undeniable evidence, and those same people who've decided to hide all of this will act.'

'But—'

'There might be a way to navigate these treacherous waters, but we must be smart about it. Trust me, in my time, I've seen too many swallowed by the tide because they miscalculated their moves.'

That seemed to be the end of it. Ash couldn't even be angry at him; Morvander had already taken an immense risk in saving Daerna's life. If word got out before they'd garnered the necessary political support for his work, he could be imprisoned or even hanged for the crime of desecrating the hallowed onyx. They *all* could be.

Then a ludicrous, desperate and terrible idea dawned in Ash's mind, one that instantly carved an empty pit inside him. There was a way for him to help Daerna, but it meant returning to his own entombed hell.

'What if there was another way to consult the Silver Book?' he asked.

'If what you're suggesting is spying on the Wardens' crypts, that's a disastrous idea,' Morvander replied coldly.

'I'm talking about a different Silver Book. A copy in Damnia's Great Library.'

'I thought everything of value was rescued from the Great Library when it flooded,' Daerna said.

'I know a lot of the books are still there, against all odds. I saw them.' A cruel shiver ran down his spine just thinking about it. 'My father found a work journal belonging to one of the Great Library's Illuminators and deduced from it that the library held a partial copy of the Silver Book. Here, let me show you.'

He reached into his satchel for the notes and his father's crude maps. One of Lord Morvander's floating masks descended to read it.

'But how to know whether it's still there?' There was curiosity in Morvander's tone now.

'My father was convinced enough to risk his life.' Ash swallowed hard. 'To risk both of our lives trying to recover it.'

The words were difficult to say aloud, but it felt good to lay the truth bare. Eoinas Allandra had believed in this. He'd gambled everything he had on the belief. For too long, Ash had thought his father had been driven by greed, but now he understood better.

It wasn't that he'd valued Ash's life too little; it was that this dream was worth everything to him. He'd been willing to die for his ideas, for a shot at changing their world, partly for his son's future.

Morvander tilted his head, weighing Ash's words.

'Daerna, will you grant us a moment alone?'

There was a flash of concern in her eyes, but she dipped her head and left the workshop.

Ash waited until she'd closed the door to speak. 'Please, I'm only asking that you let us try.'

'You really must love her if you're willing to return there.'

It hit him then, just what he was asking. 'I do love her, but this isn't just for her. I've seen your work, and I *believe* in it. I believe in the gift you want to give the people. You said it yourself, there must be more to Dreaming. If this can help either of you, it's worth my life.'

'What about your exam? They'll rescind your exemption if you don't show in time for the summons!'

'If that's what it takes to save Roshia . . .'

'The risk is too high, the reward too uncertain.' Lord Morvander shook his head. Without his patron's resources, the idea was doomed from the start. Then he remembered that, among his many sketches and documents, there was a map of the Onyxian Domain.

He bolted from the chair and rummaged through the shelves until he found it. He spread it out over the drawing desk, while Lord Morvander sent one of his masks to watch him.

'With the *Night Swan*, I could make the trip and be back on time.'

'You'd need a different crew, though, one loyal enough to keep this secret for the good of us all.'

'I can get one!' he responded. His old Lightning-Hunter crew would rather die than betray him.

'You're serious about this, aren't you?' Morvander furrowed his brow.

'If Daerna's right, if my father was right . . . this could help us cure the Wilting! Perhaps even give us the solution we seek to help Lord Brakte's people in the Valelands!'

Morvander sighed loudly. 'I wish I could deny you, but I'd be lying if I said this wouldn't change everything. If your father was right, if you bring the book back, I promise you we'll save Daerna's Sister, even if it's the last thing I do.'

* * *

Ash sent a message to his crew through Daerna, since they had to maintain utmost secrecy. He hoped they'd be ready to depart in the afternoon. The cover of night was the only way for them to evade the Academy's sentinels at the Sunken Library.

He then set to finishing his exam preparations.

The past few days, he'd been working on enhancing one of his father's designs, and now it was finally ready. He offered Lucre the final result: a metallic flower.

Lucre held the bloom with both hands. It was as long as her arm, and the stem was solid cast iron. The bulb was made of sharp iron petals folded around a hollow core that could hold a small orb-lamp. The original idea had been Ash's father's, but the elegant design was all Lucre's: each petal curved into a grappling hook that could eject or retract at will.

Too often one heard tales in the Shingle Sea of chimney-children, thatchers or Lightning-Hunters falling to the canals from a badly secured rope or a too-rusty hook that gave in in the middle of a storm. This would prevent that, and could also be used to climb walls in sieges or hulls during naval boardings.

Lucre's eyes gleamed ruby red as she examined the object with her mask. Ash braced himself for a round of harsh criticism. 'It has beauty, but I can see it all serves its purpose. And more importantly, it could have many applications in trading and in war. I think you've found it.'

Ash blinked. Had he misheard her? She returned the black metal rose carefully.

'If Josod was here, he'd chastise you for not having made it beautiful enough, or functional enough, but you've struck a fine balance, Aescyon. You should smooth the edges and polish it, but I dare say the tribunal will favour you tomorrow.'

'Thank you, Lucre. It means a lot that you've believed in me all this time.'

She smiled and clasped her cloak. 'Get some rest tonight. You'll need to be at your best during the exam. Then we'll celebrate.'

He bade her farewell and set to preparing his own equipment for the night's sortie. He wrapped the long rose in a canvas bag with a couple of orb-lamps and put on the rapier Thalder had got him, as well as a dagger. He didn't want to find himself in want of weapons if the situation arose.

As he finished putting on his boots, Omen insistently pressed one of his sharp paws against Ash's leg, as if begging.

'Don't worry, it'll be fine,' he said.

But Omen paced about the room restlessly.

Ash leaned over and pressed their foreheads together, then whispered in his ear, 'I'll be back before dawn, I promise.'

The truth was that Ash couldn't bear the thought of Omen getting lost in that hellish place, and so the cat would stay.

Ash slung the satchel over his jerkin, put on his cloak and hurried to close the door after him. He could hear Omen scratching, and as soon as Ash walked down the hallway, the panther began roaring and lashing violently at the door.

Ash went back and opened the door to reprimand him, but the panther immediately shoved his head through the crack and forced himself past Ash. Apparently, he'd decided to come whether Ash wanted him to or not.

'Very well. But you must keep quiet, do you hear me?' Omen snorted like a chided child. They hurried up the stairs towards the palace's sky dock. Boarding the skysloop, Captain Bentor's voice reached him from his cabin. He knocked at the door and Thalder opened it.

'Master? What in the entombed hells are you doing here?'

The man stretched his neck. 'Saving you from your own stupidity, it'd appear.'

'I'll leave you two,' Bentor said, clapping Ash's shoulder on his way out.

'Morvander told me what you're planning.' Thalder scratched at his grey beard. 'Lad, you're a complete *fool* if you think you can break into the Sunken Library and steal anything.'

'I know the Academy keeps watch over it. I've been there before.'

Thalder gawked at him. 'That you survived that place once was luck, Ash. Don't squander it by tempting fortune again.'

'Master, you realise the book might have the key to our work?'

'And you, boy, must realise that if there was some "cure" in that book, it'd mean they've deliberately kept it a secret?'

Ash narrowed his eyes. 'I think that weighed against some political gains, the Southern Quarter folk matter little to them. It's up to us to help ourselves.'

'So, let me get this straight. You're going to sneak into an area fabled for its Nightmares, dangle yourself in front of the Academy's sentinels for some book that might or might not be there, for a cure that it might or might not have, and even if you find it, it will only provoke the fury of the powers that be – is that right?'

Thalder had always possessed the remarkable gift of making Ash's plans sound not only reckless but downright stupid. This time, the prize was worth the odds, though.

Ash tilted up his chin. 'Are you going to stand in my way?'

'Actually,' he said, 'I think this will serve you well as a final lesson.'

'Excuse me?'

The slit of a smile appeared in Thalder's greying beard. 'That's why I'm going with you.'

Chapter Twenty-Seven

Daerna

Among the many tragedies the Sibling Strife bequeathed future generations – soiled seas, uncountable dead, ravaged lands and ruined marvels – the worst are those places that remain Vigil-blighted.

A razed battlefield might, with the years, harbour life again. A Vigil-blighted one isn't barren, but rather the contrary; it's fertile soil for cruel maladies of unreality to fester.

The very land has gone feral, shaped not by the elements but rather by the unspoken fears of those who tread upon them.

– *A Tale of the Sibling Strife* by Blessed Merele

THEY WERE ALL READY AT the agreed-upon hour, waiting atop Ash's former garret in Little Vespiria.

'Ah, a fine harvest we could gather out there,' Rudher lamented, watching the increasing drizzle. Despite his whining about lost wages, he'd been the first to accept Ash's crazy request and encourage Yaisa and Ghalod to do the same.

At last, the skysloop glided into view above them. Its descent was graceful despite the wind, and it soon berthed on the side of the roof. A stocky man clad in a leather jerkin, his greying braids and matching beard whipping in the wind, appeared portside and set down a gangplank for them.

Rudher and Yaisa darted ahead; Daerna struggled after them on the slippery rooftop. Only Ghalod trudged behind her, burdened with the Lightning-Hunter tools.

Breathing heavily, she made it to the gangplank, but the stranger stood in her way, arms crossed.

'You're not coming, Sister,' he said.

'Who are you to tell me what I can and can't do?' she asked.

'Thalder Kewildra, Ash's tutor. You're Sister Daerna Eimar – pleased to meet you. Now turn around. We don't need the extra weight.'

'Extra weight? Who put you in charge of this party?'

'Lord Nial Morvander,' he replied with a smirk.

Yaisa, who'd witnessed their exchange from the deck, yelled, 'Hey, Ash! How come you always have nagging old men around you wherever you go?'

'I'm not nagging!' Rudher said, dropping his satchel on the deck.

'Who are you calling old?' replied Thalder, almost in unison.

Yaisa chuckled. Ash finally emerged from the stern castle.

'Daerna? What's wrong?'

Thalder crossed his arms. 'Ash, could you please explain to her that this is no lark?'

'Don't you think I know that?' she snapped. 'It's my friend's life we're talking about! Now tell me, Master Thalder, do you have much experience digging through piles of books or archives?'

'You'd be surprised, Sister. Becoming a master Nightmare-Hunter requires handling plenty of bestiaries,' Thalder replied unfazed, arching an eyebrow.

'Well then,' Daerna pressed on. 'How about medical texts, or obscure theological discussions in Ancient Iskian? Are you familiar with those too?'

Thalder sucked his teeth at that.

'You don't have to do this if you don't want to,' Ash said softly.

'And send you to risk everything for me? No, I'm going,' she replied firmly.

Ash pursed his lips. 'She could be useful in the library, Thalder.'

Thalder sighed wearily. 'Have it your way! But you'll have to do exactly what I tell you to do.'

'Understood,' she said.

She and Ghalod boarded and the skyship took off, spreading its sails and picking up speed.

Daerna felt an uncomfortable tug in her heart. This would be her first time in years outside the capital. Leaving the Motherstorm's protective embrace made her fret.

They headed east, deep into the mainland of Logria. She'd passed through it once, accompanying her father on a trip to meet with some wool merchants, before their family had moved into the sugar trade in Vespiria. Her memories were of a green and pleasant land, of wooded hills and moors and cities built around old Iskian ruins.

She'd always thought that if she glimpsed the Great Library, it would be during a pilgrimage to its nearby abbey or one of the other sacred sites nearby, not to lead a sacrilegious ruin-robbing expedition.

She jumped when she felt a hand on her shoulder.

'You should get some rest. Captain Bentor says that even with these favourable winds, we won't be there before midnight,' Ash whispered.

'Come rest with me,' she said.

They lay down together, wrapped in each other's arms and Omen's thick fur. Daerna soon drifted into a deep sleep.

* * *

'There!' Ghalod's booming voice woke Daerna. 'Is that it?' He was hunched at one of the prow portholes. Daerna rose to join him. A thorny spire of black stone and pale bone rose in the distance, cutting through grey skies. The fires of a beacon lit up its sky docks.

'No,' replied Thalder, arriving from the upper deck at the same time she and Ash emerged from the bunks. 'That's the Lundeyn watchtower. You might not see it, but there's a whole fortress underneath. Even the Academy keeps a small detachment there. Mostly experienced Nightmare-Hunters and the occasional Hordemaster. A shitty post if there ever was one.'

'Shitty how?' Yaisa asked. 'Aren't they just watching some old ruins and keeping the pilgrims away?'

'"Old ruins" doesn't quite explain it. There's a reason why only ruin-robbers and the mad come here. The final battle against the Pale Prince took a heavy toll on the land.'

'Vigil-blighted,' Ash said grimly.

'Vigil-blighted?' Daerna repeated.

He kept his eyes on the sinister landscape below. 'Stuck between the waking and the Dreaming world. Two Divine Dreamers faced each other here, and the land still bleeds for it. Of all the Sibling Strife battles, this one was among the worst. The waking world's foundations are particularly brittle here.'

'What do you mean?'

'That things don't play out the way they should. Around the battle site, the natural order is unreliable, contradictory and, most importantly, perilous. If that isn't bad enough, there's also a lot of corpses in that bog.'

'Ach,' Rudher cursed loudly. 'Not sure I want to know ... but why does that make it worse?'

'The Charnel Mother's reach must be particularly strong here,' Daerna surmised aloud.

'Precisely,' Thalder said.

'I thought she'd been shredded into ashes by Geleisdra's Guardian,' Rudher replied.

'She wasn't just some Nightmare, that much I can tell you, old crow. I've seen enough corpses crawl away from plague pits and battlefields to tell you something lurks on the other side of the veil of death. Princess protect us,' Thalder said, touching his heart four times, Daerna and the others following suit. Misguided as they were, the Charnelites were right about one thing: the Sibling Strife had forever woven terrible miracles into the fabric of the world, none more terrible than the Charnel Mother Herself.

Daerna reached for Ash and noticed he had both hands tightened into fists.

'How are you holding up?' she asked.

'I'll manage,' he said, keeping his eyes on the deck.

After a while, he took a deep breath and put his arm around her shoulders. They lingered together like that until he abruptly stiffened.

'That shouldn't be there.'

She could barely make out what he'd seen. Mist-like clouds loomed ahead of them, hanging low, almost impossible to see through in the thick of night. Threads dangled beneath them like a ghostly moss.

'Master!' Ash called.

Thalder turned from speaking with Rudher, eyes widening as soon as he saw it.

'Hold fast!' he roared.

They all clung to the handgrips in the hold while Thalder sealed the doors shut with his bracelet.

'Keep it closed, or it'll kill us all!' he yelled as he disappeared up the stairs into the stern castle to alert Captain Bentor.

Daerna could hear Thalder arguing tensely with the ship's captain. A moment later, he reappeared in the hold.

Clinging to one of the fixed rings on the ceiling, he said, 'Brace yourselves. Things are about to get even rougher. Oh, and you might want to keep your eyes closed.'

His gaze went glassy as he entered the Dreaming trance, and then the skyship started shaking, and Daerna's whole body with it. Omen raced through the hold as if tracking something outside, while Ash tried in vain to calm the panther down.

She was thinking it could hardly get any worse when something began screeching outside. It wasn't the wind howling, more like a thousand claws tearing at the ship's hull. The skyship teetered perilously off-keel. Thalder, lost to the trance, fell limply to one side, and Ghalod and Rudher rushed to grab him.

Any minute, it seemed they would fall out of the sky, and then a sudden, blinding wave of flames engulfed the ship. Amidst the fire, Daerna thought she glimpsed large wings.

When the fire dimmed, the skyship regained its stability. Thalder, breathing heavily, stood up.

'By her blessed bones! What was that?' Ghalod asked.

'A feckin' assassin mist, that's what it was!' Rudher replied while rubbing his ankle. 'I think I've broken something.'

'He's not wrong,' Thalder replied. 'Luckily for you, I trained with good Nightmarists and I happen to know how to burn one down. That was a close one. We better hurry, though. If they didn't know we were here, they do now.'

'What does that mean?' Daerna asked.

Thalder frowned. 'Means they'll be sending a patrol to the library soon enough. I'll tell the captain to inform them that our skysloop's helm has been damaged and that's why we've wandered over here, but for them to eat that wyrmshit, we need to be fast.'

'We've arrived!' Captain Bentor announced from the cabin above.

Daerna and the others clambered to the prow portholes.

The Sunken Library wasn't like she'd imagined it. It wasn't some lone tower in a dismal landscape, but rather a crooked copse of colossal spires connected to a massive citadel that rose higher than even Muirtra. The hungry marshes below had swallowed the foundations, and the whole complex now tilted perilously.

'I'll tell Bentor to berth there,' Ash said, pointing at the colossus. 'You should get ready.'

'It couldn't be one of the nice ruins,' Rudher grumbled.

The skysloop folded its wings, and the swaying abated. A gentle rain fell over the island, its pattering the only sound.

'Ready?' Ghalod asked.

'Someone will have to stay behind to warn us if the ship's attacked,' said Thalder, looking at Daerna.

'I'm going in,' she replied firmly.

'Don't mind if I do,' Rudher said. 'You all come back in one piece, you hear me? Otherwise, I'll charge you the surgeon's bill.' He laughed, a shrill nervousness in his voice.

'You stay here too!' Ash commanded Omen, who was pacing nervously over the stern castle.

'Allow me,' Thalder said. Without warning, he jumped overboard, ignoring the ladder. Like some sort of mountain lion, he hit the wall and clung to it, jerking himself to a stop before pulling himself up.

'Cocky old bastard,' Yaisa said with a smile. She climbed down after him.

Ash froze when his turn came to approach the rope ladder. Daerna looked at him with a question written on her face.

'It's barely changed since the last time I saw it,' he whispered.

Chapter Twenty-Eight

Geil

The First Article – we will not allow ourselves to be further oppressed by those who claim themselves above us on account of their Dreaming gift. Oneirocrats shall only demand what just services have been paid for and agreed to by the Undreaming.

It is our will and resolution that in the future, we shall have power and authority for each community to choose and appoint their own governance.

– *The Seven Articles of the Exarchians*

Oldcourt's orphanage was larger than Geil had expected, stretching over lands and a manor house that had once belonged to some magistrate's estate. Its ample grounds lay sequestered in a dale hidden from the main road that traversed the Craghorn peninsula.

Well over a hundred children and teens lived there under the Widowed Sisters' care.

Nothing suggested it'd make a good home to the Exarchians, which meant that to find the truth, she'd have to dig beneath that pristine skin. Good thing that the Drake enjoyed using its claws so much. 'Lanteus, you say his name was?' Sister Lasara, the woman in charge, asked.

As soon as Geil had announced her presence, the head Sister had hurried to meet her. She was a wry, olive-skinned woman in her mid-years, with snowy streaks in her long braid that spoke of the toll of running this place.

'Lanteus, yes.'

'I'm sorry, I don't think I've ever met him.'

'I thought, given he'd left you a fairly generous sum in his will . . .' Geil tried again, pretending to be taken aback by her reaction.

'May his blessed soul soar within the Motherstorm's bosom, then!' she replied piously. 'We shall sing psalms in his memory!'

'Strange. His family told me he'd visited your institution before, Sister.' Geil accompanied her bluff with a hard stare.

'And he was a Skycourier, you say?' The Widow pursed her lips. 'Maybe if you described him?' The woman nervously fiddled with her braid as Geil described Lanteus.

'Actually . . . Yes, now I recall him. I do remember seeing him pass by once or twice. I never spoke to him. And he was a close friend of yours?'

'He was my companion,' Geil said, clearing her throat to force the words out.

'I'm sorry for your loss,' Sister Lasara said, placing a hand over hers. Geil thought she saw genuine grief in her gaze.

The Drake stretched inside her. *She's lying to us.*

'Perhaps someone else talked to him?' she suggested.

'I'll gladly ask around on your behalf,' Lasara said. 'Perhaps you'd care to give me an address where I can write to you?'

'That won't be necessary.'

She bade farewell to the Widow and headed back for the road. Once she was certain she wasn't being followed, she roused the Drake, letting her back shift and the wings break through, scaly, long and powerful. Then she took to the skies.

She met Mavis near the main road that swept west towards the capital. Atop a bushy hill, he'd set up an observation post.

From there, the orphanage seemed just a part of the sleepy landscape dotted with farms and verdant fields.

'Any luck?' he asked.

'No. They're lying to the point of it being ridiculous. The question is why.'

'We could go together. Lean on the Skycourier's authority and say that the Falconess demands answers.'

'Don't you worry, Mavis. I'm getting us answers one way or another.'

* * *

Night had just fallen when Geil spotted a dim lantern leaving the orphanage's main building. Even from her nearby watch post in the woods, the Drake could make out Sister Lasara's long braid as she cast furtive glances around her.

Time to hunt, the Drake whispered.

Geil trailed her through the thicket until Lasara entered an overgrown ruin, possibly a former granary. She skirted around to the back and found a pair of mules grazing on a pile of hay and a cart loaded with blankets and barrels. Supplies for the orphanage, perhaps. Why the secrecy then?

She crept forwards, doing her best not to startle the animals, and felt under the blankets. Cold, carved metal. She pulled the cover away to find a dozen swords, three breastplates and a couple of crossbows. A remarkable little arsenal, perfect for a group of brigands or assassins. Before she could check for carvings that might reveal the maker's identity, voices reached her from inside the ruin.

Geil skulked behind a wall and peered inside. The Widowed Sister was talking to a young muleteer.

'Where's Parvos?' Sister Lasara asked. 'I need to speak with him.'

'He's around,' the young lad replied. 'Are the children ready?'

'Yes. Only one this time, though.'

What in the Motherstorm's dark bosom was this all about? Was this woman trading the children she was supposed to be caring for? How could Lanteus be involved with such people?

The Drake growled hungrily.

'He should be here!' Lasara protested. 'Someone came poking around today. She asked about Lanteus.'

'Poor bastard's been dead for a while now. Do you think they're finally on to this place?'

'Someone is! That's why I need him—'

A twig snapped behind Geil. She turned to find a hulking figure moving about in the bushes.

Immediately, she jumped into a defensive stance, ready to take on the stranger. She could make out only half of his face under the hood, worn out and hard. A long scar cut from his chin to an eye of solid iron.

'Why don't you introduce yourself, friend?' he asked with a raspy voice. He held a metallic whip coiled around his hand.

That was enough to set the Drake off.

She rushed him, claws open like a hawk swooping for the kill. The stranger held his ground and cracked his whip, which suddenly had not one but a dozen tails spread in a net ready to trap her. It was Dreamchanted, exactly like the ones at the Academy.

The masters had lacerated her flesh with them – until she'd grown Drake scales, hard as steel they couldn't cut through.

Still, out of a hard-won sense of caution, she leapt away to avoid most of the whip's tails.

Drawing strength from her anger, she Dreamt her bones lighter and her muscles with the power of a mountain cat. When the whip's tails snapped closed, she'd already jumped out of their reach.

They both circled each other, looking for an opening. Until, out of the corner of her eye, Geil spotted the other two emerging from the ruin, each one wielding a dagger.

Three to one wasn't ever good odds.

The Drake had faced worse, though. *Break the weakest link and the chain will snap.*

She pretended to ignore their approach, dancing out of the whip's reach but closer to the opening in the wall they'd emerged from. With luck, the scarred man would refrain from lashing at her for fear of hitting them.

The muleteer, seeing the chance, lunged at her. His dagger came at her head, but the Drake was ready. She raised her left arm to parry.

The blow grazed her hard enough to draw a little blood through her scales. She swallowed the pain through her gritted teeth and smashed a fist into his stomach, knocking the air out of him.

She didn't let him fall. Instead, she grabbed him with her spare claw and flung him through the air towards the Sister. He crashed into her and, together, they toppled to the ground.

Finish them, now! the Drake urged.

Lungs burning, she turned, ready to rush her remaining adversary. Surprisingly, the one-eyed man was right behind her. He aimed a swooping kick at her legs, and Geil hit the ground hard.

She couldn't see anything but red, so she kept moving, rolling towards him on the ground. She tried to tackle him, to drag him down into a muddy brawl, but he pulled his knees to his chest to swiftly leap over her. He was fast. Damn fast for his age.

The Drake howled with rage. More scales covered her burning flesh. She jumped back to her feet and clawed at him, but he'd spread his whip, and although she cut two of the tails with her claws, the rest coiled into a thorny bush.

She wasn't just facing a Dreamchanted weapon. He was a Dreamer.

The realisation sank in as two of the stings dug into her thigh.

The whip's heads cut through her breeches, drawing blood. He was good, too good. Against an untrained Dreamer, she'd have an edge, but against one who knew how to fight, it'd be a coin toss.

Part of her mind begged her to escape, or at least scream for Mavis's help, but the Drake was too loud. So loud she couldn't think of anything else but killing. She'd held it off for too long, starved it too much, and now the Drake was unwilling to relinquish control.

This was to be a fight to the death.

At least there was one thing a Dreamer couldn't beat her at: she could shift, adapt, mould herself to be faster.

She Dreamt both her hands anew. Her claws grew as long as scythes and as sharp as cleavers. It was brutal but also unnatural, and her brain burned with the effort.

She launched into a barrage of attacks.

Claws splayed, she swiped left and right, slicing a tail, ripping another, then tearing two more. The bastard was still smiling, as if pleased with the challenge.

She was ready to be done with him. She jumped at him, dodging the mangled whip, but as she leapt, he made a yanking motion with his free hand. A gust of forceful wind knocked her sideways and sent her into the standing walls of the ruin.

Everything went black.

Blinking until her vision cleared, she crawled to her knees, only to see him standing over her.

A score of blades floated at his back like majestic, spread wings. They weren't beautiful, but functional and deadly, some as heavy as broadswords, some the size of daggers.

Let us go through the blades and tear out his throat. Even if we both end up dead, it'll be worth it, the Drake begged.

Her mouth tasted of blood. She might be going down, but so was he. Even if it was the last thing she did.

The man raised a hand.

'How about we talk instead?'

Breathing heavily, she forcefully reined the Drake in. The man backed off, his posture relaxing. He even sheathed the whip and put his thumbs on his belt, waiting for her to recover.

The muleteer and Sister Lasara stood up, hurrying out of sight towards the orphanage. The lad was limping.

It was just the two of them then, but she feared that if there was a second bout, she wouldn't survive it. It wasn't just the burning pain in her ribs; she was running out of rage, out of inspiration too.

He reached for a canteen on his belt. 'You fought well. You deserve a drink.' He threw it at her feet.

'I don't need anything from you.' She spat blood to punctuate the remark.

'If I ever want to kill you, you'll see me coming. I take pride in my sword-work.' He shrugged. 'You're Geil Morvander, right?'

'How do you know my name?'

'Lanteus. How else?' He looked wistful. 'Brave lad. Tough as a bear too. And a friend.'

'Funny. He never mentioned you, *Parvos*,' she tried. His smile suggested she'd guessed correctly.

'With good reason. He wanted to tell you about the children, to involve you in our struggle, but I told him not to. Not until the time was right.' His lips formed a thin line. 'I was wrong.'

She glared at him. 'Bullshit. You'd have me believe that he let you, what, run your human trade? Continue with your cowardly murders?'

Parvos sighed. 'Like I said, I take pride in my sword-work, but I don't murder the helpless, which is more than your bosses can say.'

'Who are "my bosses" supposed to be?' Geil clenched her fists but was mindful of feeding the Drake too much anger for fear of losing control again.

'Whatever our differences,' Parvos said, 'Lanteus decided to help us take many children and their families to safety. Families from the provinces that couldn't afford a dispensation and didn't want to see their daughter or son mangled by Nightmares.'

Geil paused, unbelieving. 'So, what, you snatch them from the Academy recruiters out of the kindness of your heart?

I don't believe it one fucking bit. I've seen Exarchians at work before. Stabbing soldiers at the market, poisoning entire households just to get to one governor. If you're getting the children away, it's to make your own army with them. Indoctrinate them with whatever horseshit you believe.'

His solitary eye flared for a second. 'Sometimes, when tearing off yokes, you end up injuring the ox. And yet, we do a lot more than that. Use your head! I am what I am, but Lanteus was no murderer. Why would he be helping us? When he found us, he could have taken the information to the Stone-Masks, but he saw what we were doing and thought it was good enough to help.' She had to bite her tongue. Kicking the Academy in the eye did sound like Lanteus. Helping children evade conscription, too. But most Exarchians *hated* Dreamers. What was one doing on their side?

She shook her head, though, still on guard, still on edge. 'And I'm just supposed to believe you?'

'No,' he conceded. 'Come. See for yourself.'

With that, he started towards the orphanage. The flying swords fell limply to the ground. She should use the opportunity to escape or call for Mavis. Instead, she followed him. She *had* to know.

Hadn't she come back to Onyxia with the hopes of honouring Lanteus's memory? Of changing things for the better, if not for everyone, at least for Ragdra? Since then, the tide of Onyxian society had pulled her down into its depths. Both politics and Lady Liadra had turned out to be quite the distraction.

She followed the man into the orphanage's building through a side door. Up some stairs, they reached a candle-lit study, Sister Lasara's alcove judging from the decor. The Widowed Sister was cleaning the lad's wounds there.

'What is she still doing here?' the muleteer asked.

'The letters. Where are they?'

'Have you lost your last ounce of sense, Parvos?' The Sister kept her voice low despite it simmering with anger. 'Why are you giving away everything that's taken us so long to build?'

'We've already lost this place. If she's found us, it's only a matter of time before the Stone-Masks do.'

Sister Lasara held Geil's eyes, glaring at her.

'She deserves to know,' Parvos insisted.

Sister Lasara huffed, then reached behind the desk and manipulated something unseen until there was a click. She produced a bundle of missives tied together, loosened the string and, after skimming through them, selected two for Geil.

Her lips trembled. The handwriting was Lanteus's. Letters to a nameless friend living in the countryside. Dull and wordy paragraphs of crumpled calligraphy reporting life in the capital. Unremarkable. Except they were cyphered. Someone had done part of the decryption on the margins with charcoal, highlighting words and letters and translating their secret meaning.

He really had been helping them: intercepting and delaying reports from local governors, providing names of children about to be conscripted by the Academy, of families that wanted their young to escape.

Lanteus had believed that Grandmaster Ranndra, the Academy's supreme authority, had abused their conscription powers. With High Sage Malvedra's acquiescence, she'd doubled their recruiting numbers. They'd started taking any common children with a whiff of the gift, even before they had reached the age of reason, and freely trampled any exemptions in guilds and city charters.

Lanteus had despised Grandmaster Ranndra. Geil didn't know her well; she'd been but one of her Nightmareology masters, though she had always given her the creeps because of her cold cruelty.

If Lanteus had believed she was up to something, or worse, operating with the connivance of higher powers in the Domain, his alliance with the Exarchians wasn't so hard to believe anymore.

Maybe she should have felt better, but she just felt worse. Why had he trusted these strangers and not her?

'Where do you take the children?' she asked.

'That's none of your business,' Sister Lasara snapped. 'Somewhere safe. Somewhere they can grow up to be whoever they want to be.'

'Now please, Geil, tell us how you found us,' Parvos said.

'Lanteus's testament.'

'Then we might still have some time left,' Parvos mused.

'No, you were right. This is over,' Sister Lasara said bitterly. 'If she knows, others will soon.'

Parvos turned to Geil. 'If you tell anyone, we're all as good as dead.'

'I only found you because he wanted me to. I'm sure that the legacy sum was just a way for him to get me here. He must have feared something might happen to him.'

Shaken as she was, she still picked up on the glance Sister Lasara threw at Parvos. His lips curled downwards.

'What? What else aren't you telling me?'

Parvos lowered his head.

'You said she deserved to know,' Sister Lasara said.

Parvos nodded heavily. 'What do you know of *The Dreadful Drake*?'

'I know that name,' Geil said, feeling even the Drake inside her refocus. 'That's one of the Academy's warships. Its holds can carry large hordes to battle, even fully grown fire Drakes.'

'Or something equally dangerous,' Parvos said. 'Our "friends" had alerted us that Grandmaster Ranndra was using it to bring something dangerous to the capital.'

'What?'

'We don't know its exact nature, only that Ranndra, her most talented acolytes and Davorles worked intensively and in utter secrecy on it.'

'What do you care, if it has nothing to do with children?'

'If it's of value to the Academy, it should be destroyed,' Sister Lasara remarked. 'Which is why Lanteus agreed to trail the ship.'

'And you believe that this is what got him killed?'

'I believe that Lanteus was smart enough to figure out what they were doing, and they killed him for it. But he never returned to tell me what he learned.'

Geil tried to swallow but couldn't. It felt like her heart was burning in her throat.

It wasn't the suspicion that it was the Academy behind Lanteus's murder that hurt. It was that now she could see how it had all happened.

That's where Lanteus had been. That's where he had been coming from suddenly to find her wrapped in Itraya's arms.

If he hadn't found her like that, maybe he'd have told her everything. Yet as things stood, he'd just let out a weary, broken sigh. 'I'm sorry,' he'd said. And then he'd left.

Back then, she'd thought that he was too hurt to even scream at her, but perhaps the pathetic truth was that he was disheartened at the realisation that they'd both been lying to each other for a long while.

Geil felt the room teetering and leaned onto the desk, hiding her face from them. 'What else have you learned about the ship?'

'Only that *The Dreadful Drake* anchored near the Southern Quarter but left as quickly as it came,' Parvos said. 'You could help us, Geil. If the damn Wisp was the one who killed Lanteus, it's only because he found something that they wanted to keep secret. Our friends in the capital have kept themselves busy enough with other things, and we lack the connections in the halls of power to pierce his plans, but you, on the other hand ... have plenty of friends above.'

'So now you want me to use my political connections for ... what? To spy on the Wisp? Forget it. You've got enough people I care about killed.'

Parvos pursed his chapped lips. 'Understood. That is, after all, what he thought.'

'What are you talking about?'

'Lanteus didn't want to get you involved in treason, or worse, killed. So, I'm respecting his choice. But if you change your mind, find us. We could do much good together.'

'I should leave.' Geil stormed for the exit.

Outside, the world was the same.

A trail had opened in front of her that she couldn't ignore, that she didn't want to ignore.

No more running, no more hiding. We follow. Wherever it leads. And then we kill them. This time, there's nothing stopping us, the Drake said.

Geil agreed. It was right.

She made her way through the woods until she reached Mavis's hideout. He practically jumped from a treetop to come running to her, sword in hand.

'What happened? I lost sight of you.'

'I'll tell you what I've learned, but first: tell me, word by word, what Lanteus told you the night he died.'

Chapter Twenty-Nine

Ash

Every Dreamer hides a kernel at the heart of their creations: obscure sorrows, impossible longings. Most of the time they aren't even aware of it. Discovering such a kernel is the key that unlocks a Dream's hidden provinces and locked vaults.

– Joshian the Errant

THE CITADEL MIGHT NOT HAVE changed much, but he had. He wasn't a scared boy anymore. He could Dream. At least, that's how Ash reassured himself.

He entered through the crack that opened into the crumbling ruins of an abandoned rookery. Ghalod had already lit an orb-lamp, and its dim blue light cast angular shadows against the hundreds of cages littering the chamber.

'Thalder is downstairs,' Yaisa said, checking her daggers. Ash descended a narrow stone staircase covered in mould.

Thalder was on the upper landing of the tower's central stairs, scrutinising its depths with the dim hue of his glove-lamp. Below them spread the seemingly endless tower's entrails. Worn wooden stairs interlaced the centre's immense hollow, a zigzagging maze of balconies, bisecting pathways and balustrades. The labyrinthine descent went on until it sank into abyssal blackness.

It smelled of wet wood and dusty books, but mostly of humidity and another heavy metallic scent that reminded him of his father's printing shop. Water trickled down from the cracks in the dome above, its dripping the only sound cutting through the thick silence. At least until the floor began creaking under their soft footsteps.

'Motherstorm's dark bosom! How will we ever find anything? There are thousands of books in here!' Thalder muttered beneath his breath.

'It used to be tens if not hundreds of thousands, so you can count yourself lucky,' Ash said with a grim smile. 'Now give me some light.' He reached into his satchel for his father's notes and withdrew them with shaking hands.

'If you need to take a break, lad . . .' Thalder trailed off.

'It's just the cold,' he lied, forcing his hands to still. Ash read the notes again. His father's handwriting was minuscule and cramped, making the most of every corner among the elegant sketches.

Even though Ash had studied them repeatedly over the past few days, it was difficult for him to connect the list of books with the half-transcribed and disjointed map. His father had figured it all out eventually, but the final version of his map had been lost with him the night he drowned.

To think that his bones might be floating somewhere in the underwater hallways sent him off-keel. Ash felt a rising nausea, his stomach churning with bile.

He had to focus. Allowing anguish to seize him would only get them all captured or killed. Worse, he remembered his father's words of caution regarding the Vigil-blighted library: 'Tread lightly and think quietly.'

'Empress Damnia's personal collection was split in two between her daughters. My father believed Empress Lyxeia's had been taken south to Ravkiria but that Empress Myrtele's vaults on the fifteenth floor still held many tomes. Alternatively, the library's Illuminators might have kept their copy at their workshop on the lower levels.'

'Hasn't the marsh swallowed those by now?' Thalder asked.

'They were still there seven years ago.'

'If Empress Myrtele's collection is closer . . .' Yaisa trailed off. 'But won't it be kept behind a closed gate?'

'Gates we can deal with, trust me. It's the Academy's patrol that worries me,' Thalder said. 'We should be gone by the time they show up. Let's move.'

They dimmed their lights to the bare minimum and began their descent of the creaky stairs. A few levels below the dome, darkness was already thicker and the rain just a murmur.

A loud roar, a cavernous cacophony of wood and rock, rose from the spire's depths. They all froze. Ash felt his heart rampaging in his chest.

'What the hells was that?' Ghalod whispered.

'The hells' hunger,' was Thalder's sullen reply.

Thalder stretched out his left arm, and two bats, more smoke than flesh, took shape. Lean, formidable creatures that blended perfectly into the dark and that he'd conjured seemingly effortlessly.

'Go find whatever that was,' he whispered to the bats, who flew out of the chamber. 'We keep moving.'

They soldiered on, moving faster than before. Ash had never seen the spire's heights. When he'd been here before, he'd kept himself to the levels near the water. Many were blocked off by piles of wood and rubble. He was reminded of that now; the farther they descended, the worse off the structure seemed. In some places, the inner wooden gallery around the stairs had completely collapsed.

Ash counted the levels on the map.

'This is the one,' he said.

'Which way now?' Yaisa asked.

Four arches opened around the inner gallery, each one with a different sigil carved in their keystones. At least the rusty iron gates guarding them stood ajar.

'Those are the Imperial Regalia of the Divine Empire.' Daerna pointed at the southmost keystone. She was right; Damnia's crown, sword and book were engraved on it.

Out of caution, Ash looked at the engravings on the others. One was a wreath of flowers, another a setting sun. The fourth depicted a pair of wings. 'That's a reference to Geleisdra's guardian,' he said, recognising it from a sketch in his father's notes.

'Is there any way of knowing which one is older?' Daerna wondered.

'We should check them both,' Ash resolved. 'Ghalod, come with me to the northern tower. And the rest of you check the southern one.'

'I'll guard the stairs,' Thalder said.

In silence, they set to work. The northern tower was shaped like a hexagon, with smaller chambers connected in an outer ring to the central vault. Despite the floor's strange tilting, both the chambers and the books had weathered the centuries strangely well.

Ash quickly realised something was wrong with the indexing. Here, someone had stacked treatises on mathematics next to illuminated catalogues of weapons. There, sketchbooks filled with anatomical drawings sat next to a fictional account of the journey of a mute woman into the stars. Some of the stone shelves were cluttered with junk too: dried flowers, empty jars and even rat skeletons. Hard to picture the Academy's sentinels bothering to do this, yet somebody clearly had.

'You'd think it would be easy to spot, being made of silver and all,' Ghalod lamented.

'Maybe not. Might be hidden under a different spine,' Ash said. 'We'll have to check them all. Leave the lamp here. I'll take the chambers on the left; you take the ones on the right.'

Ghalod nodded and wandered off, while Ash set the sketchbook on a blackened desk and began perusing the books. The order here followed no logic either; it was as if they'd been rearranged on a whim. But as he searched, he picked up on a strange sound.

At first, he dismissed it as the wind whistling through the empty hallways, but the longer he listened, the more he realised it had a melody.

It wasn't unlike the flute his father used to play.

'Ghalod, do you hear that?'

Ghalod didn't answer, possibly because here the rapping of the rain was louder. Ash followed the sound and came upon a narrow corridor connecting this chamber with the west one.

And there was candlelight coming from it.

Ash crept ahead, dagger now in hand.

In the battered room, he found a man with grey curls seated on a pile of books, playing a small flute with ink-stained fingers.

Ash rubbed his eyes. Was he really seeing this? The man was the spitting image of Eoinas Allandra. His father.

He certainly played like him, his fingers dancing delicately over the wooden flute.

The man's grey eyes fell on Ash, and he stopped playing.

'You took your time, didn't you?'

Chapter Thirty
Geil

Coil like the viper, spring like the hydra, devour like the wyvern.
– Davorles Family Motto

THE WAVES LAPPED HUNGRILY AT the wooden pier Geil stood upon. From here, the Scab seemed some quaint and sleepy district. Only the bodies that hung from the gibbets facing south betrayed the illusion. 'Heretic' and 'Traitor' read the crude signs hanging from their necks.

They were lucky we didn't get our claws in them, the Drake lamented. After the frustrating clash with Parvos, it had been left wanting more blood, not less.

Mavis, by her side, squinted at the tattered and ruined silhouettes of the palace. He seemed more collected, more her Talon-mate and less the pained mess he'd been recently. They were closer than ever to discovering the truth of Lanteus's death; all the rest, Exarchians included, could wait.

'Nothing. I can't make sense of it. Are you sure this is the place Lanteus summoned you to that night?' Geil asked.

'Yes,' he said, rubbing the stubble on his chin. 'Southmost quay.'

It still stung her when she thought about it. How she could have been here with him. Helped him, protected him, saved him.

'The question is, why specifically here? Were there any ships anchored nearby?'

'You mean *The Dreadful Drake*. No. Either it had already left by then or they had set anchor somewhere else. Maybe he just wanted to talk to me away from the Secret Chancellery's eyes and ears,' Mavis suggested.

'The Scab's good for clandestine meetings, but there are easier ways to avoid the lionheads. Why not the Susurrus? Or some tavern? Especially if he just wanted to drown his sorrows. No, him choosing this place has to do with what the Exarchians wanted him to investigate.'

But as Geil looked around, she saw nothing. She had to be missing something.

'Do you remember his exact words?'

'Southmost quay, by the old slaughterhouse.' Mavis pointed a gloved hand at the nearby husk of a large brick building.

'Come on,' she said, marching towards it.

The slaughterhouse's courtyard was silent, too silent. Blood-sopped bricks had been reddened further by the district's scabbing. Cracks covered the walls, like scratches would a chopping block. Doors and windows slammed shut at their approach. From an arch above, a lone woman, her eyes darkened with heavy make-up, gazed at them defiantly and spat at their passing.

Geil didn't blame her. Silence might be the shield of the slighted, yet even in silence one could show pride and disgust.

'Supposedly this is where that gang of criminals ambushed Lanteus ... not that we can question them, of course. And the locals don't seem keen on helping,' Mavis groaned. 'Though ... seems other carrion birds have flocked here since ...' He gestured at the crude painting on the wall depicting the Charnel Mother.

The Charnelite Cult had certainly benefitted from the rioting, despair and lawlessness in the Scab. She could imagine Davorles working with those lunatics or at least letting them prosper if it benefitted him. Yet none of this explained what they might have brought aboard that boat. What could possibly have been worth killing Lanteus for?

A passage cut to the southern facade, where a smaller wooden quay endured the beating of the lagoon. From there, one could see the Crumbling Quarter's vastness. Onyxia's old dreams of magnificence, revealed now for rotting husks of stone. Reefs sprouted like mushrooms from manors' corpses. Only some islets, anchored together by an elegant palace or a tangle of bridges, still stood.

'A warship isn't discreet, so we can assume they meant to unload some cargo nearby. Either very large or very dangerous given they used *The Dreadful Drake*.' Perhaps it was nothing, but thinking of her master's nagging smile … 'I wonder if Davorles had possessions nearby …'

'Given his lineage, he could own one of these islands.'

Geil arched an eyebrow at that, and Mavis continued. 'I know he's a senator, and not on account of his wealth. Since the Davorleses are one of the older families, it's likely that they were Archdreamers with their own islet.'

'The Wisp always spoke of his family with pride,' Geil said. 'Let's take a look.'

She ran towards the edge of the pier, letting the Drake's wings break through her shifting skin. She kept running, wings beating, sending her above the water. Pulled by his Skycourier breastplate, Mavis flew much slower behind her.

The palaces looked like ghostly ships moored against a bleak, choppy sea. She circled around the closest islets to the quay they'd just left. Nothing looked out of place.

She let the Drake take over her senses.

Something odd: a long, heavy silhouette stretching like a mooring line, connecting the city with one of the islets. The surface's foam and murk hid it, but the Drake could see the schools of lagoon fish swerving away from it.

'There. You see that?' she yelled to Mavis.

Mavis flicked a hand to conjure a golden orb-lamp that he then dropped into the water where she'd pointed. He glided closer to the surface, following its light. 'Is that a chain?'

'It is! And not a normal one, either.'

They traced it to one of the crumbling islets, where a lone, moss-covered manor still stood. It was ancient. Everywhere, its elegant windows and thresholds had been sealed, not just bricked up but rather fused with slabs of grey stone.

Geil circled around to find a landing spot. There was a muck-covered loading bay with grimy stairs that sank into the water, but tears in the algae bedding over the marble suggested it'd seen recent use.

'Let's take a look!' she called to Mavis, and flew down to land on a terrace atop a balustrade. He gently steered his Skycourier armour to follow.

A dome lorded over the manor. Its barred door displayed a carved symbol on the lintel above: a wyvern rampant.

'Is this what I think it is?'

'You were right!' Mavis replied, grabbing her biceps tightly. 'It's the Davorles household sigil.'

'Stand aside,' Geil said. She allowed more of the Drake out, her muscles bulging and scales covering both her arms. Her fingers burned as they hardened into steel-like talons.

'Is this a good idea?'

I can't think of anything better than pulling Davorles's entrails out, the Drake growled as she sank her talons deep into the rock below the doorway's lintel. With a groan, she cut through and began pulling at the stone. Her muscles burned with the pain from yesterday's injuries but also with rage.

The big slab cracked. Closing her eyes, she ripped it out, sending it scattering as debris.

A gaping gash had opened in the walled door's upper half. Enough for her to squeeze through.

She entered a lightless corridor. The entire palace was dark and badly mangled by scars, cracks and black growth. She reached an inner circular rainwell under the dome and let her Drake eyes adjust.

That's when she saw him.

He was pale and dishevelled in battered Skycourier armour, but she'd recognise that smile anywhere, no matter how long had passed.

'I knew you'd come,' Lanteus said.

Chapter Thirty-One

Ash

In the end, it all turns to dust. Even the Philosopher Empress's mighty wisdom was unable to prevent the fall of her lineage. So why is her Great Library still standing? It's been centuries, and yet when Joshian the Errant entered the ruins a hundred years ago, they reported that the books and scrolls left inside hadn't crumbled to dust. Why is that? Perhaps some words refuse to die.

– From the diaries of Eoinas Allandra

'H-HOW?' ASH'S VOICE QUIVERED. HIS brain scrambled to make sense of what he was seeing. He had to be hallucinating. That's what this was, a hallucination conjured by the paper-thin reality of the library.

How else could he explain his father's presence?

'We should get going,' the man said.

He set the flute on a dust-covered shelf before moving deeper into a hidden corner of the vault.

'You're not my father,' Ash said, clenching his fists.

Unless he got some good answers, he wasn't following any apparition blindly into the labyrinth out there.

The man turned. 'By her blessed bones! What are you saying? There's no time for this, Aescyon.'

'My father's dead.'

'And yet here I stand,' he replied, pursing his thin lips in the same way his father had shown his disapproval. His voice was also the same. Ash had missed it deeply. Listening to it again hurt, but it was the sting of nostalgia. The candied, warm burn of a beloved memory.

'So you've been trapped in this forsaken place for over six years? How's that even possible?'

An uneasy ripple disturbed the man's placid face. 'The truth?' Ash gave him a slight nod. 'I'm not sure. A lot's missing from my mind, entire years have vanished . . . but I remember the army, I remember Crunia, the printing shop. And you, of course.'

'Larens and Rorsen, where are they?'

'My friends, yes?' He tilted his head. 'Dead? Lost? I can't remember . . .'

'You don't remember? You expect me to believe that?'

His father shook his head, clearly exasperated. 'Think, Aescyon! How is this place still standing? Why haven't its books crumbled to dust in all these centuries?' He gestured to their surroundings. 'Empress Damnia Dreamchanted the Great Library to endure and to preserve its contents. The Vigil-blight has only made it easier to survive.'

Could it really be that? Whether you were a fervent believer or not, Empress Damnia's Dreamcraft was legendary. She Dreamt the Silver Book to contain all of the wisdom in the Empire, built a diamond citadel to study the heavens whose celestial transits could still be observed at night. She'd even pierced the Academy's Mantle with a rain of fire. Unlikely as his father's reasoning was, it was not entirely impossible. Maybe what had preserved the books had kept his father alive too.

Still, the library looked sick. All around him, the shelves were warped, twisted by humidity and decay and covered in black mould.

'Aescyon, I really am here,' he said, grabbing Ash's shoulder. His hand was clammy, also calloused. Reassuringly imperfect.

'Now, I can help you, but we *must* move quickly. The library has kept me alive, but I don't know what they'll do to you.'

'Who are you speaking of? The Academy's sentinels?'

'Sentinels? More like rabid rats. They won't let you get away a *second* time.' Noticing Ash's hesitation, he went on. 'I can always let you keep fumbling on your own, or I can show you the seed of it all. But it must be now, before they find you.' He headed for a nearby doorway.

Ash took a hesitant step after him. 'Wait! We can't go without my friends!' If his father had heard him, he didn't stop. He called for Ghalod but got no answer, and his father had opened the door at the end of the corridor and stepped through.

He couldn't squander this chance. Ash ran after him.

From the doorstep, he saw that his father had begun descending the maze of central stairs, carrying a lamp.

'Wait!'

His father turned and placed a finger over his lips, then waved for Ash to come down.

Ash followed his father down the spiral staircase to a lower vault and then through another hidden passage that led to a secondary set of stairs. In Ash's memories, the library had always stood a shadowy labyrinth, but seeing it with fresh eyes, he realised it was a maze colonised by the twisted fantasies of books. The lower they went, the more reality was replaced by the mysteries of a hungry darkness.

At least his father seemed to know his way around well enough, and they made quick progress in their descent.

'Wait!' his father called abruptly.

He gestured for them to climb up a shelf that had transmuted itself into a gnarly tree, to the point that thick branches now protruded from its upper section, heavy with cobwebs. Beneath his feet, a blanket of torn pages had fused with the warped wooden floor.

'What's going on?' Ash asked.

His father hushed him with a finger to his lips.

Below, a wolf-like figure loped into view. No, not a wolf – more like a wolf carcass, with spindly legs and dead amber eyes. It moved very quietly and disappeared into deeper shadows.

'What was that?'

'One of the sentinels' monstrosities. They're already here, Ash, searching for interlopers to kill.'

Interlopers like Ash and his friends.

'Good thing I know this place better than them,' his father said. 'They can only spend so long here before the library infects their minds. Me? I only live because the library wants me to, so I don't fear it. Come on. We should move while we can.' His father climbed down from the treetop.

'Wait! We must go back and warn the others!'

His father huffed. 'We're very close, Aescyon. This might be the only chance we get. Besides, to make it back to your friends, we'd have to go through *them*. We can't stop now!'

Perhaps his father was right. Turning back now might be foolish, and he might not be able to reach them before the Hordemaster did. But that didn't mean he couldn't warn them.

'Just give me a moment, I'll catch up with you,' Ash said, waiting a few seconds for his father to get a head start. Even now, Ash feared his judgement. His confirmation that Ash had betrayed everything they stood for by being a Dreamer.

Heavy-hearted as it made him, guilt was a fine price to pay to help keep his friends alive. Ash entered the Dreaming trance and hurried to craft the right sort of warning.

Chapter Thirty-Two
Daerna

To listen to a fiend,
Is a fool's game,
To kiss a temptress,
Is a sure way to end mouthless.

– Ancient Onyxian rhyme

DAERNA SQUINTED UNDER THE LIGHT of Yaisa's orb-lamp, trying to read the book spines. No matter how she tried, she couldn't discover any pattern, structure or logic to the collection, nothing that would help her find the Silver Book.

Ghalod burst into the room.

'Have you seen Ash?' he asked.

'Wasn't he supposed to be with you?' Yaisa replied.

'I lost track of him, and now I can't find him. Thalder hasn't seen him either.'

'How did he just disappear? Did he say anything to you?' Daerna asked.

'I turned for a moment, and he vanished. I heard him talking to someone, but thought it was Thalder.'

Heart pounding, Daerna hurried into the gallery and then into the northern vault. Thalder was already there, sword in one hand, lamp in the other.

This vault was more degraded than the one they'd been exploring. Many of the shelves had rotted, reducing the scrolls and books into mushy pulp.

'Ash?' she called.

No reply.

Daerna and the others spread out through the vault's many rooms to search for him, their lights like a swarm of lightning-flies in the air. Over and over, they called for Ash, but there was no response.

They found his orb-lamp, though, abandoned on an empty desk.

Then she heard Thalder call, 'Here!'

They followed his voice through a narrow passage that led to the western vault. He stooped over what looked like footprints on the dusty floor.

'There was someone else here,' he muttered.

'Who?' Yaisa asked.

Thalder shrugged, casting his orb-lamp's light over the marks. One set was clearly Ash's damp tread, but the others were darker and grubbier, almost muddy.

'Where did they go?'

Thalder gestured to a corner of the room where a spiral staircase opened, descending into the darkness of the lower vaults.

Daerna immediately headed for them, but Thalder stopped her.

'We have to follow them!' she said.

'Agreed, but if it's an Academy sentry down there, it's better they see me first.'

With light steps, Thalder led them down to a lower level of the vault, to a room packed with cabinets, writing utensils and empty ledgers.

The floor was warped and blackened with soot. Thalder crouched and studied the cobblestones until he picked up on some barely noticeable trail.

He led them onwards. They were almost back to the central gallery when he abruptly stopped.

'Someone's coming!' he whispered.

Following his lead, they all hid around an open archway. Light footsteps approached, then Daerna spotted a figure moving through the dark. Yaisa drew her daggers, and Daerna lamented not having brought her own.

Thalder jumped the figure as soon as they crossed the threshold, placing his blade against their neck. 'Any sudden moves and I'll cut your breath short,' he muttered.

The figure stood very still. They wore a long monastic robe of dark-wine-coloured silk. A hood hid their face.

'Let me see that ugly mug of yours,' Thalder said, pulling the hood back with the point of his sword.

It was a woman with red hair streaked with white. Half of her gaunt face and her neck were covered in tattoos.

'Who in the entombed hells are you?' Thalder asked. 'Are you with the Academy?'

'The Academy?' She shook her head weakly. 'Those brutes would burn down our Garden if they could. I'm an Illuminator, here to serve the Garden, to help it talk to you.' She gestured with one hand around her, as if that explained everything.

'Garden? You mean the library?' Daerna asked.

'A Garden of thoughts and hopes, grown out of ink, parchment and paper. What else?'

Yaisa stepped forwards, blade ready. 'Well, *Gardener*, where have you taken our friend?'

'He's walked his own path, with his own guide. Below, seeking his own answers from the Garden.'

'You want to play smart with us? Have it your way.'

'Wait, Yaisa!' Thalder yelled. He reached out to stop her but wasn't fast enough. Yaisa's blade traced an arc, grazing the woman's sternum.

The stranger gasped and covered her wound. Her dark blood soon soiled her hands and robes.

'Why did you stop me? She's got Ash!' Yaisa fought to shove Thalder aside, but Ghalod grabbed her from behind.

'Killing her won't get us any answers!'

Daerna cast her light over the woman to help her with the wound. Tattoos covered her from head to toe. Except they were . . . words, mostly in Ancient Iskian and tangled in a myriad of branches. She could imagine them spreading from a tree beneath her robes, except the words seemed to be alive on her skin, floating and rippling like clouds.

'I'm here to guide you, not mislead you,' the stranger croaked.

'Only fools listen to fiends!' Yaisa yelled, quoting the old wisdom about temptresses and fiends.

But a different tale stirred in Daerna's memory.

'Those tattoos . . .' The writing was microscopic, but she recognised some of the words because she'd seen similar ones in the Silent Abbey. 'It's like an index.'

'Indeed, all librarians carried a living index on their skin.'

'Except they all fled three centuries ago, during the siege,' Daerna replied.

'Fled?' The woman chuckled bitterly. 'We died protecting this place. We bought time with our lives for Princess Geleisdra to lift the siege.'

Yaisa snarled at the woman. 'So you admit to being dead? I knew it! She's a fucking Nightmare sent to mislead us!'

'I'm but an echo of one of them: Melkia of Asod,' she replied weakly. 'But I walk in their footsteps. The Garden needed someone to tend it, so when it found Melkia's journal, it bound me to its service.' She offered them a sad smile.

'Here, let me help you.'

Daerna tore some of her sleeve to bandage the woman's wound. Yaisa reluctantly backed off. The blood was *too* dark. Almost as dark as ink.

Thalder's eyes narrowed at that. 'So, you're an Eidolon, then? Destiny has a strange sense of humour if the library "copied" one of its copyists. Why should we trust you?'

'You,' Melkia said, addressing Daerna, 'you've communed with books before; the Garden can tell. Where? We don't know; rare is such privilege, and we wish not to squander it.'

Daerna considered her words. Melkia had to be referring to her visit to the Silent Abbey somehow, but how she knew about that was beyond her grasp.

Before she could ask anything else, Thalder raised a finger. 'Did you hear that?'

As they listened in silence, Daerna could make out a sharp warning whistle echoing through the library's hollow stairwell.

'That's Vespirian whistling language! Of the sort our guild uses,' Yaisa said. 'It must be Ash!'

'What does it mean?' Daerna asked.

'Watch out,' Ghalod said, grimly clutching his spear.

During all of this, Thalder had kept moving. He'd crouched atop a balustrade that overlooked the dark stairs below and carefully turned the sword in his hands so the blade faced downwards.

Then, without warning, he dropped into the darkness.

They heard a loud squelch and a furious growl. They raced to the balustrade and saw Thalder atop some pale, wolf-like Nightmare with far too many legs. The beast squirmed under his weight, twisting its head at an impossible angle, more insect than mammal, to bite at its attacker. Thalder drove the sword through its eye.

He pulled the blade free. The beast's maw split in two, spilling a thick white blood all over the steps.

'Blessed Merele's bones! What was that?' Yaisa asked.

Thalder, breathing heavily, kept his eyes on the darkness of the steps that led deeper into the library. 'Aracnolykos. The sentinels are here. We should hurry.'

'What about the book?' Yaisa asked.

'Is our companion where the book is?' Daerna asked the Illuminator.

The woman shook her head and pointed to her chest at the lower part of her sternum. 'The book's nestled at the heart of the Garden, but your friend has taken a different branch.' She then pointed at her left wrist.

'There's no time to find Ash and get the book, and the lad might need us now,' Thalder lamented.

'It's what we have to do!' Daerna said. 'You save Ash! I'll find the book.'

'For you to go alone is madness!' Thalder said.

'I'll stay with her,' Ghalod volunteered. 'You two find Ash.'

Thalder and Yaisa nodded.

'Take us there,' Daerna said, pointing to the Illuminator's chest, 'to the heart of the Garden.'

Chapter Thirty-Three
Geil

When we lose those we love, we lose their secrets too. The yearning to unlock them will forever haunt us. We will wonder what parts of them were hidden to us, long after each poem and each letter has turned to silent ash.

– *Contemplations on Sorrow* by Empress Myrtele

GEIL STUMBLED TOWARDS LANTEUS. HER brain choked with the impossibility of it, but she didn't pull back when he reached out to touch her chin. His hand was cold, cold enough to burn, cold enough to numb and drown.

'I have missed you so much,' she mumbled.

'So have I,' he replied, his touch drowning her: the Drake was panicking, beating furiously against the cage of her skull, trying to break free, but she leashed him. So what if his caress hurt? So what if it killed her? She didn't deserve any less.

'Geil, no!' Mavis screamed, and she felt him pulling her back.

'What are you doing?' she asked, then screamed in horror as he swung his blade, Dreamchanted in blazing flames, towards Lanteus.

Except it wasn't Lanteus. It never had been.

It was a Nightmare made of smoke and darkness, as if someone had bundled and braided blades of grass into a human shape.

Their mere presence sucked the light and warmth from the sunny morning. Others began appearing throughout the dome.

She'd seen these shadow-wisps before, at the Academy. Their icy grasp was enough to cause instant frostbite or even kill their prey.

'I can't hold them very long; we need to go!' Mavis yelled.

They circled her with perfectly silent, synchronised movements, leaving frozen footsteps in their wake.

'Stay away!' Geil called to no avail. The Drake's roaring anger rose, and she dropped into a combat stance. A shadow-wisp reached for her, its coils as cold as winter. Geil lashed out to keep it at bay, but it was like tearing at smoke. Worse, its unearthly cold bit through her scales, turning them craggy and grey.

They retreated outside, ready to take flight. Mavis leapt, his Skycourier armour pulling him beyond their reach. Geil ran towards the edge, spreading her wings. Before she could take flight, one of the shadow-wisps lunged at her, grazing a wing. Frost spread over the sensitive membrane between the bones. She lost her balance and tumbled down.

She fought, trying to Dream her wings anew, to no avail.

Down and down she spiralled. She was going to smash against the rocks at the base of the island, and that would be the end of her.

Mavis seized her beneath her arms. 'I've got you.'

She sagged into him and allowed him to pull her upwards, gaining momentum. As they flew away, she recovered her breathing, little by little, and was able to Dream a stronger membrane and recover the mobility in her wings.

'By her blessed bones!' Mavis cried. 'It was bad enough he had wisps there, but why were you leaning into them?'

'I . . . I thought it was Lanteus come to kill me.' Even the admission hurt.

'What? How?'

'I have no idea,' she muttered. Except then it struck her. The deep darkness, the fearful imaginings that took shape. She looked back to confirm her fears and saw that the water swirled grey and silent around it, as if robbed of voice and colour.

'The Mantle. That crazy bastard has a piece of Mantle here.'

* * *

Back at the quay, it took them a long while to catch their breath and dare discuss what they'd seen.

'This is what Lanteus must have found,' Mavis said. 'This must have been what *The Dreadful Drake* carried inside.'

'How is it here? Transporting a fragment of the Mantle is one thing, keeping it here a very different and difficult matter.'

'What do you mean?'

'I'm no master Nightmarist, but I can tell you that the Mantle's deeply tethered to the Academy, where it's already part of natural reality. Here, it's a tear in nature. It should have crumbled long ago under the weight of its own impossibility. If it hasn't, it's because they're constantly reinforcing its foundations, nurturing it, so to speak.'

Geil rubbed her chin with her knuckles. 'What worries me is *why*? Why go through all the effort of bringing it here and then feeding it for a year without using it?'

'To protect his palace? Or perhaps use it to breed Nightmares in the city?' Mavis ventured.

'It seems to me there are easier ways to achieve both ends. And if it's a threat to the city as the Exarchians thought, what are they waiting for to use it? No, there's something we're missing.'

'We could break in again, really explore the place.'

It was tempting, but also reckless after they'd almost ended up frozen by shadow-wisps. 'Let's be smart about this.'

'We could take it to the Falconess,' Mavis offered.

That wasn't a bad plan. 'Or even to Lady Saorla directly. She's the one who brought Davorles to the Secret Chancellery. If he's playing her, she will be the first one to want his head.'

'Assuming she's not in on it. Lady Saorla has relied more and more on the Academy this past year. It's only with the Hordemasters' aid that she was able to turn the tide in the Valelands.' Mavis set his hand on her shoulder, and she found herself leaning into his touch. 'Be careful, Geil. Whoever's behind this is willing to kill for it. I've already lost Lanteus. If Lady Saorla's in on it . . .'

The mere thought made her stomach simmer with bile. She wasn't that stupid. She'd never be duped into supporting her enemies' political plays.

Unless you've been distracted. Unless Liadra's been stringing us along all this whole time, the Drake grumbled.

'For her own good, she better not be,' Geil said.

Chapter Thirty-Four

Ash

Is it wise to bring Aescyon to the library with me, I wonder. His mother used to joke her whole family had been kissed by the Muse of Melancholy, as explanation for her occasional display of Dreaming talents. That said, if he's indeed inherited those, it's a risk. And yet, how to deny him this once-in-a-lifetime chance?

– From the diaries of Eoinas Allandra

ASH HAD TO HURRY TO catch up with his father. 'What's happened to the books?'

His father … grimaced, uncomfortable. 'You know Joshian the Errant spoke of the library Dreaming. He was almost right. It's not the library, it's the Silver Book that Dreams. It has a mind of its own, and thanks to the Vigil-blight, it can reach out. That is why this place is particularly dangerous to Dreamers.'

'But why is it doing this?' Ash asked, pointing to the leaf mould of empty pages on the floor.

'The Silver Book feeds on knowledge and stories. It used to rely on its readers for nourishment, but since it has none, it starves. Ever hungry, it stretches roots through wood, paper and books to search for answers,' Eoinas said, caressing one of the bark-like walls.

The passage narrowed, and the mesh of fused paper and wood converged on a gnarled cavity that resembled a worn-out tree hollow.

'We're here,' Ash's father said, creeping inside.

Warily, Ash reached into his satchel for an orb-lamp. Only once he'd lit it did he dare to follow through the opening.

Inside, an oval, cave-like chamber awaited him. It was like a forest, but one that had turned on itself. Wooden bookshelves had become tree branches, forming a bushy mesh above them. Flowers and fruits hung from them, except they were books, their spines now stems, their pages now leaves and petals.

Some of the pages still had words on them. These still remembered.

But nothing gleamed in the dark. No silver shine, no silver thread or bloom.

'Where's the Silver Book?' Ash asked.

'The Silver Book?' His father seemed suddenly confused. 'Is that what we're looking for? I brought you here to find answers. Isn't that what you wanted?' He began shaking.

'What's wrong?' Ash hurried to his side.

His father's face, contorted with pain, twisted further, and he let out a low groan.

'I'm losing myself. I can feel it inside my head . . . trying to get through to you.'

Ash placed his hand on his dagger. 'Father? Tell me what's happening!'

His father bent over, clutching his head. 'The Book and the library are using me, Aescyon! To get to you! It knows your blood, and it craves an end to the story!' Teeth clenched, he pointed upwards. Ash raised his orb-lamp, casting light over the warped shelf-branches above them. There, his eyes caught sight of a familiar wine-coloured spine transformed into the stem of a handwritten bloom.

'That's your journal!' Ash exclaimed.

His father nodded. 'This is why I'm here and how it knows everything. And why it wants you, to use you to write an ending to our tale! You must get out of here!'

The man let out another groan and fell to his knees. His veins bulged with a dark liquid. His eyes filled with the inky blackness.

Ash's blood ran cold. This wasn't his father; this was some nightmarish Dreamling sent to lure him here. Dreamt by the library itself, if he was to believe his words. How had he been such a fool to fall for this?

'Please, Aescyon, leave ... I feared this would happen. All those years ago. I should never have brought you here. I'd hoped that you hadn't inherited your mother's curse ...'

'What are you talking about?'

'The kiss of the Muse of Melancholy, her Dreaming gift, Aescyon.' Ash stood agape. That would explain so many things, his father's resentment against Dreamers, his unwillingness to talk about her, to explain where she'd gone once she'd left.

'I can't keep myself together much longer ...' His father's voice trembled. 'Please, leave!'

But he couldn't; there was something of his father here, a fragment of the real man, of his mind. He was a sort of Eidolon, incomplete and flawed but a living echo nonetheless. That was why the trap had been so convincing. Why the man looked like him and talked like him and played his flute like him.

Ash looked towards his father's journal above them.

'If I take the journal, will that help you?'

His face lit up with a watery hope. 'I can't ask that of you. I'm already gone ...'

To hell with that. Ash took a step towards it, his boots splashing in the viscous black puddle on the ground. He hung the orb-lamp on a branch, then took out the metal rose he'd made for his exam.

His father let out a pained growl. Ash had to hurry. He removed his right glove and let the iron stem coil around his arm like a serpent. The bud latched on to the back of his hand. He aimed and shot a petal towards a nearby bookcase, and the grapple hooked into the wood flawlessly. He assured the stability of the tether with a tug. There was nothing left but the climb.

He quickly reached the level of the journal. Carefully, he reached out and gripped the book with one hand. His heart ached to be reunited with it after all this time. With a sharp tug, he tried to pluck it, but the tree held to it tightly. As he struggled, the walls began to rumble and groan. Below, a heavy, ink-like liquid was oozing in from the lower reaches, creating a rising tide beneath his father.

Worse: the entrance had begun closing in on itself.

'You belong here with us! There's nothing outside for you except death at the Academy's hands!' the man who'd been his father yelled, but he was hardly a man anymore. He'd lost permanence. As the water rose, he started disappearing, not because he was sinking beneath the wave but because he was made of the same matter. A Nightmare born from ink, rain and long-buried words, debris from the recesses of the mind. Dreams gone mad.

The branch refused to yield to him, so Ash flung his fingers open, and the rosebud mimicked him, spreading its sharp petals. With the razor-like edges, he hacked at the stem, chopping through. The journal toppled down.

He watched it plummet in dismay. With the instincts of a rooftop rat, he threw out his left leg in desperation. It landed atop his foot.

Carefully, Ash pulled his knee upwards. As soon as the journal was in reach, he grabbed it and secured it inside his satchel. By then, the light of the orb-lamp was oscillating dangerously. He checked the exit. Still open, but half the size it had been.

The man below opened his arms, welcoming the rising waters.

'Don't fight it, Aescyon.' His voice didn't sound like his father's anymore. 'We know how cruel the world can be to yours. We can keep you safe. We can help you. We can help you achieve greatness, and make the most of your mother's gift. With our wisdom and your blood, we can write the ending your tales deserve. We just need some of your dreams . . .'

Ash shot the rose towards another of the branches. The sharp petals coiled around a gnarled protrusion, and he leapt. The Dreamchanted flower uncoiled, extending like an impossibly firm metallic vine.

He landed nimbly but sank in the muddy water up to his knees. Only the cable helped him keep his balance. He found his feet, only for hands to seize his throat.

The semblance of his father was melting away, dissolving like a tallow candle. Only a crude smile with blackened teeth remained in his melting face.

'There's no need to fight us. You'll live on, my boy, in the perfect memory of books. In our hungry constellation, ever knowing, never alone. Don't you think I would have wanted this for you?'

Ash shoved him, but his hand sank into the mud that made up the man's chest, erasing any remaining semblance of his father. The Nightmare's muddy fingers grew towards Ash's face, up his jaw and over his cheek, until they covered him. Ash clenched his teeth firmly as the mud crawled up his nostrils and filled his head.

Blinded, he struggled to operate the rose and, at the same time, enter the Dreaming, but he couldn't focus as he gagged, choking on the mud. The terrible panic of drowning seized him.

He'd be lost, erased, swallowed, as the Nightmare had said. Worse, he'd be devoured by something that had been pretending to be his father, that had worn his face like an ill-fitting skin, that had soiled his voice and profaned his memory.

This had been his fate all along. To return here to die with his father. To join him.

Except his father wouldn't have wanted him to give up. To surrender to silence, no matter how soothing.

He'd have wanted Ash to remember. To remember was to speak against the silence of death. To remember was to rebel, to breathe new life into his memory.

And Ash had a voice now, a voice to speak his Dreams aloud. He just needed the fuel. And what better fuel than grief, than anger?

He poured it all into the rose, and, nurtured by bitter loss, the petals crackled with angry lightning. He swung it like a whip, blindly lashing left and right, until he felt the choking embrace of the Nightmare give in and release him.

He jolted out of the Dreaming, coughing until he vomited a mouthful of ink, then gasping in all the air he could seize. While the Nightmare had lost all consistency, the sludge fought on, sucking at Ash's legs as he advanced towards the shrinking exit.

Every step was a battle, and when Ash was close enough, he coiled the stem to a more manageable size and hacked at the choked gap with the sharp petals. Just like with the Nightmare, the obstruction burned like paper at the touch of the lightning, Ash's anger cutting through the stagnant mass of ink.

There was something bubbling behind him. Ash flung the whip to hold it at bay, then climbed into the hole he'd cut and leapt into the passage beyond.

He tumbled into walls as he ran, all the while coughing up ink.

He was afraid that, at any moment, the entire cavern would close on him, or that something else would follow. How could he have been so stupid as to come here alone?

When he reached the landing he saw two figures blocking the exit, both armed and closing in on him.

He clenched his teeth and brandished the crackling rose-whip in his right hand. He'd cut his way through every single Nightmare if he had to.

'Come at me!' he shouted.

'Ash?' the smaller figure replied.

It was Yaisa – at least, it sounded like her, but how could he know for certain anymore?

'Out of the way or I'll roast you alive!' the other figure, Thalder, yelled. This was all the confirmation Ash needed, and he ducked out of the way.

Something was roiling down the hallway behind him, and Thalder threw a glass flask at it.

From the floor, Ash saw that a long tendril of spikes and spines, shaped exactly like his flower-whip, had crept after him; Thalder's flask hit it and exploded into flames. The tendril withered and melted, leaving nasty-smelling smoke.

'Motherstorm's dark bosom! What was that?' asked Yaisa, helping Ash to his feet.

'Nightmare,' he coughed.

'But how did it drag you here?' Thalder asked.

'It had my father's face . . .'

Yaisa and Thalder exchanged a concerned glance.

'What?' Ash asked. Then he realised Daerna and Ghalod weren't with them. 'Where's everyone else?'

Chapter Thirty-Five

Daerna

Empress Damnia's Silver Book wasn't just a symbol of legitimacy; she believed the best hope she could leave the world was wisdom, an ever-growing forest of knowledge.

Etedros, the Pale Prince, desired not to steal it for himself but rather to burn it. A testament to his belief that nothing was worth saving. This is why we had to flee with it, this is why we took it for safekeeping to the Great Library.

– *A Tale of the Sibling Strife* by Blessed Merele

As THE ILLUMINATOR LED DAERNA and Ghalod into the tower's depths, the rain's heavy drumming became a distant murmur. The wooden flights of steps were replaced by a twin set of spiral staircases that coiled around each other, made of metal and rusted by humidity and age alike. Their footsteps echoed, giving Daerna the feeling of being in a massive chamber. The air carried a smell both metallic and mossy.

The darkness was nigh absolute, but when Ghalod raised his orb-lamp, she saw that the stairs ended at a dark pool. The stairwell was waterlogged. They could go no farther.

'Is this it?' she asked.

'Almost,' the Illuminator replied.

She led them to a doorway connected to the last unsubmerged landing. Inside was a monumental vault, more a temple than a library. The Illuminators' workshop, at last.

Stone columns rose like giants, bearing the colossal spire's weight. At their feet, a veritable underwood grew. Vines swarmed over the crumbling wooden desks, overrunning the hall, strangling themselves and dying, only to be reborn in a cannibal thicket that devoured both copied and unfinished books alike.

Other strange formations rose throughout the vault: shining walls of illuminated tomes, warped into a forest of coral. Cave-like tunnels of twisted shelves, covered in leaves of written pages. Vast swathes of rustling grass, the white of blank paper.

It all paled in comparison to the workshop's heart. Where the shadows grew thickest, a flower bush had taken root, and thousands of silver flowers, all different varieties, meshed into one another.

'A beating heart,' their guide had called it. There was no doubt in Daerna's mind that this was the Silver Book – or rather, a copy left behind grown feral.

The years had mutated it, stretching its hungry roots to suck the written word away and turn it into the silver sap that now dripped from the heart of the bush.

'The Garden is waiting for you,' the Illuminator said. They followed her down a well-trodden path that meandered through the rocky outcroppings and shattered workbenches.

Daerna was so lost in the strange beauty that she let out a startled gasp when Ghalod touched her.

'Watch out,' he said in a low voice, 'we're not alone.'

He pointed at the cracks on a desk, and only then did Daerna realise they were claw marks. There were other signs of Nightmares too: broken twigs, tall etchings of impossible sizes on one of the room's columns and something in the grass that resembled a crystallised splatter of blood.

When they reached the heart of the bush, the Illuminator gestured for them to approach. She leaned in to caress a lily-like flower. 'Poets, scribes and philosophers have tried to describe it, and yet they've never fully captured its quintessence. The immensity of its knowledge can't be experienced in a single human lifetime; thus, you need to know what you seek from it.'

'I do know what I seek,' Daerna muttered, more to herself than the Illuminator. She just had to picture Roshia, twitching in her bed, or those she'd seen slowly drifting away in the hospice cots, those crushed by the disease, the poor that were being suffocated, the children wasting away at the Vespirian hospice. This would be her unbreakable certainty of what she sought. 'Just tell me how to read it.'

The Illuminator guided Daerna's hand into the depths of the bush and placed it over a smooth object, even colder than her skin. It was dry and hard but slightly spongy, and her fingers found an empty socket. She almost jerked her hand away when she realised it was a skull nestled in the vines.

'What is this? Whose skull is this?'

'The last reader who wandered lost in its labyrinth. To read a book, a reader must allow it into their thoughts. The Silver Book is different, because it's a reader too. If it finds you worthy, it'll open itself to you, but it'll also offer you many paths, too many to be followed. Chase them all and you'll wander until only your bones are left.'

'And if it doesn't find me worthy?' Daerna asked.

'Then it'll carve your knowledge out of you, leaving only a hollow husk behind,' the Illuminator said.

Daerna was reminded of the way she'd felt when she entered the Silent Abbey's vaults. How she'd felt the gate, the echo of the mind who'd Dreamt it, scrying her, trying to make heads or tails of her intentions.

'What does it want?'

'What do all books want? To share. To converse. To grow too. Are you prepared to pay that price?'

Before she could reply, the entire chamber filled with a grinding groan of stone against stone. Ghalod firmly clutched his spear and looked upwards. Their sharp, shared silence spoke volumes of their fear.

She didn't want to become captive to it, but she feared failing the sick even more. In the end, the choice was no choice at all.

'I am.'

'Your hand, please.' The Illuminator reached out, but Ghalod stepped in the way.

'Are you certain about this?' he asked.

'I'll be fine, Ghalod. Just keep an eye out for the others. I'll try to do this as quickly as possible.'

Ghalod grimaced but stepped aside.

This time, she forced herself to remain still.

A loud rustling ran through the garden, as if from a phantom wind. The branches and thorny vines began to move.

'What's happening?' Daerna asked, alarm slowly overcoming sense.

'It's waking up.'

The vines swarmed like a wave towards her. Daerna had no time to panic as something grabbed her hand and pierced her skin. She shrieked.

Chapter Thirty-Six

Ash

The Vigil-blight around the Sunken Library is particularly dangerous, for it now can reach into the waking world. Not only that, it craves Dreamers and their gifts, anything in order to reach out beyond its confines. This is why all patrols must be strictly timed, and why any interlopers with the Dreaming gift must be removed by any means necessary.

– Instructions from Master Vartus of the Academy to the Great Library's sentinels

THE DEEPER THEY SANK INTO the library's darkness, the more he feared what they'd find, especially once he and Yaisa had exchanged stories of what had happened to them.

They reached the lower levels in good time, but a water like dark ink prevented them from venturing farther. It was Thalder who found an opening in the wall, obscured by vines. Inside, the room was dark and damp, more a swamp than a cavern. This might once have been the Illuminator's copying room, but no longer. Everything was overgrown with wild plants that seemed unnatural, blooms and bushes made of dripping honey or ruby gemstones.

Hanging above it all were silver branches and shining leaves. They moved in silence towards the radiance of an orb-lamp in the distance, following a well-trodden path. But Thalder stopped abruptly and pointed at a large approaching figure.

Ash was readying his weapons when the figure waved his spear at them.

'Is that you, Ghalod?' Yaisa asked.

'Heavenly winds! About time!' Ghalod replied.

They ran the rest of the way towards him. Yaisa threw herself into his arms.

'Where's Daerna?' Ash asked.

Ghalod cleared his throat. 'Better come see for yourself.'

They followed Ghalod's long strides through the tall grasses to the origin of the light. Ash froze when he saw Daerna in front of the wild bush of shimmering silver, her pale skin radiating with the blue hue from the orb-lamp.

Then he saw the stranger, the 'Illuminator' Yaisa had told him about. Another Dreamling conjured by the library from its many books. She sat peacefully by Daerna's kneeling figure.

Ash ignored her and came to Daerna's side. 'Dae?' He tapped her shoulder.

She didn't answer.

He knelt at her side and checked her face. Though her eyes were closed, they moved rapidly, as if she were in the middle of a dream, and her mouth hung open.

'What have you done to her?' Yaisa asked the woman.

'She's reading the Garden, as the Garden reads her.'

'Bring her back!' Thalder ordered, but the Illuminator remained unfazed.

'Daerna, please, listen to me, we need to leave.'

An angry, dull roar filled the chamber. Above them, the shadows atop the columns rippled like water. The entire spire seemed to tremble with some unseen strain.

Ash felt the very air change, as if a storm were coming.

'We need to leave now!' Thalder said. 'Just grab her!'

'Wait!' the Illuminator protested. 'If you pull her out too soon, you'll leave her mind in the labyrinth.'

Ash placed a hand on Daerna's shoulder and hesitated. Before he could decide what to do, Ghalod whistled and pointed with his spear at the shifting bushes around them.

One of the wolf-like Nightmares prowled in the silvery grass.

It ran towards Yaisa, who instinctively struck with both her daggers. The creature was smart, though, and leapt to try to surpass her defence, but it wasn't smart enough to anticipate Ghalod. He thrust his spear at it, piercing the beast through.

It collapsed.

'You have quite the eye, friend!' Thalder said.

But despite the formidable blow, the Nightmare wriggled on the floor, gurgling. Thalder strode towards the fallen creature, sword in hand, and began hacking at its neck until he'd chopped its head off.

In the silence that followed, they heard answering shrieks from the upper galleries. An awful lot of them.

'That's . . . bad,' was all Thalder said. He gestured to Daerna. 'Do whatever it takes, Ash, but bring her back. We need to go!' He turned to Yaisa and Ghalod. 'You two, with me! We'll try to buy some time!'

Chapter Thirty-Seven

Daerna

Is it hard to believe the book was copied in secret? Elpia of Ravkiria, before becoming Blessed Elpia, was the most remarkable Illuminator of the Imperial Court. Traditional wisdom posits that Empress Myrtele consigned the book for Elpia to deliver to Princess Geleisdra. Yet if, like many believe, this was the empress's design, why would she entrust the book to an Illuminator unless she expected it to be copied? And why did Elpia tarry for so long in the Great Library if not to copy it?

– From the diaries of Eoinas Allandra

THE ENTIRE WORLD WAS SILENT.

In the darkness around her, the silver leaves shone brighter and brighter. Like lightning, they flashed until they blinded her. They sang too, a chorus of a million voices. It should have sounded like a thunderous cacophony, but instead it rang with the clarity of constellations. Every word was a ray of light, every book a star, all filling the hollowness of eternal silence.

Something reached out of the depths and brushed against Daerna's mind. It was a warden, a questioner, and it was hungry for knowledge.

It reminded Daerna of the Blessed Elpia who'd questioned her at the Silent Abbey, except this being was like a colossal wave about to swallow her. When Daerna tried to look into it, to give it a shape, it took one familiar to her: Geleisdra's winged lion, shimmering and with lightning crackling in his eyes.

He stood in her way, impassable and mighty as the mountains. She couldn't overpower him, so instead she spoke to him in the only way she thought possible. She sang.

It wasn't with her voice, or her words even. All of her came out as a raw note, a fragment of everything she was and everything she sought.

The lion's eyes narrowed. He prowled away, satisfied. She finally looked upon the book.

Every piece of emotion and thought collected in these pages floated in stupendous harmony. This was the eternal storm at the heart of the world made legible by the power of the word, strung together like a necklace of stars, like notes in the same melody.

It had the serene immensity of oceans, and it troubled her heart not to be able to stay within it, to make sense of it all even if it took her an entire lifetime. But she had to search for something. Not the whole truth but a fraction of it. An understanding.

She moved, flying on the currents, searching for any trace of the Wilting, any scrap of knowledge about it.

And there were many instances. Branch connected to trunk connected to root connected to forest, moving the disease from heaven to earth, to sea, to heart.

It was like reliving the memory, a painting of the past where someone had added a new layer of colour. She was there again. Because none of these things the book had witnessed, except through her eyes.

At the Broken Arches, where the flailing sick raved words of anguish. Their bodies ravaged by that which had been brought forth by the city.

She was again at the hospice in Vespiria, and there it was even more evident, how the entire naked isle was angry sorrow and despair, hidden under a cloak of sand. The bare rock suppurating its misery upwards into the masses flocking in, hungry, shattered by the loss of their homes. The bedrock of the city was feeding on this despair, catching fire with it. Ravaging their bodies with it. But the spark, the spark was coming from deep below.

She could see now.

How far it went. How deep into the city's bones, and deeper still into its very soul.

The rock emanated, radiated . . . Dreamt. Dark dreams, bitter and miserable.

Her mind darted back to the roots of the disease, and there she saw a group of courtiers gathered on the black-sand shore of some craggy coastline.

These weren't her memories, but someone else's.

A pale woman, dressed in the dark blues of the evening, had fallen to her knees, black sand coating her brocaded dress and white hands. There were tears burning trails down her cheeks.

Divine Geleisdra herself, or rather an echo of her in the book.

There was grief rising from inside her throat, but also a deep undercurrent of guilt. She saw Geleisdra scream.

Scream and shatter the world.

Onyxia's bones carried the root of it, for Geleisdra had birthed it out of her woe. It was her Wail of Stone, her sadness made manifest, in the dark onyx that had been used in every wall, road, building and foundation.

This malady had slept until the forlorn's clogged dreams woke it and shaped it.

The spores found fertile soil in the sorrows of Onyxia's people and blossomed into a disease. That was what had seized Roshia, the children of Little Vespiria, the afflicted at the Broken Arches. Their spirits echoed that primal sorrow that poisoned the brain and tangled the strings that carried the body, fossilising it, freezing it, turning it into something hollow and dead.

Daerna heard Ash calling for her, but it was a distant echo in the depths of her mind, a minuscule spark in the celestial silver.

And yet, this spark burned differently. The despair and yearning in the cry were enough to remind her that she was elsewhere. Her mind might be inside the comforting embrace of the Silver Book, but her body was not.

In Ash's urgency, she was reminded that time still existed beyond this serenity, that it threatened to run out.

But she had to find something first.

A cure.

But what cure? The city couldn't be undone; its grief and its guilt couldn't be removed. She felt the Pale Prince's hand on the Solemn Princess's shoulder, trying to reassure her, to offer a measure of peace upon their shared loss, their shared failure and guilt.

That hadn't been enough then.

Ahead, the path became a whirlwind. Divine Geleisdra's visions, already shaped. Already certain.

A whirlwind, not the Motherstorm's but not unlike Her. Skies parting to let through falling pieces of firmament, tendrils of fire and smoke, cutting through the world now that it was forever broken. And inside, Geleisdra, battling death itself.

But she wasn't afraid to face it, this woman, for she faced it for all of them at the same time. She was every woman since the beginning of time, enduring, resisting, facing the dark truth of the world: death was coming. Death of burnished gold and bronze flame. Death trying to bend her, to flay her and strip the world naked of skin.

She floated in the sky, battling death with her wits and her love, turning her despair into something grander. The Motherstorm lifted her up, her mind flashing with every thought she'd ever recorded like lightning.

This too she had seen. She'd called upon the Motherstorm to fend off the Charnel Mother's Nightmare at the Scab, but only now did she understand what the Solemn Princess had done. Above her, she saw Divine Geleisdra's Guardian roaring amidst the storm, facing the Charnel Mother, looming, towering like death itself.

One Mother of hope and solace, the other Mother of despair and destruction.

And as the woman sang, the trembling city listened. The black stone echoed her voice. And together, in synthesis, the song became an act of hope, a way to turn her immense loss into a seed for future growth.

Ash's voice reached her again, dimmer this time but also more urgent. Time had run out.

Chapter Thirty-Eight
Geil

A wise ruler enters alliances only recognising the poisoned seed hidden inside them. For when foreseen, it is easy to remedy betrayals, but if you wait until the fever blossoms, there's no longer medicine for it.

– *The Oneirarch* by Malchiavos

GEIL GLIDED TOWARDS LADY SAORLA'S Nacre Island. Her wings still burned where the shadow-wisp had grazed her, but it wasn't the only thing nagging at her.

We never should have lowered our guard with them, the Drake chided her.

Either way, she had to act before the Senate reconvened tomorrow. She could still call on favours, remove her house's support for the Reformers. And if she hadn't been played by Lady Saorla, she had to alert her immediately to the threat the shard of the Mantle posed to the city.

A pair of golden hippogriffs released a cry of alarm upon seeing her. She flew past their stables and beyond the docks to land abruptly on the grass of the palace's inner courtyard. Exhausted by the long flight, she almost collapsed to her knees. She quickly Dreamt her wings and scales back into her flesh despite the Drake's grumbling.

Three house guards with swords and breastplates that shone silver under the orb-lamps' lights hurried from the arcades. But before Geil could even introduce herself, a voice called from above.

'Geil!' Liadra peered down from the arched gallery. She was dressed in a simple chemise and embroidered cloak with her radiant golden hair falling over one shoulder. 'She's my guest,' she said to the guards, who obsequiously escorted Geil inside to a drawing room with fine tapestries on the walls.

'I didn't know you'd be calling, but this is an excellent surprise,' Liadra said, entering the room. 'Come, sit. I'll have wine and cake brought to us.' She took Geil's hand and gently pulled her towards one of the comfortable velvet chairs.

Keep your guard up, the Drake warned.

Geil really wanted to forget the whole affair and while away the hours with Liadra, sitting by her side and listening to her talk, getting lost in her aquamarine eyes. Let the wine sate her thirst, and awaken one of a different kind. But she couldn't.

'I need to talk to you,' Geil said.

'So, you already heard? We have the votes for tomorrow!' Liadra's smile was bright. When Geil stared blanky, she explained, 'Zerandra will take the High Sage position and I'll serve him as secretary to take on the creation of literacy schools! That is, with your support, of course.'

Geil pursed her lips. This should have been a triumph for both of them, and yet, she couldn't enjoy it.

Liadra raised an eyebrow. 'Aren't you happy? You encouraged me to do this, to step out from my sister's shadow, and I have.'

'We need to clear up some things first,' Geil replied.

Liadra blinked, taken aback by her coldness. 'What's this about?'

Despite her best efforts, Geil's words came out blunt and hard. 'I've just found out there's a shard of the Mantle hidden in Lord Davorles's family palace in the Crumbling Quarter. One that has been kept secret, to be used either to breed

Nightmares or torture others. So, far from reining in the Academy, it seems your sister is happy to invite them into the city.'

'Th-that can't be,' Liadra stammered. 'Whatever it's meant for, Ines wouldn't be part of such a thing.'

'Wouldn't she? She brokered a deal with the Academy to fend off the Delectian raids in the Valelands. In exchange for what, exactly? Allowing them to expand their conscription rights? Granting them more power by naming Lord Davorles as head of the Secret Chancellery?'

'I don't like it either, but Lord Davorles and the Academy are just a counterweight to the Traditionalists' ambitions to get rid of Senate rule once and for all. He's there to keep Lord Stalcar honest. Besides, tomorrow, when Zerandra becomes the new High Sage, he'll be able to rein them in!'

Liadra hadn't denied any of it. *She's been playing us.* The Drake simmered with resentment.

'So, what's the role of this in your sister's alliance? A weapon of last resort to use against a Traditionalist coup? A secret torture chamber in which he can play with your sister's enemies? What's so important that they're killing to keep it secret?'

'Killing whom?' Her face went pale. 'I assure you we have no idea of what you're talking about!'

'How would you even know? Would she even tell you?'

Liadra's eyes welled up at that. *Yes, see how she squirms. She's weak and unworthy of us*, the Drake purred.

She could tell the harm caused by her own tone, her own harshness. Liadra wasn't weak, as the Drake thought. She was good-natured and idealistic, very much like Lanteus had been.

Geil could still feel the Drake's delight, but it also felt strange to her.

'I'm sorry . . .' Geil croaked. 'I know you're not that sort of person, Liadra.'

'Then, if you trust me, trust me on this: neither is my sister. Please, you have to believe me,' Liadra begged.

She's just stalling, the Drake snarled in protest.

Believing didn't come easy to Geil anymore. And yet, her heart wrestled with the Drake's advice for once.

'I want to trust you,' she finally muttered.

Liadra tiptoed to kiss Geil somewhere between her cheek and lips. When she withdrew, they held each other's gaze. It'd been only a caress, a graze, but the warmth in Liadra's eyes, on her lips, trickled like warm honey into Geil's heart.

She'd been caught off guard, not just by her kiss but by the dormant yearning it had awoken in her. She should have kissed her back in that moment. Taken Liadra's lips as an invitation, chasing the perfume in her hair, sinking into her neck's warmth. Invited her hands to wash away this excruciating dread.

But in her hesitation, the moment sneaked past her, and the chance vanished.

'I'll prove it to you. Just wait here. I'll go into her study. If there's anything in her correspondence, I'll find it.'

* * *

Time trickled excruciatingly slowly while Geil kept watch in the hallway, scanning the shadows. Distant echoes reached her, furtive steps, hushed words.

Somebody treading where they shouldn't, the Drake ascertained.

She left her post and stepped softly on the rug towards the end of the corridor, where it turned into a different hallway. Whoever it was had gone silent.

Then she picked up a trace in the air. She inhaled deeply, detecting a sticky, saliva-like smell she knew well enough. Instantly, the Drake was awake. *Hydra*, it snarled.

The many-headed snakes were bred at the Academy by the dozen, not just to train Nightmare-Hunters in the art of killing but because both their venom and breath, equally poisonous, were useful in slaying other Nightmares. The venom itself didn't smell that much; their breath, though, clung to the nostrils. For Geil to pick up on the stench meant the beast couldn't be far.

In the dark, she marched around the corner, following the scent down a long marble corridor towards the family's private quarters. Two young servants stood guard on either side of mahogany double doors. The musky smell seeped from behind them.

'Are you lost, my lady?' the maid asked.

'Something's wrong. Open the door,' Geil demanded.

The young servants traded nervous glances in the penumbra.

'Lady Saorla isn't to be disturbed,' the maid protested.

Why were they standing there in the dark? This wasn't adding up.

Deftly, Geil sidestepped the maid. When the squire tried to grab her, Geil pulled his arm, slamming him against the maid and sending them both tumbling limply to the floor.

Stepping over their fallen bodies, she slammed the doors open. The viscid reek rolled out in a heavy wave.

These were Lady Saorla's personal quarters. Yet the windows were tightly shut and the curtains drawn closed, so she had to rely on her Drake eye to see anything. Under an engraved wooden ceiling adorned with a golden frieze sat a delicately carved bed, enclosed by curtains. Inside, Lady Ines Saorla and her husband squirmed, their breathing weak and uneasy. Something other than hydra's breath pervaded the air: the scent of rose.

This was no Nightmare.

She bent at the knees. Her eyes fell on the source. A rose, a Dreamchanted rose. Icy and white, dripping with pearly drops of something that wasn't dew. What it exuded was slowly poisoning Lady Saorla and her husband. It'd poison her too if she wasn't careful.

Geil locked the air in her lungs and Dreamt her nostrils tightly closed. Wading into the thick of the venomous cloud, she knelt and reached for the solitary flower.

Liadra's cry came from the corridor. 'Watch out!'

She spun on her heel. The squire came at her with a blade carved out of bone. She'd thought he was unconscious. A cold pang ran through her left forearm where the blade pierced her scales, drawing blood.

He furiously stabbed again, and Geil ducked under the blow and swung her fist upwards, smashing into his skull with a brutal crack.

He fell limp. This time she made sure he was properly knocked out.

In the corridor, Liadra struggled to hold the maid while screaming for the guards. Seeing Geil approach, the maid shoved Liadra into the nearby wall and bolted.

The Drake wanted to chase after the servant, but the rose was still spreading its deathly veil. Head spinning from holding her breath, Geil rushed to the bed and picked up first Lady Saorla then her husband, balancing them on each of her shoulders. Lungs burning, back aching, she marched all the way to Liadra's chambers before she placed them on her bed.

'What's wrong with them?' Liadra asked.

Geil checked for Lady Saorla's pulse. Her heart was racing out of control, and her irises were dilated and her breathing an unsteady wheezing.

'They've got poison in their lungs.'

A score of squires and other servants rushed into the bedchamber.

'Ready the *Burning Dawn*!' Liadra commanded, her voice shaking. 'We need to get them to a physician!'

Geil, for her part, took to the balcony running. Spreading her wings, she flung herself high into the night skies. Circling the palace from above, she read the movement below. Cries of alarm came from every direction. Servants, guards and gargoyles rushed inside.

There, the Drake said. A lone figure was running through the gardens, fleeing from the commotion.

Geil beat her wings to gain some altitude, then plunged towards the fugitive. She landed on the maid's back, knocking her onto the grassy ground.

Wobbling, the maid struggled to crawl back up and fumbled for a knife. Geil slapped it out of her hand. 'Talk!' she commanded.

The maid was shaking, not just with fear but also anger. Geil might have had the patience to deal with her, but the Drake didn't. It grabbed her by the neck and slammed her against a tree.

'Talk, you filthy traitor, before I break every one of your bones!' Geil warned.

The maid spat at her, so Geil slammed her against the tree harder.

'I'm not afraid! The Charnel Mother will deliver me from this cursed life soon!'

A bloody Charnelite, here? It wasn't the boldness of the attack that shocked her. They'd dared ambush those Sisters at the Scab, after all, and Geil had seen the results. It was just that their nihilistic preachings had touched the heart of Saorla's own household.

And yet ... something didn't add up. Maybe if she hadn't been Academy trained, she wouldn't have caught it.

'The Charnel Mother didn't give you that hydra's breath. Somebody else did,' Geil said. 'The same person who's taken you for a fool. That's who you're really serving, not the Charnel Mother. How do you think I found you?' It was only a bluff, one that she delivered with full conviction.

'No, no, that can't be.' Uncertainty had crept into the maid's voice.

'What did he tell you?' she gambled.

'It doesn't matter what he said! He's but an instrument of *Her* will. When the Charnel Mother's delivered back to us, we'll finally be free!'

'Delivered? What are you going on—'

Geil stopped talking as she noticed her own breath as a fine fog in the air. A sudden cold had crept in. She looked over her shoulder, searching for the cause. Too late, she saw a ripple in the shadows.

The maid shrieked and clutched her own chest, twisting in pain. A shadow-wisp had taken shape in the tree's looming branches and reached inside the young woman.

Geil pulled her away. The maid was gasping and convulsing. The shadow-wisp hovered for a second, sensing her doubt. Geil feared it'd chase after her. It didn't, instead melting away into the garden's darkness.

The maid's eyes lingered on Geil, feverish and frightful, until they went hollow.

* * *

'You need to leave too,' Geil told Liadra as she landed on the *Burning Dawn*'s deck.

Weak groans of pain came from within the quarter cabins. Servants, sailors and squires were readying the skyship at a furious pace.

'I am.' Liadra's eyes were red, but her shoulders were high and set. 'I've given them some of our precious theriac with white wine, but both are delirious and in pain. I'm taking them to the Grand Palace's resident physicians.'

'Wait.'

Geil pulled Liadra aside to whisper where they wouldn't be heard.

'The poison is part hydra's breath, which is not easy to collect, distil or preserve. The maid admitted someone else had provided it.'

'Who?'

'Just as she was about to confirm my suspicions, a shadow-wisp killed her in front of me. I assume the only reason it didn't attack me is because it'd only been given enough understanding to carry out a specific task: eliminate the assassins. Yet no doubt it'll report back to its master what it's seen. And you know exactly who manipulates shadow-wisps with the same ease as breathing.'

'Lord Davorles,' Liadra muttered.

'He's behind this attack, one way or another. And now he's covering his tracks. Which means the city isn't safe for any of you.'

Liadra nodded tensely. 'Arvira, then. The university has the best physicians and Remakers in all of the Domain.'

'Good winds, then,' Geil wished Liadra, sweeping her into a fierce hug.

'You're not coming?' Liadra asked, leaning her head against Geil's chest.

'No. I need to warn my father, the Falconess and everyone I can.'

'Please, be careful, Geil.'

Her heart beat like a loud drum: at Liadra's closeness, at her caring, yet the beating was also her own anger, a furious calling for war.

They are the ones who need to be careful, the Drake thrummed.

Chapter Thirty-Nine

Ash

I hope Aescyon defies the world by living, by clinging to his imagination.

– From the diaries of Eoinas Allandra

'PLEASE, COME BACK. PLEASE . . .' All Ash could do was call for Daerna as the howls grew louder around them.

He couldn't leave her. He wouldn't. This damn place wouldn't claim another of his loved ones.

'Daerna, please.'

Finally, something changed. A violent shiver seized her. Then she collapsed into his arms. He held her tightly, relief breaking open in his chest.

'Ash?' Her voice was weak and her eyes red.

'Are you hurt?'

She shook her head.

There was no time to rest, as much as he wanted to let her. 'We *have* to go,' he said. 'Can you walk?'

She stood, albeit on wobbly legs. He put her arm over his shoulder and led her back towards the stairs where the others were, but as they reached the landing, Yaisa came down running.

'They've trapped us! There are too many!' she screamed.

A bit farther up, Ash caught a glimpse of a horde of cadaverous animals – wolves, boars and bears – coming down the stairs, reeking of decay. They were grotesque, as if they'd been copied from the flat drawings of some ancient bestiaries but made up of rotten bones, muck and maggot-ridden pelts. Their glazed eyes, though, shone hungrily, and their bony and chitinous legs followed with ravenous swiftness.

They caught a glimpse of the Hordemaster leading them on a balcony above. He was a grizzled man with a long, frayed beard.

'We know you're here! Surrender and we'll be lenient!' he yelled.

Thalder landed at the bottom of the stairs. Ghalod was coming right behind him, his spear's tip on fire – Dreamchanted by Thalder, certainly – and he was swinging it to keep two snarling wolves at bay.

'Here's my surrender, come and get it!' Thalder yelled back at the man.

He threw a flask at the landing over Ghalod's shoulder. It shattered, releasing dark oil that burst into a fire. The blaze wasn't mindless; it had purpose and anger to it. Furious deflagrations burst out, winding a twisting path to spear the wolves. In its aftermath, a dozen different fires had spread. The Horde of Nightmares bided their time beyond them. Their sparkless eyes watched blankly.

'Ash, tell me your map has a miraculous way out of here!' Thalder yelled.

Ash sucked in a sharp breath and dug into his satchel for his father's journal. There, written in Eoinas's handwriting, was the precise path they'd both taken to enter from the spire's main gates farther down.

'This way!' he said, and led them through the writing desks turned page-covered bushes. The Nightmares chased swiftly, their insectoid chattering growing louder as they approached.

They exited the cavernous Illuminators' vault to an overgrown stairway descending all the way to the main gates. The same staircase he'd used all those years ago – except the entire landing and entrance chamber lay submerged by inky black water.

'Tell us there's another way!' Yaisa yelled.

Ash checked his father's map again, heart hammering in his throat. There was nowhere else to go. 'We'll have to swim!' He shoved the journal back into his satchel.

'Those stupid gates better still be open,' Yaisa grumbled, 'and there better not be worse things in the water!'

'It'll have to do!' Thalder roared. 'There's no time for anything else!'

They entered the water one at a time. Ghalod remained behind atop the stairs, his blazing spear in his hands. 'Go on! I'm right behind you.'

'I hate this! I hate this!' Yaisa cried. She took a deep breath, threw her satchel to the side and, with a dagger in her teeth, dived beneath the water.

Ash helped Daerna to the edge of the water with him. She dragged her feet, dazed and exhausted. It seemed unlikely she'd be able to make the swim into the outside. 'Curse my rotten luck!' Ash said.

His vision grew dark around the edges. A primordial fear seeped into his stomach, filling his chest and pushing against his lungs. He felt that if he held his breath, he'd never breathe again.

He froze, even though he knew the beasts were almost on them.

He imagined that if he strained his eyes, he'd be able to see himself. On the stairs, on the boat, sliding away as his father was dragged underwater.

'Can you do this?' Thalder asked.

Ash wanted to say yes. To say that he could. But his lips failed him. He just stood there, shivering like an idiot.

The library rumbled in the distance.

Thalder turned to the water and made a gesture, as if pulling something from the air.

'Put your hand here. I've called a string-nymph. She'll get you out.'

'Wait!' Ash called as Thalder reached for him.

His father's journal . . .

He slipped into the Dreaming and wrapped his whole satchel into a watertight skin. Then, he turned to Daerna and recalled the clear winds from the Sea of Shingles. They swirled around Daerna and him, eager and strong. It was easy to play with them, to conjure them, but not to tame them, so he just shaped them, gave them the playfulness of crowcats and beckoned them to take care of Daerna, to play with her hair, to dance with her in their trip under the water. He was still in the Dreaming when something pulled him farther into the water, up to his shoulders. He held tight to Daerna as that same something embraced him, warm and welcoming and soft.

He emerged from the trance to protest again, but Thalder was faster. 'Get them out!' he yelled.

Ghalod still hadn't arrived.

Ash only had time to take a deep breath before the string-nymph took him. He was swallowed by the numbing cold, pulled by his armpits into a black vortex. His lungs burned. He clenched his eyes closed. Was his father's body still down here? Would he find it if he looked?

He held Daerna tightly. He wasn't going to make it. He was going to suck the water into his lungs and die like his father had—

His head broke the surface, and he gasped for air.

They had emerged in the flooded plateau outside the main entrance. Daerna coughed and sputtered, conscious once again. 'It's okay,' he said, not sure if it was meant more for her or for himself. 'It's fine.'

Yaisa was there too, her teeth clattering with the cold. 'Rudher! Down here!' She whistled loudly.

Ash wanted to drift away. To rest. To forget what had happened in this cursed library.

But he'd left the others behind, to die, to drown, to be torn apart.

'I have to go back,' he told Yaisa. 'Please, get Daerna out of here.'

'Ash, wait!' Daerna protested.

He didn't wait.

He dived under the water and with forceful strokes swam through the darkness. He'd have enough strength in him, enough air too if he didn't get lost.

Inside the cold dark depths, he reached for the Dreaming and pulled a rope out of nothingness, one binding the landing he'd left behind with the gate outside. And with its help he climbed and thrashed ahead, lungs burning until he was back where he never should have been, much less returned.

He broke through the waters at the bottom of the steps.

He followed the sounds of fighting to where Thalder had rejoined Ghalod to help him fend off a vicious boar-like Nightmare. Ghalod's spear had finally snapped and he was wrestling the monstrosity's tusks, while Thalder hacked at its thick skin with his sword. This hellish place wouldn't let them go, not without claiming blood.

'We have to leave!' Ash called.

With a groan, Ghalod shoved the Nightmare away. 'Now!' he yelled.

They turned and ran, Thalder furiously throwing his last flasks behind them, setting the doorway ablaze. Ghalod loped ahead of him.

The beasts circled the blaze, trying to find an opening.

A blurry shape descended on them, as if the obscurity above were shifting, one moment darkness, the next some sort of translucent spiderweb with spiked tendrils.

This was Ash's fear, not quite shapeless, not fully formed yet either.

It was the library, twisting, turning on them, the Vigil-blight feeding from his dread and all the secret terror carved into the long-dormant pages of forgotten tomes.

'Above you! Watch out!' Ash cried.

Thalder swerved to one side but not fast enough. One of the bony tendrils had pierced him. It'd missed his heart but had run him through the shoulder. Now a blood-soaked sting protruded from it. Thalder gasped before falling to one knee.

Ash ran upstairs. Ghalod was faster, grabbing the tendril from both sides and tearing it apart. Ash only made it in time to catch Thalder before he toppled down the steps.

He reached for the Dreaming again, squeezing his dwindling hope and energy before dread devoured it all. He made the rope into a long water snake, young and nimble. Eager to escape and pull them out.

Taking a final breath, he grabbed its tail with the hand not holding Thalder.

Out of breath, out of time, he came back to his body. 'Let's go!'

Around them, the chamber groaned in anger.

Too late, Ash saw another tendril lash out at him, spiked tip thrusting like a dagger towards his face. He closed his eyes and heard the brutal, crunching blow.

He opened them to see that Ghalod had stood in its way. His chest was torn open.

'It's too deep,' he said with a sad smile. Blood trickled down his lips as he collapsed.

The sea snake pulled them away, and Ash didn't let go.

Chapter Forty

Daerna

The Iskians almost always read their scrolls aloud. That's why they deemed the oldest books as dangerous. They believed the ghost of the author took over their lips to speak for themselves.

We can't say they were entirely wrong. Books can't force a reader's lips, nor their mind, yet, sometimes, they do plant seeds in their souls. Some of these eventually bloom, forever changing the reader. That is both their danger and their allure.

– *The History of Books* by Itras Valandra

DAERNA WOKE IN ONE OF the skysloop's bunk beds. Her muscles burned and her head throbbed, but she was alive. She could hear a distant tinging, a buzzing at the edge of her perception. As if the great winged lion of the library were somehow still creeping about unseen.

Something shifted at the end of her bed. Omen perked up when he noticed she was awake. In another nearby bunk, Thalder shivered in what seemed to be some violent fever. Ash was seated by his side, wiping the sweat off his face with a cloth.

'Where's everyone else?' she asked.

Ash turned, face hardening with a pained grimace. 'Yaisa and Rudher are searching for an antidote to whatever poison's got into Thalder. He's had some flowerfall for the pain. Let's hope we can get him to a physician in the city soon. But Ghalod . . .' He didn't finish. 'We should never have gone to that forsaken place. It's all my fault.'

Daerna reached for his hand. 'I'm sorry.'

'The Silver Book. Did you find anything in it?' he asked with a cracked voice. He needed the answer.

Daerna nodded. 'The Wilting and the black mould – we were right, they are connected! Onyxia isn't just a Hallowed Dream. It's alive, like the Motherstorm, and much like the Motherstorm, it listens and mirrors our dreams back to us.'

'Are you saying the city is causing people to get sick?'

'In a way. The disease is an echo of our own doing. A terrible Nightmare inspired by the despair of those being crushed by society.'

'That can't be.' He stared with shock. 'All those people, Roshia, the children . . . They can't be doing this to themselves.'

'They're not! The disease must have been growing, festering in Onyxia for decades, but it's erupting now among those in the clutches of despair.'

Ash's eyes went wide. 'I think I understand.'

'Yes! And the anguish of the people is shaping it into something terrible.'

'Will any of this help save Roshia?'

'It has to! Understanding its root will help curb the Wilting's spread, especially if someone like Lord Morvander lends his voice to denounce it. We could save thousands of lives.' She considered the blurry mesh of images and memories in her thoughts. It was hard to remember the immensity of it all, harder even to make sense of it. After a moment, she added, 'And I saw something else in the book. The Motherstorm bringing some measure of solace to the city too.'

'But wouldn't they have tried it by now if it was as simple as Keening?'

'Something else is at play that I don't understand. The Order's Superiors have allowed the Wilting to spread and grow, claiming it's a spiritual punishment for the morally corrupt. The Secret Chancellery promised to purge it, and although this has failed, the Orders have failed to react – why?' Daerna shook her head. 'Either way, I'm not abandoning Roshia.'

They fell into silence.

'Good,' Ash finally replied. 'I'll take Thalder to the physicians, then aid you with whatever you need. Nothing else matters now.'

'Ash, isn't the tribunal reconvening today for your exam?'

'Ghalod is dead, Daerna. Thalder might not make it either.' He shook his head. 'Who cares about the damned dispensation?'

'You're of no use to anybody if the Academy arrests you. And think of all the effort Thalder put into training you!'

Ash roughly scratched at his scalp, as if trying to tear the pain away, but then he conceded. 'I'll ask the others to take Thalder to Lord Morvander's physician. But won't you need a Dreamer?'

'What I need is a Remaker. Don't worry, I'll find one even if I have to indebt myself for life.'

They lingered together in a silent embrace, taking comfort in each other. It was a small fire to keep away the numbing dread that was slowly growing inside her.

* * *

When the *Night Swan* reached the Central Quarter, Daerna went to the deck and leaned over the gunwale to search for University Square.

Nightmare hounds as large as horses were chained at the fountain. The arcades, usually bustling with students, were eerily quiet. Even the merchant barges from the mainland performed their morning dances, loading and unloading with a particular fury, as if they feared the storm would befall them any minute.

As the vessel glided to a slow sway and then a stop, Ash dropped the rope ladder, and Daerna readied to leave.

'I'm sorry I can't be there with you,' he said.

'Everything will be fine. I'll see you soon,' she replied.

He pressed a deep kiss to her lips.

* * *

She found Dirdra pacing in Roshia's room.

'Blessed thunder! You're back!' Dirdra hugged her. 'They don't know how much longer she has.'

Inside, a couple of physicians leaned over Roshia's still figure on the bed. She was pale as bone, and the two physicians seemed harrowingly grey. The woman's eyes were bleary and red, his broken and defeated. Despite their dishevelled appearance, it was clear they were Roshia's parents.

'Daerna! I trust my apprentice is well?'

Lord Morvander was there too, seated by the window with his chamberlain. To her relief, she saw a heavy chest, probably loaded with mirrormatter, by his side.

She walked over to him. 'On his way to meet the tribunal.'

'Excellent. Did you find what you were looking for?' he asked.

'We did find some answers.' She knelt by his side and dropped her voice. 'You were right about the city being a conduit. However, it's even more than that. The city's a living Dream, just like the Motherstorm. It listens to us and delivers its own miracles.'

'You're saying it's not just that the onyx is Dreamchanted; the whole city shares a sort of soul.'

'Yes! It's not some mindless reflection but a mirroring of our own despair. Just like the Hallowed Motherstorm, it can become overburdened. That's what sparks this growth, this physical malady that spreads in the shape of the black mould and ravages whatever it touches.'

'So, Sister Roshia caused this outbreak?' he asked.

She glanced over her shoulder at Roshia. 'Rather, Onyxia listened to Roshia's despair, and at some point began echoing it back through the eruptions of the cracks and the mould.'

'I fail to see why Onyxia would focus so intently on a specific individual.'

'It hasn't! It's happening everywhere. In the Scab, in Little Vespiria. This is what turned the Southern Quarter into the Scab and the Crumbling District!'

Morvander rubbed his chin, lost in thought. The Remaker finished her examination and stood.

'Sadly, she's not reacting to the vespershade,' Roshia's father, gaunt and grey, explained to the room. 'Maybe we should ask Sister Dirdra to prepare her last rites.'

'This can't be.' Roshia's mother shook her head, her voice wavering. She turned to Lord Morvander. 'What of this remedy you spoke of?'

'Do I have your permission, then?' he asked.

'Of course!' she begged.

'I'll need you to leave the room, and make sure we aren't interrupted,' Lord Morvander said. 'Not you, Daerna. There's something you can help me with.'

Roshia's parents looked at her with a mix of fear and hope before Dirdra closed the door between them.

'What do you need from me, my lord?'

'We're going to try to save her your way. If you're right, it won't be enough for me to fight the disease's physical symptoms. Even if I succeed at transferring the palsy to the mirrormatter block, we must extricate the malady's roots from her very spirit. You must be the one to attempt to do so, because you know her best.'

'How?'

'If her despair's the fire that has started this blaze, we must douse it. Use your talent for Keening.'

Daerna's stomach quivered. 'The holy canticles won't work with her.'

'Then find something else. Sing something that speaks to your Sister's soul. Be her beacon to find the way back.'

Chapter Forty-One

Ash

Those seeking dispensation must prove sufficient mastery of their gift by either producing a Dreamchanted work or creating a new being. Furthermore, the tribunal shall interview them to assess their soundness of mind and control over their own terrors.

– *Instructions on Dispensation Exams* by High Sage Malvedra

CAPTAIN BENTOR DROPPED ASH AND Omen at the Grand Palace's northern quay. He gave a silent hug in farewell to Rudher and Yaisa. Ghalod was dead, Thalder might be very soon. Ash had managed to survive that accursed library twice, but both times he'd left a piece of his heart behind. Had it been worth it?

Ash was dragging his feet towards one of the entrances when he heard someone calling for him from an approaching barge. It was Lucre, dressed in a dark scarlet gown, disembarking and hurrying towards him with a worried expression.

'Gentle Storm! You look terrible! What's happened to you?'

'Thalder's with Lord Morvander's physician,' he blurted out, as if that explained everything.

'What are you speaking of?'

'We were attacked,' he mumbled. 'It's a long story.'

'I'll request a deferment of the exam then. I'm sure these are extraordinary circumstances, the tribunal—'

'No!' He realised he'd grabbed Lucre's wrist and let it go. 'I can do it. I'm going to do it.'

She must have read the dull anger in his words. She nodded and turned to the entrance.

Suddenly, Omen's ears perked up, and Ash turned to face an oncoming stranger. A short man wearing a worn-out Academy cuirass under a damp woollen cloak approached them.

He must have been waiting under the rain for a while. If it was because of Ash, it didn't bode well. Maybe word had already got back about their incursion. 'Greetings, Aescyon Lightning-Hunter. I am here to escort you to your examination.'

'Thank you,' Ash replied.

Instead of taking them inside the complex towards the Sages' palace, the man led them down a set of stairs that stopped at one of the Grand Palace's canalside entrances barred by a heavy wrought-iron door. Ash's relief soon shifted to suspicion and his heart drummed in his head. Wherever they were being taken, the Deep Wells couldn't be far off.

'Is this the fastest way to the Sages' palace?' he asked.

'It isn't,' Lucre said curtly.

'You're correct. We're heading to the barge that'll take us to the location where we'll conduct the practical part of the exam,' the man replied.

'I thought I was only required to show a masterpiece, not show Nightmare-Hunting skills,' Ash said.

He let out a shrill laugh. 'Don't you worry, it's a mere formality. Now, let's hurry, the tribunal doesn't like waiting!' he said with a big smile.

Ash took a hesitant step, but Omen blocked him and let out a low growl.

'Easy,' Ash said, but the panther didn't shift his stance one bit.

'Surely you can use a leash. It'd be a pity if I had to hurt it.' The man chuckled grimly.

Something didn't add up. Ash turned to Lucre, hoping she'd offer guidance.

Lucre arched an eyebrow. 'This is all very unusual. I suppose you don't mind if I check with your superiors at the High Sage's office?'

'It might take you the entire day, but be my guest,' he replied, annoyed.

'Wait here, Ash,' Lucre said, and immediately headed back up the stairs towards the palace.

Omen growled again, louder this time.

'Do something about your Nightmare now, or I shall,' the stranger said.

'It's alright, Omen.' Ash knelt to reassure him. Omen's stance was tense, his every muscle ready to spring. Something had the panther on edge.

He followed Omen's gaze and noticed the man reaching very slowly inside his cloak with his left arm.

'What are you doing?' Ash asked.

Too late, Ash realised that the man's eyes had gone vitreous, lost in the Dreaming trance.

Ash heard a splash from the nearby canal. The man pulled out a multi-tailed whip, but Omen lunged at him with swipes from both paws, shattering the weapon and tearing a gash in the man's knee.

Ash turned, only to find that a mudghast, a Nightmare shaped of grey refuse and mud, had crept out of the canal. Its pupil-less, crab-like eyes fixed on him, and it fanned its rocky claws to embrace him.

Ash tried to reach into the Dreaming, but the beast was faster and sank one of its pincers into his shoulder. He screamed as a bone snapped and blood ran down his chest.

Omen turned and leapt onto the Nightmare's arm, tearing a big chunk out of it with his teeth. The mudghast squirmed in pain but didn't release Ash.

Instead, it flung him aside like a broken ragdoll. Ash flew through the air and crashed into the canal. He sank into the darkness.

Chapter Forty-Two

Daerna

Peace, which flourishes under prudent and wise justice, can also be born from fear and power. In Onyxia, peace is only an absence of unrest, enforced through secrecy and vigilance. Dreamchanted lionheads gaze upon squares, canal and bridges, the Secret Chancellery watching through their eyes, its Stone-Masks ready to hunt the Domain's enemies.

– *Secrets of the Domain* by Stevanus Manvel

Daerna was singing – not Keening one of the holy canticles but singing in a way she hadn't in ages.

She sang joyful songs without obsessing about their intensity or the amount of sorrow she poured into them. She sang children's songs, folk rhymes to a tune and ballads to be belted out with a drink by a warm hearth during the Ascent masquerades.

To sing such mirthful songs with Roshia on the verge of death felt wrong, but she forced herself to do it anyway. She needed to reach her friend, to break the ever-encroaching silence of loss, to remind her of the importance she held to her, to others, to the world.

Even if she wasn't singing one of the holy canticles, Daerna found herself relying on Keening's familiar rhythms, shaping her music through them. She wasn't trying to reach the Motherstorm's Hallowed heart, just somebody she loved, someone who lacked a path through her despair.

And yet, she felt something stirring in the air, as if the abbey held its breath to listen. Its arches and flying buttresses trembling imperceptibly, ready to carry her song. She felt vertigo at this sensation. Still, she took the plunge. She lent whatever strength she had to the song, breathing herself into it.

Outside, the rain shuddered, shifting from icy sorrow to cool wistfulness. Muirtra's very skin seemed to quaver an exhalation. A breeze blowing freely through the room. Hopefully, it'd sweep away the ashes suffocating Roshia's heart.

She sang and sang, until something else stirred in her hand. Roshia's fingers had twitched.

'Dae?' she asked. Her eyes no longer wandered but landed on Daerna.

'Roshia?'

'You were singing . . .'

Roshia reached out for Daerna, and Daerna fell into the bed to hug her. They lay embraced together for what seemed a long while and yet not nearly long enough, until Daerna felt a hand on her shoulder.

Lord Morvander's face was pearled with sweat. 'You should both get some rest.'

'You did it! Is she safe?'

'The circulatory swelling and the clotting have been removed from her body.' He pointed to the mirrormatter block, where a replica of Roshia lay frozen in silent pain. 'Though more importantly, I can no longer perceive the disease. It washed away without my doing, and the fever with it.'

Was that what she'd felt? The oppressive dread washing away?

'So, we were right?'

'*You* were right, yes. Something in the city, in our surroundings, sparks the disease. Which means we can work on stopping it from spreading. This is the beginning of a cure.'

'Thank you, thank you, my lord!' Daerna kissed his gloved hand. 'How can I ever repay you?'

'Your help's been reward enough. With what we've achieved here today, we might help so many more! For now, I shall deliver the news to Sister Dirdra, then alert the proper authorities.'

'What of your fears that this might be deemed heresy?'

'Given the circumstances, my fears no longer matter,' he replied in a firm voice. 'These cruel quarantines must stop at once, and an inquiry should be opened to see why this has been allowed to spread. And please, accept my invitation to my house tonight. I'm sure there'll be much to celebrate.'

With that, he left, helped by Balchod. She closed the door after him before crawling back into bed to lie beside Roshia.

'I thought everything had faded away.'

'It's alright now,' Daerna whispered to Roshia, but her Sister pressed on.

'These last few weeks ... seeing all those people die. I felt I couldn't waste a single second doing anything but fighting the disease, but the more I fought, the more each defeat weighed on me. And then when you almost died, I felt I had failed you. Failed everyone. Everything fell down on me ... Then I heard your song and realised that I wasn't alone in the fight.'

'You're not, little sister,' she said, and kissed Roshia's forehead.

The doors opened and Roshia's parents came in. Their faces underwent a miraculous transformation. From weeping with utter dread, they now shed tears of joy. The two of them fell upon Roshia and held her as they placed a dozen kisses on her face.

* * *

After bidding her farewells, Daerna hurried to the street. She might still be able to make it for Ash's exam, and even if she didn't, she still wanted to be with him to face the results.

Descending the abbey's steps, she noticed a crowd gathered around the nearby water stairs. She approached the commotion warily only to find Lord Morvander's chamberlain shouting at a group of armed figures who were blocking them from boarding their gondola.

A shiver ran down her spine as she spotted their grey leather half-masks.

'This is an outrage! Do you know who my lord is?' Balchod shouted.

'Lord Morvander has nothing to fear if he's innocent,' a woman, her Stone-Mask cracked by shimmering purple veins, replied.

Daerna merged with the crowd of spectators. An artisan with the white cap of the Reformers watched intently, clutching her hammer with badly disguised anger.

'What's happening?' Daerna asked her.

'The Stone-Masks are accusing Lord Morvander of conspiring to assassinate Lady Saorla!'

'What? That's ridiculous!' Daerna said. Cool fear pooled in her stomach. Whatever conspiracy they were discussing, she was certain the charges had to be trumped up.

'Let us call for the magistrate, or even better, call for Lady Saorla! We'll see what she thinks of this unlawful arrest!' Balchod commanded the young bargeman.

The artisan and some others in the crowd jeered at the masked men. 'Release him!'

Lord Morvander's bargeman tried to leave the boat, but a masked man wearing a cloak of smoke blocked his passage and unsheathed two curved blades from his belt.

'Come with us and there won't be need for violence,' the masked woman said.

'You don't want to do this,' Lord Morvander replied.

'You have no right to arrest a senator!' Daerna yelled.

'This is tyranny!' the artisan by her side shouted. Some in the crowd, taking heart, began encroaching on the group.

'Grab him!' the woman ordered her subordinates.

The Stone-Mask blocking the path punched Balchod with his gauntleted fist and sent him to the ground. Lord Morvander stumbled to reach his fallen chamberlain.

The barge boy swung his pole at the Stone-Mask, but the man turned into a wisp of black smoke, whirled past him and reformed behind the lad. The boy spun to face what was coming, but he wasn't fast enough. Daerna smothered a scream as the man stabbed him in the neck, and the lad fell, sputtering blood. With a boot, the Stone-Mask pushed the boy overboard.

Another Stone-Mask tried grabbing Lord Morvander, but as soon as he touched the lord's cloak, he fell backwards, screaming and rolling as if he'd been set on fire. The crowd's patience too had gone up in smoke.

Cobbles were flung at the Stone-Masks. The artisan and others even charged the woman, and Daerna followed.

The veins on the woman's mask shimmered as she cracked the whip in her hand. She didn't attack Lord Morvander, though.

Instead, a wave of fire rolled towards the crowd, a strange fire of purplish flames that caught on the plaza's flagstones. The mob's charge broke down into a panicked stampede. Daerna turned to run but was shoved to the ground.

As the fire ate away at whatever it found on the flagstones, Daerna crawled back up, only to have someone trip on her and knock her down again. Smoke filled her nose and throat, burning.

From the ground, she saw Lord Morvander extend his arm. A sudden blast of icy blizzard fell like a punch from the heavens. In the blink of an eye, the flames had been extinguished.

She'd have cheered, but the woman cracked her whip again. This time, it shifted into a long scorpion's tail. Its sting landed on Lord Morvander's neck, and he staggered and then collapsed limply over Balchod.

The woman barked another command to her companions. 'Arrest the agitators too!'

Daerna sucked in a sharp breath, crawled upwards and ran.

She had to warn Ash.

Chapter Forty-Three
Geil

The Oneirarch must be merciless in the pursuit and purging of their enemies, for there are fewer dreams as perilous as those of vengeance.

– *The Oneirarch* by Malchiavos

WHEN GEIL FINALLY REACHED THE Susurrus's skies, her relief vanished as soon as she realised the Quietude offered no sanctuary.

The palace was closed off. The upper balconies had disappeared, swallowed like tongues by featureless black stone faces. Heavy iron shutters had fallen over the skywharf's entrance, as if ready to withstand a siege.

Half a dozen city watch commanded each of the bridges.

As she glided down seeking an entrance, she spotted figures hidden from view in the nearby arcades. Two were large gargoyles, their amethyst eyes burning against the shadows. The other one wore the stone half-mask of the Secret Chancellery's agents.

The Stone-Mask pointed at her: 'There she is! Seize her!' Two of the guards drew their crossbows and took aim. At *her*.

Dive! the Drake growled in her head. She reflexively folded her wings and dropped like a rock.

Bolts flew past her, exploding into capture nets.

She plummeted towards the canal at full speed. At the last moment, when the edges of the tall walls were close enough for her to read the etchings on them, she spread her wings and channelled her momentum into speed to veer away from hard stone.

Cries of alarm filled the surrounding streets, and gargoyle shrieks responded. They were clearly after her. She was tired and injured, so fighting wasn't really an option. Her fate rested on the dock's gate being open.

The canals were too narrow for her to manoeuvre easily. Crossbow bolts whistled by. She desperately dodged them, until an incandescent bolt of lead pierced her left wing.

She screamed and swayed perilously close to the canal looming darkly below her. She might not make it to the dock after all.

Unable to regain altitude, she glided towards the palace's back wall. Upon rounding a corner, she saw the grates of the quay were closed and the black stone that stretched into the water deserted.

Her wing hurt. She couldn't fly any farther so had to land on the dock. It was a terrible plan, but maybe someone would see her and let her inside.

Despite flexing her legs as she was trained to do to absorb the shock, her ankles burned with the bad landing. She stumbled forwards and slammed into the grates with her bracelet bearing the house sigil, hoping they'd open up in recognition.

'Balchod! Father!'

Another Dreamchanted bolt buzzed past and cracked against the wall above her head. This one exploded into a thorny vine, but before it could spread, the wall swallowed it, cutting the growth in half.

Of course, the quay was only deserted because the guards had left some of their own watching over it. Above, a stout woman hurriedly reloaded her crossbow. 'Geil Morvander!

Surrender yourself to the city watch and you won't be harmed!' she called.

Just like Lady Saorla hadn't been harmed – no, she didn't trust anything that came out of the guards' mouths. If she let them put her in chains, Davorles's Stone-Masks would find it easy enough to slit her throat.

The Drake only understood rage and blood. And Motherstorm, was it was angry.

She turned to face the oncoming gargoyles. Feeding her anger to the Drake, her scales came to the surface, the stone-blue hue spreading like a ripple over her skin, covering her in its sturdy embrace.

But she was exhausted and had burned through much of her inspiration in the past long night, so the pattern was weak, too unevenly spread to provide a perfect armour and not thick enough to keep her safe from a crossbow bolt.

The first gargoyle flung itself at her, its hind claws snatching at her like prey. Geil tipped her fingers with talons as large as the gargoyle's and latched on to its stony leg. Channelling its weight and speed, she swung it over her head and slammed it against the ground. The gargoyle's back cracked loudly against the dock, and the Nightmare rolled limply into the canal.

Geil turned to face the other. Exhaustion made her slow and, too late, she spotted the claws hurtling towards her neck.

A blur cut through the air, and the gargoyle shrieked.

Tarna, the Quietude's warden, stood between them, a sword covered in the gargoyle's black blood in her right hand. The Nightmare's paw lay on the ground, oozing.

'Quickly, inside!' Tarna commanded, and Geil saw that the grating had been pulled up halfway, enough for her to crawl beneath.

Exhausted, she leapt at the gap, but only had half of her body through when she heard the twang of crossbows.

Bolts bit the walls of the Quietude. One clanged loudly as it hit Tarna in the chest and pierced her breastplate. Tarna fell to one knee, then, straining, pulled the bolt out.

Geil didn't waste the chance and threw herself inside the palace. Tarna followed, sliding swiftly beneath the grating, which immediately fell down after her.

In answer, the Quietude's walls rippled and expanded as if made of mercury, covering the entire grate and turning it into another solid wall. Darkness swallowed them as the lights of the city disappeared from view.

For a moment, Geil stood shaking, breathing uncontrolled. She was both furious and terrified. Slowly, she calmed, and her Drake sight adjusted to the scant light coming from the upper floors.

'Are you alright, Tarna?'

The door warden stood up and nodded. Her once-smooth breastplate had a hole, but her skin underneath was as smooth and pale as ever.

'Apologies, it took me too long to get to you, Lady Geil. Do you need any assistance?'

Geil examined herself. Despite the thick stone, she could still hear the bolts smashing against the outside landing.

'They won't get inside for a while. At least until they bring thunder-cannons, and even then, the Quietude is ready to resist.'

'Where's my father?'

'Lord Morvander left this morning for Muirtra Abbey. He hasn't returned, but about an hour ago, he used his bracelet to command that I lock down the palace and guard it with my life. Then the guards came.' Tarna reached into her blackened doublet for a folded letter. 'The guards delivered this when they first asked me to surrender the palace. I fear for his safety.'

Geil took the letter. It was an order for her arrest and for that of her father and their known associates. Vice-Chancellor Davorles had accused them of being behind Lady Saorla's assassination attempt.

It seemed the Wisp had finally removed her from the board. She knew too much, and she'd seen too much.

We'll have his head for this! the Drake roared.

She wanted nothing more. Taking him on directly was a stupid idea, though. Reaching Lord Brakte's manor to ask him to publicly denounce Davorles in front of the Senate would be better if it wasn't for the Stone-Masks angling for her.

No, she'd let Davorles beat her to the punch once; she had to be smarter than him this time ...

Geil was roused by the sound of the watch ramming the Quietude's main gates.

Between their ceaseless pounding and the Drake's bloodthirst, it was difficult to think clearly. She needed allies, but there wasn't any trace of Aescyon or Thalder, and their names had been in the warrant too, which didn't bode well. For all she knew, they'd already been arrested.

She could try to reach Liadra and explain, yet that might be the fastest way for the Wisp to realise Lady Saorla still lived.

The Falconess, her old mentor, would be an ideal choice, except that sneaking past the guards outside was risky, and if she failed, it'd be straight to the Secret Chancellery's dungeons for her, assuming they didn't kill her before that. No, she needed to hedge her bets. Figure out whether Lady Saorla was safe, and who she could count on to stop Davorles.

Lord Orles Brakte came to mind again. He'd been supporting her father's work, and he was a senator. She realised she didn't need to abandon the Quietude's safety to talk to him.

Leaving Tarna in charge of defences, she ran upstairs to the workshop. There, among the charts and sketches of the mirror-matter, she searched through her father's twinned journals, ledgers she'd seen him Dreamchant as means of communication with allies, and located Lord Brakte's.

The twinned tome was filled with pages of thickly scribbled code. That might have stopped her when she was younger, but she had the advantage of knowing which mask her father usually wore when reading the journal, an ugly iron thing with no slits for the eyes.

She donned it, and immediately the book's interior lit up and became as translucent as glass, allowing her to read the decrypted words. She thumbed her way through the recent messages, but there wasn't anything particularly revealing, so instead she took over a blank page and wrote:

Lord Brakte, this is Geil Morvander writing to you from the Quietude. What have you heard about the attack on Captain Regent Saorla?

The page sucked the ink dry, a sign that it had worked and that her message had been transferred to the recipient. Would he dare reply, though? Nothing made friends vanish faster than a political purge. She'd seen families disappear from the jet-black city from one day to the next when they'd incurred the wrath of one too many powerful Oneirocrats.

After a few minutes, the page shifted, revealing new words.

What a relief to read you, Lady Geil! I just heard about the outlandish accusations against your family, that you're all behind some sort of conspiracy to kill Lady Saorla. I refuse to believe any of it, especially since Lord Davorles is soon to address the Senate; rumour has it, to request extraordinary powers to ensure the Domain's safety.

Anger sparked in her. At least she could see what the damn Wisp was trying to do.

It is Lord Davorles who's behind the assassination attempt. He's only fabricated these charges to prevent me from publicly denouncing his treason. His hunting dogs are at my gates, trying to break in to arrest me.

The reply came quickly.

I won't desert your father. Neither will I abandon you.

Geil finally allowed herself to breathe deeply. If Lord Brakte was still on their side, not everything was lost. He could help spread the news of Davorles's attack, maybe even use his political leverage to get them a fair hearing with the justices. Such hopes were cut short when newer lines appeared on the page.

They have your father on the Isle of Sighs, so I must ask you to keep this secret and remain in hiding for now. I've heard he will be shipped to the Academy tomorrow morning with the next cohort of conscripts. I fear this might be a way of forcing you to remain silent. If you speak publicly, you risk all kinds of harm coming to him. But despair not, I'll try to force his liberation through other allies. In the meantime, it's best if you stay within the safety of the Quietude's walls.

And with that, the pages went silent.

Geil removed the mask and paced around the room like a caged Manticore. Lord Brakte was right that it was foolish to wander outside just to risk capture or worse.

We'll gut the Wisp, split him open and milk every drop of vile, cold blood he's got inside him, the Drake fumed. At the same time, dread trickled down her insides. While her father was in Onyxia, they wouldn't dare harm him, but as soon as he was behind the Mantle, they could subject him to all kinds of torment.

She felt the bracelet ring again, this time with the distinct chime of the *Night Swan*. Imprecise as it was, she knew it meant Captain Bentor was close.

Setting up a pick-up point would be easy. Getting out of the Quietude wouldn't.

* * *

With the gargoyles upstairs trying to break in and Captain Bentor so close, there was no time to waste. Accompanied by Tarna, Geil hurried to the Quietude's underground dock.

She descended through the palace dressed only in a black sea-drake diving suit she hadn't worn since her time in the Academy. It was a bit too tight on her, but other than that, it was perfect for this kind of sortie. She only had to call the Drake fully to the surface and then twist herself a little further to have a seaborn shape.

She expanded her lungs and Dreamt webbing on her hands and feet. Her eyes shifted into black orbs. She sank into the cold water of the inner dock.

'Good luck, Tarna. I shall return before dawn. If I don't, I entrust the Quietude to Aescyon or Balchod, whoever returns first.'

'Good luck, Lady Geil. Rest assured that while there's a spark of your father's life in me, I shall fight to keep this place safe.'

The door warden commanded the walls with a gesture. Geil felt the waters around her cooling, mingling with the canal. Tarna had opened an exit for her.

Geil dived beneath the water and into the dark canal.

Dim sounds reached her from the surface. Yelling and shrieking, now strangely warped. Of course, she should have known that the Stone-Masks had Dreamt some sort of alarm to warn them when the palace's walls changed. Soon, a heavy barge glided into view, casting hazes of light into the murky waters.

She fled into a furrow of blocky foundations. There, she coiled into a foetal position, averting her eyes from the light and holding her breath.

'Wait!' a Stone-Mask yelled, voice distorted.

A ray of light fell over her. Had they spotted her? If she didn't bolt now, she wouldn't be able to outrun them.

She ignored the Drake's insistence to flee and stayed still, hoping her shape would be disguise enough to confound them.

Long, thin shapes slid into the water. They slithered furiously in several directions. *Dreamchanted bolts?* the Drake wondered. But she then caught sight of the amber sting at the end of one's tail as it trailed her by like an arrow. *No, scorpion-snakes. Best grow scales, then . . .*

She felt a sharp tang in her thigh. Too late, she realised one had approached her from the bottom of the canal. As the sting dug deep into her flesh, Geil almost screamed. Almost.

She managed to clench her teeth in time, but not before she let some air out. Which was as bad. If they spotted her, the snake and its poison would be the least of her concerns.

She stretched taut, ignoring the viper burrowing its sting even deeper, and managed to reach the bubbles with her palm, breaking them before they reached the surface.

Then, still without breathing, she gripped the scorpion-snake's head.

Above, she heard angry voices, but after an eternity, the light moved away. Only then did she pull the sting out and fling the snake away. Ignoring the burning in her leg and the increasing weakness in her kicks, she swam in the opposite direction of the barge.

When she reached a nearby canal, she dared surface. From there, she cut through to the lagoon, where she swam, diving in and out, dolphin-like, towards the northern eaves.

Once she'd swum out far enough to not be seen by pursuers, she tapped her message into the bracelet, then Dreamt herself some crude scales to block the worst of the bleeding and paddled weakly to stay afloat.

She was too tired to think, too weakened by the injury and the poison to do anything other than float.

She was so addled that she only noticed the dark silhouette above her when it filled half her field of vision. Either her friends or the enemies of her house had found her.

This time, though, she wouldn't be able to do much but go down swinging. Luckily, when she looked closely, she had to smile despite herself. It was the *Night Swan*.

Chapter Forty-Four

Daerna

All of Lord Nial Morvander's kin and associates are to be delivered to the Secret Chancellery. This includes his daughter, Lady Geil Morvander, Master Thalder Kewildra, his apprentice, Aescyon Allandra, and Sister Daerna Eimar.

– From an arrest warrant signed by
Vice-Chancellor Davorles

Daerna's pace slowed at the sight of the Grand Palace's domes. She was wary of walking into the wolf's den, but needed to find Ash.

Climbing the palace's western steps, she entered a bustling hall. Veil down to hide her face, she abused the habit to jump the queue for one of the reception desks.

'Please, I need to find where the Sages's tribunal has gathered.'

The clerk frowned. 'All exams are done for the day.'

'Could you please check again? I'm looking for Aescyon Allandra.'

The clerk consulted her ledger. 'He did have an appointment today, but he didn't report for it.'

Her blood ran cold. 'What? Why?'

'It doesn't say,' was the clerk's curt reply. 'What did you say your name was?' the woman asked.

She swallowed. 'Sister Andaras of Yelm,' she said, using the name of Muirtra's Cellarer Sister.

The woman eyed her shiftily. 'Would you mind waiting here? There are some people who have some questions for you.'

Daerna felt a growing knot in her throat. 'I'm afraid I'm in a hurry,' she apologised. 'May Her gentle tears bless you.' She dipped her head and turned away. She had to force herself not to run.

On the palace steps, hidden among the towering columns, she stopped to check her veil and catch her breath. Was this because of their raid on the Sunken Library? And was that why Ash hadn't made it to his exam? Had he already been arrested?

She scrutinised the nearby streets. The rain was falling hard, blanketing the surrounding alleys and viaducts in a sinister shroud. Trails of citizens trickled through the streets, burrowed in thick cloaks and hidden by wide-brimmed hats.

Looking up, she noticed a familiar shadow skulking on a rooftop across the canal: a large feline, seemingly fixated on her.

Omen.

It took a while, making sure that no one was tailing her, to find a way up. Using some rotten wooden scaffolding abandoned by a crumbling house, she climbed towards the rooftops.

Her muscles burned with the effort. Her scar ached, along with the weariness of built-up exhaustion. She wanted nothing more than to sleep. Once she was on top of the crumbling house, it was a short walk over the shingles to the nearby rooftop. To her relief, Omen was still there.

His ears perked up as she approached.

'I'm happy to see you too!' she said, rubbing the creature's neck. He tugged her wrist with a gentle bite.

Omen hurried ahead, and she followed him to the shadowed base of an oratory's arches. There, unconscious, with a crude, blood-sopped bandage around his shoulder, was Ash.

'Ash?' she tried.

He groaned, but slowly regained consciousness.

'Daerna? What . . . ?'

'I was hoping you'd tell me. We're near the Petitioners' Pavilion in the Grand Palace. It's a miracle I found you. What happened?'

'A man tried to kill me. I fell into the canal. I barely managed to swim to safety, and only with Omen's help,' he said, rubbing the panther's scruff.

'The wound looks bad. We need to get you to a doctor. How are you feeling?'

Slowly, he pushed himself into a sitting position. 'Better now that you're here,' he said with a pained smile. 'How's Roshia?'

'Alive!' That, at least, gave her relief. 'Lord Morvander was able to remove the ailment . . .' She faltered.

'Dae? What happened?' Ash asked.

'Stone-Masks arrested Lord Morvander while he was leaving Muirtra.'

'The Secret Chancellery? What do they want with him?' He swallowed and winced with the pain.

'I've been thinking about this a lot and reached one conclusion: whoever's behind all of this – ambushing you, arresting Lord Morvander – it must be the same individuals trying to hide the truth about the Wilting by any means necessary.'

'They must have been on to us for a while.' Ash looked away, clearly troubled.

She swallowed hard at that. Ash might have said 'on to us', but she'd been the one to drag everyone through the thorns and brambles in her investigation of the disease. If the Order's Superiors wanted to keep the Wilting quiet, she should have known it was for powerful political reasons.

How could she have been so careless and naive? She couldn't see how keeping thousands sick and in need was for anyone's benefit, but they were about to fall victim to a political purge meant to keep the affair silent.

'Listen to me, Dae. What matters is that you are well and that Roshia's alive thanks to you. Besides, you didn't put Lord Morvander in chains or hurt me. They did.' When she didn't answer, he continued. 'Whatever this is, it can wait. We have to go somewhere the Academy and the Secret Chancellery have no power. Deep in the Highlands, or farther to Evenfall Forest or Ilea, if that's what it takes.'

Fleeing was the sensible thing to do.

And yet, Daerna couldn't convince herself to do it. It wasn't that she wouldn't be able to bear life in exile; she'd already entertained the errant life of the Wanderers. It wasn't even that she wouldn't bear the loss of her life; she'd separated herself from her family to become a Wailing Sister. It was that she couldn't unsee what she'd seen, couldn't unlearn what she'd understood in the library.

Not when there were so many who needed the truth.

The *Song of Sorrows* had taught her to embrace loss, to make it a prized treasure, to extract power, meaning and significance from that which had been taken from her. But the Song didn't preach that one had to surrender to fatality, to succumb to despair.

'We can't,' she said.

'What do you mean? I still have money to buy us passage on a skyship.'

'It's not that! I keep having these dreams about what's tormenting the city. About the Charnel Mother's reach growing because of it. I don't understand it all. What I do understand, though, is that we saved Roshia and we could save so many others, Ash.'

His eyes sank. 'My father used to think the Silver Book would change the world, that it'd truly free the people . . .'

'Your father was right!'

'My father got himself killed, and got me thrown in a prison cell,' Ash concluded bitterly.

Daerna remained silent. She couldn't force him to accept this. He'd lost his father, and Ghalod, to the Sunken Library. Master Thalder might not make it either. She had lost nothing.

'I'm sorry . . . I just don't want to lose you too . . .' He rubbed his forehead. 'Do you really believe we can save more people with this?'

Daerna considered his words. Was it wise? No. But was it necessary? Yes.

Could she ask Ash to walk this path, to risk losing more? No. But she couldn't lie to him.

'With all my heart.'

'Then . . . let us stay and fight.'

She kissed him hard, unscathed by doubt or despair.

Chapter Forty-Five

Ash

Under the downpour and lightning fall, we stick together. Above and below, we're our only haven.

– Lightning-Hunter saying

If ash wanted to fight back against their enemies, he had to survive the day, which was easier said than done. The Lightning-Hunters' tower would offer a good place to hide – even if the Secret Chancellery could stomp all over their guild charter, he could count on the guild's notorious uncooperativeness with the authorities. All they had to do was persuade Master Esmus that he was worth the trouble.

And, of course, get there first.

The lionheads throughout the city had come alive, their eyes gleaming with the pale hue of lightning, signifying that the Secret Chancellery was now watching over every bridge and viaduct. Traversing the Shingle Sea was their best bet, even if their pursuers were there too.

High above, gargoyles and guards on hippogriffs circled. The Dreamling mounts were a rare and dangerous sight in the skies, so each time Ash spotted a patrol, they hid in the shadows of nearby spires. His fever was getting worse, and he didn't Dream because he wanted to preserve what little energy he had left in case they found themselves in a truly desperate spot.

As they stood in the shelter of a large manor's dome, his arm tingled at the same time he heard the toll of a distant bell. At first, he thought the fever was making him imagine it, but when it happened a second time, he was certain that his household bracelet had vibrated alongside the sound.

'What's wrong?' Daerna asked. Neither she nor Omen seemed to have heard or felt anything.

'The bracelet's ringing like a bell. I thought it only worked close to the Quietude.'

'They could be using it as a means of communication,' Daerna suggested. 'It's not rare that Oneirocrats Dreamchant their bracelets to command or react to the same master creations.'

Daerna not only knew better than him the inner workings of Oneirocratic households, her guess was very sound. Especially since Captain Bentor, Thalder and Geil all sported such bracelets.

Could this be Captain Bentor trying to contact him? If so, Ash had no idea how to answer the call. The jet-black city was too vast for him to Dream something capable of scouring it all. Maybe if he were more rested, less desperate, more inspired, he could pull it off, but not now.

On the other hand, he could take a page from Thalder's book. When facing an unassailable adversary, it was best to pick the battlefield. In this case, he could find a place and a sign for the *Night Swan* to find them.

He scanned the Sea of Shingles and found a nearby dome.

A large lightning-trap had been set right above its oculus. He could use the trapped lightning instead of burning through his meagre inspiration, even though he feared the trap's owners might be close by.

'I have a plan, but I need your help,' Ash said.

Daerna nodded nervously. 'What do you need me to do?'

'Just keep watch while I climb up there.'

Wobbly from pain and fever, Ash's crawl up the slippery dome was slow. The trap above was large, and given the good location, the hunting ground had to belong to one of the big crews, the sort that would beat him if they caught him stealing. Luckily, its orbs were already lit with a fresh catch. He carefully unscrewed an orb and cradled it in his right arm by his bracelet.

Inside the Dreaming, the skies were a purple whirlwind, raining petals and poison. With his mind, he cracked the orb's surface, brittle as an eggshell, and sank his fingers into the coiled lightning, weaving his own bell chime into the flash before releasing it.

It shattered the sky with its thunderous shrieking.

His mind flowed, adrift, the passage of time seemingly slower as he took in the city.

The heavens swirled above him, out of anyone's control. A billion raindrops fell at different speeds, landing on rocks, on rooftops, on the cool lagoon waters. One fell on a bare lover's skin, and another on the unblinking eyes of a guardian gargoyle.

Still no trace of the skysloop. He whispered to the orb-lamp again, and another bolt of lightning flew free, chiming like a bell in his mind. The rush of uncaging a feral bird that yearned to be free swept over him.

With a brush of his hands, he peeled away the layers of clouds, one after another, and gazed into the face of the heavens. A mournful murmur rumbled above, ready to erase whatever it touched, desperate to run free through the jet-black maze below. Still, there was no response to his lightning.

But he picked up on a distant yet familiar thunder coming from below. He dared a glance, and saw Omen pacing around his still body while Daerna pleaded loudly with a large Lightning-Hunter crew, led by a hirsute man with a wide-brimmed hat.

He dived back to the surface, slamming into his body.

By then a dozen soaked, angry men and women had surrounded the dome. They were yelling. A shingle flew past his head. Only Omen, pacing about and snarling, kept them at bay, and sooner or later, he would lash out at them.

Daerna kept trying to calm them down, but their boss snorted derisively. 'Get your spears, lads!' he commanded. 'Come down! I'll show you how we deal with thieves around these parts!' he yelled at Ash.

'Wait, I'll pay for your catch, Master Bencos!' Ash yelled, finally managing to conjure the man's name from the mists of memory.

'If you know who I am, you'll know this isn't about money – you can't just—'

A ripple passed through the Lightning-Hunters. A group of city guards had appeared on the palace's roof. If they'd found him, the Secret Chancellery's agents couldn't be far behind.

'Aescyon Lightning-Hunter, give yourself up!' a sergeant shouted over the drizzle.

The gang boss's eyes widened. 'You're that Aescyon? The Dreamer?'

The young crew stared at Ash.

'There's a reward for that man!' the officer yelled, leading a handful of armed men in a slow climb.

'What do you say, boss?' a large hauler lass asked, copper spear in hand.

'I say, "Under the downpour and lightning fall, we stick together,"' the boss declared.

Almost immediately, the gang cheered back: '"Above and below, we're our only haven!"'

The boss's thick beard parted to show a proud smile. 'Fuck the floor-feet that come here giving orders and thinking they own the place. Send 'em back where they belong!'

Cheering from the gang soon turned into a full-blown assault on the guards. The Lightning-Hunters threw pellets, rocks, shingles and even bird droppings at the bailiffs from up on the roof's slope.

'You better run though, lad,' the boss said to Ash.

'Thank you,' he said.

Taking Daerna's hand, he leapt off the other side of the dome and raced for the closest rooftop. They were moving fast, but Ash felt near to the point of collapse, and the crossbow twangs rang ever closer.

They were almost at the rooftop's edge when Omen stopped and turned back to let out a furious growl. Something was coming at them from above.

Ash looked up, fearing he'd see a pack of gargoyles swooping in, but it was a skysloop. A rope ladder fell towards him, followed by a harness. Up above he saw a familiar grey face, and, with relief washing over him, smiled up at old Rudher.

'Come on, we don't have all night!'

Chapter Forty-Six

Geil

An empress must be wise in counsel and steadfast in her plans. She must show firmness towards the soldiers and stern discipline to those who stray from their posts, but also display magnanimity when necessity calls. Even to those who once were her enemies.

– *On Rule* by Empress Damnia

'IT'S GOOD TO SEE THAT we got to you in time,' Geil said, tying off a bandage around her pierced thigh. She still felt dizzy and the injury was spasming, but at least with the healing ointments kept on board, she hoped it wouldn't become infected. As for the poison, she'd Dreamt herself a burning fever to fight it as best she could.

'I could have used you earlier,' Ash replied with a bitter chuckle from across the captain's cabin.

He didn't look good either. Daerna was in the middle of changing the dressing on an ugly wound on his shoulder. Other than Omen, the three of them were alone. Ash's companions were above, on the piloting deck with Captain Bentor.

Geil listened to their tale in silence. Daerna's investigation into the Wilting had led them into dangerous truths indeed. Just as she had begun unravelling a thread, Geil had been unravelling another. All this time, they'd both been picking apart Davorles's carefully laid deceptions.

Geil then recounted her own findings regarding the Scab. How she believed Lanteus had discovered Davorles's hidden shard of the Mantle and been murdered for it. How Davorles had had a hand in all the Scab's troubles that had followed ever since.

'Davorles is somehow in league with the Charnelites. If a Dreamer as powerful as that "Midwife" you've spoken of is operating in the Scab, it's only because the Secret Chancellery has allowed it. Davorles might have even advocated for the brutal treatment of the Wilting-afflicted, knowing it'd push those trapped there into the Charnelites' hands.'

'I fear he might have even sown the seeds of the Wilting to begin with,' Daerna said.

Geil looked at her. 'What do you mean?'

'You said that your companion Lanteus thought he'd found this secret Mantle when it was brought to the Crumbling Quarter, what, a year ago?'

Geil nodded as a shiver ran down her spine.

'That's about the time the outbreak also began in the Southern Quarter.' At seeing Geil's confused face, Daerna added, 'The Sister Superiors were right all along in one thing: the disease is spiritual. Except it isn't caused by the moral failings of the masses, but rather an innate sorrow in the city that sparks these "diseases". The timing, the location of this Mantle – it all matches. You are familiar with the Mantle. Could they have used it to torment the city and engineer this outbreak?'

'That's precisely what the Mantle does best,' Geil said with a nod. 'Turns all your dreams into nightmares, then vomits them deep into your soul.'

Daerna's face lit up. 'That's it. Not only has the city been listening to its inhabitants' woes without respite, this shard of the Mantle was also brought here to torment it. For all we know, this is what sparked the Wilting!'

It was all finally making sense. This was the secret worth killing Lanteus for. 'Lord Davorles has dedicated his life to refining the art of tormenting and terrorising others: children, students and now a whole city. What I'm less certain of is what he intends to gain from all of this. Judging from his swiftness at claiming special powers to protect the Domain, I'd guess he never cared for the Wilting other than as a tool to spread chaos. I can't see the whole picture yet, but I'm certain that what he's doing, he's doing to undermine the Domain.' The ploy sounded devious to the point of madness. But this was the Wisp they were talking about.

'Why turn on Lady Saorla, though?' Ash asked.

Geil sighed. 'I must have forced his hand. First by finding the shard of the Mantle, then by trying to take that news to the Captain Regent. Still, his betrayal was only a matter of time, I believe.'

'We could just wait this out, then, like Lord Brakte suggested,' Ash said.

'Who's not to say Lord Stalcar won't crush him for us, either?' Daerna wondered.

'That worries me too. This inner strife might be what Lord Stalcar needs to impose his own tyranny. With Saorla recovering, he's sole Regent now, after all. But we won't be safe anywhere until Davorles is removed from power. But for that to happen, I must rescue my father.'

'Rescue him?' Ash stiffened.

'Only once he's free and safe will we be free to act. If we move too quickly, we forfeit his life.' She swallowed hard.

A heavy silence fell over them.

'What're you thinking?' Ash asked.

'We descend on the Isle of Sighs, tonight. Hit them in the dark.'

'Just the two of you?' Daerna looked between them. 'Neither of you is in shape to fight, much less to storm that cursed fortress.'

Ash slouched in his chair. 'And the garrison will be strengthened since they brought in the Hordemasters to enforce the curfew after unrest in the Scab.'

'Daerna's right. We're wounded, and even with the *Night Swan* and a surprise attack, I don't like our odds. They'll easily outnumber us.' Geil picked at her scales. 'I suppose I should be grateful we've spared Thalder all this mess.'

'At least he's alive,' Ash replied.

Geil reached over to squeeze his shoulder.

'You have us too, lad,' a hoarse voice said. Rudher and Yaisa descended from the deck. The old man's eyes were reddened, and there were trails of tears on his sweaty face.

'If it's to stab those bastards of the Academy, count on me too.' The young woman's eyes burned with an unfocused, quiet anger.

'Thank you,' Ash replied with a sad smile. 'I'm afraid we'd need a good dozen of us to have a chance.'

Listening to the Lightning-Hunters, it suddenly struck Geil that there were others willing to spit in the Academy's eye. Others who Lanteus had trusted, and were already on Davorles's trail, trying to undo whatever he'd been planning.

'Geil?' Ash asked.

With a wave of her bracelet, she rang the bell and summoned the captain below deck.

'Set a course northeast,' she commanded him. 'We're going to Oldcourt's Orphanage.'

'An orphanage?' Ash asked.

'What better place to find the desperate people we need?'

* * *

When, a few hours later, they found themselves surrounded by grim, armed Exarchians, Geil feared they'd made a big mistake.

At least Ash and his Lightning-Hunter crew were with her as she entered the ruins near the orphanage. The Drake boiled beneath her skin, ready to tear out the bowels of the man closest to her, but inside, there were only a couple dozen people camped in the dark, huddled together in the cool night – families, not the murderous brigands she'd expected. Sister Lasara was there, loading their belongings onto some nearby horses.

'You're leaving?' Geil asked.

'Haven't you heard? They've given the Chancellery of Secrets special powers to quell the unrest. The Stone-Masks are making arrests all over the city. We aren't safe here anymore,' Sister Lasara replied.

The burly Parvos suddenly emerged from behind her, running a hand over his closely cropped black hair. 'We won't be here when the masked men come for us.'

'That's unfortunately why I'm here. Traitors from the Academy have taken my father, and I need your help getting him back.' Both Exarchians looked at her as if she were mad.

'You'd need an army to storm the Isle of Sighs,' Parvos said, pursing his chapped lips.

'I don't need an army, just a handful of fighters willing to watch my back while I storm the Academy's transport en route. That way there won't be any reinforcements coming.' She could feel eyes widening at that. Now she had their attention.

Sister Lasara spat angrily on the ground. 'Forget it.'

'You can keep their ship as well as any loot.'

'Did you not hear me?'

'It's not impossible if we work together.' Geil hated the begging tone her voice took on.

Sister Lasara chuckled. 'What do we think we are? Pirates? Mercenaries? We don't fight for Oneirocrats, only for our cause. Let others die for him if they so wish!'

'You're wrong about Nial Morvander,' Ash said gravely. 'He was at the Widows' hospice after the riots in the Scab broke out, working to save as many as he could. He's even helped the Sisters find a cure for the Wilting!'

Parvos arched an eyebrow. 'That'd be a remarkable feat were we to believe you. Your loyalty is commendable, lad. Still, I see no reason for us to gamble our lives for him.'

They're wasting our time. The Drake wanted to quarrel or storm away, but Geil forced it silent. Strength or anger alone wouldn't win her anything.

'Wait. Don't do it for my father or me. Do it for Lanteus. You wanted to know why they killed him, didn't you? I'll tell you why . . .'

She told them of what Lanteus had found, of the Mantle shard and how it'd helped poison the city's dreams, causing the Wilting to spread and the Charnelites to fester in the open wound. 'You might like the prospect of a weakened Onyxia, but you don't want the Wisp unchained. Think the Academy's pushing the limits now? Wait until they have an all-powerful Secret Chancellery behind them.' She thought of Ragdra and all the other children that would be broken by the Academy if Davorles had unlimited powers. 'If you help us, I swear my house will move heaven and earth to put an end to conscription, even if it's the last thing we do. Isn't that what you want?'

'What I want is the Oneirocrats' yoke forever torn to splinters,' Sister Lasara muttered, 'and the Academy burned to the ground.'

Parvos looked at Geil searchingly.

'You risked Lanteus's life for this: a chance to find out what the Academy was planning and to stop it. This is that chance.'

The Exarchians exchanged glances. Lasara leaned in.

'We need some time to discuss this.'

* * *

Geil waited with the others outside the ruins. Inside, the Exarchians conferred with each other. Each aspect of their plan was incessantly put to debate, sometimes in hushed tones, sometimes with loud screaming.

'They bicker like crowcats!' Yaisa said, taking her frustration out on a piece of wood she was relentlessly whittling away.

Rudher, for his part, had unshod himself and lain down to nap in the grass.

Ash kept staring at the stars. He was, if anything, in a more sombre mood than Geil. She picked at her scales, then paced about, then milled about some more. Anything to keep her mind from the possibility of them saying no.

After a long hour of wait, Parvos emerged. A dozen trickled behind him.

'Well?' Geil asked.

'Our assembly has decided we won't be servants of the Oneirocrats on this matter,' Parvos announced solemnly.

'That's it?' she asked tersely.

Parvos grinned. 'Yes. Luckily for you, our assembly has also decided that we want to see the Academy's transport burn.'

Chapter Forty-Seven
Daerna

Even in the middle of the worst storm, even with one oar, keep rowing for shore.

– Onyxian Mariner saying

DAERNA HAD BEEN TRYING TO sleep, but as soon as she'd drifted into a dream, she'd caught glimpses of the dark veins that ran underground, poisoning the city, and anguish brought her back to wakefulness. After a while, she gave up and clambered back to the deck.

The *Night Swan* was still anchored above the orphanage, sail-wings tucked to the sides to limit its movement to a gentle swaying because of the breeze.

She found Ash seated on the bowsprit, keeping watch over the camp in the ruins. Omen softly snored close to him.

'Couldn't sleep?' he asked.

'Not really. How did it go?'

'Geil seems to have convinced them.'

'Do you trust them?'

He shook his head wearily. 'I don't know who to trust anymore. It's not like we have many alternatives.' He reached for her arm. 'If they help us, you should stay here with Omen. No point in risking everyone if things go wrong.'

Seeing the concern in his eyes only made what she was about to say harder. 'I'm going back to the city, Ash.'

'What? Why?'

'I won't make a difference with you, but the Wanderers and my friends in the Orders need to learn what we've discovered, about both how to heal the Wilting and how Vice-Chancellor Davorles and the Academy are letting it spread. What saved Roshia could help so many others!'

'Dae, you heard what Geil said. They've given the Secret Chancellery extraordinary powers to hunt us! It's not just the city watch anymore, not even just the Stone-Masks. Going back is reckless!'

'Reckless? I'm not the one about to pick a fight with the Academy.'

Ash frowned and clenched his fists. She scowled at him. Clearly their exhaustion and dread weren't doing them any favours.

'You're right,' he finally said. 'I'm sorry. But wouldn't it be safer to send them a message? I could Dream something that carries your words.'

'It'll be difficult enough for them to believe me even if they hear it from my lips. Though that could be a great help to gather them together . . .' She paused to collect her thoughts. 'After healing Roshia, I think I know how to beat the disease.'

'How? I thought we needed the mirrormatter for that.'

'When Lord Morvander was healing Roshia, I sang to her and felt the oppression that was choking her giving in. I also can't shake what I saw in the Silver Book. The vision of the city withering, drowning in its own guilt and misery. It clings to me, in dreams even. I feel that I've been asked to stop this . . . I have seen Blessed Elpia come to me.'

'Like an apparition?'

'Like a sacred vision. And Blessed Elpia asked me to somehow put an end to the city's suffering.'

'But that's . . .'

'Ridiculous? Delirious? Don't you think I know that? The thing is . . . It doesn't really matter what it is, Ash, because it's still the right thing to do. The entire city dreams together in a divine miracle. From its tallest spire to its filthiest gutter, Onyxia is hallowed.' Daerna rubbed her forehead. 'If I'm right, we Wailing Sisters could speak to Onyxia's soul through the Motherstorm. That's why I need to go back: to show them what I've learned. To prove it can be done, and to teach them how to do it.'

A long silence followed. She could feel him considering her words. This too was a test. If she couldn't persuade Ash, after everything he'd seen, after everything they'd done, her efforts would be doomed from the start.

'It's worth attempting. I'll go with you.'

It was tempting to accept his offer. So very tempting. Just the two of them against the world, that was how they'd go on. But there was a sting of guilt at the thought of abandoning Lord Morvander and Geil.

'Ash, Lord Morvander's done a lot for you, for both of us. There's no shame in caring for him in return.'

'What about you?' He averted his gaze. 'I don't want to desert you . . .' He took her hand. He was warm to the touch, possibly because of the fever. When she laced her fingers through his, he finally met her gaze.

'You aren't,' she promised him. 'If you succeed in freeing Lord Morvander, he can help stop Davorles. It's all very well finding a cure – but not if there's someone out there who'll do everything in their power to prevent it.'

He let out a heavy sigh. 'What's your plan?'

'Can you Dream a messenger raven for me? I need to reach Sister Pierla.'

Ash smiled weakly. He looked away, his gaze glassy and lost. In the blink of an eye, a large raven was suddenly perched on his shoulder, as if it'd been there all along. Its burning cerulean eyes watched Daerna with curiosity.

'I'll get inside the city and share everything I know about the Wilting with the Wanderers. There has to be a way to cleanse it from the Scab forever.' Before he could protest, she added, 'Alone and disguised, I might have a chance. If I leave now, I should make it to the city by dawn, when they open the gates.'

'At least allow us to take you as close as we can.'

Daerna hesitated but, exhausted as she was, she could use the help. Besides, this would give them a few more moments together. 'Agreed.'

She then whispered her message into the raven's ear, after which, it took off in a rush of feathers.

They watched it fly away until it was lost to the distance, then, still holding hands, fell into each other's embrace. Ash pressed his forehead to hers, then tenderly kissed her lips, her cheek, her neck, as if afraid this might be the last time he would hold her. She released a sigh as her body lit with a desperate desire.

'Come,' she said, and pulled him below deck to a sleeping cabin.

* * *

The *Night Swan* dropped Daerna in the hidden outskirts of the Craghorn peninsula. She and Ash bade each other farewell with a kiss, too brief, despite its length, to be their last.

Dawn was beginning to break, and Daerna feared she'd stand out in the deserted streets as she joined the crowds of muleteers, merchants and farmers flowing over the large bridge crossing from the Craghorn.

Dressed in the simple grey uniform of a Widowed Sister that Sister Lasara had given her, she hoped to fool the watchful gazes of the stone lionheads carved into the viaduct's arches. But as she neared the heart of the city, she realised reaching the Broken Arches wasn't going to be easy.

Armed mobs had taken to the streets of the plateau, seizing bridges and crossings. It seemed that both senatorial parties had rallied their followers and allies. Now guildmembers and merchants had taken to the streets, some wearing the Reformers' white caps, some Lord Stalcar's Traditionalist blue, but all armed with improvised weapons. On her way south, Daerna saw many outbursts of violence.

The spark set by Lord Morvander's arrest had flared into a full blaze that engulfed the city in angry madness. Cobbles flew at houses, shops and palaces. Incendiary graffiti appeared everywhere. *Depose Stalcar the tyrant!* was written in the Reformer neighbourhoods, while *Saorla, traitor!* appeared on Traditionalist domains.

The guards were barely able to keep both groups from cracking open each other's skulls, which at least meant they were too busy to pay attention to her. Hiding in colonnades and avoiding the bigger mobs, she made good progress until she reached the bridge that connected to the university.

Nightmares resembling monstruous, hunched hyenas stood guard, their serrated jaws drooling, their gnarly fingers sharpening their claws on the bridge's stone.

She let out a dejected groan and turned on her heel. Finding another way could take hours. Then she heard a funerary procession's chants a few streets over. A chance, but not without risk.

Daerna hurried ahead of the procession, adjusted her veil and began humming a funerary hymn, playing oblivious to the scene as she approached the bridge – at least until she noticed that two Nightmares were gnawing on the remnants of a human arm.

The stench of death punched Daerna in the nose, and she fought to suppress a violent urge to vomit. The Nightmares' reptilian eyes fell on her. One licked its chops.

Their Hordemaster, who'd been crouching nearby, had to crack her multi-tailed whip to rein them in. She was thin and grim like her creations and wore plated armour.

'Turn back, Sister. The Broken Arches are filled with rebels and criminals.'

'Someone must minister to the ill, even in these times.' She spoke in a hushed tone, hoping to disguise her voice. She didn't think the lionheads were able to hear her, but at this point, she was unwilling to try her luck.

'For your own safety, I can't let you enter.'

'My Sisters are coming to collect the bodies. The least you can do is let me talk to the people here to make sure their deceased receive proper deliverance. Or will you deny them the Motherstorm's mercy?'

The chants had grown louder as the funerary procession neared, and at that, the Hordemaster's lip twisted. 'As you wish.'

She cracked her whip, and the Nightmares scattered. Daerna hurried to the other side of the bridge.

The place she'd known was a dismal sight. Around University Square, the students had erected barricades. She approached with her arms up. 'I'm here to help! Where's Sister Agonea?' she cried.

Hurriedly, they cleared a barricade for her to pass through.

Her respite was short-lived. Everywhere she looked, violence had left scars. Cracked chunks of the beautiful square littered the floor and pools of blood had watered the dark flagstones. Not to mention that the isle's residents had turned the square into a veritable fort. Students had armed themselves with clubs fashioned from the legs of chairs and tables, and the Broken Arches residents had shown up with hatchets and daggers.

More than a dozen bodies filled one of the courtyard's colonnades. The bloodstains on the improvised shrouds told Daerna they were recent.

'You're a balm for sore eyes, Daerna,' Agonea called from nearby.

Daerna turned to find her in another part of the arcade where the Wanderers had set up a battlefield hospital. Agonea was seated on a stool, covered in much blood.

'Are you alright?' Daerna asked.

'Fear not. Only this blood is mine.' Agonea grimaced, revealing a bandage on her left calf.

'What happened here?'

'Hordemasters and the watch came to arrest the new High Sage, a lecturer named Zerandra. As they dragged him away, the students started pelting them with vases, wooden benches, orb-lamps, books even. Word got to the Broken Arches. When those monstrous hyenas started maiming the students, the lecturer found some nerve and Dreamt swarms of bees to attack the Hordemasters. And that's when things really went to hell. Some of our Exarchian friends joined in the fight. They killed some of their beasts and even took down a Hordemaster. Many fell, though. Since then, they've retreated to the northern side of the bridge, sending only some of their monsters to poke at the barricades. Some say this is the beginning of a full revolt, and I . . . I'm just trying to keep as many alive as I can.'

'This isn't just about the students or the university's printing press. If they're coming for the High Sage, they're trying to install some sort of tyranny. I never expected things to become this bad.'

'Why are you back here?'

'I . . .' Daerna's whole plan seemed sort of ridiculous in light of what was happening. Yet, she'd come this far, and those afflicted by the Wilting weren't going to get any better without help. Sometimes, even in the middle of the worst storm, the only thing you could do was keep rowing for shore. 'I might have found a way to help the Wilting-sick.'

Agonea sighed and offered her the saddest smile she'd seen. 'Tell me, but tomorrow, when and if the smoke clears. Until then, just stay alive, Daerna. We'll see more blood before the day's out.'

A sound came from behind Daerna. She turned, drawing her anelace dagger.

'Charcoal?'

'Sister Daerna! I was afraid that you wouldn't make it!' The sparkler boy ran to hug her.

'I'm glad to see you're well! Wait, how did you know I was coming?'

'Sister Pierla told me. She's waiting for you on the quay. Come!'

'Go,' Agonea said. 'You've given me enough, girl. Just make sure you return to us.'

Daerna followed Charcoal, relieved that he was safe and her message to Pierla had arrived.

'She had me deliver messages through the city, just like you wanted.'

'Thank you, Charcoal.' She reached for her belt purse, but he waved her away.

'No need, Sister Daerna. The people know who their friends are.' He winked. 'You just make sure you're safe out there.'

'Oh, don't you worry,' somebody replied from the nearby quay. Pierla was standing on an old gondola, clinging to the pole. 'She'll have me watching over her.'

Daerna leapt into the gondola, and they hugged.

'Now tell me, Dae. What beautiful trouble awaits us?'

Chapter Forty-Eight
Ash

When a band of skirmishers face a superior army or a particularly dangerous Dreamer, only surprise attacks can ensure victory.
– *Strategikon* by Jerem of Ymis

BY NOON, THE *NIGHT SWAN* had picked up their quarry's trail. Parvos had Dreamt a dozen seagulls sent in different directions with innate instructions to report back if they spotted the Academy's skyship. Captain Bentor steered them at high altitudes, leaving them cold and miserable but hopefully hidden from sight.

Ash waited downstairs in the cabin hold, dozing on and off, unable to fully fall asleep because of the nightmares.

It was mid-morning when Geil woke him from a half-slumber. She was wearing the elegant plates of a Skycourier over her doublet and breeches. 'We found them,' she said. 'We should ready ourselves.'

He climbed after her to the deck, and then onto the stern castle, where Parvos was feeding fish to two of his seagulls. The air was fiercely cold and perilously thin.

'How many are there on board?' Geil asked.

'I've counted at least one, possibly two, Academy Talons. Young cadets all.'

'The Academy must be stretched thin if this is all they have protecting their transports,' Ash said.

'It isn't,' Parvos replied, sombre. 'They have Stone-Masks on deck.'

'This confirms that my father must be on board, then,' Geil said, clapping Ash's back.

'I can help with the Stone-brains; you get rid of the cadets,' Parvos said.

'What's the plan?' Ash asked, feeling uneasy. With less luck, he could have been one of those cadets. Entombed hells, he might still be, even if they won.

'We hit them hard and fast,' Parvos replied. 'Once they're in view, we fire our thunderers from above, taking out as many as we can. Meanwhile, you, lad, Geil and myself drop right behind and finish the job.'

'We could shoot some of them down, give you a distraction,' offered Yaisa, who'd sneaked into their conversation. The thought made Ash sick. 'There has to be another way!' he said.

They all looked at him. Parvos stood up, his iron eye harsh. 'What's wrong, Lightning-Hunter? Is your stomach about to drop its cargo?'

Ash chuckled bitterly. 'No cargo to surrender.' He carefully held the man's gaze. 'This isn't about that. We Dreamers can make anything, and yet you speak of filling them with arrows? There must be a better way.'

'The tools of war leave us few options.' Parvos gestured to the swords he carried. Two on his back, one on each side, another in his hand. All set to one purpose.

Ash had long denounced the brutality of Dreamers; now it was his chance to prove he could do better.

'Then let's use different tools.' He pointed to the swaying orb-lamp hanging from the ceiling.

'Lightning?' Parvos asked, arching an eyebrow. 'So you plan to set their boat on fire? How's that more merciful?'

Geil's eyes had brightened. She'd seen it too.

'Lightning *and* surprise,' she said. 'Enough to give us a chance to get them to surrender.'

'If this fails,' Parvos said, 'we'll be warning them. We'll be boarding a well-prepared ship, instead of attacking in stealth. Nigh impossible odds. They'll shoot us down before we reach the deck.'

'We'll make it work,' Ash said resolutely.

'If we don't, I'll be their first target,' Geil said with a grim smirk.

Parvos let out a long sigh but finally nodded, and Ash set to work. He instructed Rudher to keep an eye on Omen and then climbed to the deck, then he sat with his back to the mast and prepared himself.

* * *

A seagull cry alerted them of the proximity of their prey.

The Academy's skyship was a thing of terror, with bones for masts and grey sails like a bat's wings that stretched the length of the ship. It flew fast, but full as it was with all kinds of supplies from grain to cloth and medicine, all things that a place built for horror couldn't ever produce, it kept at a middling height over the dark waters below.

Ash couldn't help the shiver that ran down his spine.

The Exarchians began assembling on deck, many armed with bows and crossbows. They even had two light arm-thunders, probably smuggled from Amalga, judging by their design.

Parvos turned to address them. 'Wait until we've engaged them. Only then may you reveal yourselves. When you do, pick your targets, but shoot to kill.' While he expanded on his instructions, Geil leaned over to whisper to Ash:

'I always knew the day to openly fight the Academy would come. Didn't expect it to be to free my father, though,' she said. 'Either way, I'm counting on you, Ash.'

It was time.

Ash's mind drifted into Dreaming. He floated, weightless, above himself before casting his mind through the sea of clouds. He wove a silver coil after him – one made of courage and grit, something he could use to catch and wrangle yet-unborn lightning.

He coaxed the lightning from its nest, and it trickled into the coil. He poured his own anger into it, and it twisted, snake-like, forming long fangs with vicious venom.

Then he dived down, his angry catch trailing him, until he saw the vessel through the shades of the Dreaming in its full, glorious horror.

Colossal as a wave, the ship was covered with armoured plate to protect it from an attack from above. It had two thunder-cannons mounted on each side. He couldn't find any gaps in the cover, and their plan seemed more reckless and foolish than ever.

He still had to try.

'Now!' he yelled through lips far away, hoping that Geil would hear him and take flight.

He spread the coil like a cloud of silver smoke, a playful kite that floated alongside the Academy vessel.

Geil said something, and her voice reached him, a distorted echo wading through the wind. He didn't understand her, but he couldn't stop now to find out what she'd said.

He flung the coil like a whip, casting its contents against the Academy ship. Like a nest of serpents, scales burning blue, fangs of flickering gold, five claps of thunder roared in unison.

They hissed and spat as they clashed with the ship's metal frame, and one slithered beneath the cover and hit the central mast, which lit up with blue flames.

Ash crept back into his own shivering skin aboard the *Night Swan*.

The blinding explosion had left the enemy combatants stunned. Some crouched, out of formation, while others rubbed their pained eyes.

It would take them a moment to recover. Hopefully, that'd be enough for his allies to land in their midst and keep them scrambling. Ash leaned over the gunwale and saw Geil was already diving towards them.

'Ready?' Parvos asked, grabbing him by the armpits. Ash nodded. 'Don't let go, then,' he warned. Out of nowhere, a gale propelled him upwards, and he pulled Ash with him.

Ash held his breath and tensed up. Even if Parvos didn't drop him into the nothingness below, they could still be brought down with bolts or spears.

As the dark mass of the enemy skyship came increasingly closer, he feared instead that Parvos's gale would send them into the ship's side, smashing them against the spikes there.

They hit the deck hard in the middle of the cowering cadets. Geil spread her wings to slow her fall, then absorbed the rest by flexing her legs. When she rose, she shone silver in her Skycourier armour.

'Surrender this vessel in the name of the Senate! You're committing an act of treason!' she boomed in her most commanding voice.

It was a bluff, of course, but one she could pull off convincingly. Most of the cadets looked at her, confused and dazzled, then turned to their leaders. The Stone-Masks sprang into action.

Their commander, a wiry woman with an amethyst-veined mask, uncoiled a whip that ended with a scorpion sting.

'Stop right there!' Geil shouted, but the woman ignored her and ate up the distance between them with an impossible leap. Geil was lifting her arms, covered in scales, to meet her attack when a dagger struck the woman mid-jump.

In an instant, Parvos had Dreamt a dozen swords and daggers that hovered in the air around him, like a halo of sharp steel.

The commander hit the deck, bleeding but not dead. 'Kill them!' she screamed.

The other two Stone-Masks drew their weapons and immediately threw themselves at Parvos, but he moved deftly, guiding his blades with his hands, parrying the barrage of blows and attacking back.

The Stone-Masks circled Parvos's ring like a pair of falcons hunting together. One wielded a multi-tailed whip and a dagger, the other twin curved blades and a cloak of smoke that engulfed and transported him out of Parvos's reach.

Somehow, Parvos managed to keep one step ahead. He read distances like an architect, then reacted with the swiftness of a tiger.

When the one cloaked in smoke reformed inside Parvos's ring, Ash feared he was lost. Yet Parvos ducked one of his blades, locked the other with one of his bracers and then kneed the Stone-Mask with such force he fell backwards into the whirling circle of blades.

A dagger pierced his calf and then a short sword skewered him from side to side.

The other Stone-Mask redoubled his efforts with the whip and called for aid.

Some of the cadets began closing in on them. Ash stood in their way, holding his hands up high. 'Stay back! Right now, they're the only criminals on board!'

'Don't listen to him!' the Stone-Mask commander yelled from the other side of the deck. 'Kill them all, and Vice-Chancellor Davorles will reward—' Geil took advantage of her distraction and clubbed her on the head from behind with both hands.

She collapsed to the deck.

'Lay down your weapons!' Geil yelled. 'Do you even *know* who you carry on board? Lord Nial Morvander of the Quietude! A senator of Onyxia, an Archdreamer!'

The cadets wavered, and turned to the prow as someone emerged from below deck.

Ash turned to see a man wearing the Academy's ribecage-like cuirass.

'Look who we have here.' Dain smirked at Ash. 'The roof-rat has joined a gang of pirates.'

'Geil, go find your father. I can take care of this.' Ash hid his lack of confidence behind a nervous smile.

Geil cast him a regretful look, nodded and dashed down the stairs, deflecting a grab from Dain.

'Hey, still kidnapping innocents, Dain?' Ash yelled, turning the sergeant's attention back to him. 'Why don't you go back to fondling crabs instead of helping traitors to the Domain?'

Using a half-remembered insult from Thalder worked – too well, in fact. Dain swung his war hammer at him, splintering the deck where Ash had stood a moment before.

There was no more time to Dream or talk. Dain swung at him again and again, while Ash did his best to defend himself, deflecting and parrying with his sword.

At least Thalder had trained him well enough to make it difficult for Dain to kill him. But Dain was fresh, well rested and full of energy, and he certainly knew how to use a war hammer. Moreover, he was a far more experienced and crueller Dreamer than Ash. He feinted a swing towards Ash's left, and when Ash reached to parry, Dain closed the space on Ash's right.

Ash had run out of distance to keep Dain away. Cornered against the prow, unable to cut wide arcs, it was only a matter of time before the hammer gained the upper hand. Dain pushed him towards the bowsprit. Ash was tempted to Dream a fire-wall, armour, anything to keep Dain away, but the second that would take him would be enough for Dain to crush his head.

All those training sessions with Thalder had been for naught. He wasn't good enough. And although he quickly shoved the thought away, the second of distraction was all it took to change the tide of battle.

Dain sidestepped Ash's swing, shoved the tip of his blade away with his war hammer's head and, wielding his weapon sideways, struck Ash in the stomach.

It knocked the air out of him, and Dain doubled down by elbowing him in the face. He could only see white and lost the grip on his sword.

Blood ran down his face, and his whole torso throbbed with pain. When Dain raised his war hammer again, Ash jumped onto the carved horn that served as bowsprit for the ship. Splinters flew as the steel head shattered the gunwale he'd been leaning against seconds ago.

'Run, roof-rat!' Dain called after him.

The horn was wet, and Ash's feet weren't planted firmly enough. Blood rushed into his eyes, and he had no free hand to wipe it away.

Dain climbed onto the cracked gunwale with a scornful smirk on his face. 'A coward until the end . . .'

This was it. A shameful end for a fool who'd believed he could change anything.

The war hammer traced a deadly arc towards him, and Ash clenched his teeth, dreading the pain of the blow. Then a black shape struck Dain's back, and he toppled sideways against the prow. His war hammer slipped from his grasp and he reached over the gunwale to grab it.

Ash kicked. His boot struck Dain's temple, and he fell overboard, pulled down by the weight of his weapon.

Dain spun downwards, a look of confusion and fear etched on his face, until he disappeared into the dark clouds.

Above Ash on the gunwale stood a black panther, lashing his tail furiously.

'Omen!'

Ash crawled back to the prow castle and threw his arms around Omen's neck. Omen knocked his head against Ash's, and Ash grunted from the wound on his eyebrow. 'Ow . . .' Still, he couldn't help but smile.

The *Night Swan* had come up beside them, its archers aiming at the cadets. Completely leaderless, the cadets threw down their weapons.

Chapter Forty-Nine
Geil

Breeding Nightmares was a necessary evil when training Nightmare-Hunters, and yet it was difficult to contain them. Thus, the Mantle, and its capacity to conjure horrendous fears, was Dreamt to keep the Academy's own monstrosities and Nightmares inside the confines of their island.

A marvel from the Guild Age: a thousand dark fumes braided together, sucking away light and air. Let us be glad that this abomination is confined to the Academy, the only place where it is natural. For if it were able to grow and engulf the world, what other forms of cruel madness and despair would it reap?

– *The Rise and Fall of the Dreamer Guilds* by Henriod Esturios

BELOW DECK, GEIL SEARCHED FOR her father. The captain's cabin was empty but held numerous documents that would deserve closer inspection later. She rummaged through the drawers of a desk, finding the master keys, then crossed over the deserted sleeping quarters and descended into the prison hold.

A dozen terrified recruits, children of all ages, squirmed inside their cages. This was part of the process of breaking them, treating them like beasts. She remembered it well. A cursory glance told her they were well enough – afraid but not injured. *Soon*, the Drake promised.

Ahead was an armoured vault, the sort of place they put prisoners being sent to the Academy's torturers. It was empty except for a lone steel sarcophagus in the darkness.

These sarcophagi were employed only for dangerous Dreamers. Not only were they designed to isolate the prisoner in a sensory vacuum, but they were Dreamchanted with harrowing hallucinations that enhanced the effect of whatever mind-addling drugs the captive Dreamer had been given.

With shaking hands, Geil tried every key in the lock. Finally, it clicked, and she unlatched the lid. A pale figure lay inside, still as a statue. Her father's nakedness allowed her to see fresh fang marks on his skin and blood-soaked bandages. Geleisdra's tears, what had they done to him?

She pulled him out. To her relief, he was still breathing, albeit weakly. She tried shaking him awake, but stopped when she heard someone approaching at a run.

'The ship's ours!' Ash exclaimed from the door, but his elation left him upon seeing her father's state. 'Is he . . .?'

'Not yet! They must have drugged or poisoned him. Find me cold water, we need to wake him up!'

Ash soon returned with a canteen of water and fresh compresses. He and Geil worked in silence, cleaning the worst of the wounds with the cool water, and Morvander stirred.

'G-Geil?' he mumbled, drooling and only half opening his eyes.

'I'm here, Father,' she said, holding him against her. With Ash on her heels, she carried him up to one of the crew's beds to wrap him in a blanket. At least his breathing was steady now.

'Keep an eye on him,' Geil said. 'I still have one last thing to do.'

Ash nodded.

Geil returned to the prisoners' deck. The Drake growled at the sight of the children, and she let it rise to the surface. Its anger fed her muscles, which burned as she tore the locks apart with her bare hands.

She had come for her father, but seeing these children, freeing them, was an unexpected victory that left her weightless.

Hesitantly, the children emerged, first one but soon others. There were a dozen of them, all sooty and miserable. A blonde child, hardly more than six years old, was the youngest. She hid her face in the grey Highlander garb of an older girl.

'Geil?' the Highlander asked.

'Ragdra?' Geil gasped in shock.

Ragdra ran towards her and threw her arms around Geil's waist.

'Why are you here? You should be home—'

'There's no home anymore.' Ragdra averted her gaze. 'The Academy came a few weeks ago, and we had to flee. Mama took us to Ayron, to wait for a ship. They arrested us at the docks. I haven't seen Mama in days.'

Geil crouched and forcefully hugged the young girl.

'Don't worry, you're safe with me now. We'll find your mama.'

'And me?' asked Ragdra's young companion. All of the children were looking at Geil, their large eyes full of hope.

She opened her mouth to respond, but found no words. What could she possibly do? Until she cleared her name, she was a traitor, one that had to flee. She was hardly in a position to help anybody, much less to offer shelter or hope.

Yet wasn't this precisely what she'd wanted? What had brought her back to Onyxia? Geil couldn't just leave these children here. Sister Lasara tentatively came down the stairs and stopped, looking in horror at the holding cells.

'The Sister here will take you to her orphanage.' She pointed at Sister Lasara. 'She'll help you contact your families and return you to them. Those who want to go elsewhere, the Academy or a different place, will be free to do so.'

The Widowed Sister gave an approving look to Geil and nodded. 'You have my word on that.'

As Sister Lasara started to group the children together, Geil gave Ragdra one quick embrace before returning above deck. A dozen cadets huddled together, kneeling on the deck with Parvos's swords hanging over them and the Exarchians' crossbows pointed at their heads.

She was glad they'd found a way to take the ship without killing them in a senseless skirmish.

Weaklings. Should have fought to the death. What do we care? the Drake muttered.

The truth was that she did care. These cadets were young, likely about to graduate, with lofty notions of sacrifice and loyalty beaten into their heads and hearts. Moulded, as she'd been, to be loyal tools for retribution. Yet try as the Academy might, they weren't tools. Unlike tools, they could question their purpose and set themselves to new ones.

'Do you know who I am?' she asked, looming over them.

'You're Geil Morvander,' replied an amber-skinned lass with a shadow-raven perched on her shoulder.

'Then you must know I too have loyally served the Domain. I have no intention of harming you or of making you betray your oaths.'

The girl stared at Geil coldly. A muscular lad spoke up. 'Really? Master Dain would argue differently, if you hadn't thrown him overboard.'

These two were likely the Talon sergeants, and wherever they went, the others would follow.

'The only traitors here are Davorles's henchmen, trying to kidnap my father on unlawful charges,' Geil snarled.

'Words are cheap. We don't serve Lord Davorles, so why don't you let us go?' the raven lass replied.

Geil ran her tongue over her teeth. *She'll stab us in the back*, the Drake whispered. *They're not children anymore. If they're here, it's because the masters have already broken them. Why trust them at all?*

'Fair is fair. I give you my word that I'll release you as soon as we reach the city. If you try to escape before that, we'll show you no mercy. Do we have an understanding?'

The blond lad spat on the deck. 'I'll never stop fighting you!'

Before Geil could reply, the raven lass punched him in the back of the head. He toppled sideways to the deck.

'Understood,' she said, rubbing her hand. 'And whoever disagrees can sort it out with me.'

'What's your name, Cadet?' Geil asked.

'Anehelira. Lira for short,' she replied.

'Lira,' Geil said with a respectful nod, 'you're in charge of both Talons now. If your people need anything, you come to me. Don't mess with us and we'll release you soon. Now, do we have an understanding?'

'We do.'

'Excellent.' Geil smiled at her. If the girl was going to stab her in the back, at least she was working hard to earn it.

She walked over to Parvos, who stood guarding the unconscious Secret Chancellery agent.

'We didn't agree to this,' he said.

'What else would you have me do?'

'I'm just saying, don't count on us to help you when they turn on you.'

'I can take care of myself. What about this one?' Geil nudged the masked woman with her boot.

'Throw her overboard for all I care,' Parvos said with a shrug. 'Just look at this before you go easy on her.' He handed Geil a folded document.

To Geil's surprise, the letter wasn't encrypted, but she soon realised why. It was an edict from Vice-Chancellor Davorles. He'd claimed extraordinary powers to protect the Domain from traitors and conspirators. Moreover, he exhorted all of the Domain's enforcers, from the city watch to the Skycouriers, to bring in certain senators, guildmasters and their families, 'for their own protection'. A lengthy list of about a hundred names ranked by importance followed, Lord Orles Brakte among them.

'We might have underestimated the depths of the Academy's ambition. If he can pull this off and bring the Senate to heel, he might be able to declare himself Regent.'

'He's overplayed his hand,' Geil said softly. 'Nobody will go willingly to become hostages. By doing this, he's causing a rebellion.'

'What if the Leviathan-Maker's in on it?'

'Even if he was, there's only one squadron at the city's docks. It'd take him weeks to gather its full strength. How does he expect to control the city until then?' She could only hope that would work in their favour. 'And in the meantime, the Reformers will fight back.'

Parvos crossed his hefty arms. 'Maybe. Fighting back is one thing. To win against the Secret Chancellery, the Hordemasters and whoever's on their side, they need somebody to lead them. With Saorla taken off the board, and all these senators fleeing for their lives, it's unclear who'll do it . . .'

'Lady Saorla's still alive.' Or she was the last time Geil had seen her.

She scanned the list of names again, starting at the bottom. Geil's heart sank when she saw what she'd feared all along:

> *. . . Lady Liadra Saorla, last seen at Arvira. She's to be interrogated regarding the whereabouts of her sister so we may offer adequate protection to the Captain Regent . . .*

Even if Lady Saorla had recovered, Davorles was clearly on to her and Liadra's tracks. The list also served as a grim reminder that Davorles and the Academy weren't afraid to drag people away in chains in their attempts at usurping power or undermining the Domain.

Liadra would have to be either captured to help control Lady Saorla or killed to ensure she didn't become a rallying cry.

'We should go to Arvira. Lady Saorla is there,' Geil said. 'She's the fastest way of removing Davorles from power.'

'This is where we part ways, then,' Parvos said.

'Wait! Don't you see what this means? If we save Lady Saorla's family, you can exact political concessions from them. Think of it: full pardons for your people! Perhaps even exemptions from recruitment!'

Parvos let out a bitter laugh. 'We don't want their crumbs. Besides, I'm sure they'll find a way to poison whatever they offer. You should just let them rip each other's throats out, Geil. This is your chance to escape.'

The Drake mumbled its agreement. They could flee north and secure an alliance with Marchioness Nisdre before Davorles and whoever was behind him realised what had happened.

Except she was tired of this, tired of running, tired of surviving and letting the world continue to collapse. She couldn't do it. Not now that she'd seen the faces of all those children freed from their cages.

'I can't,' she said at last. 'If I survive this coup, I'll have a real chance of changing things.'

Parvos sighed. 'You've fought well, Geil,' he said, and offered his hand.

'You too,' she said, shaking it.

Chapter Fifty

Daerna

The Charnelites believe that their false goddess, born from the might of the Pale Prince's Divine Dreams, still crawls under the surface of our world. Ushering in her return is thus the main drive of their actions. Such promise, and the boons they allege would come from it, is what allows the cult to prey on both the feeble-minded and the desperate.

– *The Charnelite Heresy* by Sister Warden Marras

Daerna's boat slid slowly down the Great Canal.

'Any time now,' Pierla said, keeping her eyes on the northern bank.

The truth was that Daerna wouldn't really blame her friends if they didn't show up. Pierla's messages might not have reached them in time. Not to mention Roshia should still be recovering and Indre, brave as she was, knew enough to see Daerna was going to drag them all into deeper trouble.

Yet, as they neared the canal's end, three Sisters stood waiting at the water stairs by the watch's barracks.

Roshia still looked sickly pale but had the strength to greet Daerna with a heartfelt hug, and so did Indre.

'It's so good to see you both. I'll never forget this.' Turning to Dirdra, Daerna added, 'You too, Sister.'

Sister Dirdra's face was darkened by a concerned scowl.

'I'm only here to understand what you've got yourself into,' she replied. 'Did you know that the Secret Chancellery came to Muirtra with some serious accusations? Her Sorrowfulness has ordered you to immediately report to Muirtra and submit to her mercy. Otherwise, you'll be on your own.'

Daerna nodded gravely.

'I will. But first, there's something I have to do.'

'What are you speaking of?' Sister Dirdra asked.

'I believe there's a way to end the spread of the Wilting.'

* * *

When she finished explaining the Silver Book's revelations, everyone but Roshia looked at her with a mixture of confusion, hope and disbelief . . .

'Please, I can't do this alone. I need your help. The city needs your help.'

'Even if you're right, the canticles weren't designed for this,' Sister Dirdra said. 'Our Keening elevates the sorrows and the souls to the Motherstorm. I can believe in the mysterious complexities of Divine Geleisdra's miracles, yet even if she imbued Onyxia with a Divine Soul, there's no certainty we can either reach or soothe it.'

'I know for a fact that a year ago the Academy brought a shard of the Mantle to a palace near Hollowshrine. Right when the Wilting began worsening, as if that was enough to send the city into this torment, this outburst of the disease.' Daerna gestured around then pressed on. 'If I'm right, they drove the city's dreams to cruel nightmares with the Mantle. If they reached the city's dreams, who's not to say we can? And shouldn't we at least try?'

Sister Dirdra dropped her voice to a whisper, as if speaking to herself more than them. 'If such a thing were possible . . .'

Daerna stood unflinching under Dirdra's hard gaze. 'Please, Sister, you said that I had a gift, that few could truly deliver their hearts into the songs like me. I'm heeding your advice. I'm asking you for help because I believe we're the only ones who can make a difference.' Of all the Sisters of rank at the abbey, she trusted that Dirdra would understand.

After a long pause, Sister Dirdra sighed. 'Very well, then. Let us see if the city will listen to us.'

Chapter Fifty-One
Geil

Truth is strength.

– Arvira University motto

THE *NIGHT SWAN* SAILED TOWARDS Arvira, loaded with freed recruits and captive cadets. After an hour, lush, rolling hills opened into a green valley latticed by silvery rivulets. Arvira stretched over a river crossing, honeycombed by college cloisters and ruled by a lone keep atop a grassy knoll. The golden-gilded *Burning Dawn* perched on its skydock, yet it was the plume of smoke rising east of the city that drew their attention. One of the large halls of what seemed an abbey had caught ablaze.

Heart drumming with dread, Geil followed it downwards with a spyglass. Large windowpanes framed a tableau of horror. On one side of a long hall, mudghasts tore through beds and wooden panels. The fire ate away at their sludge, but not quickly enough to stop flames from spreading; on the other side, Widowed Sisters and robed students hurried to carry the injured and infirm to the gardens outside.

This wasn't just some abbey but the city's hospital.

We're too late, the Drake murmured in warning. But she ignored it; she had to find Liadra.

Thinking that they'd hurt Liadra – or worse, killed her – made her boil with rage. *We'll paint this river red with their blood*, the Drake promised. Heaving angrily, she was about to swoop into the blazing infirmary when Ash grabbed her.

'Wait!' he begged. 'What if this is a trap?'

'What are you saying?'

'I recognise the Imprint in those things! Some Hordemaster tried killing me at the palace with one of them. I don't see him though, nor do I see Lady Saorla. What if they're just using the fire to draw her out?'

She didn't want to listen to this. The Drake thrashed in her mind, yearning to give in to the blissful immediacy of ripping everyone and everything apart. But Ash was right. This wasn't about her; she'd come here to save Liadra, and the first step was to find her.

'There!' said a young voice from behind them.

Geil turned to face Lira, the Talon leader who'd helped take control of the Academy ship. She stroked the sooty-looking raven perched on her gloved arm. 'My feathery friend here's noticed something's off with the oratory tower.'

The blaze hadn't caught the tower yet, but Geil could see what the raven had. Its stones glinted golden. 'Just like the Starspun Maiden's halo,' she said. 'She's probably Dreamchanted the tower to resist the fire.'

'We're not the only ones to notice,' Ash replied.

Panicked cries came from the gardens below as three more putrid mudghasts, emerging from their hideout on the opposite side of the cloister's arcades, rushed for the tower.

'Tell Captain Bentor to lower the *Night Swan*, and make sure you get Lady Saorla and her family out. Then fly away and don't look back.'

'Wait, what will you do?'

'I'll draw them away to give you a chance to escape. Don't waste it.'

Geil jumped overboard. She called her wings and flung them open to make herself visible. She needed their eyes on her and away from the tower, so she landed forcefully on top of one of the mudghasts, smashing it into cracked bits of hardened muck under her weight.

Another swung at her. She barely had the time to Dream scales over her forearms and parry its fury of blows.

A third mudghast came for her head, but Geil ducked swiftly beneath it and sank her claws into its belly, tearing it open.

'Where's your maggot of a maker?' she called, defiant. More of the beasts came loping toward her from the arcade, herded by a cloaked man with a whip.

At least she'd succeeded in drawing the killer's attention.

Don't let them gang up on us, the Drake warned.

The mudghasts flung themselves at her and Geil danced through them, cutting and parrying, drawing them away from the tower.

Before the loping mudghasts fully encircled her, she beat her wings and took flight.

She circled as the horde swarmed the courtyard, their crude, malformed limbs stretching after her. There were far too many for her to take by herself. Their master, though, was alone.

As she circled one last time, gaining altitude, she saw the man flash a pearly grin.

He won't smirk for long, the Drake growled.

Too late, she caught sight of a blur behind her. A grey mud gargoyle had appeared, a crude thing, barely capable of flying, yet capable enough of tearing through Geil's wings with its claws.

She spun, throwing the gargoyle off her, but her tattered wings beat uselessly at the air. Hurtling downwards with little control, she steered her fall towards the covered arcade and had just enough time to throw up an arm to cushion her blow before she slammed against its roof.

A sharp bolt of pain shot through her. She tried to dig her claws in, but momentum kept her rolling until she fell off one side towards the waiting ground below.

Everything went black.

She blinked. She was somewhere in the garden. Her arm was throbbing, and her nose was bleeding. Her ribs and back ached. There were figures all around her. She stood and started swinging and slicing, fighting to crawl away. If the horde of mudghasts grabbed her, they'd drown her in seconds.

'Lady Morvander,' a figure called.

As the colours and shapes around her resolved into a person, she realised it wasn't one of the mudghasts but Lira. Her Talonmates had spread out around Geil, fending off the Nightmares with blazing swords. There was no trace of the Stone-Mask.

'What are you doing here?' Geil asked.

'We thought we'd even the odds,' Lira replied, helping her up. 'We were tasked with fighting traitors, so that's precisely what we're doing.'

A javelin of lightning arced down from above, hitting one of the mudghasts and shattering it into dust. Geil looked up and saw Ash at one of the tower's windows. He waved for her to approach.

Geil was dizzy, but with Lira's help, she reached the tower entrance.

Her heart thundering in her chest, she flung the door open. A sudden, fiery glimmer blinded her, and she heard cries of alarm. She allowed her eyes to slip back to their human shape, quick enough to spot someone aiming a crossbow at her. On instinct, she ducked.

The bolt whistled above her head.

'Geil?' Liadra called. 'Lower your weapons!' she ordered. The golden radiance faded enough for Geil to see. Two of Lady Saorla's house guards parted for Liadra to emerge.

Liadra ran and embraced her. Her arms wrapped around her ribs so hard it hurt, yet it was nothing compared to feeling that she was safe, like there was a measure of harmony in the world again.

'Blessed Motherstorm, I'm so happy you're safe!' Geil said, gazing into the deep opaline of Liadra's eyes. Her hand had risen to cup her cheek before she realised what she was doing.

Heedlessly, Liadra stood on tiptoe to plant a kiss at the edge of her mouth.

Geil staggered, saw Liadra's eyes fill with confusion and fear. Liadra was about to turn away when Geil stopped her. She seized the back of her neck and pulled her forwards, caught her mouth with tongue and teeth.

Warmth washed through her from the burning fire of Liadra's lips; it ran down her body in waves, washing away exhaustion and woe, setting her heart ablaze, lighting up every piece of her soul she'd thought broken, lost or forgotten.

This time, the moment didn't pass by. They both seized it, their hearts beating in unison. There'd be questions, conversations, concerns – but they could all wait.

* * *

The *Burning Dawn* had avoided capture by Davorles's agents, so a rendezvous point was arranged near Onyxia. On their way, an impromptu war council was hastily convened in the crammed captain's quarters of the *Night Swan*.

Lady Saorla presided over it, dressed in a regal golden cuirass. She looked pale and wan, and spoke softly. Even moving about required considerable energy.

'Our senators report Lord Davorles has used his powers to impose his control over the entire Grand Palace,' Lady Saorla said dourly. 'There are gangs of Blues and our own in the streets fighting and looting, but the watch has been requisitioned to protect all accesses to the Grand Palace. I'll make my way to the city and order him to relinquish his powers, but we need to be ready in case he doesn't surrender and we need to dislodge him from the palace by force.' Despite everything, she kept her serenity, and seeing her, dressed in her golden armour, coldly tracking the shapes on the shifting and changing map, was reassuring. She wasn't going down without a fight.

Neither was Geil, but the Regent was right. If Lord Davorles didn't willingly surrender, a handful of cadets and House Saorla's guards wouldn't be enough to storm the palace, let alone restore order.

'Who still supports us in the city?' Liadra asked from her sister's side.

'We've received messages from Lord Brakte and some other senators. They've called on their allies and supporters in the Western Quarter and the Craghorn. They're as good as ours,' said the man at Lady Saorla's right. It took Geil a moment to place him; he was less dashing than he'd been at Lady Saorla's party, but that was to be expected after he'd been targeted alongside his wife. 'If you give the order as Captain Regent, the magistrates can arm them.'

'I can call on the support of the Susurrus's magistrate and its guilds. That's another foothold,' Geil said.

'Just a foothold? We have the numbers!' Liadra said.

'Numbers aren't sufficient if he can shuffle the Academy's Hordemasters to plug any breakthroughs with Nightmares,' Lady Saorla said grimly. 'And according to our friends in the College of Seafarers, Lord Stalcar has taken refuge at the navy's arsenal docks. Five of his war vessels are there with him, not to mention his Leviathans. We need to tread carefully. I have yet to see that he's not in league with that viper Davorles.'

'He wouldn't dare stop you!' her husband said. 'If we take back the Grand Palace, you'll be the one who restored power to the Senate.'

The door slammed open and Ash ushered Geil's father in, pale and bent. He was wearing an old surcoat over a loose shirt and breeches Captain Bentor had lent him.

'Father!' Geil stood and helped him into a chair. 'You should be resting. The drug's still in your veins.'

'There's no time for rest, not after hearing what you're planning.' His eyes jerked from Geil to Lady Saorla. 'Your errors of judgement have cost us a lot. I'm not letting you risk my daughter's life too.' Despite the exhaustion, the cold anger was unmistakable.

'Nial, please! I've suffered the consequences of my poor judgement myself!' Lady Saorla said, offering an open hand. 'Let me make amends and reward you for your service to the Domain.'

'It's too late for rewards or amends,' he muttered bitterly.

'I can't undo my mistakes.' Lady Saorla squared her shoulders. 'But once we restore power to the Senate, this calls for a reform, of everything from the Chancellery to even the Regency Council.'

'And who's going to make sure that happens?' her father asked.

'I will,' Geil said.

'You?' A bushy eyebrow climbed up his forehead. 'Why?'

Geil was afraid to say it out loud. Voicing her dreams would give them weight. Once spoken, they could be broken. But Geil knew her world was at a crossroads. Ahead awaited bloody, uncertain battle, but walking away from it was a sure way to lose. So, if she was to fight, she might as well fight for the things she believed in.

'Because we can't just go back to the way things were. If the Academy, the Domain even, is to endure, they need to change. And now is the time. I'm not asking you to place your faith in Lady Saorla.' She reached for her father's papery hand. 'Place your faith in me.'

Morvander pursed his lips thoughtfully. Geil felt the weight of his doubt, but the hard lines of his face gradually gave way to something else: curiosity, pride, perhaps even hope.

'You have my promise to offer Lady Geil Morvander ample powers to lead the reformation of the Academy, assuming there's even one left after this. Now, can the Domain count on you, Lord Morvander?' Lady Saorla asked.

Slowly, he nodded. 'And my ship, as well as my own aid.'

'Excellent,' Lady Saorla said, to the great relief of those present. 'Now, to put down this unrest and restore order, we'll seize the Central Quarter from many points at the same time. The only path to triumph is overwhelming their forces on all fronts . . .'

As she went on to outline her plan, Geil felt something bubbling in her stomach. This felt wrong, and it wasn't about the odds. Ash had been right about sparing the cadets. To achieve victory, they'd be cutting through thousands of citizens. An even larger number would find their homes and livelihoods ravaged. The thought of the blood that would be spilled made her queasy. Birthing a new age in terror was the Academy's way, not hers.

'Wait. I have another request to make,' Geil said.

All eyes fell on her. 'Speak,' Lady Saorla said.

'There must be a way to take the fight to the Grand Palace directly. What about skyships? Your senators must have their own, as well as some of the guilds,' Geil said.

'That is a bold gamble,' Lady Saorla replied, eyes stuck to her map. 'As long as Davorles controls the Secret Chancellery's lionheads, he'll see it coming, and he'll try to take the fight to the skies. With skyships falling in flames all over the city, the resulting disaster would be as terrible.'

'Then allow me to lead a vanguard into the Grand Palace first,' Geil said. 'I want to see if I can win over the Skycouriers to our cause. I'm certain the Falconess won't heed Davorles's edict until she knows which way the wind's blowing.'

All around, faces turned from disbelief to shock. Her father clutched her hand forcefully. 'You realise that's walking into the wolf's den. What's to stop the Falconess from delivering you to Davorles?'

Lady Saorla seconded his concerns. 'The old bird is both stubborn and unpredictable. There's enough bad blood for her to not be wooed by Lord Davorles, but she might equally bar you from crossing the palace's heights.'

'I'm aware of the risks,' Geil replied. 'If we convince them, we could sweep the palace out from beneath Davorles's feet in a single stroke! Imagine the bloodshed we'd prevent.'

Lady Saorla nodded. 'You'd do the Domain a great service with this, Geil. Lord Morvander, what do you think?'

Her father's pale face filled with deep furrows of concern.

'My daughter's willing to gamble her life out of loyalty to the Domain . . .' He inhaled loudly. 'I shall have to follow her example. I'll head to the navy's arsenal to meet with the Admiral Regent.'

'You really don't think he's in on this?' Lady Saorla asked.

'I don't. You know him well, Ines. They might be offering him the city on a plate, but this feels like the Academy's play, not his. And he despises them more than he despises us.'

Lady Saorla nodded. 'The temptation might be too strong for him to resist, though.'

'I can be very persuasive: why become a tyrant when he can become the saviour of the Domain? I'm certain that even if it just serves to buy you some time, it'll be worth it.'

It was hard to imagine her father, weak as he was, on the front lines.

'Certain enough to risk your life?' Geil asked.

He squeezed her hand with all his frail strength. 'Certain enough that I'm willing to give my daughter the best shot I can.'

Chapter Fifty-Two

Daerna

The graves were empty, the charnel houses hollow, and the dead, they feasted and smiled, they danced and filled the cities. Across the continent's battlefields, the Charnelite Midwives coaxed the freshly fallen to rise again, rats and maggots still clinging to them like finery. They rallied under the Pale Prince's banner. And where they led, woe followed.

– *A History of the Sibling Strife* by Blessed Merele

DAERNA WAS UNSURPRISED THE WILTING had begun in the Scab. The towering steel columns nailed into the islets had been part of the torment inflicted on the city's bones for so long.

'This is as far as I can take us into Hollowshrine,' Pierla said, docking them by some mossy steps half swallowed by the waterway. 'They've Dreamt locks to block access to the rest of the district's canals.'

As the others disembarked, Daerna felt her stomach clench. To step into the very streets where she'd almost died seemed a sure way to invite death again.

They all crept into the Scab's knotted heart. The alleys were quieter than she'd expected. Everywhere they looked were signs of fighting: smashed barricades, houses with their doors torn off the hinges, shattered glass. The locals stayed out of their way, either watching them warily from behind barred windows or marching in arms to fight elsewhere.

It was easy to see why when they crossed paths with a horde of mudghasts. The Nightmares sniffed the air and turned their eyeless heads towards the group. Their crude semblance of reason was enough for them to understand they weren't enemies but little more. And even then, they ended up taking side alleys to avoid tempting luck.

They soon reached the Hollowshrine islet, where the rotten facades of the houses crowded up against each other, their wounded dreams knotting together.

'This is either terribly foolish or terribly brave,' Roshia said.

'You can go back to the boat, Roshia. You've done enough,' Daerna said.

'This one? She's having the time of her life!' Pierla jested.

That won a smile from Roshia. 'It seems your recklessness has started to rub off on me after all this time.'

They laughed together.

'There.' Indre signalled ahead.

Warily, they reached the same secluded square as before. The fresco was still there, except it'd been splattered with muck and manure.

Something else presided over the ruins instead: half a dozen corpses of the executed Charnelites, some of them badly mangled, had been left hanging for the scavengers to pick clean. Notable among them was the reeking cadaver of the bearded priest.

They had almost killed her, and yet she found no joy in the macabre sight of their bloated bodies.

Here, the dread was so heavy, one could almost breathe it in like smoke. Even the Motherstorm above had grown eerily quiet – no rain, no rumble, no wind.

'There's something in this place, I can tell,' Dirdra said.

'You too?' It was a relief for Daerna to hear she wasn't imagining these things. That Dirdra, with her skills and her own connection to the Motherstorm, felt something amiss as well. 'It's even worse than last time.' She lifted a loose cobblestone from the ground with the tip of her boot. It was covered in the black mould that she'd grown to fear so much. It seemed to be oozing directly from the island's naked rock.

'What is it exactly that you want us to do?' Dirdra asked.

'I've been thinking about what you said. The canticles weren't written to reach the city, but the Motherstorm,' Daerna replied. 'So let us ask for Her aid. Let us ask the Motherstorm to help us wash this rot away with Her tears.'

'Sister Indre and I will keep an eye on the surroundings,' Pierla said, while the others stepped into the centre of the ruins.

Together, the Wailers formed a triangle and took to their warm-up vocal exercises.

Dirdra had picked Geleisdra's 'Blinding Lightning' canticle for them. It was a responsory that spoke of lightning tearing the veil of despair placed over one's eyes by death. It felt like an apt choice to try to alleviate Onyxia's burdens, and she and Roshia took to it eagerly.

Above, the Motherstorm was stirring, releasing some cool droplets onto their heads.

When the song ended, Daerna felt nothing had changed. Roshia shook her head as well. She sighed in frustration.

'Again, from the beginning,' Dirdra said, undaunted.

This time, Dirdra joined in, and her deep voice carried their song high above other sounds. But it went beyond that; soon Dirdra was improvising around the base, weaving her own harmonies into the song, crafting her own cadences. It was a beautiful performance, one that inspired Daerna to follow along with her own improvisations. And then, their song became something else.

The air around them felt charged. The Motherstorm was shifting, letting Her breath follow theirs. The rainfall followed this vortex, and Daerna felt carried by it.

It was an exhilarating sensation that brought tears to her eyes. It reminded Daerna of the first time she'd managed to move the Motherstorm as a novice. She felt the same unbridled hope, the same blissful certainty she had then.

Wherever these tears touched the earth, they carried a lightness, a silence, a relief. Close to the soil, they descended even deeper into the roots of the islet.

Something almighty was waking up below, and to feel such expansive magnificence was thrilling.

And then it ended, a sudden, abrupt silence swallowing it all. The rain cut off as if someone had dropped a lock on a river, choking the stream.

The connection was still there, but it carried a sharp tang of pain, enough to send them to their knees. From there, they looked at each other in confusion. Not far above, the clouds were parting, as if shoved aside by invisible hands.

'What is that?' Roshia asked, sweaty and voice trembling.

'Impossible,' Pierla said.

Daerna only saw Dirdra pointing behind her at the hanged corpses.

She turned around.

The bearded priest's mauled cadaver, with its stony hue of dead flesh and blackened injuries, was seized by spasms.

'Is he really moving?' Roshia asked.

Almost in reply, his eyes snapped open. They were hollow and glassy, eggshells cracked bloody by the blunt impact of death. And yet, they landed on Daerna with a precise knowing.

'How is this possible?' Daerna asked.

Indre approached, raising her orb-lamp to look from up close. Around them, shadows fell, as if all light had been sucked from the day.

'Keep away from it!' Pierla yelled.

Sister Indre ignored her and leaned closer to examine the corpse. 'Chroniclers tell that Charnelite Midwives would embed corpses with Dreamchanted bones that reanimated them, giving them a semblance of life. This,' Indre said, pointing, 'means the Midwife wasn't killed by the city watch.'

'Cursed heretics!' Pierla snarled, stepping to Daerna's side and unsheathing her sword. 'I should finish what the Hordemasters couldn't!'

To their terrified surprise, a roar rose like a thundering wave over the city. The cacophony was deep enough to vibrate in Daerna's bones.

'What in the entombed hells is that?' Pierla shouted.

Daerna spotted the answer in the courtyard: a worn-out, moss-covered lionhead roared with the sound of grinding stone.

A hundred stone throats were screaming in unison throughout the city. Their roar was loud as the heavens, as mighty as the mountains.

Before she could ask more, the stone chorus bellowed again, and this time, a deafening crack reverberated throughout the empty courtyard. Shards of rock and dust rose up from the ground. It was rain, but a rain of stone that fell upwards, pulled towards the heavens like plumes of smoke.

The Wilting had shattered the city's bones, but something else was pulling at the bedrock of onyx.

High above, a form was taking shape, a cloud made of strands of smoke and shadow, a swirling nest of snakes coiling into each other and feeding on the rock that rose towards them.

Daerna feared, more than anything, what – or who – was growing over the city.

The hanging corpses stirred in a desperate dance. The Sisters huddled together at the centre of the ruins.

A voice came from a nearby doorway. 'Your return pleases us.'

The Midwife was suddenly standing there. Her twisted features shone in the half-light, accentuating her cadaveric appearance.

'Stay away!' Pierla yelled, brandishing her sword.

Surprisingly, the Midwife didn't attack. Instead, she caressed a jagged column, scratching the surface, drawing even more black mould that flowed upwards.

'What do you want?' Daerna asked, reaching for her own blade.

'We've come to bask in her glorious return.'

'"Her glorious return"?' Dirdra repeated.

'The Charnel Mother's,' Indre replied with hushed tones.

This drew a blackened and serrated smile from the Midwife. 'Yes! Yes! She's crossing the many veils to return to us! Witness Her miracle, little birds. Sing, sing for Her. And She'll take you soon.'

'Come on then, maggoty numbskull!' Pierla barked. 'Either the Hordemasters will string you up like your miserable followers, or I will!'

The Midwife's fleshless lips curled with delight.

'Watch now, foolish child.' As she spoke, she reached with her left hand into her tunic through a lateral opening, so deeply she seemed to be rummaging inside her belly. She withdrew a skull of solid gold, or perhaps a helmet carved to resemble one. It seemed to shine, or rather, it sucked up what little light of day remained. 'Gaze upon these jubilant dead, and marvel at this one last service that shall offer them deliverance.'

She raised two fingers as if calling them to attention. And in reply, the corpses wheezed out screams as high and loud as their broken larynxes allowed.

The worst part was that the lionheads roared in reply.

Their suffering cry came in waves from all over the city. With each inhuman bellow, the whole Scab shook as if having a seizure, and the ground below bled more of its mould-choked dust. The courtyard was slowly being engulfed by the black, dusty plumes as they rose towards the heavens.

Above them, the vortex swirled, until it was large enough to block the Motherstorm. Daerna felt the world around them swirling too, a heavy dizziness hitting her, as if the very city had been thrown off its axis.

In the distance, the Motherstorm rumbled, all thunder with no lightning. Daerna could feel Her pain; the pillar of misery was like an open wound in Her bosom. It pulled at Her edges, sucking the air from Her.

The Hallowed Motherstorm couldn't be destroyed, but it could be shattered and it could be hurt. And that thought was terrifying.

'What madness is this?' Dirdra asked.

'She's calling up the city's suffering,' Daerna replied. 'Feeding it to the Charnel Mother.'

'That can't be,' Dirdra replied, confused. 'She was vanquished.'

'Vanquished, but not erased from the world. She's a divine miracle too,' Indre replied, keeping her eyes on the Midwife, who tilted her head to listen to the cacophony of sounds.

Her fellow Sisters were trembling, staring at the sky with naked fear, but Daerna steeled herself, refusing to give up.

'We must try one last time!' she said, and began chanting the 'Canticle of the Burning Dawn'. Her muscles were sore, and her heart still heavy with dread, but she fought through it all. This was for Onyxia, for Ash, for her own family.

She reached out to the Motherstorm. She was there, but She felt far away, farther away than ever.

Daerna tried to focus on the canticle, but her singing had become disjointed and meandering. She elevated the verses to the heavens, but there was nobody listening. A colossal shadow had fallen on her, one that didn't care for her harmonies or gentle sorrows.

One that only understood the language of sharp bones and hearts turned to ash.

'We thought you'd learned your lesson, little bird, but fear not. We'll pray for your deliverance.' The Midwife spoke in Iskian now, addressing Daerna over the roar and the upwards rain of dust. Daerna heard her praying then: 'Deliver her, deliver her from the sorrows of the world, tear the soul from her skin and spare her . . .'

The Midwife's voice droned on, and a creeping cold assaulted Daerna. It wasn't physical, and yet it made her shiver.

There was something else there in the square with her, an invisible presence like the Motherstorm's, except this one prodded at her mind. She could feel its long fingers, sharp as sickles, grazing her skull, probing for a fissure, an opportunity to infect her.

She couldn't see the Charnel Mother, but she could feel Her ready to cut through the air. Ready to pry her ribcage open and free her from this mortal coil.

Fear rose in Daerna's throat, and her Keening wavered. Breathing was becoming difficult, and her mind went blank. She lacked the strength to continue, her will and fury sapped.

Daerna fell to her knees, unable to breathe.

Chapter Fifty-Three

Geil

Under the Motherstorm's embrace, over a Wail of Stone, with the will of Her people.

– Inscription at the Onyxian Senate's gates

THE *NIGHT SWAN* SLIPPED THROUGH the ashen skies until they reached the grey mist over the Grand Palace. With every gate tightly shut, the colossal building looked more like a mausoleum.

Lady Saorla's house guard and a handful of cadets had gathered on deck around Geil. Soon they'd be fighting inside the palace, perhaps even against the Skycouriers if things didn't go the way she expected.

She could see that Omen had suddenly grown restless, growling and pacing about on the prow castle.

'Something's wrong with him,' Ash said. 'With the Motherstorm too,' he added, pointing at it.

The Motherstorm was ominously silent. And there was an eye opening over the Southern Quarter.

'What does that mean?' she asked.

'That the Motherstorm is about to birth a new Kinstorm. But that's usually accompanied by increased downpour. This . . .

I've never seen anything like it. It's almost as if She's holding Her breath. What is happening out there?'

Omen stood on his hind quarters and peeked over the gunwale. He let out a loud yowl, as if he'd noticed something they couldn't see.

'Omen?' Ash crouched by the creature's side. 'What's wrong, boy?' His eyes went glassy. 'Something's forming in the skies there, giant plumes of dark smoke rising high into the heavens, cutting into the Motherstorm,' he said, shaking out the Dreaming trance. 'They're coalescing into a vortex. That's what we're seeing.'

'Plumes of dark smoke? You mean like the Mantle?' she asked.

'Could be.' He scratched his neck while still petting Omen's scruff. 'It does resemble the cloak I saw Davorles wearing.'

Geil grimaced. 'Maybe he's released what he had in his palace.'

'Why, though?'

'As a distraction, perhaps. Either way, it doesn't change what we're here to do. If anything, it means we should hurry.'

As the *Night Swan* finally came close to the palace, they realised the fight had started without them.

Gangs of armed men wearing the Traditionalists' blue ran through the courtyards, littered with fallen bodies.

The screams of fighting reached them through smashed windows from nearby pavilions and domes. The Skycouriers' pavilion, though, remained quiet, except for the occasional order barked from the mess and the guttural croaks of the gargoyles guarding it.

'With me!' Geil commanded, jumping overboard, followed by Lira's Talon.

Her Skycourier armour slowed her fall to a gentle glide. The cadets followed. Some had Dreamt powerful eagle wings or Dreamchanted cloaks with which to glide; others simply rappelled down.

The pavilion's gargoyles reacted swiftly to their appearance. As soon as Geil's group landed, the stone beasts encroached on them, brandishing their thick stone claws in warning.

Geil's party stood still, encircled by the unblinking parliament of gargoyles. The Dreamlings easily outnumbered them and were led by a hulking gargoyle Geil recognised.

'Leave at once!' it roared.

'We come in peace, Moss-Eyes! I'm here to see the Falconess!' She bowed her head to it. They said that no matter how many times it'd been remade, it forgot nothing.

'Sergeant!' Moss-Eyes called.

Someone else – not the Falconess – emerged from the Sky Pavilion: Itraya. Her full plate armour was charred black in some places, and there was a bolt protruding from her left side. The broadsword against her shoulder was bloodied too, except with blood too dark to be human.

'What are you doing here, Geil?' Itraya asked coldly.

'I came here to put an end to Davorles's betrayal, but it seems that you're already one step ahead.'

'The Falconess suspected him from the start. When Mavis came to us with the news of what you'd found at his palace, she warned us all to be on guard, so when he claimed extraordinary powers to restore order, we were ready. She's had us warn and move some of the senators, guildmasters and their families out of the city, though many were still caught at the Senate meeting this morning. She went there in person to try to persuade Lady Malvedra to let the hostages go, but that plan has now gone tits-up.'

'What does Lady Malvedra have to do with anything?'

'Try to keep up, Geil!' Itraya huffed. 'Damned old Wisp appointed her High Justice and put her in charge of the palace before he left. That vulture Malvedra threw the Falconess in chains instead of listening to sense. With her out of the action and the Blues running rampant in the streets and threatening to storm the palace, it's been utter chaos. I'd try to break her out, but I'm still gathering our scattered forces.'

'Where's Mavis and the others?'

She waved around. 'Stopping the damned Blues after they stormed one of the city watch garrisons and armed themselves. Which is why it's been hard to stop them without killing them. Or getting killed by them.' Itraya clenched her teeth.

'Let us help, then,' Geil said. 'We'll get the Falconess out.'

Itraya huffed, blowing a golden tress out of her sweaty face. 'Can't. I don't trust you, Geil Morvander. I can't have you watching my back if I don't trust you.'

'Trust something else then,' Geil begged. 'Trust that I love the Falconess and the Skycouriers. Trust that I'm a stubborn bitch that's only here to thwart Davorles.'

Itraya huffled a laugh and shook her head. 'Ah, to the entombed hells with it.'

* * *

Geil, leading Lira's Talon, followed Itraya in a short flight towards the Senate's dome, where they landed near the apex. Through the darkened oculus at its peak, Geil saw that at least two scores of senators – some of them Dreamers, others just powerful merchants – were being held captive, blindfolded and with their hands tied behind their backs. Two Stone-Masks kept them under heavy watch, and palace guards manned a barricade in the hallway that led to the main entrance.

Misshapen Nightmares, twisted gargoyles with still-human faces and half a dozen stone arms, stood guard at the circulate colonnade. In the centre of the Senate floor, Lady Malvedra addressed her captives like a teacher scolding unruly children.

'How do we do this?' Itraya asked.

'I strike from above, and you storm the gates,' Geil suggested.

'If we fail, the Falconess and the hostages will end up dead,' Itraya warned her.

'Then let's not fail,' Geil replied.

Itraya let out a chortle.

'With me!' Geil called.

Let's break them. Let's burn them, the Drake snarled.

She Dreamt herself thick armour, strong arms and sturdy claws. And then, she smashed the oculus glass and dived down.

From behind the basilica's main nave, some of the palace guards fired crossbows at her and the cadets. Geil ducked to avoid a bolt and then barely had time to veer away from lightning fired from an arm-thunderer.

Chunks of masonry fell behind her as she pressed forwards.

'You damned upst—' Lady Malvedra cursed loudly before Geil landed on her, knocking her out.

'Hit the gates!' Geil yelled at Lira and the cadets as they glided towards the entrance, unleashing fire and lightning to scatter the guards there.

One of the stone Nightmares came at Geil like a loping bear. Geil held her ground and, at the last moment, leapt upwards, propelling herself with her wings and her Skycourier armour. The stone arms reached for her, barely missing her ankle. Then she dived between the Nightmare's shoulders, toppling its overextended body. Crossbow bolts came whizzing at her, and Geil hit the Senate's floor, rolling until she struck one of the senators' stone seats. Taking cover behind it, she heard the gates finally being blown open.

'For the Falconess, for Onyxia!' Itraya cried. She was the first through the gates. The Skycouriers she'd gathered came in on her heels, hurling javelins at the guards in their path.

The Stone-Masks unleashed their large Nightmares on them, trying to stanch the wound they'd opened, but Itraya was unstoppable. Engulfed in a flaming halo and swinging her broadsword with the fury of a gale, they were unable to get past her.

'I have your back!' Geil called.

Rallying Lira's cadets again, Geil led another charge, now on the Stone-Masks themselves.

One summoned his stone Nightmare to shield him. Geil rushed them, ramming the many-armed monstrosity, then dancing out of its reach as it toppled onto its master.

When Itraya reached the second Stone-Mask and ran him through with her sword, the remaining palace guards threw down their weapons and surrendered.

From behind a cracked stone senatorial seat, the Falconess emerged, spitting the last of the rope she'd chewed through.

'It's good to see you again, Falconess,' Geil said.

'It's good to see you too, Drakelet, even if you've been gambling with my neck.'

'Apologies, Falconess. You know how good I am at rolling the dice and making dramatic entrances.'

Mathana's lips curled first into a grin but then broke into a burst of croaky laughter. 'Now tell me, Drakelet, what took you so long?'

Geil was about to explain when a great rumble shook them, momentarily freezing their movement.

It wasn't an explosion like the ones they'd heard throughout the palace. It was more like a cavernous roar carried by the wind. But what could—

'Lady Morvander!' Lira landed by her side. 'The vortex in the Scab is getting worse!'

'He's unleashed his shard of the Mantle,' the Falconess surmised.

'What is he trying to do though? Use it as a distraction?'

'I fear it might be worse than that. *This* might have been the distraction. Whether he ever intended to stage a coup or not doesn't matter; he's moved on to a different game, and if he's got a losing hand, he'll burn the entire deck.' The Falconess pursed her lips.

Before Geil could answer, Mathana placed a gloved hand on her shoulder. 'You listen to me now. I'm old. Old enough to know this city won't be the same. There's no going back, only forwards. Are you certain you want to enter this new world?'

There was no hesitation when Geil answered, 'I am.'

'Then let's go. Lead us, and we will follow.'

Chapter Fifty-Four

Ash

Repent and you'll receive the swift deliverance of unbirth. Rebel and meet Her grim embrace.

– Graffiti near the Scab's old slaughterhouse

HEADING SOUTH, ASH CLUNG TO the gunwale hard enough to turn his knuckles white, letting the cool air wake his sore muscles.

Behind him, the *Night Swan*'s deck swarmed with Geil and all of the Skycouriers that had flocked to her banner. Not just Lira and the other cadets but also the Couriermaster herself and twenty of her Skycouriers, many injured and exhausted.

He'd fought alongside them, or rather helped some of them contain the Traditionalist mobs at the palace's entrances. He'd Dreamt mud walls and pulled up the water of the canals into rolling waves. For the most part, he'd avoided being injured, except for a brick that had hit him in the chest, which was now sore and bruised. His brain burned with the effort, and he felt dizzy, on the verge of physical collapse.

And yet, he also felt exhilarated, brimming with inspiration. For far too long, he'd been fighting just to survive, but today, he was fighting for others, as a Dreamer, yes, but for the people he loved, both his family and the city. The air felt charged with a crispness that spoke of possibility.

The *Night Swan* glided into the Southern Quarter's grey skies, heading once again into the fray.

Omen grew even more restless and began breathing heavily, despite Ash's attempt to reassure him. He seemed fixated on the ominous vortex that hovered above the Crumbling Quarter. Was it wider than before? Seagulls, sparrows and crowcats cried and fled in swarms from it. Even daylight looked like it was being sucked in.

Below, Onyxia writhed in pain.

From the skyship's deck, Ash watched the streets, trapped in complete pandemonium.

The onyx lionheads spread throughout the city screamed. Their roars rolled from the south in waves. At least, most people they'd encountered had abandoned the street skirmishes and run, seeking shelter inside houses.

Those who'd remained in the streets seemed to have grown even more brutal and feral. Reason had crumbled, leaving only rabid beasts that growled, howled and killed. On a balcony, two men wearing the Traditionalists' blue fought to strangle each other, their shared allegiance forgotten. Below, a sizeable group tore at each other's flesh with only their nails and teeth as weapons.

Geil had explained that this was what the Mantle did: it crept into your brain, digging out all the fears and nightmares you kept hidden from yourself, only to vomit them back into you.

Nightmares were spontaneously sprouting, fresh from the terrified minds of not just whatever Dreamer the Mantle had caught in itself but also from many of the common folk that were, at that moment, little more than children casting their night terrors into the streets.

At the Barley Market, a baker was furiously hacking at his cart, now filled with pearly, crab-like creatures instead of loaves. A few yards away, a guard collapsed to his knees covered in black spores and started seizing. Not far off, an old woman ran over a bridge, naked except for the flames that burned over her skin to what seemed her great delight. Grey sludge centipedes crawled up the facades of buildings while hairy spiders picked their way through corpses and slugs with human faces oozed in the canals. This wasn't Onyxia anymore, it was a Nightmare-ridden landscape.

Ash searched for Geil, who was in a war council with the others.

'Couriermaster Mathana will create a distraction by swooping in from above, while . . .' She turned to face him. 'Ash?'

'I need a word,' he said.

Geil took him aside, not far from where Rudher and Yaisa were talking to some Skycouriers. 'If this is about your friends, don't worry. They can stay behind.'

Ash shook his head. 'It's Dae. She was planning on heading to the Scab to fight the root of the Wilting.'

'And you're worried that with the Mantle being unleashed on the streets . . .'

'Yes.'

Geil opened her mouth, but then let out a loud sigh. 'Pity. We could have used you taking down Davorles, but go. Make sure she's safe.'

'Thank you, Geil.'

'Don't thank me yet. I'll need someone to come to our rescue if everything goes to hell in the palace.'

* * *

As soon as the *Night Swan* dropped them off near the old slaughterhouse, Geil took her cadets into the waterways, while Ash started towards the vortex swirling above them.

Omen bolted, running ahead with a determined trot, only to stop and turn around at a bridge to make sure Ash was following.

Whatever this was, he had a plan.

'Go ahead, friend. I'm with you.'

They ran into the depths of the Scab.

Chapter Fifty-Five

Geil

Everything that dreams can be tormented. The better tailored the harrowing, the deeper the nightmares.
– *Instruction of the Hordemaster* by Master Davorles

GEIL SWAM DEEPER INTO THE canal beneath Davorles's palace alongside Mavis and Lira's Talon.

This time, she'd taken the cautious approach. No point in reusing the same entry point as before. She hoped the Mantle didn't reach here.

They'd emerged onto the water stairs of an internal dock. As she'd suspected, this too showed signs of often, recent use: fresh ropes, clean docks, even a lone, dimmed orb-lamp.

One of the young cadets was about to crawl ahead when Mavis grabbed their arm.

'Wait until the Falconess strikes from above,' he said. While they waited, Geil instructed Lira to send her shadow-raven to scout ahead.

Now, they were finally within a stone's throw of the enemy.

After what seemed an eternity, they heard sounds of fighting in the distance. The Falconess was meant to draw Davorles's defences while they sneaked in from below. But Geil knew better than to be overconfident around the Wisp.

Lira's raven returned and perched upon its master's shoulder. She listened to its garbled croaking and then translated for the rest. 'The shadow-wisps are all flocking to the palace's heights. There are two Stone-Masks ahead.'

'Davorles?'

'I don't think so, but the upper floors of the palace are dark. Unnaturally dark. Swathed by the Mantle. My raven didn't dare go that far.'

Strange that Davorles had cornered himself this way. There had to be a trap, a twist, a catch of sorts ahead. Even so, they had to strike at what they could reach.

Cautiously, they crept forwards. The subterranean docks were devoured by cracks and black mould. They emerged into what should have been the ground floor, only to stop short at a strange sight.

Chains, spread over the walls and ceiling like a spider's web. Some must have been the oxidated and rusty chains used to slow down the collapse of the Crumbling Quarter, but others were new. Parts were nailed to the floor with thorny iron spikes. Their strange, asymmetrical links and engravings suggested they hadn't been forged but rather Dreamt.

'I know this Imprint,' Lira said. 'Master Alra, she's . . .'

'One of the Dreamchanters of torture instruments at the Academy,' Geil finished.

As they moved in the darkness, trying to avoid the web, Geil saw the whole thing was suffused with black drops, like ink, or perhaps blood. On closer inspection, they were just water droplets darkened by the mould.

Daerna had been right after all; this had been the way they'd kept the Mantle 'fed'. By channelling this mould, all the while it tormented the city. An ever-growing blaze, feeding deeper and deeper on the roots of Onyxia.

It was tempting to shatter the web, but Geil knew better than to trifle with complicated Dreamchantment patterns unless she knew exactly what the dangers were. Instead, they moved ahead, following the chains towards the tower with the dome.

They climbed up the marble steps in silence until they reached the upper floor. The abundance of frescoes, carved stuccoes and sculpted columns spoke of a proud lineage. The blackened silhouettes that inhabited the paintings now, though, showed its decline. Had Davorles grown up amidst these ruins? Easy to see where his obsession with shadows and sculpting came from if so.

Lira's raven raced back to her screeching. 'Shadow-wisps ... They're coming! We should move or they'll corner us here!' she warned.

'Hold them!' Geil commanded Lira, and hurried ahead until she reached the base of a round tower.

All of the tower's windows had been barred, so she had to rely on her Drake eyes. The chains curled like vines around the columns, reaching all the way to the darkened dome at the top, blending into a lattice made of shadows. At its centre, hovering like a gorged spider, floated Davorles.

He was engulfed by a pocket of the Mantle, and he seemed to be wrestling with it, dancing, pulling from it and against it. His pasty face sweated; his teeth were clenched like a fisherman hauling in a big catch.

She Dreamt her wings and rose in the stale air, beat them and braced herself for the impact as she entered his Mantle.

To her surprise, she was able to land on the balustrade of the spiralling stairs without feeling its pressure.

'Davorles,' she snarled.

His masked eyes fell on her, and for a second, there was a look of fatigue.

'We know what you're doing. Your coup has been defeated at the palace, and now, like the sore loser you are, you're making one last, desperate gamble to burn down the city that has proved too strong for you to tame. Is that it?'

'You're in the game, yet you still don't understand it. I've been outplayed, Geil, but not by you. If you're smart enough to have made it here, you know now is not the time ...'

Kill him, smash every bone in his body! the Drake roared.

'Not the time? Should I wait until your shard of the Mantle ravages the Southern Quarter entirely, then?' Geil replied, spreading out her claws. 'You have one last chance to surrender!'

His lips curled into a bitter smile.

'That damned Charnelite has wrestled the Mantle shard out my control! She's the one using it now. We should have known better than to deal with that treacherous fanatic.'

'How convenient that she's doing exactly what you want her to do.'

'What *I* want her to do? She's bringing her damned divinity back into our world. Come now, you must feel her too.'

'So, what, I should just let you regain control of the Mantle shard so you're the one ravaging the city? I don't think so ...'

The Drake was roaring: *Take his blood!*

She leapt for him.

Cursing, Davorles sent out a tendril of darkness to engulf her.

She whirled, skirting past it, and hurled Davorles against the wall at his back. He fumbled for a dagger in his belt, and she slammed him back a second time. Still, he managed to chuckle. 'Pity you weren't there to help poor Lanteus ...'

Geil shrieked and rammed Davorles into the wall so hard it cracked, blowing dust over them. *Kill him!* the Drake urged, and she dug her claw into his belly. Dark blood spilled out, rolling down his breeches. It was warm on her skin and even warmer inside her heart. Her muscles felt as heavy as the earth, but at least her hatred kept her nimble.

Blood ran down his chin, but that wasn't Davorles's mouth. She knew those lips, had kissed them so many times. The man in her hands was no longer the scrawny, grey-haired man who had been her master at the Academy but someone far dearer to her.

'Why did you let me go, Geil?' Lanteus asked. His eyes were devoid of light and filled with hurt and loss. Just like she remembered them. 'If we'd stayed together . . .'

The Drake thrashed inside her. *You know it's not him! Lanteus is dead! He always was too gentle-hearted, dragging us down, dragging himself down!*

He'd done this before. Or rather, his Mantle had. It made her see things, tormented her. Disguised the truth. She could only hope she was wrestling with the real him.

'I'll shut you up once and for all!'

She furiously smashed his head against the wall. A rain of dust and shards of rock fell over them both. When she released him, she expected him to collapse at her feet, but while his nose had sunk into his skull and his jaw hung loose, he was still standing.

If he wasn't dying, it was because this wasn't the real him. Or maybe it was the real him but the Mantle was playing tricks on her.

It doesn't matter! Kill this mirage, kill the real him. Tear them both apart! Kill them all! the Drake snarled.

She lurched at him, but Lanteus ducked to the side. His broken body was covered in blood, yet he moved swiftly. And she was tired. So tired. Somewhere along the way, she'd cracked scales and broken claws. Her whole hand burned with pain.

She thought she heard someone calling for her, but she ignored the voice. *Bring down the tower and there's no way he'll survive. Bury us all alive if that's what it takes!* the Drake demanded.

'Fear not, love, we'll soon be reunited,' Lanteus said, and she caught his throat with a claw. But despite the dark blood flowing from the slice, he stabbed her in the arm before dancing away. She roared in pain and anger, but when she threw herself at him, he spun out of reach, forcing them both to circle as they tried to find an opening.

'Geil!' the nagging voice repeated. Was it Mavis?

The Drake growled. *Don't listen to that cowering, pathetic thing.*

She listened to the Drake. It was the only one strong enough to carry her through all of this. It always had been. She just had to let it fill every thought in her head, pump its acid blood through her veins, cover her heart with scales.

She feigned a stumble, and her opponent leapt at her back. She spun at the last moment, wrapping her arms around his neck and her legs around his arms. He wasn't going to escape her, not this time. She squeezed hard, hoping to crush his windpipe – except her adversary wasn't Lanteus anymore.

The mangled creature she'd caught was herself. Skin cracked and broken, bleeding to death from a dozen cuts. Somehow, she was still alive, smiling at herself with bloodied teeth.

'We both know you won't do it,' the other her choked out. 'No matter how much you hurt, you've always been too much of a coward to just end it!'

But the Drake was willing to see it through. It had the strength she lacked. She just had to let go, to give in, to burn through her weak shell of humanity once and for all.

She could still hear someone calling for her. She couldn't shake their voice, nor the fear that she wasn't seeing the whole picture. Her brain was sluggish and she felt she was trapped in one of Davorles's games, like she'd been forced to play at the Academy.

She tried Dreaming her eyes anew, to read the shadows for her former master, but ... she couldn't. The Drake wouldn't relinquish its hold over them.

What are you doing? Focus! Finish the deed! Kill him a thousand times if that's what it takes!

Her arm tightened against her will, and, trembling, Geil forced herself to hold still. Clenching her teeth until it felt like her jaw was about to snap, she wrestled enough control back from the Drake to reshape one of her eyes. It wasn't much, but it was enough.

The icy cloud of darkness wasn't just obscuring everything, it was also pouring into her lungs and twisting her head.

Just kill him first. If that coward Mavis can't hold on until then, he doesn't deserve to survive!

'Lady Geil!'

Another voice again, coming from below. This time it was Lira, calling for her.

Mavis too. 'Geil, we have to leave!'

The Talon needed her help, and they needed it now.

If they aren't strong enough to save themselves, let them sink! Let them all die so we can finally kill Davorles! Bring this whole palace down if that's what it takes!

Geil's blood curdled at the Drake's thoughts. When had it started to sound exactly like Davorles?

What was the point of all this strength if she was to become him? To sacrifice everyone else for revenge?

Lungs burning, she released her prey and stumbled down the circular stairway. Everything hurt, and without the rage powering her, she was just a broken body at the end of her rope.

And yet, despite the pain of a thousand blades every time she took a step, she soldiered on, floundering towards the Talon of cadets and Mavis – her own Talon-mate.

She could see them ahead, fighting, desperately banding together to hold against the oncoming slaughter of the shadows.

'Leaving so soon, my dear?' This time, it was clearly Davorles's voice. He sounded close, but she couldn't pinpoint his exact location.

Not that she'd stop to fight him. She wasn't him. She was getting out. She was getting the cadets out. She was getting Mavis out, like Lanteus would want her to.

And as she took another step away from him, from this man she hated, who had taken so much from her, she snapped out of it. Shook out of the Mantle's hold on her mind.

'What a disappointment you've turned out to be. Lanteus was too brave and Mavis too gentle, but you, you had the needed ruthlessness in you. You could have been here, helping me. Yet your idiotic meddling has cost us.' Davorles stood on the stairs above, the Mantle dispersing quickly. His nose was gushing blood. Maybe some of her blows had landed on the real him after all. 'The city won't just be remade; it'll be a Vigil-blighted ossuary. That crazed Charnelite is going to turn every single being in this city into a new host for her mad goddess.'

'Should have run when you could,' Geil replied, tensing her stance. The Drake's vigour was fading from her bones, but a cooler kind of anger still endured, a flame at the centre of her own heart.

'Fear not, there's still time for me. Can't say the same about you.'

The temperature plummeted, and her limbs grew numb. She soon saw why: a swirling vortex of shadow-wisps were converging, encroaching on her from all angles. Coalescing to crush her with their cruel blizzard of hatred.

The spiral surged towards her, the icy darkness swallowing her.

She sheltered herself with her arms, but what good were scales for that? What could she burn with her dwindling flame?

She was going to fail them all.

She couldn't think anymore. The cold was creeping into her very mind, freezing who she was, erasing her under its stone-like frost.

'Geil!' Mavis called. His voice was a dull echo, coming from below.

'Lady Geil!' Lira's voice. 'Hold on! We won't leave you!'

Her Drake eye saw a bright flare. Someone was wielding a sword of fire, and like a phoenix, it crashed against the icy serpent.

Despite the fact that they were barely still standing, they were willing to risk their lives for her. If they hadn't given up, who was she to do so?

She harnessed whatever little of herself she still had. Her hatred was spent, but there was that little flame in her own heart – hope. Hope that there were enough brave souls willing to take up the fight, to protect each other, to burn together even when facing sheer hatred.

The Drake might be enough to survive, but if she had to lean on others in order to save those in trouble, that was a price she was willing to pay.

The fire began inside her belly, dry like a burning coal. She held it, feeding the flame, until it was enough. She let it radiate to the surface. Her scales were sturdy, but to fight the cold of Davorles's shadow-wisps, she had to become something else.

She shed her scales for the ruby feathers of a firebird, warm as a blaze but impervious to ice, burning through the darkness.

He was right . . . We're too weak. You're too weak. This will break you, the Drake warned her.

But she wasn't afraid. She was willing to break, maybe even die, to burn brighter than those who wanted to drown her. Scars, shards and cracks – she could work with those if that's what it took. So long as she could keep Dreaming – keep living – she could become something new.

'Brace yourselves!' she shouted.

The cadets threw themselves to the ground.

She filled the chamber with her fire, with the firebird's flame, burning like a conflagration and cutting a fiery hole in the night.

The spiral of shadow-wisps shrank, collapsing in on itself. It lashed at her with a dozen icy claws, but it couldn't cut deep enough, nor cold enough, to stop her fire.

She heard a roar – not hers but Davorles's as he tried to rise above her. But this time, he was constrained by the frailty of his own shape, his view made narrow by the mask. As the fire engulfed them, the whole world shimmered, and she finally caught a glimpse of him, raising his arms to defend himself. He shrieked as his mask cracked, and then he fell into a still silence on the floor. His mask had shattered into a hundred pieces.

Chapter Fifty-Six

Daerna

Spare us sinful breathing,
Deliver us to your healing silence,
To the loud clamour of the grave,
Grant us the gift of your unbirth.

– Ancient Charnelite psalm

DAERNA GASPED FOR AIR, BUT breathing was like fighting a giant fist clutched around her middle. Filling her lungs took all her effort.

A loud crack made Daerna freeze. For a second, she feared it was something of hers that had shattered, but from the ground, she saw that Pierla had swung her sword at the Midwife and sent her staggering backwards.

Now, she could breathe again. She could think. Around her, her companions crawled to their knees.

Pierla slammed the blade against the Midwife's face again, sending some of her teeth flying. When she tried to lift her clawed hand, Pierla hacked at that as well. 'You think you have any right to take more from the world? Curse your miserable, rotten heart!' she screamed.

Coughing, Daerna went to help Dirdra to her feet, while Indre did the same with Roshia.

'Ignore the canticle,' Dirdra said, catching her breath. 'To reach the city like Daerna has, the canticles won't work, but the Motherstorm will listen to you if you give Her something powerful, something to draw Her away from the misery.'

Daerna looked at her in confusion. 'What?'

'When you healed Roshia, you didn't use a canticle, Daerna. You always had a gift, and now it's led you to find a new path. You must walk it, weave yourself into your own song. And we must use it to call on Her to aid us.'

'Daerna!' Pierla yelled.

She'd been hacking at the broken Midwife, cornering her, but the hanged men were now swinging violently. In unison, the ropes snapped.

Pierla turned and slashed at one and then another. They fell, only to rise again. Heaving, Pierla manoeuvred to stand in their way in a defensive stance. 'Whatever you're doing, hurry up!'

If this was really the Charnel Mother reaching from beyond the veil, they were already lost. Divine Geleisdra wasn't here, nor was her winged guardian. How would Daerna be able to fight something so immense, so terrible?

The only thing they could do was to reach for the Motherstorm's aid again, but how, without the canticles?

Dirdra and Roshia formed the chorus, while Indre gathered some loose cobblestones and started throwing them at the rotting corpses that encroached on Pierla.

In the distance, the lionheads still roared in pain.

Theirs was a hollow song, devoid of breath but winged by despair. Their misery, the city's misery, was loud as the heavens, as mighty as the mountains.

Dirdra began a base with her deep voice, and Roshia joined in, but even as close as she was, Daerna could barely hear them. The chorus of lionheads was drowning them out.

They couldn't rise above them.

Still, she didn't give up. No matter the odds, she rejected their furious, broken dream. Because she *chose* to believe in something else. That even despite misery and despair, life was worth living. She rejected them because her art had given her a way of fighting the meaningless of it all, of taking back from loss itself.

She might not be able to sing louder than the lionheads, but perhaps there was a way of making the city listen by sharing a piece of her own heart with it.

So there, in the dark, with nothing to offer but her truth, she sang. Except this time, she sang her own song.

She sang, her voice as tense as a bowstring about to snap. She poured her heart into it – her misery, her exhaustion and her dread turned rebellious hope. Hope that she could reach what lay beyond, something that could defeat the hollowness of the lionheads' roar. Something that could ease pain and erase misery.

It lacked lyrics, but not a soul. She poured her emotions into the patterns and scales, all the grief she'd witnessed, all the suffering and anger. And above all, she poured in her own pain, transforming it into something else.

She felt something coil around her ribs and chose to ignore it. The same sharp hand that she'd felt scratching at her skull and the edge of her mind was now wrapping around her lungs.

Threatening to cut her in two.

But she didn't stop. She didn't stop singing, because in the singing, she could rise above her own pain. Because if she was to die, this was the best way to do so, soaring on the wings of her song.

Chapter Fifty-Seven

Ash

Imagination is the fire that never dies. It lights blazes that not even death will put down.

– *A Hidden History of Arvira* by Bekah of Belba

OMEN CLEARLY KNEW WHERE HE was going as he ran ahead, leading Ash over the bridges and twisted streets of the Scab.

Risking glances at the sky, Ash saw the vortex worsen as the lionheads cried their dull roars of pain. It resembled the Motherstorm's birthing throes, except this was sickly and far more sinister. The vortex opened into a thick and still obscurity. It wasn't the mournful black of storm clouds; this was a hollow night, the black belly of a beast.

Strange to think that just a few months ago, Omen had been created on a night similar but so different to this one.

Omen was the first to catch the sounds of singing and sped up, and Ash struggled after him. The islet they'd entered, brutally ravaged by time as it was, now offered the strangest of miracles. Dust rose from the ground in columns, black sand falling upwards. He felt lightheaded as he slowed his run.

Nothing could explain this. The world had been turned upside down. Rain was now onyx dust rising into the heavens, instead of clear raindrops falling from the skies.

Omen lowered himself into a hunter's stance, crouching as if stalking prey.

Ash squatted behind the panther. Ahead, he could hear Daerna singing, but also the clanging and thudding of fighting. He crept forwards until he could see, amidst broken columns, Daerna singing, raising her hands to the heavens, oblivious to what was coming at her.

Dirdra and Roshia stood by her side, while a tall Whisperer threw cobbles at a group of men hounding Pierla. Except they weren't men, but half-rotten carcasses.

Pierla fought well, swinging a sword in big arcs, keeping the blade in perpetual motion, to hold them at bay. Until one of the dead men took a daring step forwards and the blade fell and lodged in his shoulder. He let out a growl of pain, grabbing the cross-guard with his free hand to hold the sword. The rest swarmed Pierla.

Ash entered into the Dreaming.

Reality rippled like a pond that had been darkened with oily blood. It was permeable, making it easier to create something larger, more unnatural.

He needed to weave fast. He worked quickly, pulling blinding lighting from memory, sharpening it with the hungry despair that permeated the air like sweat, wrestling with it to cage it into the blade in Pierla's hand. It burned in him, through *him, and then he released it into the fray.*

From the Dreaming trance, the skirmish was a blur. One moment Pierla was down on one knee, the next she was swinging her sword in lateral strikes over her head with two hands. Embedded with the lightning's wrath, the blade cut fiercely.

As soon as Pierla was free from the threat of the corpses, Ash fell back to his body. He was tired, his head throbbed with the effort, and he had to lean against the wall not to fall. Then he saw an unmistakable gaunt figure. The same woman Daerna had described to him after her attack: twisted features, elongated phalanges and archaic tunic. She cursed at Ash in an old Iskian he was only barely able to comprehend. The Charnelite Midwife.

Out of the plumes of smoke, something took shape: mantis-like, except with dust pressed into a long ribcage of a body, a fanged skull for a head and a dozen forelegs of sharp bone.

The huge bone-mantis came skittering at him. Ash fumbled for his weapon but realised with choking dread the futility of the motion as the spindly Nightmare rose to impale him with half its hooked limbs.

Omen struck it from the side, and the two went rolling, desperate to tear into each other.

The Midwife, indifferent to their efforts, raised an engraved golden skull to the heavens, praying in Ancient Iskian.

Despite her wounds, her shining face looked elated at some impending apotheosis. Ash hurled himself back into the Dreaming.

The air in the Dreaming was foul, infested with hate and the stench of death. The Midwife gleamed inside it, radiant and blissful in its embrace. She swayed and danced and reached for the heavens. And the heavens reached back.

A colossal figure ripped its way into being above the courtyard. Outside the Dreaming, the Charnel Mother might be invisible, but here She was a towering giant, cutting into the fabric of the world.

Just gazing upon Her hurt. He could taste blood on his lips as the Mantle's shards cut into his brain.

Only Daerna offered some respite against her suffocating presence. Her song was a small hearth in the night, enough to cast some light but not enough to erase her intrusion. At least not by herself.

But she wasn't alone.

He reached boldly for her song. He didn't need to centre himself, only carry her song's truth, no matter how bloody and painful.

He'd burned through all his energy, and hatred wouldn't sustain him. But in his soul, he carried the dreams of others.

His inspiration was his father's dream to illuminate the world and nourish every mind with the truth.

His inspiration was Omen's unbending courage, his stubborn unwillingness to give up when he was protecting someone. Instinctively, as when he'd Dreamt Omen, he shaped this Dream like a great cat, this one like Geleisdra's guardian of old.

And with this new-found energy, he carried Daerna's song, the truth bleeding into a Dream of lightning. It didn't need to be louder than the city's roars of pain, because it could speak to the Motherstorm in its very own language. It could be a messenger shaped of pure and blinding firstfall-lightning, its roar surpassing any storm.

For a moment, the lion's great eyes looked into him, and he felt he hadn't so much as Dreamt the creature as called for him.

With his last effort, Ash set him loose. Then the lion spread his radiant wings and leapt towards the heavens.

The vortex lashed at him as he ascended, carrying Daerna's song, but he was too strong, too fierce to be restrained, and he burned through their embrace. When he reached the Motherstorm, the skies lit up, entire and bright.

Silver sprites of lightning tore apart the vortex and garnet rain-drops followed, cutting through the colossal figure of smoke that was the Charnel Mother.

Fire filled his vision, purifying and magnificent, before everything went black. And then his vision dissolved.

Chapter Fifty-Eight

Daerna

. . . Of the people she loved, more were dead than alive. That's when she realised she was afraid, not just of forgetting but of the eternal heartache filling her chest. She feared that the loss would be the only thing she recalled, instead of the lost themselves. Thus, she decided the Song of Sorrows *wasn't enough. That remembrance wasn't enough. That her quest to heal the world would only end when death itself was undone and removed from existence.*

– The Life of Divine Geleisdra, the Solemn Princess
by Blessed Elpia

DAERNA HAD GIVEN HERSELF OVER to the singing, ignoring the world around her. The roar, the dust, the Midwife's own dark psalms, she forced it all out.

The shattered courtyard's acoustics helped amplify her voice, and she felt the ascending plumes of dust slow. It was a miracle, this thread connecting life and death, stone and storm, yet not what they needed now.

She needed something else, like Dirdra had said: to make the city listen to her. To believe that healing was possible, that its broken bones could be mended, that hope could take root and blossom, even here. Especially here, since the Scab was fashioned out of grief, of guilt, of sheer despair.

Daerna reached inside herself, just as Dirdra had said, for everything that made her who she was: her longing to stop the Wilting, her yearning for Ash's lips, her unabashed joy at having saved Roshia. Her resolute will at fighting to save those afflicted. Her anger at those who'd leave them behind.

Intoning only melodies that mattered to her, she elevated her yearning and hope. Part of her felt ashamed to sing them to the world, especially when it seemed to be crumbling around her.

Even then, she wanted to believe that Dirdra was right. That the city might listen to her and to her small, humble dreams.

She drew hope from all of them, like water from a stone. Hope against reason, *beyond* reason. Desire for a peaceful future for everyone in the city. A boldness to reject the inevitability of misery.

As she sang and the others followed, she felt their song finally reaching high enough, loud enough. Touching the Motherstorm's heart above.

The thunder roared, loud enough to shake their hearts in their chests and make them tremble.

Even the lionheads went quiet, cowering, and the plumes of dust dispersed.

The Midwife faltered, and Daerna risked a glance around her without ceasing her song.

Omen was there, bleeding on one flank, keeping a grotesque, mantis-like Nightmare at bay, a terrible thing of bone and blades that, even half broken by the panther's claws, fought on.

Yet she wasn't afraid; in fact, she felt her head clearing, her heart elevating again to the Motherstorm's sublime heights. Above, she saw shimmering flashes of lightning converging around the vortex.

Her hands rose and swayed with the Motherstorm's celestial dance. Below, her feet remained grounded, anchoring her to the city.

The Midwife hissed. 'Insolent child! This shall not be undone!' She held the golden skull above her head and renewed her prayers with desperate fervour.

Indre went to help Pierla, bruised and bloody, but all Daerna could focus on was the Midwife's golden skull.

The Motherstorm was swallowing the vortex now, and she'd felt the skies clear, but the other presence, the choking fumes of the Charnel Mother, suddenly redoubled.

It was as if She'd descended from the heavens into the courtyard, and the golden skull took on a sickly radiance, glowing with black flame.

Daerna felt the long-curled claws of death reaching into her, trying to carve their way through. The world was a blurry, dark picture around her, shattered glass held together only by the thinnest of threads.

It threatened to collapse on her, to crush her soul into pieces, but still she sang.

She should have been afraid, but instead felt liberated. She was the axis, the bridge elevating the city's grief to the Motherstorm's soothing solace. But she was also their anger.

Her song weaved in passages of the Righteous Thunder, and the rain began falling, loud, angry drops smashing against the muddy ground.

'Take her!' the Midwife screeched. 'Reap her heart!'

The black flame that wreathed the golden skull ignited in the corpses, and though they lay headless and mangled on the floor, somehow, at her command, they began moving again. Chopped limbs crawled like bugs, any pretence of resurrection now dispelled. The mantis-limbed Nightmare also managed to pull itself forwards, with whatever bone arms still remained.

Daerna breathed in, summoning the fury at what they'd done to the Scab, the Broken Arches and Little Vespiria. It'd been bottled up inside her all along, and now she could harness it and turn it on one of those responsible.

Swathes of rain became hail, striking the Midwife's Nightmares. Sharp rocks of ice fell, snapping limbs and tearing rotten flesh. The many-legged monstrosity tried to clamber forwards, only to be impaled by a javelin-like piece of ice that nailed it to the ground. This time, when Omen leapt on it, it came apart like a tattered doll.

Around her, her friends were only soaked, the hail turning to water the moment it neared them. Dirdra, encouraged, joined in her chorus, and then so did Roshia. Indre shielded the wounded Pierla with her body.

The golden skull flickered, the black flame guttering. The Midwife tucked it away protectively into her ancient dress, perhaps unwilling to lose that piece of the Charnel Mother´s power completely, then ran at Daerna, the hail unable to do anything but slow her down. Her claws spread, the same ones that had almost killed Daerna once. She should have been afraid; instead, she focused her fury on her.

The barrage of hail that followed was so brutal that even the Midwife, in all her might, fell to her knees.

Through the shroud of icy downpour, Daerna saw the Midwife's eyes burning black with hatred. Her face was bloodied, her lips torn, her teeth broken.

And then she was gone, crawling through a dark archway and into the night.

Whatever had been growing in the skies above blew away like tattered mist.

As the dust settled, Daerna saw that the patches of naked rock around her were smooth and cleaned, the scabs and mould peeled away.

Epilogue

Bleeding and crying are the price of living on. Blood can be replenished, tears can refill the eye. Cry to your heart's content, for it is breath that can't be replaced.

– Old Remaker proverb

When ash came back to his senses, he was in one of the beds on the *Night Swan*'s lower deck. He opened his eyes to find Omen looking at him expectantly.

'Omen!' He threw open his arms for the panther, and Omen bumped his head against Ash's.

'I missed you too,' he said, hugging his friend.

Omen began making a deep, rumbling sound. It took Ash a moment to realise the panther was purring.

Everything swayed when Ash stood, but he managed to find a jug of water that helped to dispel some of the hammering in his head. Then, with Omen stuck to his side, he dragged his feet onto the deck to discover that the ship was docked at the Grand Palace's Sky Pavilion. A dozen other skyships surrounded them, Lady Saorla's *Burning Dawn* among them.

He disembarked, avoiding the bustling ship crews, as well as the Skycouriers guarding prisoners on the rooftop. At least the city seemed at peace. He couldn't make out much with it being the dead of night, but he felt the Motherstorm raining placidly. Where were Daerna and the others?

He reached the Sky Pavilion's main hall, now an impromptu hospital with dozens of wounded lying across the wooden tables. Omen quickly took off without explanation, and Ash chased after the creature into what looked like a mess hall for the Skycouriers' barracks.

At the very end of the room, hunched over some sort of drink, was a Sister. Omen trotted towards her.

Daerna turned, and Ash's heart took what felt like its first beat since they'd parted. They ran towards each other and collided like two waves in the middle of the room. He threw his arms around her, and she him, and they clung to each other, kissing breathlessly.

There weren't any words, only joy and relief.

* * *

The rapping on the door forced Geil awake. She rolled out of bed and put on her wrinkled shirt before opening it.

'We're ready to leave,' Captain Bentor said.

'Wait for me,' she replied.

She closed the door and hurriedly put on some boots.

'What is it?' Liadra mumbled, half asleep.

After two whole days of running around the Grand Palace's chancelleries and the Senate floor, they were both exhausted. There'd been many testimonies to give, much evidence to share and many more accusations to make.

Luckily, for now, it seemed Lord Stalcar was on their side. He'd been only too happy to claim some of the merit for their efforts, and his clamouring for both disbanding the Academy and harnessing its power against a full war with the King of Thorns was now louder than ever.

The Wisp was done for. He'd been locked in the worst sarcophagus at the bottom of the Deep Wells while he waited for his trial and certain execution. His Stone-Masks had either been arrested or were dead. The Hordemasters and the city watch members who'd followed his commands, though, claimed to have been following a legitimate authority, so, despite some protestations, they received pardons, as had those who'd joined in with the street mobs. The rule of the Senate had been revealed as surprisingly brittle, but Lady Saorla claimed she needed to consolidate her power before deeper actions could be taken.

The thorny matter of how to deal with the Academy remained. Grandmaster Ranndra had denied any knowledge of Lord Davorles's actions, so a thorough investigation was needed. If they didn't prove their innocence, Lord Stalcar would have their heads, and most likely they'd revolt before that, which was why Geil had volunteered for a duty she'd never expected.

This was the best chance she'd get at forcing them to change their ways. Yet it would also mean walking into the Nightmares' nest to poke them and then sleep by their side.

'I'm just going to say goodbye,' Geil explained.

'I'll come too. I just need a minute.'

'Take your time.' Geil pressed a warm kiss on Liadra's golden curls.

She hurried up the Quietude's cold passageways. At least the exhaustion helped dull the pain of her wounds and the soreness in her muscles.

Still rubbing her eyes, she emerged onto the balcony that led to the skywharf. From the arcade, Tarna watched over Bentor's crew loading up the *Night Swan*, but there was no sign of Ragdra or her mother.

Before Geil could ask the door warden, something slammed against her back.

In her old skin, the ever-paranoid Drake would have reacted violently, or at least, quickly disentangled. The firebird burned at a slower pace, and she had time to catch Ragdra's scent of warm pastries. Geil gently turned to face the girl's embrace.

'Easy with my ribs,' she protested.

'Sorry,' Ragdra said, immediately loosening her hold.

The clothes she'd borrowed from Geil were too baggy on her, and she had a spot of clotted cream at the edge of her lips, but other than that, she seemed as good as she could be.

'You promise you'll come visit?'

'Ragdra, I'll be busy these next few months—'

'No, no excuses!'

Not so long ago, Geil had lied to her about their odds of meeting again. But now, she wasn't afraid of their re-encounter. In fact, it was a consolation to think that this wasn't the last they'd see of each other.

'I promise I'll make every effort.' And then, seeing Ragdra's long face, 'And if we haven't seen each other by the end of summer, I'll send the *Night Swan* to bring you over for a few weeks. You can spend harvest season with us.'

'You promise?'

'I promise.'

'You'll teach me how to grow wings as well?'

'I promise I'll teach you a thing or two about flying,' Geil replied.

'Swear it on the bird?' she said, proudly displaying the wristband with the silver charm of the firebird that Geil had given her months ago.

'But how do you . . . ? Didn't the recruiters take it from you?'

'You told me not to let anybody take it, and I've been practising my Dreaming with it,' she said with a mischievous smile.

Geil leaned over, beaming proudly, and kissed the charm.

Ragdra hugged her again. Geil felt a fire burning inside her, one that, unlike the Drake's, didn't burn with anger but the clean, fresh feeling of a life starting anew.

* * *

'This it?' Rudher asked. He was seated on the stairs that descended into the basement. Omen groomed himself at his feet.

The cold cellar sprawled in front of them, musty and badly lit despite the bronze streaks in the skies outside, but Ash couldn't help but be delighted by its possibilities.

'This is it!' Ash said, spreading his arms. 'Enough to fit a large printing press, and perhaps even its own type foundry!'

'I don't get it,' Daerna said, stroking Omen's thick fur. 'Of all the places in the city, why here? I thought you hated the Craghorn.'

'I did hate my life here, but this isn't about me.'

Ash leaned closer to one of the narrow windows that opened at street level. He could barely make out the outside world through the soot. But what he could see was the hurried pace of those who were still afraid, the slow drag of those with a heavy heart.

'It's also time to finish what my father started. If we're to build a different future, we need the right tools. Weapons build empires, but we need ideas to build what will come after.' Ash could imagine his father beside him. 'I say it's time to seed some.'

'Printing what, exactly?' Rudher replied.

Smiling despite himself, he turned to face his friends. 'Books, of course! Little books, dense books, whimsical and philosophical, written and Dreamt. All of them!'

Yaisa clapped her hands, sending dust pluming over the pile of wooden crates she'd been examining. 'You're really set on this?' she asked. 'I thought you'd stay and keep working for mighty Lord Morvander.'

Ash looked at Daerna, who offered an encouraging nod. She already knew everything about his upcoming trip and the risks associated with it. It was strange to think he'd be leaving not to evade conscription but to aid an Oneirocrat. At least the High Council had awarded him a dispensation on account of his service. He was free from that shadow forever.

'Of course we want to help him finish his work on the mirrormatter. But we can't count on the Oneirocrats, or even the guilds, to fight all of our battles. Especially right now.'

'But we stopped the coup! What's so bad about right now?' Yaisa asked.

'Haven't you heard, lass?' Rudher said. 'People say we'll see either an uprising headed by the Academy or a war with Delectia before the year is over. Possibly both, if everything they say about the Wisp is true. Lad, are you sure it's wise to get mixed up in politics?'

Ash sighed. 'My plan is only to help the Craghorn find new dreams, better dreams for our future. Either way, you can all see why I'm going to need you to help me.'

'Help you? Doing what?' Yaisa asked.

'Are you offering us work? We don't need no charity, lad.' Rudher arched an eyebrow.

'Not charity but good, honest work. As for the what . . . How about helping me run this place? And more importantly: keeping me sane.'

'Can't let you turn into another floor-foot, can we?' Rudher chuckled. 'You know you can count on us, lad. You don't need to pay for our time.'

'I know. But I mean it. The upcoming months will be difficult. And I could use you two to watch my back. So, what do you say?'

'If the pay's good . . .' Rudher mused.

'It won't be,' Ash replied teasingly.

'Ach . . . You drive a hard bargain, Master Printer. What say you, Yaisa?'

'I say we'd better discuss this with some ale.' She winked. 'Ash is paying, of course.'

* * *

Daerna's chorus closed its circle around the funerary pyre in University Square. Her throat was very sore, but she'd refused to miss this opportunity.

She was going to lead the Keening on a crucial night that signalled the beginning of the city's healing. To her, it also served as a reminder to Abbess Forlaitra and the Traditionalists in the Orders that she wouldn't be silenced.

Daerna and the others had tried warning them that the Midwife had escaped. She feared that the Charnel Mother now burned like an ember inside that golden skull and prayed to the Motherstorm that it would not prove a devouring blaze.

To her and Dirdra's shock, the Wailing Sister leadership had decried these warnings as senseless. Not only that, Prioress Balachdra had even accused them of making the entire incident up, using the tale to seek notoriety and spreading it with the help of the Wanderers.

But when Lord Morvander stepped up to back her and others had denounced Abbess Forlaitra for consorting with Davorles to allow the Charnelites free rein, the matter had become controversial enough for many voices in the Orders to question the Abbess Superiors. To appease them, a Cloistered Council had been called to meet in a month.

Abbesses and anchoresses would come from all over the Domain. The portent-readers would consult the Silver Book, and Daerna herself would be asked to testify. She just hoped it wouldn't be too late to prevent further disasters.

In the coming weeks, the Orders' politics would consume everything, but tonight she was happy to focus on their spiritual duties.

'We're ready,' Pierla said.

The Widow was among those assigned to prepare the pyre, and despite the swelling of her face, she beamed with the same cocky smile she'd worn when they'd first met. Daerna tipped her head back.

'I'm so nervous,' mumbled Roshia by her side.

'More nervous now than when we sneaked out to the Broken Arches?'

'No, but . . .'

'More than when we sneaked into the archives?'

Roshia sighed. 'I see your point.'

'You'll do fine.'

She gestured to Indre, who, in turn, invited the nearby crew of Lightning-Hunters to unleash their freshly caught lightning.

They hurled their loaded spears to the pyre, setting it ablaze. There was a collective exhalation when the fire rose in a fierce column that illuminated the square. The crowd around them was large – not just students and locals but also others who'd come from all over the plateau, the Scab and Little Vespiria.

In the days since the Charnel Mother's visitation, many had been terrified to leave their homes. Tonight, it was different. With the Motherstorm's blessing, they were challenging the night.

She looked around at the expectant faces, at the people waiting for the Wailers' song. This was a pyre for all those who had been lost, and she would lead them in remembering the sorrow and joy of those lives.

Daerna began to sing, and her chorus joined her.

She hoped the city would listen. She hoped the dead would listen too.

* * *

'Ach. Pity of a wasted night,' Rudher grumbled.

'It's only wasted if you don't shut up,' Yaisa snapped.

Ash warmly squeezed both of their shoulders. Yaisa might not understand that Rudher was ashamed of his grief, but Ash had seen his eyes glistening when he'd spoken of Ghalod.

Somebody tapped his shoulder weakly, and Ash turned to see Thalder, leaning on a staff. Deep shadows of exhaustion had grown around his eyes.

'Master! Shouldn't you still be resting?'

'The physician would agree with you, and my legs are still wobbly, but a man honours his debts.' He offered a bitter smile.

Ash helped him join their ranks.

They all lowered their heads. Even Omen, oblivious to the nuances of what they were doing, stood solemn and watchful.

They were quiet as they watched the funereal fires.

'To Ghalod!' Yaisa shouted. 'I miss you, big brother.'

'To Ghalod!' Ash raised his glass to the night sky.

He thought of Ghalod, and of all the stupid and pointless bloodshed that this had cost them. He thought of his father too, of his dreams, too big, too bold, for a humble printer.

Perhaps Ash would see them live and find a way to illuminate the people. To teach everyone who wanted to learn.

They might even be able to prevent another senseless war, or put an end to death like Lord Morvander wanted. Together, they'd reverse the river of time itself, allowing new beginnings to advance without endings.

Tonight, he was content with living on.

Acknowledgements

Every novel is a living dream made of ink and imagination. This dream is about fantasy itself, or rather about my love of fantasy, from modern and ancient epics to the pre-Raphaelite longings and dark imaginings of 90s comics and roleplaying books, all woven together with the windswept melancholy of Atlantic legends. Bringing this dream to the world required a vast number of brilliant dreamers, whom I wish to thank:

Firstly, my agent, Julie Crisp, battle-hardened warrioress and sage wizard all in one. She understood Onyxia so well that she unearthed secrets I didn't even know existed, secrets I can't wait to share with you.

Kelly Smith, human whirlwind of an editor, who conjured the perfect vision of what this book could be and worked relentlessly to make it real. Behind her stood the formidable Zaffre team and their fierce work. Special nods to Rianna Houghton for teaching me some of the ropes and Toby Selwyn for lending me his dexterous copyediting blade.

Jeanne Cavelos, lady of wonder and possibly the best teacher of imagination and Dreamcraft I could have ever asked for. Also, my Odyssey '16 family, whose talent and feedback taught me so much. Special mention to the Tomatoes: Joshua Johnson, Rebecca Kuang, Farah Naz Rishi, Jeremy Sim and Richard Errington. Not only did they read early drafts of this book, but also helped me find paths through its many labyrinths. Their own incredible books remain my constant inspiration.

Massive thanks to two of my brilliant mentors: Gareth Hanrahan and Karin Tidbeck. It was their contagious passion for the craft and generous advice that set me on the path to begin with.

Those who, through the magic of roleplaying, helped me find the Nirian shores many years ago: Nast, Enrique, Néstor, Rosendo, Esteban, Javi Oca, Javi Dorta, Cripzy, Urbano, Marisa, Leo, Ana, Ale and Luis. Susana Arroyo especially, who doubled as fellow adventurer and trusted beta reader.

My parents, Juan Antonio and María, who taught me to love books; my brothers, Jacobo and Juan, who helped me weather many storms. Bebin, Phoenix and Stark, wild dragons that walked themselves into these pages without asking for permission.

Finally, Linden, the Evenstar who strayed into my dreams to for ever light them with her radiance. You inspire all things worth pursuing.

And thank you, reader, as well. If this dream lives, it's only through the might and generosity of your imagination. I hope that you've enjoyed this journey and that you will join me on the one to come as shadows fall over the Nirian continent, from the Mantle to the bloody thorns of the Delectian court . . .

Glossary

Academy: The home to the ancient Dreamer-Guild of Nightmare-Hunters, now the leading institution to train and school Dreamers in Onyxia.

Charnel Mother: An ancient deity-like Nightmare that ravaged the continent during the Sibling Strife.

Charnelite Cult: The nihilistic religion built around the Charnel Mother.

Conscription: The right of the Academy to forcefully recruit those with the Dreaming gift.

Divine Empire: The now-defunct empire, founded by Divine Damnia. Replaced by a myriad princedoms and confederations, the Onyxian Domain among them.

Divine Lineage: The ruling lineage of the empire of the same name. Renowned for their powerful Dreams, many of which endure after centuries.

Domain: The lands under the rule of Onyxia. That is, Eirune, Gallecia, the Highland Marches, the Loengrian Peninsula, the Valelands and the Walled Sea islands.

Dream (Capitalised): *(Aka the Dreaming gift)* The magical act of conjuring something out of one's imagination.

Dreamblooded: A person born from the union of a human and a human-like Dreamling. Often possessing the ability to shift and transform their body.

Dreamchantment: A Dream, woven into a physical object, conferring it with magical properties.

Dreamer: One possessing the gift to manifest their imaginings into the physical world.

Dreamer-Guilds: The ancient guilds that brought down the Iskian Empire.

Dreaming trance: The state of half-consciousness that Dreamers enter in which to shape their imaginings before summoning them into reality.

Dreamling: A creature *Dreamt* into existence. Dreamlings can possess magic-like unnatural qualities and human-like shape or intellect, but can't Dream.

Eidolon: A Dreamling, created as a replica of a dying or deceased person.

Entombed Hells: The place of eternal torment in which Prince Arcos and his court are forever trapped in the sunken ruins of the old Imperial Capital.

Exarchian: A political movement advocating for the liberation of the Undreaming from Dreamer/Oneirocrat rule.

Gargoyles: Dreamlings made of living stone, often winged, that guard Onyxian palaces.

Hordemaster: Dreamers trained by the Academy to create Nightmares and control them.

Imprint: A Dreamer's signature, often manifesting itself in a set of recurring visual marks.

Inspiration: The creative energy that powers Dreaming.

Iskian Empire: *(Aka the Ancient Iskians)* The first Oneirocrat empire to spread from Ravkiria to rule over the Nirian continent.

Keening: The mystical art of singing that allows Wailers to elevate souls to the Motherstorm. Motherstorm instituted the Sisterhoods.

Lightning-Hunters: *(Aka Lightning-Catchers or Rooftop-rats)* A guild operating on the Shingle Sea, the rooftops of Onyxia's buildings.

Mantle: An enchanted expanse of darkness surrounding the island home to the Academy.

Motherstorm: A spiritual entity that preserves the souls of the deceased, manifesting as a perpetual storm over Onyxia. One of the Divine Dreams of Princess Geleisdra.

Nightmare: A Dreamling of monstrous shape, often Dreamt to torment or attack others. The collective name is *Horde*.

Nightmare-Hunter: Dreamers trained by the Academy in the hunting and killing of Nightmares.

Niria: The continental lands.

Onyxia: *(Aka the Jet-Black City)* The large city made of interconnected islands built over a lagoon. Capitol to the Domain.

Oneirocrat: A lady/lord belonging to a noble lineage of Dreamers. Often, the ruling class across the continent.

Reformers: *(Aka The Whites)* A political party in the Onyxian Senate advocating for more rights for the Undreaming, Guilds and Merchants.

Remaker: A Dreamer specialised in healing by forcefully 'remaking' injured parts of the body.

Sisterhoods: The religious orders open to women that deal with spiritual matters in the Domain.

Skyship: A vessel Dreamchanted for aerial navigation.

Song of Sorrows: The sacred text of the Sisterhoods.

Stone-Masks: Agents of the Onxyia's Secret Chancellery.

Suffering Masses: Followers of the Song of Sorrows and the Sisterhoods's religion.

Talon: A group of Academy students belonging to the same unit.

Traditionalists: *(Aka the Blues)* A political party in the Onyxian Senate advocating for strict morals and protecting the privileges and power of the Oneirocrats.

Undreaming: Those humans lacking the Dreaming gift.

Vigil-blight: A state in which reality has become fractured, and Dreams manifest spontaneously.

Wailers: *(Aka Wailing Sisters, Sisters of Sorrow)* The Sisterhood dedicated to the art of Keening, as well as education.

Wardens: *(Aka Whispering Sisters, Sisters of Solemnity)* The Sisterhood dedicated to watching over Divine Geleisdra's resting place and her relics on the Solemn Isle.

Whisperers: *(Aka Whispering Sisters, Sisters of Silence)* The Sisterhood dedicated to preserving the stories and memories of the deceased.

Widows: *(Aka Widowed Sisters, Sisters of Solitude)* The Sisterhood dedicated to charity and tending to funerary arrangements.

Wilting: A disease that causes fevers, rashes, a weakening of the body, ravings and, ultimately, death.

The story continues in

NIGHTMARE OF THE EVENFALL FOREST

Coming soon